I0650619

The Coral Throne

The Coral Throne, Volume 2

Elizabeth Schechter

Published by Elizabeth Schechter, 2026.

The Coral Throne

Copyright © 2026 Elizabeth Schechter

All rights reserved, including the right to reproduce this book, or portion thereof, in any form.

This is a work of fiction. Any references to historical events, real people, or real locales are used fictitiously. Other names, characters, places, and incidents are the product of the author's imagination, and any resemblance to actual events or locales or persons, living or dead, is entirely coincidental.

No part of this book may be used or reproduced in any manner for the purpose of training artificial intelligence technologies or systems.

Published by Raven's Wing Books

Editor: Michael Schechter

Sensitivity Reader: Kendra Herber

Cover design by GetCovers

Raven's Wing Books

ravens-wing-books.com

Table of Contents

Chapter One
Awakening

THE EARLY MORNING SKY and the sea were almost the same shade of white-streaked crystalline blue. The wind was strong, the sails billowing overhead, and there was nothing visible in any direction for as far as the eye could see. The sun was warm on Tarjiaan's back, and it was easy to believe that the *Wave Runner* was the only ship left in the world. He could hear people singing somewhere on deck, the cadence marking the time of whatever they were doing. He recognized the song as one of his own. He smiled, taking a deep breath and letting it out slowly, savoring the salt and the wind and the quiet. It wouldn't last. It never lasted. But for now, the sea, the ship, and the captain were all at peace.

He corrected course slightly, feeling a shiver along his spine. He concentrated on the sensation, trying to translate the feeling into something he could understand. The idea of being a Reckoner was still new, and he was still trying to learn what each seemingly random itch, tingle and shiver meant. This one... oh. He corrected course again, and watched the pod of Great Mothers surfacing just off the port side of the ship. He watched them rise and fall, then turned his attention back to the helm. And to the couple coming up the stairs to join him. The pair of them looked sleep rumpled, and he guessed that one of them had woken up, seen he was missing, and awakened the other to come find him.

"Good morning," he called.

1

"You are awake very early," Nika said as she came to stand by his side. His right side, and he smiled as he leaned down to kiss her quickly. Then he turned to his left, and into another kiss, laughing as Daanir's still-new facial hair tickled his lips. Daanir smiled and rested his hand on Tarjiaan's back.

"We missed you. You don't ever get up before me. I'm not even sure how you got past me, or got into your armor without waking me up," he said. "Have you eaten?"

"Not yet," Tarjiaan answered. "I couldn't sleep, so I came up to watch the sun rise, and just be with the sea for a time." He looked out toward the horizon. "When it's quiet like this, you can forget everything about the war. There's just... us." He took another deep breath. "But we need to make plans. Comms on." His earpiece crackled slightly as the comms went live. "Marikaar. I want all my officers for a meeting in the day cabin as soon as possible. It's time we all understood what we're facing."

"*Understood, Captain. I'll send Destirian to relieve you. Should I have food served as well? I don't think you've eaten yet, and you need to. You're still recovering.*"

"Yes, please. Pass my compliments on to Aranti and ask her if she can attend. And tell Nimas that if he's able, I want him at the meeting, too. Now stop mothering me. Comms off." Tarjiaan heard laughter as the comms turned off.

"I think we both could hear him laughing," Daanir said. "What was funny?"

"Marikaar appears to have decided that he's going to take care of me in Logiri's absence." Tarjiaan took a deep breath. "If either of you want to try and dissuade him, you're welcome to do so. I don't want him stepping on either of you."

Nika rested her hand on Tarjiaan's arm. "If it becomes an issue, I will speak to him. Who are Nimas and Aranti?"

"Nimas is our purser," Tarjiaan answered. "And Aranti is his wife, and our cook."

"I have not met either of them yet," Nika said. "And I do not know what a purser does?"

"The purser is in charge of all supplies for the ship," Tarjiaan said. "His skills lie in organization and provisioning. He's also unofficially in charge of hydroponics."

"He has a second rank?" Daanir asked. "That's unusual."

"Unusual describes Nimas very well. He's a fantastic hand to hand fighter, but he won't come above deck if he can help it. The sky scares him — he's young enough that he'd never been above before he was assigned to the *Wave Runner*. He only stayed because he won't leave Ara. They're both very good at what they do — he and Ara can somehow stretch a single grain of rice into a meal to feed the entire ship. And he adores working in hydroponics."

"So he's good?"

"Daan, he can grow root vegetables." Tarjiaan grinned at the look of shock on Daanir's face, then turned to Nika. "You're not supposed to be able to do that, but Nimas manages it. Those systems are his pride and joy, and it destroyed him when he couldn't find the problem and had to hand it over to Ishantar to repair."

"And he is afraid of the sky?" Nika looked up. "I... he is like you, in reverse."

Tarjiaan blinked. "I... I never thought of it like that, but yes. I try not to put too much stress on him. I rarely ask his attendance at officer meetings, but I need to know how we're provisioned and what our options are. Which means he has to come to the day cabin."

"He can't use the access passage?" Daanir asked.

"The what?" Tarjiaan turned to look at the mancer. "There's an access passage? In the day cabin?"

"The *Wave Runner* is full of access passages. I designed her that way," Daanir said, nodding enthusiastically. "There's one that comes up in the back of that tall cabinet in the day cabin. The one on the right. I'll show you."

"And then you'll show Nimas," Tarjiaan said. "There's Destirian. I want to see these passages."

"They are small," Nika said hesitantly. Tarjiaan understood why. "Will you able to see them?"

Tarjiaan smiled. "I'll be brief, and I'll be back under the sky. There won't be anything stopping me. I think I'll be fine." He leaned down and kissed her. "Thank you."

In the day cabin, Tarjiaan followed Daanir to the tall cabinet in the corner, his armored footsteps echoing slightly. "There's a passage in here?"

Daanir nodded. "I designed her so that someone... me... so that I could get from one end of the ship to the other without ever coming above. It was me hoping that I would be the mancer assigned to her, and being selfish. It saved our necks when we sneaked onboard after the Imps took the ship." He looked over his shoulder. "You're sure you're ready for this?"

Tarjiaan nodded. "Show me."

Daanir hesitated, looking at Tarjiaan intently. Then he nodded and pointed at the rear panel. "The controls are here," he said, and tapped what looked like a knot in the wood. The panel receded, then slid away, revealing a narrow space and a ladder.

"That is so small," Nika said. "Jiaan, I do not think you are going to fit."

"Let me see." Tarjiaan waited for Daanir to step out of the way, then stepped into the cabinet, ducking his head to fit. The sides of the cabinet pressed against his shoulders...

The next thing he knew, he was flat on his back on the deck, and Nika was kneeling over him, her hands on his chest.

"Jiaan!"

"I..." He sat up slowly, grimacing as his head spun. "What happened?"

"You tell us," Daanir said, crouching next to him. "You stepped into the cabinet, stopped, and fell over backwards."

"You *fainted*," Nika said, her voice shaking. "Your heart is racing. Jiaan, what happened?"

Tarjiaan shook his head, swallowing, trying to slow his breathing. "I... I don't know."

"Oh," Daanir breathed. "I think I do." He got up and went to the cabinet, measuring the space with his hands. Then he came back, straddling Tarjiaan's legs as he held his hands up to Tarjiaan's shoulders. He nodded. "Roughly the same size," he said.

"As what?" Nika asked. She looked at the cabinet, and her brows rose. "Oh!"

"The same size?" Tarjiaan looked at the cabinet, and this time saw phantom shackles dangling from the ceiling. He shuddered and looked away. "As... as the box," he said softly. "The one they locked me in."

"The walls against your shoulders was enough to make your mind think you were trapped again, and your body reacted." Nika took his hand. "You are calming. This is good. Jiaan, you are safe. You are not trapped. You are here, with us."

Tarjiaan squeezed her fingers and looked from her to Daanir. "I..."

"It's only been two days," Daanir said softly. "You kept us alive through the fighting and the storm. You were distracted. Now you're not, and you're still not recovered. You have to deal with what they did to you."

"And how you will react," Nika finished. "We must talk to Wilaanger. He will know what you must do."

"We're not out of danger yet," Tarjiaan protested. "It can wait—" He fell silent under the weight of two identical looks of pure scorn. "I don't have time!"

"Your body is saying otherwise," Nika said. "If you do not take the time, your body will take it for you. You will get sick, and that will be disaster for all of us."

"She's right," Daanir said. "Talk to Wil."

Tarjiaan took a deep breath. "Fine. After the meeting. Now... I need to get ready for this meeting. Let me up, Daan."

Daanir helped him to his feet, steadying him as he found his balance, then looked at the cabinet. "Where do I find Nimas? I'll go get him and show him the passages."

"I apologize for forcing you to share your secret," Tarjiaan said. "If you'll excuse me, Nika? I'm going to wash up. The others will be here soon." He turned toward the door that led into the bedroom, hearing Nika's footsteps behind him. He smiled as he took off his coat and hung it on a peg. "Nika, I'm fine."

"You are not fine. And I am not letting you out of my sight." She took his hand as she came up next to him. "You are still hurting, and I hate that."

He raised her hand to his lips and kissed her fingers. "My darling healer. I don't want to worry you. More than I already do, anyway." He gestured to the rumpled bed. "Remind me to do something about this? I'm too used to having someone around to tidy up. I completely forgot yesterday."

Nika shook her head. "You have important things to do. I can tidy while you work. There is not much else I can do to help you."

"You should be resting, love," Tarjiaan said. "For the baby."

She giggled. "I am not so pregnant that I cannot tidy the bedclothes, Jiaan!" She made shooing motions. "Go and wash. I will tidy. Am I to be in your meeting?"

Tarjiaan hesitated with his hand on the door. "I think... yes. You and the children. Your reports on what you witnessed, in addition to the data disk Aanaji gave to the children, those will carry a great deal of weight."

She nodded, turning toward the bed and starting to plump the pillows. Tarjiaan walked into the washroom, closed the door, and leaned against the basin, giving into the shaking he'd been repressing by sheer force of will.

As bad as his reactions were to being below, to being trapped, this was so much worse. When he went below, he usually had at least a few hours before the walls started closing in. Days before the panic hit. This...there'd been no warning at all. What else was going to trigger this kind of reaction? How quickly could he learn to manage his reactions, and how could he protect his people until he knew?

Nika and Daan were right. He needed to talk to Wilaanger.

He took a deep breath, washed his face, then studied himself in the mirror. Even to his own eyes, he looked pale, and the sight of his short hair was still jarring. If they intended to use the shorn hair for magical tokens, they'd lost their chance — his hair was gone to the bottom of the sea with the mage who'd taken it. He ran one hand over the soft fuzz, noticing just how much gray there was mixed in. There had been gray in his beard for years now, but he'd never seen any in his hair before. There was a soft tapping on the door, which opened behind him.

"I'm getting old," he said. "My hair is going gray. People will mistake me for our child's grandfather."

"You are thirty-four," Nika said from behind him. "You are not old. Come out and sit. Let me look at you when I am able to see all of you."

Tarjiaan chuckled and followed her out of the washroom, sitting down in his heavy chair. She stood between his knees and studied him, her head cocked slightly to the side, her golden eyes half-lidded.

"I very much like the gray," she said. "It is very distinguished. There is also gray in your beard." She smiled and reached up, trailing her finger over the line of his jaw. "Here. It catches the light when you turn your head."

Tarjiaan smiled and relaxed as her fingertips ran over his cheekbone, down the line of his throat. Her touch was soothing, and he wondered if it was her healing power, or just that he knew in his bones that Nika was safe. That she loved him.

"You are still far too thin," she added. "And too pale. I want to speak to... Aranti, was it? I want to speak to her about making certain you eat, and put some weight back on." She stopped with her hand on his chest. "You do not look old," she repeated. "At this moment, you look tired. You look as if you have recently been ill. But that will change. When it does, you will look as you did when I first saw you." She ran her hand back up to cup his cheek. "Strong and kind and powerful and so very handsome."

"I look like that, hm?" Tarjiaan covered Nika's hand with his, turning so he could kiss her palm. "Then I have a lot to live up to."

"You know you do that by breathing."

Tarjiaan turned toward the door. "How long have you been standing there?"

Daanir smiled. "Just came in. I heard Nika describing you perfectly. Not sure what brought it on, but I agree with her."

"Tarjiaan thought he looked old."

Daanir snorted. "Old? Why? Because you have gray hair?"

"You noticed?" Tarjiaan asked. "I never saw it until my hair was cut."

"Jiaan, you had gray hair at sixteen."

Tarjiaan blinked. "I... I did?"

"You didn't know?" Daanir looked thoughtful. "To be fair, it was on the back of your head, but yes. I liked it. I was hoping it would come in stronger and look like a stripe."

"It may still," Nika said. "We will see when Jiaan's hair grows back in. Did you find Nimas?"

Daanir laughed. "Yes, and found out that he's already been using the passages. He found them a year ago, he told me. He showed me his map, and he's got almost all of them marked down. He just wasn't going to use this one without permission."

"He has that now." Tarjiaan took a deep breath. "They'll all be here soon. Nika, let me up."

She smiled. "You have to pay a toll for passage."

Tarjiaan blinked. "A what?" Then he realized what she meant, and grinned, pulling her in for a kiss. She giggled and let him stand up. "Is that how they say it on land?" he asked.

She looked thoughtful, then nodded. "I did not think of that. You would not have tolls here. You have no roads. What is your way of saying that?"

"That you have to salute the officer on deck," Tarjiaan answered.

"Oh! Is that what she meant?" Daanir asked. "I didn't make the connection."

Tarjiaan picked up his coat as he walked out into the day cabin, putting it on before he took his seat at the table. "Daan, do you have that data disk?"

"One is in your lockbox. The other... I told Kaapi to make it secure. I don't know where she put it."

Tarjiaan nodded. "Get it out and set up a monitor. It's time to show everyone what really happened. And send for Naajir and Kaapi. They should both report on what they witnessed."

"I thought you might say that," Daanir said. "So I already asked Ishantar to bring them." He went to the rear wall, and opened one of the doors in the long cabinet underneath the windows, taking out a small monitor. He brought it to the table, then went to another cabinet. Tarjiaan knew that it was locked — that cabinet was always locked — but Daanir opened it as if the lock didn't exist. He rummaged around inside, then brought a data disk to Tarjiaan.

"I don't know why I bother to lock things around you," Tarjiaan said as he took the disk. Daanir smiled and took his place at the table. Nika brought a pitcher of water and cups to the table, claiming a kiss from Daanir in return for a cup. She filled another cup for Tarjiaan, looking up as someone knocked on the door.

"Do I answer?"

"No. Sit down, love." Tarjiaan raised his voice. "Come in!"

The door opened, and Wilaanger came in, followed by Antivar and Navi. Antivar stopped just inside the door and bowed.

"Prince-Captain," he said as he straightened. "Am I supposed to be part of this meeting? We were with the honored Wilaanger when you sent for him, and he told us to come, but I'm not certain it's my place to be here."

Tarjiaan smiled and gestured to the table. "Please, stay. I value your input, and I think your insight as to what is happening in the Empire will help." He turned to Navi. "Are you helping in the infirmary?"

Navi's relaxed smile reminded him of Nika's, making it obvious that they were twins. "Helping. Learning. Be...ing useful." He licked his lips. "Prac...ti...cing talking."

"Very good," Wilaanger said. He took a seat and rested his hands on the table. "Sometimes, after a brain injury robs a person of their voice, their mind can be... retrained. It's a slow process, but we have time. And Ysnavin is more than willing to do the work."

Navi laughed. "Good at working." He cocked his head to the side, and frowned slightly as he looked at Tarjiaan. "Brother? Not well?"

Tarjiaan shook his head and laughed. "I should have known better than to sit down with healers and think I could hide anything. Wil, I'll need to talk to you after this meeting." He rested one hand on Daan's arm, the other on Nika's hand. "I frightened everyone this morning."

Wilaanger sat up straight. "What happened?"

"After the meeting, Wil. I'm fine for right now. And we need to start making plans." Tarjiaan looked over at a knock on the door. "Come in and leave it open!"

A few minutes later, the table was crowded. Marikaar and Ishantar sat facing Wilaanger and Navi, while Aranti and Nimas took places facing each other at the foot of the table. Newly-minted apprentice Mancers Naajir and Kaapi stood behind Ishantar's chair, while Antivar leaned against the wall near the door.

"Food will be up soon, Captain," Aranti said as she took a seat. She towered over Navi, who was sitting next to her, and the breadth of her shoulders rivaled Tarjiaan's own. Navi looked up at her, his eyes wide, but he calmed when she smiled at him. "You need some meat on your bones, lad. Come by the galley. I'll feed you up. And... begging your pardon, Captain, but you need feeding up, too."

"I'll eat, Aranti. Thank you." Tarjiaan looked around the table. "Antivar, come and sit. You're part of this meeting." He waited for Antivar to take the last open chair. "We're not out of danger yet. We have a long way to sail before we are, and there will be more fighting between here and there. But before we get there, you need to know where it started and why. And before we start, I want it known that this is my first time seeing this as well." He turned to Daanir. "Play the disk."

Chapter Two
Meeting

EVEN AFTER HAVING BEEN told what was on the disk, it was hard for Tarjiaan to watch his last meeting with his uncle and see what happened after he'd succumbed to the drugged tea. He thought he remembered Ilaris smashing the machines that kept Ikaanaji alive, but seeing the confirmation, knowing that it wasn't a dream, hurt more than he was expecting. Then seeing his sister, disheveled and frightened, confessing to what she'd done, how Ilaris had used her. How he had betrayed her trust and destroyed her family. He must have made some sound, because Nika took his hand in hers and squeezed his fingers.

Then it was over, and everyone at the table turned to look at him. He took his hand from Nika's and picked up his cup, taking a sip of water to try and delay having to speak

"I... I don't understand," Marikaar stammered. "The Mancer Royal told me that Ilaris had betrayed us, but this... Mothers Below, *why*?"

"There is more," Tarjiaan said, his voice surprisingly steady to his ears. "Wilaanger, if you would?"

Wilaanger took a deep breath. "Aanaji told you all that Ilaris is a mage. What I doubt that she knows is that Ilaris is Ikaanaji's son."

"Nika told me that," Tarjiaan said. "I never knew my uncle had any children."

"He had none by his wife, and he never acknowledged Ilaris as his own. Your aunt Alyaan... their marriage was in name only. When the tension between them was too high, she would tour the belowships, and would often be gone for weeks at a time. It was when she was on one of those tours that Ika took a mistress, a young healer in the royal retinue. Larina was a sweet girl, and she loved your uncle. I know that Ika suspected Ilaris was his. We spoke of it, and his plans to put Alyaan aside and marry Larina if she would allow him to prove that Ilaris was his son. I don't know why Larina refused the tests. I think that perhaps she was frightened of Alyaan. And she might have had reason — Larina died very shortly after Alyaan returned from one of her tours. After Larina died, Alyaan had Ilaris sent to the crèche. He was eight when his mother died, and he was in the crèche for seven years, until Ikaanaji adopted him into the royal household after Alyaan died."

"Did the Queen kill her rival?" Antivar asked.

Wilaanger shrugged, then spread his hands. "I honestly don't know. When Alyaan returned to the *Chimaera* after her tours, very often I was... elsewhere—"

"What?" Daanir gasped. "You weren't with him?"

"He ordered it, Daanir," Wilaanger said. "Alyaan hated me, and if she was angry at me, she would take that out on Ika. It was easiest on him, no matter how much I hated leaving him to face her alone. I wasn't there when she returned, and I wasn't there when Larina died. I didn't know that Ilaris had been sent away until I returned. I tried to keep an eye on him, but he was sent to a crèche on one of the outer belowships—"

"Let me guess," Daanir interjected, lacing his fingers together on the tabletop. "She sent him to the *Corsair.*"

Wilaanger looked shocked. "How did you know?"

"Because I came up on the *Corsair,* and so did Kaapi. It's the last ship in the fleet, in the worst repair, and with the most corruption.

Remember how I told you we never had anything on the table fresh? It was all preserved or ration biscuits? That was normal on the *Corsair*." Daanir shook his head. "She sent him to the worst crèche in the fleet. She buried him, the same way Ilaris buried me on Station Six."

Tarjiaan looked at Nika, and was surprised to see the horrified look on her face, and the fury in her eyes. Clearly he was missing something.

"The more I learn of this, the angrier I am. When we are able," she said, her voice clearly showing that anger, "the *Corsair* shall be the first ship we visit. This will not be allowed to continue." She turned toward Wilaanger, and Tarjiaan put his hand on her arm.

"Nika, we have things to do before you upend the fleet," he said. "So that you can upend the fleet. We'll take care of the *Corsair* once we've secured the throne."

She looked back at him. "First thing?"

He nodded. "The very first thing. Agreed?"

She drew herself up and nodded. "Agreed."

"Thank you." He looked around the table. "What has Ilaris told the fleet?" he asked. "Marikaar?"

"The only report we had was that the Mancer Royal went mad and murdered you, the King and the Physician Royal," Marikaar answered. "Which... we've all heard stories of mancers who went too far into the machines and lost their wits. It was believable. But then the Imps showed up and tried to take the *Wave Runner* as a trophy, and that's when we found out that you were alive. If they'd taken you right back to Imperial waters, we'd never have known you were alive, or that they had you."

"And they would not have gotten back to land," Antivar added. "Not with that storm. His Majesty would have been lost."

"First, all of you can stop calling me Your Majesty," Tarjiaan interjected. "It's an empty title until I take the throne back. Understood?"

"Yes, Captain," Marikaar said. "That mage destroyed our long-range comms to keep us from calling for help. Which means we have no idea what reports are coming from the throne, or what they're claiming."

"That's going to make going to the floating dockyards risky," Ishantar said. "But we don't have a choice. We took too much damage. We won't survive another battle like the last one."

"Which I doubt we'll see. At least, not from my... from the Imperial fleet," Antivar said. "I think most of the Imperial Navy was out there before the storm, and they're all gone."

"Seriously?" Marikaar asked. "The Imp fleet was that small?"

Antivar nodded, his expression somber. "For as long as I can remember, when the Imperial fleet sailed out, maybe one in four ships would come back. We all knew that. We were always told that the Butcher of Meradon took no prisoners and scuttled any ship that engaged. I know now that they were lying to us, but back when I first sailed? No one I served with had ever met anyone who survived. We had no one to prove the stories were fake." He folded his hands on the tabletop. "I don't know much about shipbuilding, but you need trees for the wood, don't you? Big ones?" He looked at Daanir. "Is that right?"

Daanir nodded. "If you're building wooden ships, then yes. It's not how we do it anymore, but it's how we used to. I think that's how the Imps still build their ships."

"Not anymore. The Imperial shipyards are deserted now. My last ship, and the others like her? Those were the last ones built, and they were smaller by necessity. No one is building ships in the Empire anymore, because there aren't enough big trees left in Tyraca, in Lestalt, or in what was once Meradon to replace the ships that didn't come back," Antivar said. "And anyone who tries to fell trees in Sualiman? *They* don't come back. The Sualimani guard their borders like a brindle on a bone." He paused, then smiled. "That's a guard dog, in case none of you have ever seen one."

Tarjiaan smiled. "Thank you, Antivar. Regardless of the state of the Imperial Navy, this ship needs repairs, and our only chance of them is the floating dockyards. Ishantar, what are the chances of fixing the comms?"

Ishantar grimaced. "Slim, but if the Mancer Royal can help? Perhaps we can at least get an incoming signal and find out what we are facing."

Tarjiaan nodded. "Daan, if you would?"

"Could we help?" Naajir asked. "There's not much else we can do to help. Neither of us knows much about being above. But we can do this."

"So long as you follow Mancer Daanir or Mancer Ishantar's direction," Tarjiaan answered. "If you don't, you'll learn to swab the decks. Understood?"

"Yes, Uncle," Naajir answered, his eyes wide. "I... did you have to do that?"

"And other, dirtier jobs. Remember, I was younger than you when I first came above the waves. I had to learn it all." Tarjiaan turned to look down the table. "Now, Nimas, how are we set for supplies?"

At the end of the table, Nimas frowned slightly, looking down at his notes. He had always reminded Tarjiaan of the tame birds that some Sualimani nobility kept as pets. Delicate-looking, easily startled, wide eyes and a long nose — his appearance meant people tended to underestimate him, expecting him to faint away at the first sign of a fight. They were all wrong — Aranti looked imposing, but was gentle as a Great Mother. Nimas, on the other hand... after his first fistfight, no one on the *Wave Runner* ever underestimated

Nimas in a fight again. He paged through his ledger, then looked across at Aranti. She nodded, and he cleared his throat.

"We're thin, and no mistake there," he answered. "We were thin going into the wedding, and not having the hydroponics or our pod is making it worse." He looked down at his ledger again. "Given the current numbers, I think we can keep everyone fed for another... twelve days before going onto ration biscuits. We're well supplied with those, thank the Mothers. But looking at actual food? It'll be salmag by day seven, and whatever salt fish and hardtack we have left by twelve. Ara?"

Aranti nodded. "We're already scraping the bottom of the barrels on rice and flour. Fresh produce is going off, and I was going to turn it into chutney and pickles tonight." She looked distant, then nodded. "I can maybe get us to fourteen days before we have to start issuing the ration biscuits. How long until we get to the dockyards?"

Marikaar drummed his fingers on the tabletop. "Ah... assuming they're still where we left them? And assuming we don't run into any fights and keep a good wind? Ten days. Maybe eleven."

Tarjiaan nodded. "So it sounds as if we'll be cutting things very fine."

"Yes, Captain," Nimas said, nodding. "We can make it work, but things might be... tight by the time we get to the dockyards." He took a deep breath. "Antivar, is it? Tell me, I've heard that Imperial ships will supplement their supplies with fishing. Is that true?"

"Yes," Antivar answered. "You don't?"

"We usually don't need to," Nimas answered. "Our ships usually have a support pod of belowships that includes a farm ship. Now, I know we have several of your men on board. Do any of them fish?"

"Of course," Antivar answered. "If it's allowed, I volunteer to help arrange fishing expeditions. Your skiffs are faster than ours, so we should be able to do this without losing speed."

"Marikaar, work with Nimas and Antivar to arrange that," Tarjiaan said. "We need every advantage that we can catch, especially if Ilaris actually sent the orders I gave before he betrayed us." He looked around the table. "As the disk says, I ordered and then rescinded Deep Scatter and Great Migration. Uncle ordered Ilaris to issue the orders in his name. If he did, then the floating dockyards may not be where we think they are."

Marikaar hissed softly. "If they went on migration, we'll never find them."

"They were in their regular waters when we went hunting for the *Wave Runner* after we escaped the *Chimaera*," Daanir said. "The orders said that the *Wave Runner* was supposed to escort the dockyards, so we thought the *Wave Runner* would be there, or at least en route. We found you when we backtracked." He drummed his fingers on the tabletop. "They might have moved by now. We don't know."

"We have to try," Tarjiaan said. "We don't have another option. Now, we have plans, but we also have breakfast. Ara, will you serve so that we can get to work?"

"Of course, Captain." Aranti stood up. "Children, you find places to sit. It's not good to eat standing."

Tarjiaan forced himself to ignore the memories of hunger, and the urge to bolt his food. He made himself eat slowly and chew his food thoroughly. He was very much aware that Nika was watching him eat, and quite probably recording every morsel. He paused, sipped his tea, then looked at his plate.

"Jiaan, you have to eat," Nika murmured, exactly as he'd expected.

"I am," he replied in a low voice, reaching out and taking her hand. He kissed her fingers, then let her go. "I don't want to eat too fast. And you've barely eaten at all. Nika, I'm not the only one who needs to eat."

She smiled. Then she closed her eyes briefly, swallowed, and whispered, "Excuse me, please." She got up and hurried away from the table. Wilaanger got up and followed her.

"Nika?" Navi turned in his chair to look after them. "Nika sick?"

Tarjiaan licked his lips and looked at Daanir, who grinned. "Might as well. Something else to fight for."

Tarjiaan nodded. "No, Navi. She's not sick."

"Mothers Below, the Queen is pregnant!" Aranti gasped. "Isn't she?"

"She is," Tarjiaan said.

Aranti laughed aloud. "How wonderful! Congratulations, Captain!" She paused, looking thoughtful. She nodded, then continued, "I have a recipe for a tea that will help with settling the stomach, and for easing the pregnancy sickness. And I'm certain we have what I need to make it. I'll bring a pot up once we're done here, and something light to settle her stomach."

Tarjiaan smiled. "Thank you. I'm sure Nika will appreciate that." He turned back to Navi, who was staring at him. "Navi?"

"Babies?" Navi whispered. Tarjiaan blinked. It hadn't occurred to him that there might be more than one. But Nika was a twin, and he had twins in his own line. It was entirely possible... and completely terrifying.

"Might be too soon to tell if it's babies," Daanir said. "Maybe we assume one until we know better?"

"Good idea," Wilaanger said as he came back to the table. "It's definitely too soon to tell. Tarjiaan, I'll have Chel come up and check on Nika again once we're done. She's lying down right now, and she'll be back to the table shortly."

"Aranti is going to bring up some tea that she says will help." Tarjiaan rested his hands on the tabletop, then stood up. "I think everyone is done. There's nothing else that needs to be said. Let's get to work."

The meeting broke up, with everyone stopping to pass on their congratulations. Wilaanger promised to come back once he'd spoke to Chel, and Daanir kissed Tarjiaan twice before he left with Ishantar and Kaapi, telling him to give one to Nika. Finally, the only person left in the great cabin was Naajir.

"Uncle, could we talk?" he asked. "Before I go help?"

"Of course," Tarjiaan replied. "What is it?"

Naajir hesitated, then blurted, "I want to abdicate my place as your heir."

Tarjiaan stared at his nephew. "What? Naji, why?"

Naajir wrung his hands, took a deep breath, then sighed. "I want your child to be the heir," he said. "I don't think I should be your heir. I mean... my mother betrayed Meradon. Once people know that, no one will follow me. You're saving Meradon. I won't be the one to destroy it." He took a deep breath and shook his head. "Let me be a mancer, and let me make my own way."

Tarjiaan leaned against the table. "You've given this some thought."

"It's been in my head since we first watched that disk on the submersible," Naajir admitted. "But I didn't think I could abdicate. I mean... how could I just walk away? I was all you had. But now..."

"Until the baby is born, you're still all I have," Tarjiaan pointed out. "Naji, I understand what you are saying, and I hear you. If this is what you want, then I will ask you to do one thing."

Naajir glanced at the bedroom door. "Wait for the baby?"

Tarjiaan nodded. "Exactly."

Naajir smiled slightly. "That won't be that long. I can wait. And I can help while I'm waiting."

"And learn," Tarjiaan added. "You need to learn what to do in case you do have to stay in that role, or in case you need to help your aunt hold the throne and protect your cousin while they're still too young to inherit. Or, Mothers forbid, if you have to hold the throne and protect your cousin in her place."

"I..." Naajir went pale. "You're saying... in case something happens to you?"

"In case something happens to me." Tarjiaan stepped back and sat down in his heavy chair, gesturing for Naajir to sit. He poured tea for them both, and waited until Naajir had taken a sip before continuing. "If something happens to me, if I am incapacitated in some way, the weight of the crown will fall to Nika. She's already shown that she's more than capable, and Daanir will support her however he can. But I want you there as well, even if you aren't the heir. I'm not going to make the mistakes my uncle made. I want you full trained, and fully educated, even if you're not next in line. Partly as a safety measure, in case the unthinkable happens. And partly because I can think of no better role model for my child than my beloved nephew."

Naajir sat up straighter, his cheeks turning ever-so-slightly pink. "You mean that?"

"I mean that," Tarjiaan said.

Naajir bit his lip and looked down, then blurted, "Mama said the same thing about you. She wanted me to follow your example."

Tarjiaan blinked. "I... I'm sorry? What?"

Naajir smiled and relaxed, wrapping his hands around his teacup. "When I was small, Mama showed me a recording of you playing light-harp, and I told her that I wanted to be you when I grew up. So I learned. I play flute, viol, small lute and light-harp."

Tarjiaan stared at him, then laughed. "I had no idea! When did you start?"

"I was four when I started lessons. Flute first, then viol and small lute. I started playing light harp last year. I don't have an instrument now, though. Everything got left behind on the *Allegiant*."

Tarjiaan nodded. "I have a light-harp here—"

"And a double-neck," Naajir interjected, sounding excited. "We saw the recording. Will you teach me double-neck?"

"You favor your right hand, no? Spread your left hand." Tarjiaan rested his left hand on the tabletop, spreading his fingers wide. Naajir did the same — Tarjiaan moved so that his hand was fingertip to fingertip with Naajir's. His hand was larger than his nephew's, but not by much. "Hrm... next year, I think. You don't quite have the handspan yet. You're going to be tall when you have your full growth, Naji." He leaned back and picked up his tea. "Once we make the floating dockyards, we'll see about getting you a new instrument. A small lute, or a viol? You can use my light-harp, but you should have your own instrument."

"We will?" Naajir squeaked. "But... how?"

"There's a ship carpenter who served on the *Marauder* who lives on the dockyards now, and he's an exceptionally good musician." Tarjiaan smiled. "He was my music teacher on the *Marauder*. I'll have to see if we can find a music teacher for you."

"You had a music teacher on the *Marauder*?" Naajir repeated. "Really?"

"Until he was injured and requested to be reassigned to the dockyards. His name is Owain, and he was a fantastic teacher. And an amazing luthier — he made my first small lute, and my chitarra. Both of which I need to replace. The small lute died with the *Marauder*, and the chitarra was smashed in a storm last year."

Tarjiaan looked over as the bedroom door opened. Nika came out, looking around the day cabin.

"I missed the rest of the meeting?" she asked.

"You didn't miss very much," Tarjiaan answered. "We'd already covered everything that needed to be covered. Daan is off helping get the comms online. Aranti is bringing up a pot of tea for you that she says will help settle your stomach, and something light to eat. And Wil is coming back with Chel."

"And you have not yet spoken to him?" Nika joined him, resting her hand on his shoulder.

"Not yet. Naji and I needed to talk first."

Naajir nodded, his eyes wide. "I... I had questions. And we started talking, and... you... you're really going to get me something *new*?" He sounded stunned. "I've never had a new instrument before."

"I owe you a good many natal gifts, Naji. I think a new small lute or viol is a good start. And once you've got your growth in, we'll start on double-neck." Tarjiaan leaned forward and rested his forearms on the table. "I want you to understand that I'm not trying to distract you. Or bribe you. Once the baby comes, we'll revisit this conversation. And regardless of the outcome of that conversation, you're going to have the education you should have already started as a prince of the royal house of Meradon. Is that acceptable?"

Naajir nodded. "I... yes, Uncle. Thank you." He looked thoughtful. "Can Kaapi have those lessons, too?"

"I..." Tarjiaan stopped and looked at Nika. "I'd like to discuss that with her father first, but I don't see a reason why not. Why do you ask?"

"We work really well together," Naajir answered. "And if we're learning at the same time, we can help each other with the learning. And..." He stopped, blushing furiously.

Tarjiaan nodded. "Antivar asked me if you two were betrothed," he said softly.

"He *asked* that?" Naajir whimpered. "I... Mother is going to be furious!"

"I think your mother might surprise you," Nika said. "Based on what we saw on the disk, I think that very much. I think that all she wants is for you to be happy, Naajir. And if Kaapi makes you happy, then when you are old enough, I cannot see her objecting."

Naajir looked at Nika, and Tarjiaan could see the doubt lurking behind his eyes. "I have no objections," he added. "And I am your guardian. But again, we need to discuss with Kaapi's father."

Naajir smiled. "I... thank you, Uncle."

"One more question, Naji," Tarjiaan said. "Before I send you off to help the other mancers. What fight training have you had?"

Naajir grimaced. "Light sword, mostly. My fight teachers said that because I was small and fast, it was the best approach. And I learned dual dagger, and I can shoot."

"Good! Very good," Tarjiaan said. He smiled, mostly from relief. He hadn't been looking forward to starting Naajir off from the beginnings if he'd never picked up a blade. "Talk to Marikaar about adding practice to your onboard duties."

"Yes, Captain," Naajir said with a grin. "Is that all?"

Tarjiaan nodded. "That's all, Naajir. Dismissed. And if you see the Physician Royal, if you would tell him that I'm free?"

Naajir nodded. He stood up, bowed, then left the day cabin.

Chapter Three
Healing

TARJIAAN LEANED BACK as Nika took Naajir's abandoned seat.

"What was the conversation?" she asked.

"He asked if he could abdicate his position as heir," Tarjiaan answered. "And I've asked him to wait until we have an heir to have that conversation. He's agreed."

Nika nodded. "I was expecting that he would ask," she said. "He said he feared that he would be a liability, once it is known what his mother did."

"It wasn't her fault."

Nika nodded. "It was not, but truly, will people listen to that? It may be better for them both if he is not in line for the throne. It will give her the space she needs to heal. But there is time to have that conversation."

Tarjiaan reached for her hand and shifted forward to kiss her fingers. "There is. Now, how are you feeling?"

"Somewhat... shaky," she admitted. "As if my legs are two different lengths. I do not like it."

"You can talk to Chel about that. Or Aranti. They'll both be back shortly."

Nika nodded. "Do either of them have children?"

Tarjiaan thought about the question. "If Chel and Lysson have children, they've never told me, and I'll be annoyed that they didn't. Nimas and Aranti have two boys. Both of them live with Nimas' mother on the *Plenty*. That's the name of our farm ship," he added, answering the question before Nika could ask it. "So they're safe right now. Our pod was reassigned to the *Dauntless* before any of this started."

Nika looked puzzled. "Why?"

"Because when we were first attacked by Imperial ships, the *Wave Runner* was on the way to the floating dockyards for maintenance." Tarjiaan laughed as he realized something. "We keep trying to fix this blasted ship, and things keep happening that stop us!"

Nika arched a brow. "Is that funny?"

"Not funny. Ridiculous." Tarjiaan took a deep breath and shook his head. "We'll get the *Wave Runner* repaired. We'll take back the *Chimaera*. We'll find a way."

"Those are problems for later. For right now, did you eat enough? You were eating so slowly."

Tarjiaan smiled. "For now. I'll eat again later. I know I have weight to put back on. I just... Nika, I was eating slowly so that I wouldn't make myself sick."

She frowned. "I do not understand."

"I was ready to swallow that entire plate without chewing." Tarjiaan looked at the ceiling. "I'm still not entirely recovered. I know that. Whatever it was that kept me alive in that box without food or water, it didn't stop the damage. I still feel the... the ache."

"It will take time for your body to heal. And your mind." Nika reached out and took his hand. She closed her eyes and cocked her head to the side. "You do need to eat more."

"How do we balance that with making sure we have enough for everyone else until we reach the dockyards?" Tarjiaan asked.

"Can you eat the ration biscuits?" Nika asked, opening her eyes. She started massaging his hand with both of hers. "Daanir said that they are enough to sustain."

"And Aranti said that we have plenty of them," Tarjiaan murmured. "I... when Wil gets here, we'll ask him." He tugged Nika's hand. "Come here."

She smiled and stood, coming around the table and sitting in Tarjiaan's lap. She twined her arms around his neck and smiled. "Is this what you want?"

"It's a start." He kissed her twice, and when she looked at him, her brows slightly furrowed, he added, "One of those was from Daan. He went to go help with the comms." Tarjiaan put his arms around her and leaned back, smiling and closing his eyes as she rested against his chest. "Navi asked an interesting question, and I can't wait to see the answer."

"What was the question?" Nika asked.

"It was only one word." He opened his eyes and looked down to see Nika looking up at him. "Babies?"

Her eyes widened. "I... oh!" She looked down at her still-flat stomach. "I..."

"You're a twin. I have twins in my line. It's possible." He shifted his arms and started rubbing her back. "Wil says it's too soon tell. So we'll know eventually."

"Twins," Nika repeated. "I... that would be wondrous. And terrifying."

"Agreed. But it's a good terrifying. Like sailing into a storm."

"I did not think that was a good terrifying," Nika grumbled. She sniffed, then added, "At first. It was very exciting."

"And you did magnificently. Which reminds me. Do you want me to pierce your ear for your earring? It's traditional for the Captain to do it, but not required. Which is good, because the entire crew earned that earring, and if I'm the only one doing it, it'll take weeks. If you want Wil to do it, he can numb your ear."

"My earring?" Nika sat up and looked at him, touching her earlobe with one hand. "I will be off balance if I only have one."

Tarjiaan chuckled. "Well, we could find another storm...."

"No!"

Tarjiaan tipped his head back and laughed, hugging her tightly to his chest.

"It is good that you laugh at me," Nika said when he stopped laughing.

Tarjiaan blinked. "I'm not laughing at you!" he protested. "Nika, I wouldn't!"

"I said something wrong?" Nika smoothed his coat with her hand. "I made you laugh, so you are laughing at me. And I think it is a good thing that you laugh at me. But you do not?"

"No," Tarjiaan said firmly. "Sweetheart, I think this is a translation problem. When you say laughing at you, you mean that you made me laugh. Is that what it means in Imperial?"

"It is. Is it not in Common?"

"No," Tarjiaan answered. "When you say that in Common, it means I'm mocking you. I would never do that."

She frowned. "That is not what I meant. I amused you, so you laugh. I know you are not being cruel. You would never hurt me." She pursed her lips. "I thought I understood Common."

Tarjiaan chuckled. "Your Common is still better than my Imperial," he pointed out, making her smile.

"That would not be difficult," she teased. He laughed again and kissed her again.

"I know my faults," he said. "I've never been good with languages, and I know it. I speak Common and Sualimani, and that's all. So if my lack of skill amuses you? I'm glad that I can make you laugh."

"Is that how I would say it? I make you laugh?"

"Yes, that's how you say it."

Nika nodded. "Then it is good that I make you laugh. You need to laugh more."

Tarjiaan nodded. "We all do. And I can't wait until that's all we have to worry about." He raised his head as someone knocked on the door. "Do you want to be sitting in my lap when they come in?"

"I should move," Nika said. She kissed Tarjiaan, then slipped from his lap and stood up, smoothing her skirts as she moved to her chair. Once she was seated, Tarjiaan raised his voice.

"Come in!"

The door opened, and Wilaanger came in, followed by Chel. Chel smiled when she saw them.

"Uncle said I should come and look in on you," she said. "A touch of pregnancy sickness?"

Nika nodded. "It came on me all of a sudden. I was fine, and then I felt terrible."

"Had you eaten yet?" Chel asked. "Having something on your stomach will help."

"I had not. And that seems wrong," Nika said. "Will it not make me sick?"

"No, because what's making you feel sick is the fact that your stomach is empty. That's why it happens first thing in the morning. Keep something next to the bed, and eat before you get up." She smiled. "I don't think Tarjiaan will mind crumbs."

"I can shake them out of the sheets when I make the bed," Tarjiaan said. "Chel, what would you recommend?"

Chel looked thoughtful. "I think... Nika, you liked the ration biscuits, didn't you?"

"I did," Nika said. "And we were going to speak to you about them, but for Tarjiaan."

"About ration biscuits?" Wilaanger looked puzzled. "Why?"

"Because Nika thinks that I need to be eating more frequently to help with recovery. Balancing that with our lack of supplies means ration biscuits. I can keep them in my coat pocket so I have them on me at all times."

Wilaanger nodded slowly. "That's a very good idea," he said. "I'll tell Nimas to have some sent over. Just remember to drink."

Tarjiaan nodded. "Wil, that isn't the only thing I needed to talk to you about."

"So you said," Wilaanger replied. He moved to a chair, waiting for Tarjiaan to nod before sitting down. "You said you frightened everyone?"

Tarjiaan nodded. "Daanir wanted to show me that there's an entrance to his passages in the cabinet." He gestured over his shoulder. "I stepped in to look, and woke up on the floor. Nika says I fainted." He shook his head and rested his hands on the table. "Daanir said that the cabinet was about the same size as... as the box. He thinks I reacted to the feeling of having the sides pressed against my shoulders."

"I see." Wilaanger rubbed one hand over his face. "How do you feel now?"

"Not... not bad. Not bothered by anything. Still not well, but... not terrible. If that makes any sense?" Tarjiaan took Nika's hand. She sniffed.

"Your heartrate is elevated, but that is because we are talking about this. You still need to eat. Is there anything left, or did Aranti take the food away?"

"I think we finished it," Wilaanger said. "I'll send for the biscuits when we're done. Tarjiaan, tell me your thinking."

"I'm worried," Tarjiaan admitted. "I don't know what will set this off. Before, I knew that if I was in the belowships for too long, I would start having nightmares. This... I've never fainted from being in a small space before! I've never fainted before, and if I fall the wrong way in my armor, I'll hurt myself. Or someone else." He paused, then shook his head. "This is new, and we have no time for me to learn how to manage this new... this new weakness." He saw the scowl start and had to smile. "Don't start. I know you don't think they're weaknesses."

"They're not, and I won't hear you call yourself weak," Wilaanger said. "We've sailed this current how many times? A weak man would never have survived what you have. A weak man would never have been able to do everything that you've done."

"I know, Wil," Tarjiaan replied. "And I'm not saying I'm weak. I'm saying... I'm not at my best right now, and this is...a new complication that I need to learn to address in less-than-optimal conditions." He paused, then smiled. "Better phrasing?"

"Not much, but yes," Wilaanger grumbled. He drummed his fingers on the tabletop. "And we don't have the time or the flexibility to work through desensitizing you. Not until we're safe."

Tarjiaan grimaced, remembering the first time he and Wil had tried to work through his problems with small spaces. "Exactly."

"Jiaan, what does that mean?" Nika asked. "De...what?"

"Desensitization," Tarjiaan repeated. "It's a way to deal with overwhelming fears. I have trouble with small spaces. So, the last time we did this, it was by exposing me to a small space for increasing amounts of time. Once I was comfortable, we moved to a smaller space. It worked, to a point."

Nika went ashen, her eyes wide. "I... how is that not considered torture?"

Tarjiaan looked at Wilaanger, who shrugged. "It wasn't pleasant," Wilaanger said. "It never is. But Tarjiaan and I discussed it beforehand. We went into it knowing it would be unpleasant at best, and we never went past his endurance. There was recovery time between sessions, and... well, it worked. To a point."

"To a point," Tarjiaan repeated. "The point that I could be functional below. Nika, I told you that I drank to excess. Part of that was to help with the craving for the drugs Aanaji... Ilaris had been making Aanaji feed me. Part of it was to deal with the feeling that the walls were closing in. If I was drunk, I didn't care. Once I was sober..." He paused and took a deep breath. "You saw what my nightmares could be like. Working through it with Wil... made it so I could sleep at night. And once I was sleeping, I could better recover."

"And when he had recovered and was strong enough to start using his armor, he spent a year fostering in the Sualimani court," Wilaanger added.

"You lived on land?"

Tarjiaan looked up to see Daanir standing in the doorway. "That's where I learned to walk again, and to use my armor. Although I spent my first three weeks on land feeling as if the ground was rocking under me,"

"I never thought about that." Daanir came around the table, resting his hand on Tarjiaan's shoulder. "But you'd have had to learn it somewhere else, for the same reason you can't wear it below now."

Tarjiaan nodded. "Uncle sent me to the Sualimani court to finish my recovery, and Falian assigned a Mancer to come with me and teach me to use the armor. Which is how we got Ishantar — she broke through while we were in court." He grinned. "It was my first time ever living on land, and I was landsick for days. Queen Ysnia thought I was insane."

"You have met my grandmother?" Nika asked.

"Yes, and I can't wait for you to meet her. You'll love her." He turned to Daanir. "How are the comms?"

"A mess," Daanir said as he sat down. "I'm going back in a minute. I wanted to be here when you talked to Wil. Did you tell him about what happened?"

"Yes," Nika answered before Tarjiaan could. "And now they are talking about torture."

Daanir coughed and sat up straighter, his hands balling into fists. "I'm sorry? What?"

"Desensitization therapy," Tarjiaan said. "I've done it before." He reached out and rested his hand on Daanir's forearm, feeling the tension. "It's fine, Daan."

"It is going to hurt you," Nika protested. "It is not fine!"

Tarjiaan closed his eyes and took a deep breath. "Wil, tell her about my broken arm?"

"Broken... oh!" Wilaanger laughed. "I remember that."

"The one you broke when we were just starting training?" Daanir asked. "I... oh, I see."

"What broken arm?" Nika asked. "How is that important?"

"Because Tarjiaan broke his left arm in training practice when he was eleven. A bad break, and the physician on the *Marauder* set the bone wrong." Wilaanger gestured for Nika's hand, then traced a line across her forearm. "The bones here weren't aligned correctly, and it was causing Tarjiaan pain. So Taarik sent Tarjiaan to me, and in order for the arm to heal properly, I had to rebreak the bones."

Nika frowned, then turned in her chair and held her hand out to Tarjiaan. He was expecting it, and put his left hand into hers. She ran her other hand up his arm, stopping right over where the bones had been broken.

"I... I did not know that was something that was done," she said slowly.

"Sometimes, you have to break something to mend it," Tarjiaan said. He covered her hand with his. "Nika, I won't lie. It's not going to be pleasant. But it will help."

"Once you start, what do we expect?" Daanir asked. "And how do we help?"

Tarjiaan leaned back in his chair, frowning slightly. Remembering. "I'm wondering if it won't be as bad this time," he said slowly. "I'll be able to get back under the sky on the dockyards. I won't be going from a small space to a slightly larger small space."

"This is true," Wilaanger said, nodding. "You'll have more of a respite between sessions."

"You're doing this... where?" Daanir asked.

"Once we're at the dockyards," Tarjiaan answered. "And what to expect? We may not be getting much sleep for a bit. Or you and Nika might want to sleep in the royal apartments in the dockyards."

"I am not leaving you alone with your nightmares," Nika said, her voice firm. Daanir nodded and pointed at her.

"What she said."

Tarjiaan smiled. "I love you both. Thank you. How you can help? Ah... Wil?"

"Let me think on that," Wilaanger said. "There is some evidence that introducing a new, positive association with whatever is causing the reaction can help. Perhaps that might be where you two come in."

"Positive association with small spaces, you mean?" Nika said. She looked distant, thoughtful, nodding gently. "I... yes, I can see how that may help."

"We'll discuss this further once we're safely at the dockyards," Wilaanger said. "In the meantime—"

A whistle sounded in Tarjiaan's ear. He held up one hand while tapping his earpiece with the other. "Marikaar, report."

"*Captain, ship on the horizon!*" Marikaar replied. "*Looks like a Meradonese hull. And I'm fairly certain they've seen us.*"

Tarjiaan swallowed. "All hands, beat to quarters. Try to evade. Ishantar, can you hear me?"

"*Yes, Captain.*"

"Get those comms online!"

"That's my hint," Daanir said, standing up. "Tell her I'm on my way." He kissed Tarjiaan, then Nika, then hurried out of the cabin.

"I heard him. Thank you, Captain."

"Where do you want me, Jiaan?" Nika asked.

"The infirmary," Tarjiaan answered, standing up. "Be ready. I hate the thought that we might have to fight our own people, but we don't know what they've been told."

Nika nodded and stood up, coming to his side. He leaned down and kissed her, smiling as she caressed his cheek.

"Be careful," she warned.

"You, too." He watched them leave, then went to one of the wall cabinets. He buttoned his coat, then opened the cabinet and took out his belt, cinching it around his waist. He clipped his saber to the belt, then took out his force pistol and checked the charge. He wasn't going to put on his chest armor. Not unless he had to. Putting it on would tell his men that he expected an attack from their own people.

Hopefully, it wouldn't come to that. He tapped his earpiece.

"Mancers?"

"This thing isn't even good for parts," Daanir said. *"But we have an idea..."*

"Meet me at the helm."

Chapter Four
Dauntless

TARJIAAN LOWERED HIS spyglass and grimaced.

"It's the *Dauntless*," he said over his shoulder. "And they're definitely closing on us." He tapped his earpiece. "Marikaar, shorten the sails and send up the distress flag. Let's see if we can stop this before it starts." He tapped the earpiece again, closed the glass and turned to look at Daanir and Kaapi. "What's this idea?"

"We don't have comms," Daanir said. "But the submersible does. Kaapi suggested we take it out, and once we're in range, we show them the disk."

"They'll have to accept your signal, and if they've been told you murdered me, the King and the Physician Royal, that's the last thing they'll do," Tarjiaan pointed out. "How are you... wait. You're going to tap into the *Dauntless'* systems? From the sub?"

Daanir nodded. "I did it when we reached the *Wave Runner*," he said. "It's how we found out what was going on and where you were."

"And you were functional after that how?" Tarjiaan demanded.

"Mama Nika made Papa rest after he did it," Kaapi answered, smiling up at her father when he mock-glared at her. Tarjiaan smiled. Mama Nika? He'd have to tell her.

"She did, hm?" he replied. "And he listened?"

"He was sleeping hard enough that he was snoring." Kaapi grinned. "I've never heard him snore before."

"It's an impressive sound, isn't it?" Tarjiaan looked back out over the water toward the other ship. "You can't do this and pilot. And you should have a healer with you. Who are you taking with you? Besides Nika?"

"Why do you think I'm taking Nika?" Daanir asked. He took the spyglass from Tarjiaan's hand and looked out at the *Dauntless*. "They're definitely moving to intercept. So...." He handed the glass back to Tarjiaan. "Why am I taking Nika?"

"Because she tells you to rest and you listen." Tarjiaan tapped his bicep with the glass, fighting to keep his other reason out of his face — if everything went wrong, Daanir and Nika would be safe.

"Fair." Daanir nodded. "And she's a decent pilot, too."

Tarjiaan blinked and turned to face Daanir. "She is?"

"She's got a good touch. Still needs to work on her confidence, get a bit more practice in, but she's good." Daanir grinned. "And we never told you, did we?"

"No, you did not!" Tarjiaan shook his head and sighed. "You can tell me later. Nika is going with you as a healer and relief pilot. Pick a pilot and promise me you won't die."

Daanir laughed. "I promise we'll try not to. And I'm assuming you have instructions for me in case everything goes wrong?"

Tarjiaan grimaced. "You know me too well. Yes, I do. Or rather, I would have."

"You'd have left them in the submersible?"

"Yes." Tarjiaan answered. "If everything goes wrong, go to Sualiman. Tell Ysnia what happened and show her the disk."

Daanir nodded, looking out at the water and the other ship. He reached out and rested his hand on Kaapi's shoulder and said, "Then I'm taking the children, too. Just in case." He turned to look at Tarjiaan. "You made me promise. You have to promise, too."

"I promise that I'll try not to die," Tarjiaan replied. "Kaapi, will you make sure that Nika doesn't push too hard?"

"Because of the baby?" Kaapi asked. She nodded. "I can do that."

"Go find Naajir. Meet us at the submersible. I'll get Nika. And..." Daanir frowned. "Who's the best pilot?"

Tarjiaan nodded and tapped his earpiece again. "Marikaar, have Lorithi get ready to pilot the submersible."

"And go where?"

"Meet me at the helm. I'll fill you in." He tapped the earpiece again, then turned to Daanir. "Be careful, Daan. And later... I want you to tell me everything we haven't had time for. Teaching Nika to pilot, and tapping into the *Wave Runner* from the sub?"

Daanir nodded. "And she answered. In *words*, Jiaan!"

Tarjiaan stared at him for a moment, then shook his head and laughed. "I want to hear all of this. Later. I love you."

Daanir smiled. "I love you, too." He stepped in close, clearly waiting for something. Tarjiaan nodded, leaned down, and kissed him twice.

"One for Nika," he said as he straightened. "She was pleased you sent one for her. You know where the disk is. Be careful, Daan."

"I'll keep her safe. I'll keep all of us safe. We'll be back." Daanir rested his hand on Tarjiaan's chest. "Stay safe. And don't hurt my ship."

"My ship," Tarjiaan replied.

"She doesn't talk to you," Daanir said. "Come on, Kaap."

"Where are we going?" Nika asked.

"I'll explain once we're all together," Daanir said as they reached the docking bay. A young man was waiting at the submersible. "You're Lorithi?"

"Yes, sir. I'm your pilot. Ah... I wasn't told much of anything. Commander Marikaar just said to follow your orders. Where are we going?"

Daanir smiled. "I'll explain once we're together," he repeated, "so I only have to do it once. Kaapi and Naajir will be here shortly, and we'll get underway." He turned toward the hatch. "They're in the corridor. Get ready to go. "

A few minutes later, the submersible launched, and Daanir moved to stand behind Lorithi's chair. "Take us toward the *Dauntless*. We're going to tap into their systems from here."

"The way you did to the *Wave Runner*?" Nika asked. "And that is why I am here?"

"Exactly. Because, according to Tarjiaan and to Kaapi, you tell me to rest and I listen." Daanir grinned at Kaapi, who laughed.

"Why?" Naajir asked. "Are we looking for something?"

"No," Daanir answered. "I'm going to take over their systems and push through the information on this." He held up the disk. "We're going to give them the truth."

Lorithi looked up. "What's on the disk?"

"You'll see," Daanir said. He sat down in the other seat at the controls. "I'll take us in to the right distance, and then hand off to you."

"Yes, sir," Lorithi said. He looked back at the others. "We have a healer. Why do we have the boys?"

"I'm not a boy!" Kaapi protested. Daanir chuckled.

"It's a rank, Kaap. Youngest crewmembers on a ship are boys, even if they're girls. I have no idea why. It's tradition."

"Oh, so like calling us powder monkeys?" Naajir asked. "Daanir, why *are* we here?" He paused. "Oh, wait. We're with you because that puts us out of the line of fire?"

"And before you get angry at Tarjiaan for coddling you, it was my idea," Daanir said. He nodded slowly. "Right. Keep it at this depth, Lorithi, and once we're directly underneath the *Dauntless*, come about and keep pace with her. Try to keep out of range of her support pod." He slid the disk into the reader on the control panel, then stood up. "I'm going to get ready. I'm not sure how long this will take. *Dauntless* doesn't know me like the *Wave Runner* does."

"Does the *Dauntless* know the *Wave Runner*?" Nika asked. "If you tell the *Dauntless* that you are the *Wave Runner's*... father? Would she listen to you the way that the *Wave Runner* does?"

Daanir sat down on the long couch and stared at Nika. "I... I don't know how to answer that."

"Then you should answer me once you know." Nika came over to stand in front of him, leaned down, and kissed his forehead. "Try not to hurt yourself. Do we have more of the mancer juice?"

"I'll get it ready, Mama," Kaapi said, then clapped a hand over her mouth. Nika looked at her, clearly surprised, and Kaapi turned pink. "I...."

"Do not apologize, Kaapi," Nika said. "I told you. You are family. You may certainly call me Mama. Now go and get the juice ready. Daan? Be careful."

Daanir nodded. He stretched out on the couch, closed his eyes, and reached out past the submersible. He didn't know the *Dauntless*, didn't know what her central core felt like. Would he be able to find her before he got lost in the depths.

No. No room for doubts. He had to do this. He reached, and felt something touch his thoughts.

[Who are you?]

Daanir fought back the giddy elation — he'd found the *Dauntless*, and she was just as alert as the *Wave Runner*. *"Hello,"* Daanir answered. *"I am Daanir."*

[Wave Runner's Daanir? Wave Runner told me about her Daanir.]

The ships *talked* to each other? "*Yes. I need to show your Captain something. May I give it to you?*"

A pause. [*Why not use comms?*]

"*Because the* Wave Runner *is hurt, and her comms aren't working. We need help, and we need to tell your Captain the truth. Will you help me?*"

[*Wave Runner is hurt?*] Daanir could feel the *Dauntless'* distress. [*Yes. I will help* Wave Runner. *What are your orders?*]

"*Thank you, my lovely. I'm going to give you a file. Please play it on all screens. Once your captain has seen it, open a comms channel to the submersible below you.*"

[*Understood. Let me have it.*]

Daanir tapped into the submersible systems, pulling a copy of the file and passing to the *Dauntless*. For an infinite moment, there was nothing. Then Daanir felt an unmistakable wave of mirth.

[*Captain is making funny noises. Go back. Comms will open when you are ready.*]

Daanir opened his eyes and winced. "It's done," he croaked. "And yes." He sat up slowly, feeling Nika's hands on his shoulders as she steadied him.

"Here," she said. "Drink this slowly." She took his hand and put a cup into it; he sipped the mancer juice and closed his eyes.

"*Dauntless* said it was done," he said. "And she said she'll open the comms when we're ready." He looked at Nika and grinned. "And they do talk to each other. The ships. *Dauntless* said that *Wave Runner* told her about me." He sipped more of the juice and took a deep breath.

"Mancer, there's something odd out here," Lorithi said. "Or rather, there's something odd not here. You told me to keep away from the *Dauntless'* pod. But there's no pod out here. She's the only vessel."

"What?" Daanir blinked. "That doesn't make sense." He got to his feet and staggered over to the pilot's chair, staring at the controls. "I... where are they?"

"We can ask, once this is done." Nika joined him at the controls. "Now what?"

"Now, we open comms and talk..." Daanir blinked as the comms started to beep. "They're hailing us?"

"Wide band, all frequencies," Lorithi answered. "They know we're here, but not where, I don't think. Accept the signal?"

"Please," Nika replied. Lorithi tapped the console, and an angry male voice filled the submersible.

"*...don't know who the fuck is out there or what this recording is, but I want answers, and I want them now!*"

Daanir opened his mouth, then stopped as Nika put her hand on his arm.

"What is his name?" she asked.

"Theonus," Daanir answered. "Why?"

Nika smiled at him, then drew herself up to her full, scant height. "Open the comms," she ordered.

Lorithi looked up. "Comms opened, ma'am."

Nika nodded, then squared her shoulders. "Captain Theonus, this is not the behavior I would expect from a Captain of the Meradonese fleet," she said, her voice crisp and even. The comms fell silent, and Daanir heard muttering. Then Theonus came back on.

"*Who... with whom am I speaking?*"

Nika smiled slightly. "Much better. I am Princess Ysnika, wife of the Sea Prince Tarjiaan. The *Wave Runner* has been badly damaged in battle, and our comms were destroyed. What you have seen is the truth of what happened to our beloved King Ikaanaji. Anything you have been told otherwise is a lie."

"*I... that recording was* real? *Tarjiaan is alive?*"

"He very nearly was not — Ilaris handed him over to Imperial forces. He was imprisoned and tortured for twenty-three days before we retook the *Wave Runner* and rescued him."

"*Ma'am.... Your Highness... I... we were told that the Mancer Royal betrayed and murdered the King, the Physician Royal, and the Sea Prince. We were told that he went mad—*"

"Another lie," Nika replied. "If it were not for the Mancer Royal, I would be dead. Tarjiaan would be dead. The *Wave Runner* would have been destroyed, and Meradon would be... what is the phrase? Seafoam and memory?" She paused. "Do you know Daanir, Captain? Do you know Tarjiaan?"

"*I... I trained with them, Ma'am, but I've known Tarjiaan since we were in the crèche together.*"

"Then you know the bond that he has with his battle companion. Do you honestly believe that Daanir could even for a moment harbor the thought of hurting Tarjiaan?" Nika looked up at Daanir and smiled. "Do you think that even in madness, that thought could exist within his heart?"

Silence. Daanir swallowed, stepping back and watching as Nika rested her hands on Lorithi's chair. Watching her taking command... he wished Tarjiaan could see her. And wondered if Tarjiaan would find it just as arousing as he did.

"*Ma'am? May I offer my invitation to have you come aboard?*"

Nika frowned slightly, then glanced at Daanir for the first time. He shook his head, and she nodded. "Thank you, Captain," she replied. "But until I am certain of your loyalty, I shall remain where I am. You are welcome to meet with us on the *Wave Runner.*"

"*Thank you, Ma'am. I... you don't have comms on the* Wave Runner?"

"Local only," Daanir murmured. "Tell him that."

"I am told that we only have local comms. I think that means only aboard the ship?" Nika glanced at Daanir again; he nodded.

"If you have a submersible, you may follow us back to the *Wave Runner,* and we will escort you to my husband." She paused. "There is more here than you know, Captain."

"*I... I see that, Ma'am.*" A pause. "*It will take us a few minutes to get a sub underway. The party will be myself, my battle companion, and our Mancer.*"

Nika nodded. "Very good, Captain. Signal us when you are ready. And... Captain, where is your... what is it? Your support pod?"

"*Ah... long story, Ma'am. May I wait until I'm onboard the* Wave Runner *so I only have to tell it once?*"

"Of course. Signal us when you are ready." She tapped Lorithi on the shoulder. He nodded, then looked up.

"Comms closed, ma'am."

"Thank you." Nika turned, and her eyes widened when she saw Daanir watching her. "What?"

Daanir smiled. "Nothing. Just wishing that Jiaan could have seen that. I mean... you made the hard choices when we escaped, but this is the first time I've seen you really take command and be the Queen."

"I am not the Queen. Not yet." Nika licked her lips. "As Jiaan says, it is an empty title until he holds the throne." She smiled. "But I am learning. It was... part of how I see Jiaan with his men, and part of how I saw King Ikaanaji at the wedding."

"And I think that quite a lot of that was you being yourself." Daanir added. "Being who Masthaka's daughter was always meant to be." He watched as her eyes widened. As her shoulders squared and she stood just a little taller. She held her hand out to him, and he took it and raised it to his lips, kissing her palm. She caressed his cheek, scratching her nails against his beard, then turned back toward the console.

"Lorithi, once the signal comes in, take us home."

"Yes, Your Majesty."

Daanir followed Nika and the children out of the submersible, and gestured to the docking bay that he'd opened for their guests. "Jiaan is on his way, and they'll be docking in a moment. Do you want me here?"

Nika looked puzzled. "Why would you be anywhere else?"

"Because we're still not sure they believe us?" Daanir answered slowly. "If they think I'm threatening you, things might get... exciting."

Nika nodded. "Then... do not let them leave their submersible until Jiaan is here."

"And hide behind him?" Daanir grinned. "Sounds backwards."

"No, it puts you in the proper order of favored males." Nika turned at the sound of heavy footsteps. "There he is."

Tarjiaan came around the corner. He looked tense, and Daanir grimaced.

"Corridor?"

Tarjiaan nodded. "It never seemed this long before. Where are they?"

Daanir glanced at the hatch, unlocking it without touching the panel. It slid open, revealing a familiar man, with an equally familiar woman at his left.

"Ah... permission to come aboard?" Theonus asked. "Sorry, we'd have been out sooner, but the hatch wouldn't open."

Tarjiaan arched a brow at Daanir, who smiled.

"The Queen's orders," he answered. "She said to wait for you."

"Nika, you didn't have to wait for me," Tarjiaan said. "I've known this walking bait bucket since we were boys."

Nika looked up at him. "I did not know that, and I thought otherwise. We can discuss it later."

"Fine." Tarjiaan turned to the hatch. "Permission granted. Theo, it's good to see you." He held his hand out to the other captain, who clasped it, then pulled him in for a brief embrace.

"Good to see you, Jiaan." He looked Tarjiaan up and down. "Impressive armor. You can tell me about it later. And... forgive me, my friend, but you look like chum."

Tarjiaan laughed. "In truth, I came far closer than I'd like to being chum." He looked past Theonus. "Nyssa, it's good to see you, too."

"Prince-Captain," the woman said. She bowed, then straightened. "Or should I be calling you Your Majesty?"

"Not yet," Tarjiaan said. "Now, come to the great cabin. We have to talk."

"I brought our mancer," Theonus said, gesturing behind him to an older man. "Thought he could be of use to you."

Daanir looked past the captain and his battle companion, then blinked, feeling his stomach start to churn as he recognized the older man. "Oh. Mancer Gellan. It's been some time."

"Daanir. You've come up in the world." Gellan looked him up and down. "Honestly, I can't imagine how. It's a disgrace — the Mancer Royal badge on the chest of a hopped-up crèche brat—"

"Excuse me?" Tarjiaan growled. "Is there something wrong with being a crèche brat, Mancer Gellan? Be wary of how you answer that — in case you forgot, I came up in the crèche."

"As did I, Gellan," Theonus added. "And I've already warned you to stop that snobbery. I won't have it on my ship."

Gellan sniffed. "Captain, he earned that rank on his face and you know it—"

"Captain Theonus." Nika's voice was sharp. "Send your Mancer back to your own ship. He is not welcome here."

Tarjiaan looked at her, then nodded. "I agree with my wife. Mancer Gellan, you are dismissed."

"Your Highness, I—"

"Be sure to tell the *Dauntless* what you think of the *Wave Runner's* father," Nika added. "I am certain she will have an opinion about that, and it will not be what you think. I think she will be quite cross. In fact, I think that your ship may never speak to you again."

Gellan went pale. "I... what?" he gasped. "I... tell her? And she'll speak to me? You think I can talk to her? Woman, who's been telling you those stories?"

"They're not stories." Daanir looked surprised. "You don't talk to *Dauntless*? She doesn't answer? She answered me. That's how I got the signal to broadcast. I asked her, and she let me."

"I... that's just a *story*. Ships don't... they can't...." Gellan stammered.

"They can," Daanir replied. He looked up and decided to take a chance. "Can't you, my lovely? Would you show Mancer Gellan?"

He hadn't really expected an answer. Hadn't expected more than perhaps the lights dimming. So when a mechanical voice cracked over the speaker, Daanir had to fight to keep from laughing in sheer, giddy glee.

[I do not like him. He is not nice.] The hatch door started to close. [Go away!]

"*Wave Runner!*" Daanir chided as he stopped the door closing.

[I don't want him here!]

"That's up to the Captain, *Wave Runner.*" Daanir turned to Tarjiaan. "Captain? Your orders?"

Gellan went pale. "I... no! That wasn't... that was the *ship*?"

"I already gave them," Tarjiaan said, ignoring Gellan. "Mancer Gellan, you are dismissed." He turned to Daanir. "Daan, perhaps you would warn me before you teach my ship new tricks? That truly was her?"

"Sorry. Yes, that truly was the *Wave Runner*." Daanir snickered at the look on Tarjiaan's face, wondering if it mirrored the one on his own. "Our ship. The one I designed and built, and the one that you love. The one that knows me, knows her captain, and knows her own mind. Maybe you're not as strong as you think, Gellan. Or you should start being nicer to your ship."

"But... you... you talked? To *my* ship? How?" Gellan looked horrified.

"He is the Mancer Royal. All of Meradon's ships answer to him," Nika answered, and her tone said clearly that this was the only answer anyone should ever need. She rested her hand on Tarjiaan's arm. "Now, shall we go? The corridor is no place to have a discussion."

Chapter Five
Mutiny

TARJIAAN TOOK HIS REGULAR seat at the table in the great cabin, with Nika on his right. Daanir's place was empty — he'd opted to take the apprentices back to work on the comms.

"I apologize for that," Theonus said as he and Nyssa sat down. "Gellan hasn't been assigned to us for very long. And from what I understand, he's always been somewhat... abrasive. I thought he'd be able to help with your repairs, but... I didn't know about his history with Daanir."

"Neither did I," Tarjiaan answered. He picked up the water pitcher and filled cups, passing them out. "But there's a lot I don't know about what and where Daanir has been for the past fifteen years. He and I were separated after the *Marauder*. We've only just been reunited." He shook his head at the surprised look on Theonus' face. "Long story, Theo. And we have more pressing issues."

"I'll wait, then," Theonus said. "But I want to hear all of it. It's been so long. There's so much I want to hear. Including how Daanir learned that ships really can talk! But this is more important. Could you explain more of what's happened now?"

"First, tell me. You've seen the recording?" Tarjiaan asked.

Theonus nodded. "Yes. I couldn't have avoided it if I'd tried. It was on every screen and speaker on the *Dauntless*. Gellan was beside himself. He couldn't tell where it was coming from, only that *Dauntless* was getting the signal from somewhere. And I'm afraid I got a little... uncivil." He turned back to Nika. "Your Highness..."

"Please, call me Nika," Nika said.

Theonus smiled. "Thank you. It's lovely to meet you, Nika. And I apologize for my behavior earlier."

"You are forgiven," Nika said. "You've known Jiaan a long time?" She looked at Tarjiaan. "Bait bucket seems a rude thing to call someone."

Theonus grinned. "It's not. I promise. And yes, I've known Jiaan... almost thirty years now, isn't it? When new kids come into the crèche, they get assigned someone to help them learn how things work. It's called being their guide. I was Tarjiaan's, back when he first came to the crèche."

"I was seven," Tarjiaan added. "Theo was eight, and... am I remembering right? You were the only one in the royal crèche who didn't have a tagalong?"

The other captain nodded. "That's right. So I got you, and when your father brought you up to the *Marauder*, I came up, too. We trained together, then I went to the *Dauntless*. And I never left. We've seen each other in passing over the years, but... never for long enough to catch up." He turned back to Tarjiaan. "Jiaan, tell us what we're missing. And what's the plan?" He grinned at Nika. "And why wasn't I invited to the wedding? I'm crushed."

Tarjiaan snorted. "Starting with the last question, you weren't invited because... let me see. I had roughly two hours of warning that I was getting married? Maybe three. My uncle asked me to marry, because he thought there was a chance for peace. But it wasn't so much a request as an order."

"That... doesn't sound like something the Sea King would do," Nyssa said slowly. "He was always so kind. Granted, I last saw him ages ago. But still..."

"I know. Theo, Nyssa, this information doesn't leave this table." Tarjiaan waited for them both to agree before he took a deep breath. "My uncle was dying. He wanted to stand on land once more before he died, and this marriage and the associated treaty were his path to do so. He was... well, desperate. So he boxed me in."

"It seems to have worked out well," Theonus said. "Your lady is... honestly, from the conversation I had with her in the submersible, I was expecting someone more... imposing. I should know better than to underestimate the little ones, though."

"You should." Tarjiaan looked at Nika and smiled, taking her hand. "It turns out that our marriage was the only thing that was real out of that entire mission. There was no treaty, and the emissary wasn't sent by the Emperor. He was actually the Emperor's son and Nika's father. He raised an army to overthrow the Emperor, and he wanted us to ally with him. But everything went wrong, and then..." He paused. "Then Ilaris betrayed us. You saw that on the recording. And you heard my sister. He's been betraying us for years. He gave me to the Imperial High Priest, and I was their prisoner until my crew, my companion, and my wife saved my life."

"Ilaris did this?" Nyssa said. "He... why? Why would he do this?"

Tarjiaan shook his head. "I honestly don't understand the why. Not completely. I know he's bitter. He has reason to be, which... that's not my story to tell. Suffice it to say, he has reason to be angry. But to destroy everything we've worked for... I can't imagine what he hopes to accomplish. And now... he has hostages on the *Chimaera*, and we have all of Meradon to think of."

"What's the plan?" Theonus repeated.

"Right now? Repairs," Tarjiaan answered. "The *Wave Runner* has seen more battle in the past month than it has in the past year. We sailed through that ship-killer, Theo, and fought the Imperial navy. And... well, I've seen things in the past few days that I've never seen before. That I never thought were possible." He looked down. "Nika, tell them the story you told me."

"About the *Marauder*?" Nika asked. "It is said in the Empire that there is a ghost ship that haunts Imperial waters. That it is called the *Marauder*, and that it is manned by the Demon Captain and his first mate. That it leaves no survivors."

Nyssa chuckled. "Oh, Captain Taarik would have loved that!"

"That's exactly what I thought," Tarjiaan said. "And... Nyssa, it's not a story. I *saw* them. We all saw them. You can ask any sailor on this ship, and they will tell you that the *Marauder* was there. It was real, and it fought with us. We wouldn't be there without their help." He swallowed, then smiled. "And I finally had a chance to say goodbye to my father."

Theonus reached out and squeezed Tarjiaan's forearm. "Jiaan, that's... you've never lied to me. For all that you were a singer and a storyteller, you never told tales. I... is he still out there?"

"I do not think he is," Nika said. "Because there is no Imperial navy anymore. Between the *Marauder* and the storm, I believe his mission is done."

"No navy?" Nyssa breathed. "The Imps have no ships left?" She touched Theonus' arm. "We can win?"

"I'm not worried about that course yet," Tarjiaan said. "First, we have to take back Meradon. And for that... we need to get the truth out to the fleet."

Theonus nodded. "Of course. Can you make a copy of that recording for us?" He glanced at Nyssa. "We'll have to get Gellan to boost the comm signals to broadcast on a wide band. That's going to be a fun conversation to have."

"When I commed you to hand off our pod, your Mancer was Westin," Tarjiaan said. "How did you end up with a mancer that annoys a ship enough that she refuses to let them board?"

"And that's a line of words that I'd never expected anyone to cast," Theonus said. He shook his head. "The ships talk. And have opinions."

"Mancers have been saying that for years," Nyssa added. "You know my father swore that his ship sang to him."

"And Daan is the Mancer Royal. So it makes sense that they all talk to him." Tarjiaan sipped his water. "Granted, though, I had no idea it was that obvious. But I know I'm missing details that weren't important to our survival. Things I'll find out later." He looked at Nika. "You were going to tell me, weren't you?"

"Of course!" Nika sounded shocked. "Either I would or Daanir would. When there was time."

"Which we haven't had." Tarjiaan turned back to Theonus. "Now, where did Gellan come from?"

"Westin was reassigned, and we got Gellan... it's not even been a month." He paused, a look of horror on his face; he looked at Nyssa, who looked alarmed.

"Theo...."

He nodded. "I heard it when I said it, Nys." He turned to Nika. "You told us that the Imps had Tarjiaan for how long?"

"Twenty-three days," she answered. She frowned. "Why?"

"Because twenty-one days ago was when we were told that the Mancer Royal had gone insane, had murdered the King, the Physician Royal, and Tarjiaan, and that Aanaji was acting as regent for her son." Theonus paused. "That was him, wasn't it? The quiet young man in the docking bay?"

"That was Naajir, yes." Tarjiaan said.

"He looks so much like Ranji—"

"Don't say that around him," Tarjiaan interjected. "He's apparently been told that his entire life, and he hates it."

"Like you and Tisling," Nyssa murmured. Theonus growled at her, and she laughed.

"Where is Tisling these days?" Tarjiaan asked. "I haven't seen her since the *Sea Wolf.*"

"She's First Mate on the *Intrepid.*" Theonus answered. "She seems to prefer being below."

Tarjiaan nodded. "When you talk to her next, tell her I send my regards. Now, back to our current mess. Right after Ilaris betrayed us, you had your Mancer replaced, and you were told a pack of lies."

"And they reassigned our pod," Nyssa added. "Our support pod and yours."

"What?" Tarjiaan closed his eyes and sent his thoughts below, then shook his head. "I hadn't even realized you were alone. But then again, I was distracted by the idea that you might attack."

"The orders said they were being recalled for safety, but now...." Theonus shook his head. "Now he has more hostages, doesn't he? Because it was across the fleet. None of the above ships have support pods now. And with our mancers reassigned? That means that we can't even count on our own ships."

"That's a frightening thought. If the shipboard mancers can control the signals incoming, then it doesn't matter what truth we have. We can't get it to them." Tarjiaan glanced at Nika, to see her nodding thoughtfully.

"I think we must talk to Daanir about this," Nika said.

"We'll have to. He might have answers."

"You really thought we were going to attack?" Nyssa frowned, then nodded. "Fair. Especially since you weren't answering our hails. Your comms are completely destroyed?"

"Daan says that the comms aren't good for anything but parts. We're down our solar sails and most of our guns. The sails were scuttled to keep the Imps from taking the ship as a prize, and the guns were damaged in the fighting. We're also low on supplies, and our hydroponics were off-line before any of this started. And we have a full complement of refugees from an Imperial ship that turned on the others to help us."

Theonus looked startled. "Really? One of them turned?"

"I'll introduce you to one of the most promising young Imperial officers I've ever had the pleasure to meet," Tarjiaan said. "Now, you're both very alarmed about Gellan being assigned to you. What are you thinking?"

Theonus laced his fingers together and rested hands on the table. "Nothing I could set a course by, but... honestly, I don't know how Gellan ever became a senior mancer. He just isn't as good a mancer as Westin. It's to the point that I have trouble believing he was actually a trainer, because how could he teach someone more powerful than he is? And every other above ship mancer I've ever met seems more powerful than he is. Now, he's not incompetent, but there has to be a reason he was sent out to Station Six—"

"Station Six?" Nika interrupted. She looked at Tarjiaan, horror on her face. "Oh..."

"Oh, indeed." Tarjiaan looked at her. "That answers what their history is. Nika, would you go and see if Daanir is all right?"

"Of course." Nika smiled and stood up, kissing Tarjiaan before she left the cabin.

"I missed something," Nyssa said. "What does Station Six have to do with anything? Does it have anything to do with it being gone?"

"Gone?" Tarjiaan repeated. "What do you mean gone?"

"Station Six was overrun by Imp forces. Happened just over a month ago, and only Gellan and the station commander escaped."

Daanir scowled up into the scorched mass of wires and tried to will them whole. The effort was making his eyes itch when he heard Nika's voice.

"Daanir?"

"Busy!" he called.

"You are not. Jiaan says that you told him this was good for nothing but parts. Come out."

Daanir scowled at the wires again, then sighed and slid out from underneath the console, He sat up and looked up at Nika. "Yes?"

She held her hand out. "Come with me."

Daanir frowned. "What?"

She arched a brow. "Come with me."

Daanir rested his arms on his raised knees. "Do I get to know why?"

"Once you come with me."

Daanir sighed and got up, dusting off his trousers. "Kaap, I'll be back shortly," he called. Then he followed Nika out of the comm room. She didn't seem to have a destination in mind, and they walked entirely around the deck before they finally stopped near the rail, looking out toward the *Dauntless*.

"Does she sound like the *Wave Runner*?" Nika asked. "Her voice."

"I..." Daanir frowned. "I'm not sure. They feel different, but I'm not sure if that qualifies as sounding different. This is what you wanted to talk about?"

"And other things." Nika looked up at him. "The woman with Captain Theonus. Nyssa. Is she his wife?"

"Yes. And his battle companion," Daanir answered. "I trained with Nyssa. She's fantastic. I honestly thought she was going to be picked to pair with Tarjiaan. She's that good."

"But you are better," Nika said.

"Not in close quarters fighting. Theonus is lucky to have her."

"And we are lucky to have you." Nika paused, then asked, "Was he your trainer? That horrible Mancer? He taught you?"

"Ah," Daanir murmured. He grimaced and sighed. "I should have expected that question. Yes. Sort of." He glanced at her. "He was part of the problem. He tried to break me. Tried to convince me that I was never going to amount to anything as a mancer, that I had no real power. But... I *knew* he was wrong. I'd already seen what I could do, seen that the machines would listen to me and do what I asked. And I knew that if I was going to get back to Jiaan, I needed to be the best." He took a deep breath. "He undermined every bit of my work, sabotaged my studies, took the credit for my successes... and Ishian let him get away with it."

"But you beat him," Nika said, taking his arm. She pressed her cheek against his bicep. "You got away from them."

"I..." Daanir paused and licked his lips. "I almost didn't. Ishian told me I was going to be permanently assigned to Station Six, and... I forged transfer orders and stowed away on the first ship out of the station." He took a deep breath and blew out. "Never said that out loud before. Never admitted it to anyone. I suppose I'll have to tell Jiaan that at some point. I wasn't supposed to be assigned to the dockyards, but... once they got me and saw what I could do, they weren't letting me go. I'm not sure what Mancer Narrick at the dockyards did, what favors he called in, but he got Mancer Royal Falian to officially assign me to the dockyards." He looked down at Nika. "I never thought I'd have to see Gellan again. And... seeing him here? On my ship?" He covered her hand with his. "Thank you for defending me."

"It was the truth," Nika said. "You are the Mancer Royal. All the ships of Meradon answer to you." She looked back out over the water, then frowned. "Daan? Is the *Dauntless* moving?"

"What?" Daanir turned, seeing the wake starting to appear behind the *Dauntless*. "He's stealing the ship!" He turned his comm earpiece on with a thought. "All hands! Prepare to engage!"

"*Mancer! Report!*" Tarjiaan's voice rang in his ear.

"*Dauntless* is underway!" Daanir watched the ship slowly moving, noticing the position of her sails. Something wasn't right... "And I think she's fighting back," he added.

"*On our way!*"

"What do we do?" Nika asked. "We are not going to let him take the ship, are we?"

"Not if I have anything to say about it," Daanir answered, turning to see Tarjiaan, Theonus and Nyssa running toward them.

"What's he doing to my ship?" Theonus demanded. "I... I see what you mean about fighting back. They're not going anywhere with the sails set like that!"

"Mancer, do you have a plan?" Tarjiaan asked.

Daanir stared at him for a moment, then looked back at the ship. "I... same way we got into the *Wave Runner*," he said slowly. "Sub, and I override the systems from outside. Get her to take us aboard. And I can take control from Gellan once I'm onboard." He looked at Tarjiaan. "I'll need a guard. And a healer that isn't Nika."

"Why not me?" Nika demanded. "

"Because we're going into a possible fight and you only just learned to shoot," Daanir answered. "You are staying here and staying safe." He saw the stubborn look on her face and held up one finger. "Let me amend that. You are staying here and keeping the baby safe."

Her eyes widened, and her jaw dropped. "I... oh."

"Thank you," Tarjiaan murmured. He tapped his earpiece. "Marikaar! I need an armed guard and a healer in the docking bay immediately." He turned to Theonus. "You take care of Daanir, Theo."

Theonus nodded. "Nyssa will guard him as well as she guards me."

"On my honor, Captain," Nyssa said. She bowed. "Daan, show us the way."

Daanir nodded and turned to Tarjiaan. "Captain, by your leave?"

"Granted. Be careful, Daan." Tarjiaan said. He pulled Daanir in close and kissed him, then stepped back and let Nika come forward.

Daanir leaned down and kissed her, then arched a brow. "What?"

"You do not fight fair," she grumbled.

"Where you're concerned?" Daanir said. "I'll cheat every minute of every day to keep you and him and that baby safe." He pointed from her to Tarjiaan, and back to her. "Understood?"

She nodded. "I love you, too. Be careful."

"You'll barely know I'm gone." Daanir turned and gestured to Theonus and Nyssa. "This way."

Chapter Six
Counterstrike

"I'LL PILOT," THEONUS said, sliding into the seat at the controls. "Tell me what to do."

"You're going to get up as close as you can to her," Daanir answered, resting his hand on the back of the seat. "But we need to wait for the guard and the healer."

"Who I think are here," Nyssa called.

Daanir turned and blinked. "Antivar? Navi? What are you doing here?"

"You needed a guard and a healer, Marikaar said." Antivar smiled. "I want to make myself useful, so I volunteered as a guard. Brief us?"

Daanir nodded, gesturing for Navi to sit down. "Theonus, take us out. Antivar, Navi, this is Nyssa, and our pilot is Theonus. He's captain of the *Dauntless*. Their mancer has gone rogue, and is trying to make off with the ship, but the ship is fighting back."

Antivar's eyes widened. "Your ships can do that? They're alive?"

"Ah..." Daanir coughed. "We'll debate that one later. Let's leave it as they're aware. And *Dauntless* is not letting Gellan get away without a fight. We're going to go help her."

Antivar nodded. "And what do you need from us?"

"I'm going to reach *Dauntless* from the submersible, get her to open her bay and let us in." He looked at Navi. "That's why we need you, Navi. Did anyone tell you what to expect?"

"Chel told," Navi answered. "I know already. Mages fall down. Mancers fall down. Same same."

Daanir blinked. "Interesting. Another thing to talk about later. Once we're on the *Dauntless*, Theonus and Nyssa will take their ship back. I'll need to stop the mancer. Antivar, that's where you come in."

"To watch your back?" Antivar nodded. "Wise. In case it's not just the mancer who has turned."

"I... what?" Nyssa gasped. "Are you saying our *crew* might turn?"

"Perhaps not, but..." Antivar looked thoughtful. "Captain, my Lady, Marikaar said you only just got this mancer on your ship. Were any other crew members changed at the same time?"

Theonus didn't turn from the controls when he answered, "Yes. But... how did you know?"

"It's an Imperial way of keeping a ship from mutiny — rotating the crews regularly. Don't let them form bonds, don't let them fully trust each other." Antivar grimaced. "You'll need to get word to the crew who have served you longer, because the new crew almost certainly will side with this rogue mage."

Nyssa nodded. "You're the promising Imperial officer who helped save the *Wave Runner*? I can see why Tarjiaan thinks so highly of you."

Antivar's cheeks darkened. "The Captain exaggerates."

"The Captain most certainly does not," Daanir retorted. "That's something I don't think we knew. Or that we thought of."

Antivar frowned. "If you did not think of that, then why did you want a guard?"

Daanir nodded. "Good question. I'll be fighting him with mancery, but while he's paying attention to me, he won't be paying attention to you."

"Ah." Antivar rested his hand on his saber. "Do you want him dead? Or do you want him able to stand trial?" He took something from his coat pocket with his other hand, showing Daanir the wide, gold chain. "Marikaar gave me this. He said I would need it if we take him alive." He looked down at it. "A slave collar?"

"Ah... no. It's a limiter. It locks down a mancer's power, keeps them from controlling anything." Daanir shuddered. "It's not pleasant. Ah... I'll leave it to your best judgment. Don't risk yourself or the ship to take him down alive if killing him would be safer."

"Understood, sir." Antivar frowned slightly as he tucked the limiter back into his pocket. "I... I have a question."

"Go ahead," Theonus said. "We have a few minutes before we're in position."

"Captain, you and the Lady Nyssa are going to take the ship back. I am guarding Mancer Daanir. Who stays with Navi?"

"Oh," Nyssa murmured.

Navi made a rude noise. "Can fight."

"With what weapon?" Antivar countered. "You're unarmed."

Navi looked at him and laughed. "*Am* a weapon!"

"What?" Daanir looked at Navi, then realized what the healer was saying. "Oh. Oh, you are, aren't you? I never... oh, you have to tell Nika that."

Navi smiled. "Will tell. Will teach. Don't worry."

"I missed something," Nyssa said. "Several somethings. How is he a weapon?"

"He has the Sualimani healing gift," Daanir answered. He checked the controls and nodded. "We're almost there. Let me..."

[Help!]

The *Dauntless'* voice echoed in Daanir's head, making him wince. He shook his head. "*Not so loud, my lovely. We're here. We're coming. Open the docking bay.*"

[Bay four. My captain is safe?]

"He's right here with me. And Nyssa is here, too." Daanir tapped Theonus' shoulder. "She says bay four. And she's worried for you."

"Tell her we're fine. Heading in." Theonus rested his hands on the controls and started to guide the submersible in.

Daanir sat down next to him, tipping his head back and closing his eyes, reaching for the *Dauntless*. *"What should we expect?"*

[Bad mancer and ten crew trying to make me leave. Told everyone Wave Runner's *Captain killed our captain. First Mate said no. Said wait, because how can a dead man kill someone? Mancer turned on him. First Mate is hurt. Maybe dead.]*

"We'll make them stop, my lovely. Coming in." He opened his eyes and shook his head, feeling the submersible spinning around him. A hand settled on his shoulder, and warmth spread out from the touch, chasing away the dizziness. He looked up to see Navi standing behind him.

"Better?"

"Yes," Daanir answered. He turned back toward the screens, watching as they approached the lights of the docking bay. *"Dauntless* says that your first mate is hurt, possible killed. He tried to stop Gellan. And she confirmed that there are ten crew members following Gellan.

Theonus growled softly. "You know, I used to think that keelhauling was barbaric. But now... I'm open to seeing for myself..."

"I've seen it," Antivar said, his voice flat. "It is barbaric."

Theonus winced. "I apologize, Antivar."

"You are angry. I understand. This... mutiny is a desecration." Antivar came to stand next to Navi. "Are those doors closing?"

"Gellan noticed us." Daanir reached, leaning forward in his seat as he reached, wrestling the bay controls away from Gellan. The doors opened again, and Theonus guided the submersible into the bay. Daanir let the doors close, listening as the submersible's systems started to sync with *Dauntless,* monitoring them until he was certain that there was nothing amiss with the air circulators.

"They know we're here," he said. "They're coming."

"Give me a comm channel," Theonus said, turning in his seat.

Daanir nodded, concentrated on the controls, then smiled. "*Dauntless* is listening. She's secured the comms for you already."

Theonus looked up. "Well, we'll have to have more conversations later, won't we? If I'd known we could, I'd have done it already. Open all comms, wide band, broadcast ship-wide." A soft chime echoed through the submersible, and Theonus smiled. "Thank you." He paused, and when he spoke, his voice was harder. "All hands! This is your captain. Disregard any orders given by Mancer Gellan. I repeat, disregard any orders given by Mancer Gellan. Gellan and any man who follows him are to be taken into custody. With prejudice." He nodded once, then got up, drawing his pistol. "Let's go take back our ship."

Daanir stood up slowly, and was immediately blocked from moving further by Navi. The healer looked at him, then held out his hand.

"I'm fine," Daanir protested.

"Are not." Navi offered his hand again. Daanir rolled his eyes and winced as it made his head start to pound.

"Fine," he grumbled, and gave Navi his hand. Warmth spread up his arm, through his chest and neck, and the pain in his head faded away. Navi nodded slowly, then let his hand go.

"Ready."

"Stay behind me in the corridor," Daanir said, drawing his own pistol. "Antivar, take the rear."

They filed out of the submersible and into the corridor. Nyssa led the way, pistol in one hand. She raised her other arm, and a buckler spiraled out of her bracer. They met no resistance as they made their way through the ship, which struck Daanir as strange.

He wasn't the only one. "Shouldn't someone be trying to stop us?" Antivar called.

"They should, but if there are only ten people following Gellan, they might have their hands full elsewhere." Daanir stopped and looked up. "Let me take a look." He rested his hand on the wall and closed his eyes, reaching into the systems to see the cameras...

Gellan was waiting, striking through the machines before Daanir even knew he was there. Daanir managed to parry most of the attack, but he was aware of his body falling, of Navi and Theonus trying to help him. There was nothing they could do — not while what made him Daanir was in the machines. He gathered himself and spread out through the *Dauntless*, feeling her systems moving to help.

"Where is he, my lovely?"

Dauntless showed him — Gellan was in the central core chamber, hands resting on the controls, sweat dripping from his face. There was something on the control board between his hands, a box with no outer markings. There were no ports or cables, and it hadn't been patched into the systems. There was no way for Daanir to see what the box was, or what it did when Gellan rested his hand on the surface.

"Did he say what the box will do?" Daanir asked.

There was no answer, and Daanir realized that the *Dauntless'* consciousness had vanished the moment Gellan touched the box. That the systems were slowly growing dark around him.

That if he didn't get back to his own body, he'd be trapped.

Suddenly frightened, he fled the darkness, following his own spark back to the source....

He wheezed, feeling the air filling his lungs like it was burning ice.

"Hold!" Navi snapped. "Hold."

Daanir knew the command from his training, responded as if it were his fight master, freezing in place. He felt warmth filling him, chasing away the cold. It got easier to breathe, easier to move, and he opened his eyes.

"What happened?" Theonus demanded. "You went down like you were dead!"

"Gellan was waiting in the system for me," Daanir croaked. "Can I move?"

"Easy. Slow." Navi sat back on his heels as Daanir sat up.

"He was waiting," Daanir repeated. "He's in the central core chamber, and he's got... I don't know. Something, some kind of device. And it took all the systems down. *Dauntless*... I can't hear her anymore!"

"*Dauntless*..." Theonus looked up, resting his hand on the wall. Then he looked back at Daanir. "Are you saying that Gellan killed my ship?"

"I... I don't think so." Daanir rubbed his hand over his face. "I think... oh... it's a limiter! It's stopping *Dauntless* from helping us, cut out all her systems, but she's still in there!"

Theonus nodded slowly. "You up to a fight, Daan?" He held his hand out. "Come on. Let's go get my ship back. Antivar? When we take that bastard down, do me the favor of shoving that chain down his throat?"

Antivar helped Navi up. "Just down his throat?" he asked without looking up. Then he looked past Theonus and blanched. "I should not have said—"

"If you thinking of shoving it down his throat and ripping it out his arse, I'd like to see it," Nyssa said. She chuckled. "Not a lady, Antivar. I'm a sailor, a soldier, and a battle companion. There's probably nothing you could come up with that I haven't heard in one form or another."

Antivar stared at her for a moment, then smiled weakly. "That... is going to take some getting used to."

"Right. Enough talking. Is everyone hale enough to move?" Theonus drew his saber. "I'm guessing that the mutineers are guarding the central core chamber. Shall we go find out?"

The central core chamber was at the heart of the ship, in the most protected area, and impossible to reach from the docking bays. Theonus and Nyssa led them up to the deck, where Theonus started shouting and his crew started running in response to his orders. One of them ran toward them, saluted, then blurted, "Captain, what is happening?"

"Gellan and the men who are following him are traitors," Theonus answered. "He's taken the central core chamber and locked down the ship. We need to get him out of there." He looked around. "How is Jhensen?"

"The physicians are doing what they can, but... when he refused to order the ship to get underway, Gellan shot him. Point blank range."

Daanir turned to Navi. "Can you do something?"

Navi nodded. "Will try. Where?"

The crewman looked at Navi, then at Theonus. "Captain?"

"Tarrick, this is Navi. He's a Sualimani healer. Take him to the infirmary and guard him with your life. Understood?"

"Especially since his sister is Captain Tarjiaan's wife," Antivar added.

"Stop fussing," Navi chided. He turned and rested his hand on Antivar's chest. "Be careful."

Antivar nodded. "You, too."

Navi grinned and turned to Tarrick. "Where?"

"This way." Tarrick gestured, then started running. Navi followed him, and Theonus turned to face Daanir and Antivar.

"Right. Close quarters fighting to get to the core. How are we doing this?"

"If we attack the door outright," Antivar said, "this traitor will destroy anything inside with him. Could he destroy the ship from in there?"

Daanir grimaced. "He could hurt her, but he couldn't kill her. Not without the kill switch."

Theonus took a deep breath. "Oh."

"A... kill switch?" Antivar said. "What does that mean?"

"Safety feature, to keep Meradon hulls from falling into Imperial hands," Daanir answered. "It's a last resort — if there's no way for a crew to win or to escape, there's the kill switch. It's... explosive." He looked around. "He can't set it off from the central core, though. He has to be in the same room as the switch, and the only thing I know for certain is that the switch is never near the central core. It's in a different place on every ship, and I don't know where it is on the *Dauntless*."

"You can't tell?" Antivar asked. "But... you are a machine mage—"

Daanir decided not to correct him. There was time to teach him the difference later. "And the kill switch is as low tech as they can make it and still have it work," he answered. "Mancers can't flip them remotely. Just in case a mancer loses their grip on their wits."

Antivar nodded. "That's a problem with mages, too. Where is it? Should it be guarded?"

"We shouldn't need to. Only the captain, their first mate, and their mancer know where it is on a ship. Wait... Theo, have you even *told* him where it is?"

Theonus paused, then shook his head. "No! I haven't had time! Which, thank the Mothers for that. He couldn't tell any of the mutineers." He frowned. "So how do we *do* this?" he repeated.

Daanir considered their options, and sighed. "Circulation. It's our best option. I can cut the air intake to the central core and seal the room." He frowned, trying to figure out how long it would take for a man to die in a sealed room, then shook his head. He understood machinery, not biology. He'd have to ask Navi.

Or Antivar. "How large a room?" Antivar asked. "If the room is about the same size as the quarters Navi and I were given, then it will take days for someone to die if you seal it and don't let air in. He'll die of dehydration first."

"I... how do you know that?" Nyssa asked. "How could you possibly know that?"

Antivar sniffed. "I served the Emperor, may Sun and Sand forget his name."

Theonus frowned. "I... that makes sense, given what I've heard from some of our other refugees." He paused, then nodded. "We don't have to kill him. Tarjiaan will probably want him, anyway. So if we seal the room, then we can pipe in sleeping gas and not get the rest of the ship. We'll just have to deal with the other mutineers first." He turned. "Nys, we need an assault team. And the comms are offline."

"I'll arrange it." Nyssa turned and started snapping orders, walking away across the deck.

"We'll need sleeping gas," Daanir said. "And... do you have the schematics for the air handlers? I'll need to see where best to put the capsule."

Theonus nodded. "Antivar, will you get the sleeping gas? The physicians have it in the infirmary, in case they need it for surgery. You can check on your Navi while you're there."

Antivar looked around, then pointed. "That way? Close to where it would be on the King's ship?"

"It's going to take me time to get used to *Wave Runner* being the King's ship, but yes." Theonus turned to Daanir. "Come with me. Schematics are in Gellan's workroom."

They hurried belowdecks and through corridors until they reached the workroom. Daanir took a deep breath and swallowed, walking into a long room that was messy in an uncomfortably familiar way. Everything was exactly the way it had been in the workrooms on Station Six.

"Since when is Gellan your mancer?" he asked as he went to the cabinet against the walls. Long drawers contained the schematics for all of the ship's systems, and if they were filed properly, the environmental systems would be... there. "He was at Six—"

"You weren't there when we told Tarjiaan and Nika," Theonus said. "Station Six is gone. They were overrun... not even a month ago. Only survivors were Gellan and Commander Ishian."

Daanir looked up from the papers he was taking from the drawer. "You're joking."

"I wish I was," Theonus answered. "I have yet to hear a good explanation of why the rest of the station was lost—"

"Oh, I can tell you why," Daanir interjected, his voice tight. "It's because the evacuation submersibles that did work were sold off as pleasure vessels to anyone who could pay, and the ones that didn't work were scavenged for parts. The only submersible on the station that saw any regular maintenance was the commander's." He snorted. "I should know. I serviced the blasted thing enough times."

"What were you doing on Station Six?" Theonus asked. "I mean... you had to have been, to have a history with Gellan. But... you should have been with Tarjiaan. He said you were separated, but didn't go into details, and I didn't have time to ask."

Daanir found the pages he needed and pulled them out, sweeping a space clear on the table with one arm. "It's a long story, Theo," he said, studying the diagram. "I'll tell you the whole of it later, but... to keep it short, the *Marauder* happened. And then Ilaris happened." He glanced up. "Did Jiaan tell you anything?"

"Just that you've only just been reunited," Theonus answered. "That's... what, fourteen years?"

"Fifteen." Daanir answered absently, tracing a path through the diagram. "Right. Got it. Let's go get the gas capsules."

Chapter Seven
Mancer Royal

NYSSA MET THEM BY THE main mast, leading a team of five men and women.

"We won't have a lot of room," she explained when Theonus arched a brow at her. "I chose the best sharpshooters. Are we giving them a chance to surrender?"

Theonus looked thoughtful, then shook his head. "They're mutineers. If they surrender, I'll consider accepting it. But I won't ask for it."

"At least let them know that you're not dead," Daanir suggested. "Once they know that Gellan lied about that, they might figure he lied about everything else."

"It's worth a try," Nyssa added.

"I'll try," Theonus agreed. He turned to face the sharpshooters. "Right. We wait to hear what they have to say. If they start shooting, drop them all. Understood?"

"Yes, Captain."

They made their way back belowdecks, through empty corridors and down toward the heart of the ship, the exact center of the vessel. The layout of this part of the ship had corridors running the full length of the port and starboard sides between the gun house mechanisms and the holds, allowing passage from one end of the ship to the other around the core chamber, which could only be entered from a single door accessed by a corridor that connected both sides of the ship. It was now a glaringly obvious design flaw, but Daanir doubted that anyone had considered that the cross corridor might be used as cover for mutineers guarding the mancer holding the ship's core hostage.

The walls and floors here were much thicker than in the rest of the ship, and the only way an enemy attack would penetrate far enough to destroy the core would be with an impossibly powerful shot and an inordinate amount of colossal bad luck. On the *Wave Runner,* Daanir had been able to hear his own heart beating when he'd been in the corridor outside the central core, and he was certain that if he'd been alone, it would have been the same here on the *Dauntless.* With seven other people, their footsteps sounded like thunder, and he knew that the mutineers at the end of the corridor had to know they were coming. He looked at the long corridor, with its complete lack of cover, and realized something.

"Captain," he said. "They're not shooting. They have to know we're here."

"I know," Theonus said. "They should be, and they're not." He stopped. "I know you hear us!" he called. "You know who I am."

A voice called back down the hall. "Captain? But... you're dead!"

"Clearly, I'm not," Theonus called back. "Look for yourself."

Daanir saw a head pop around the corner, then retreat, and heard distant, muffled voices. Then someone stepped out into view, a young man who held a force pistol pointed at the deck.

"Captain, the Mancer told us you were dead," he said. "He told us that... that Tarjiaan killed you. But the message said that the Sea Prince was dead, and how... you aren't dead!"

"Did you see the recording?" Daanir called.

"That was real?" The crewman looked over his shoulder. "That was real?"

"It was real. King Ikaanaji is dead. Tarjiaan is on the *Wave Runner*," Theonus called. "The Sea Prince is alive. And he needs every man of us at his back. Where do you stand?"

The young man hesitated, then stepped forward. "I'll stand with my Ki—"

A shot rang out, deafening in the corridor, and the young man fell. Nyssa darted to stand in front of Theonus, her buckler raised, and the sharpshooters moved in front of her, returning fire.

"Fall back!" Nyssa shouted. "Daanir, you and Antivar get back!" She winced, and Daanir saw a line of red along her shoulder. He growled and reached down, twisting his power into the deck plates. Rivets popped free as the plate seam closest to them rose to form a shield in front of them. Charges pinged off the shield for a moment, then stopped.

"By the Mothers!" Theonus gasped. "Daan!"

Daanir glanced at him. "Should I end this?"

"End it how?" Theonus asked.

"The way I should have, so that boy didn't need to die." Daanir closed his eyes and sent his power racing through the floors, spreading out to the parallel corridor, finding the intersection and ripping the deck plates free on either end, filling the gap from floor to ceiling with deck material. As the metal slammed into place, the screams of the men imprisoned within were cut off, and in the silence that followed, he could hear his own heart beating.

Then Antivar coughed. "That... Sun and Sand, that was impressive to watch!"

"And impossible," Nyssa added, her voice shaking. "That... that wasn't a machine. That was bare metal. How did you get *bare metal* to answer you?"

Theonus answered before Daanir could. "Not important. Let's get this done. Daan, what's the next step?"

Daanir closed his eyes and pictured the schematics. "There's a vent inside the chamber, and there's one in the corridor. I'll place the capsule, close the rest of the vents, and knock them all out." He restored the deck, calling the popped rivets back into place, then opened his eyes to see Nyssa watching him, a wary look on her face. He looked away, searching for the panel he needed.

"Mancer? Should I see to the boy?" Antivar asked. "He may not be dead."

"Please," Daanir answered. "If he's alive, get him to the physicians."

"Yes, sir." Antivar brushed past him, going to one knee next to the prone body. He looked up. "He's alive!"

"Nyssa, help Antivar," Theonus ordered, then turned and pointed. "You and you. Help them."

"Captain—" Nyssa started to protest, then stopped when Theonus held his hand up.

"I gave an order," he said, his voice flat. Nyssa blinked. Then she bowed and went to Antivar, followed by the two crewmen who Theonus had told to help. Between them, they lifted the fallen crewman and carried him away. Once they were gone, Theonus turned to Daanir.

"I apologize," he said. "That was uncalled for."

Daanir shrugged. "It's nothing. Nyssa never liked things she couldn't explain. I remember that. Let me get this done." He went to the panel and touched it — it popped open immediately. He studied it for a moment, opened the air handler, then touched the mechanism and closed all the vents except for the two he needed. "Is there anyone else down here?" he asked. "In the holds, or in a place where they might open a vent I've just closed?"

"There shouldn't be," Theonus answered, coming up behind Daanir. "There aren't any regular duty stations down here, and if there's anyone in the gun houses, they're late for their duties."

"And the gun houses are open to the outside, so it shouldn't be an issue." Daanir set the capsule inside the air handler, closed it, then looked over his shoulder. "Step back. And if I go down because there's a leak, well... worse things have happened because I made a mistake."

"What am I looking for if there is a leak?" Theonus asked.

"Green smoke," Daanir answered.

"Right. If I see green smoke, I'll try to catch you if you go down."

Daanir smiled. He triggered the capsule, looking for telltale puffs of green smoke. Seeing nothing, he stepped back, bumping into Theonus, who was standing closer than he expected.

"Why did they make it green?" Theonus asked. "The sleeping gas. Why is it green?"

"So you can see it and know it isn't regular smoke or steam." Daanir looked down the corridor. "That'll take... maybe three minutes or so. Then I'll flush the air and put the floor back in place."

"I appreciate that. Having a core chamber we can't reach is inconvenient."

They waited in silence for three minutes, then Daanir set the air systems to draw from the two open vents, pulling the gas out and flushing it outside. He restarted the system, closed the panel, then turned to look at the sealed corridor. "You'll want guards. And we sent Antivar off with the limiter."

"Let's get the limiter off *Dauntless* and get the comms back online, and I'll call for guards and get another one." Theonus looked back at the other three crewmen. "You all be ready in case anyone is still awake in there."

"Yes, sir."

"Good point," Daanir said. "I'll put this side down first. If they're all unconscious, I'll fix the other side." He rested his hand on the corridor wall and sent his power into the metal, watching the floor slide back down into place like wet sand, watching the rivets scuttle back into place like small crabs. Once the corridor looked the way it had before he'd started, he stepped back, letting the three crewmen pass him.

"They're all unconscious, Mancer!" one of them called. "Should I open the door?"

"Cover me while I do," Daanir answered. He joined them, stepping carefully over the bodies of the sleeping mutineers to reach the door to the chamber. "You couldn't open it anyway. It's locked to the Captain's handprint."

"And the Mancer's," Theonus added. "Blast it."

Daanir smiled. "And the Mancer's," he agreed. He rested his hand on the door and unlocked it, then stepped out of the way before letting the door slide open. The moment the door was fully open, a shot from a force pistol hit the opposite wall; Daanir yelped as metal shards flew in all directions, too fast for him to stop, showering him with sharp, hot shrapnel. More shots, as three crewmen fired into the chamber. "Careful!" he shouted. "Don't hit the core!"

Silence fell, and Daanir looked at the crewmen, then peered around the edge of the door. Gellan lay on his back on the floor, a breather covering his mouth and nose. His chest was marked by a tight collection of gunshots. Daanir looked back at the crewmen. "I apologize. I forgot Nyssa said you were sharpshooters. That's a very nice grouping."

The one closest to him grinned and nodded. "Apology accepted, Mancer. And thank you."

The inside of the chamber still smelled faintly of sleeping gas, mixed with the unmistakable burned flesh smell of force pistol wounds. The panels and controls were all dark, a sight that made

Daanir feel sicker than the smell ever could. He walked over to the control panels and studied the limiter device that Gellan had used.

"Can you remove it?" Theonus asked from behind him.

"I'm not entirely sure how he hooked it into the system." Daanir crouched so that he was on eye level with the bottom of the device. "No cables. No ports, unless they're on the bottom." He reached out and poked the machine, and it resisted slightly before it moved. "Huh... connected by magnetic contacts? Maybe?" He stood up. "There's not enough room in there for explosives, I don't think."

"Filian," Theonus said. "We need a rope."

"Yes, Captain!" One of the sharpshooters ran out of the room. She came back after a moment with a coil. "Is this enough?"

"Should be." Theonus shook out the coil, made a noose on one end, and tightened it around the device. "Everyone out!"

They left the chamber, and Theonus took his place on one side of the open door, the rope held in one hand. Daanir stood on the other side of the open door, watching Theonus. The captain met his eyes, took a deep breath, and tugged. They heard a metallic crash... and nothing else. Daanir felt the systems coming back online, like the pins and needles when his feet fell asleep if he'd been sitting on them for too long.

"No explosives," Theonus said. He peered around the door. "Lights are coming on. Is my ship alive?"

"Let me see." Daanir went into the chamber and rested his hand on the control panel. "*Dauntless*? It's over, my lovely. You're safe."

There was no answer for a terrifying length of time — nearly two seconds. Then an almost childlike wail nearly knocked Daanir off his feet. He felt someone catch him, and he shook his head and closed his eyes, concentrating on the *Dauntless*.

"*It's over*," he thought. "*You're safe. He's dead.*"

[Dead?]

"*Yes, my lovely, Gellan is dead, and good riddance to him.*"

An almost-human sounding sniffle. [*I see my captain. Will he feed Gellan to the sharks?*]

Daanir laughed. "That would be cruel to the sharks, don't you think?"

Theonus coughed. "Did... is she asking if we're feeding Gellan to the sharks?"

"She did," Daanir answered. "Let me guess? She heard it from you?"

"From Nyssa," Theonus answered. He looked up. "*Dauntless?* Will you be talking to me now, the way *Wave Runner* does to Tarjiaan? I would like that."

A speaker hissed, and a mechanical voice said, [You would?]

Theonus smiled. "I would, my sweet girl. Now, we need to find you a new Mancer to take care of you. We'll see if we can't get Westin back from wherever they sent him, but that might take us some time." He looked down. "And we need to get rid of this piece of chum. *Dauntless*, comms, please. I'll need a cleanup crew to take the mutineers into custody."

[Yes, sir.]

While Theonus dealt with the mutineers and the body, Daanir repaired the other corridor, then sat with *Dauntless*, carefully checking and rechecking, making sure that Gellan hadn't left anything behind that would hurt her.

"Do you ever talk to Westin?" he asked, sitting back in his chair. He closed his eyes and yawned. "Could he hear you?"

[*He was not certain that he was truly hearing me. He would say that he was imagining it when I did.*]

Daanir chuckled. "When I see him, I'll tell him that he wasn't imagining things. You're healthy, my lovely."

[*Thank you. Who will be my mancer until you find Westin? Can it be you?*]

Daanir shook his head, wincing slightly as the movement made his ears ring. "No, my lovely. I have to take care of the *Wave Runner,* Tarjiaan and Nika. I'll see what we can do. If you escort us to the dockyards, I can come back and forth, and so can Ishantar—"

[*Who is Ishantar?*]

Daanir looked up. "She's the Mancer assigned to the *Wave Runner.* And I haven't had the chance to ask her if she hears *Wave Runner.* I'll do that when I go back." He heard footsteps outside the core chamber, and turned to see Nyssa, Antivar and Navi. "Come in. Say hello to *Dauntless.*"

Nyssa looked up. "Say hello?"

[*Hello, Nyssa!*]

Nyssa went pale. "What? Daanir, that's not funny!"

"It's not me," Daanir said. He gestured. "It's her. She's like *Wave Runner.* She's aware. And chatty. Didn't Theo tell you?"

Nyssa swallowed. "I... I thought he was joking!" She looked up again. "My father... he wasn't making up stories about his ship singing to him?"

[*I do not know how to sing,*] *Dauntless* answered. [*Will you teach me to sing?*]

Nyssa's jaw dropped. "I... do you want to learn?"

[*Yes, please!*]

"Do I have to come down here, or can we do this anywhere?"

[*Anywhere you can hear me, I can hear you.*] A long pause. [*Thank you, Healer Navi, for saving First Mate.*]

Navi smiled. "You are welcome."

[*Now take care of Daanir. He has blood on his face hair, and on his coat.*]

"I do?" Daanir reached up and touched his cheek, feeling sore spots through his beard. "Must have been when Gellan shot the wall." He looked up at Navi. "If you're not too tired?"

"Nika will fuss," Navi said. "Will fix."

"We're ready to take you back to the *Wave Runner,* if you're ready to go," Nyssa said. "And we'll be escorting you to the dockyards."

"Good," Daanir said. "Ishantar and I can split our time between *Dauntless* and the *Wave Runner,* to make sure they're both taken care of. Which means I should come back to introduce Ishtantar to *Dauntless.*" He looked up. "Do you speak Sualimani, *Dauntless?*"

[I have the Sualimani language in my memory, but I have never spoken it.]

"Ask Ishantar. She'll teach you." Daanir moved to stand up, and sat back down hard as his head spun. Immediately, Navi was in front of him, a hand on his shoulder. Warmth washed over him, pushing back the fatigue and the headache.

"Overdone. No food."

"I was busy, Navi," Daanir protested.

"Fall over help no one."

Daanir laughed. "Yes, Healer. I'll eat once we get back."

"Then sleep." Navi looked up. "*Dauntless?* Tomorrow meeting?"

[I can wait until tomorrow. Nyssa can teach me to sing!]

"That sounds like a plan." Nyssa stepped back, letting Antivar come forward to help steady Daanir as he stood up. "I'm taking them back, *Dauntless.* I'll be back soon."

They made their way down to the submersible bay, and Daanir sat down, letting Navi fuss over him and heal the cuts from the shrapnel. He didn't say anything until they'd launched, then he sighed. "I'd always thought they were stories!"

"So did I," Nyssa said from the pilot seat. "I'll have to apologize to my father."

"Wait until things are settled before you do," Antivar suggested. "The fewer people know the truth, the better. We should hand no one a weapon of this nature."

Daanir looked up. "Explain."

Antivar shrugged. "The ship... she sounds like a child. A very smart child, but a child. Did you not think so?" He looked from Daanir to Nyssa. "A child is easily manipulated. Easily fooled. And easily harmed. We saw that today. If it is known to the traitor that your ships are as children, do you not think he will use that to his advantage? Better to keep the secret close."

"I'm very glad you're on our side," Nyssa murmured. "Right. There's no point in signaling the *Wave Runner*. Daanir, will you open the bay?"

They docked in silence, and the overhead hissing as pressure equalized was like a siren song calling Daanir home. He smiled as the hatch opened, following Antivar and Navi toward it. Nyssa's hand on his arm stopped him.

"A moment? Please?" she said.

"What is it?" Daanir asked.

"I... I still don't understand," she said. "What you did today. I don't understand how you did it! My father is a mancer, and even though I'm not, I know about what a mancer can and can't do. It's...you made *bare metal* do what you wanted. What you did... that's just not possible!" Nyssa stared at him, then blurted, "What kind of mancer are you?"

Daanir fought the urge to flinch away from her and the words that cut too close to his own self-doubt. What kind of a mancer was he? According to his teachers, he was a fraud who should never have been allowed anywhere near a ship of this magnitude. He was a failure who hadn't protected his prince...

But Tarjiaan, the man he loved and who he had sworn to protect, was sure in his bones that if it hadn't been for Daanir and his mancer abilities, they would all be dead and Meradon would have fallen. Captain Taarik, the man who held a place in his heart as the closest he'd ever had to a father, said none of it was his fault. Riguaarin told him often he was far too good at what he did to spend his life exiled to a backwater station or serving in the dockyards.

And his Queen declared to the world exactly what kind of mancer he was. The weight of it settled on him, in him, an awareness that felt comfortable in a way that it never had before.

"I am the Mancer Royal," he said simply. "Go on back. Theo needs you. I'll bring Ishantar over tomorrow."

Chapter Eight
Impossible

TARJIAAN AND NIKA WERE waiting on the deck with Navi and Antivar when Daanir finally appeared. Tarjiaan smiled, but the smile quickly faded. "Daan? Why do you have blood on your collar?" He looked closer. "And in your beard?"

"I—"

"Food first," Navi interrupted. "You said."

Daanir grinned. "I did say I was going to eat once I got here. I'll report while I eat." He looked at Navi. "Fair?"

Navi nodded. "Fair." He yawned and leaned against Antivar.

"I'm putting you to bed, Navi," Antivar said. "Daanir isn't the only one who is overdone."

"Food first?'

"Food first." Antivar nodded to Tarjiaan. "Captain?"

Tarjiaan waved them on. "Take care of your man, Antivar. And thank you for taking care of mine." He held his hand out to Daanir. "Come on. Let's get you fed, and you can tell us what happened."

Daanir took Tarjiaan's hand, letting his presence dispel the last vestiges of tension. When Nika took his other hand, he sighed happily.

"I'm glad to be back."

"You were not gone long," Nika said. "Was it so very bad?"

"After food, Nika," Tarjiaan said. "He's looking stretched thin."

"Then I will go on ahead and send for Aranti. Should I ask for enough for all of us?"

"Please," Tarjiaan answered. "And tell her we have a Mancer who's been working hard. She'll know what that means."

Nika squeezed Daanir's hand, then let him go and hurried toward the great cabin. Daanir let Tarjiaan lead him at a slower pace.

"You're not hurt?" Tarjiaan asked.

"Scratches," Daanir answered. "Navi took care of them. I'm fine." He took a deep breath. "Tired. I'm going to emulate Navi and take a nap. Once I talk to Ishantar." He nudged Tarjiaan's arm with his own. "And I'll tell you why I'm talking to Ishantar once there's food."

Inside the great cabin, Daanir settled into his chair with a somewhat heavy thump.

"Aranti said that she will have food for us shortly," Nika said as she sat down facing him. "Now tell."

Daanir waited until Tarjiaan was seated before starting. "Gellan is dead. He tried to kill me twice. Once in the machines, and once when I opened the door to the central core chamber. Theo has some excellent sharpshooters on his crew. They'll be escorting us to the dockyards, so Ishantar and I can see to both ships until we get there, and I promised *Dauntless* that I'd find her Westin and get him back onboard."

"You promised *Dauntless*?" Tarjiaan repeated slowly.

Daanir grinned. "She's very talkative." He looked up. "Now that we know, are you going to be that talkative, my lovely?"

The overhead speaker clicked. [I am not talkative. I will talk when I have something to say. I have to share my mancers?]

"Only until we get another Mancer to take care of *Dauntless*." Daanir looked back at Tarjiaan and Nika, both of whom looked stunned.

"I... see," Tarjiaan murmured. "And will you talk to me when Daan isn't around?"

[Will you keep playing music for me?] There was no hiding *Wave Runner*'s eagerness. [I like the music.]

Tarjiaan looked down, covering his lower face with his hand. Possibly to hide laughter, but Daanir wasn't entirely certain. When he looked up again, he was smiling. "I'm happy to keep playing for you, my dear," he answered. "But only once our work is done."

[Of course! And... when is Logiri coming back? He would talk to me, tell me stories while he worked. I miss him.]

Tarjiaan's smile vanished. "I do, too," he said. "And I hope soon. You've been listening, haven't you? You understand what is happening?"

[A bad man is doing bad things. He hurt you. But you're here now, and you have Nika and Daanir to take care of you.] Wave Runner paused. [I am sorry I am small in places and it makes you hurt.]

"That is not your fault," Nika said. "You cannot help how you were made. And you were beautifully made. We will work with Tarjiaan to make him more comfortable in small spaces."

Tarjiaan took a deep breath and turned back to Daanir. "What else?"

"According to Nyssa, I did the impossible," Daanir answered. "She's a mancer's daughter, and she told me that what I was doing was something a mancer shouldn't be able to do. She wanted to know what kind of mancer I was."

To his shock, Tarjiaan snorted.

"Doing the impossible? Again? Daan, you do the impossible on a regular basis." He looked at Daanir, and his eyes narrowed. "But this time it bothers you. What did you do?"

"I did mancery on bare metal," Daanir answered. "I created a shield when the mutineers fired on us, and I trapped them in the corridor outside the central core chamber. Then I flooded the chamber and the corridor with sleeping gas. But Gellan had a breather. So when we went to the chamber to get him out, he started shooting, and that's where the blood came from. Theo's sharpshooters killed him."

Tarjiaan nodded slowly. "I'll want you to start at the beginning, and tell me all of it. But... Daan, you've been commanding bare metal since your powers first woke. To hear you tell it, it's how you saved my life. Why is it bothering you now?"

Daanir leaned back in his chair, looking up at the ceiling and wondering. Tarjiaan was right. His very first action as a mancer had been to command the metal wreckage of the Executioner to form around the remains of Tarjiaan's legs and keep him from bleeding out.

"I think... because no one ever told me before that what I was doing was outside of what a mancer could do," he said slowly. "Gellan didn't think I could turn a lamp on by hand, let along with mancery. I taught myself most of what I needed to know, so... I didn't know that I shouldn't be doing it."

"And therefore, you did it," Nika said. "Much like Naajir and Kaapi, no?"

Daanir stared at her, trying to make sense of what she was saying. Then he realized what she meant. "I... I don't think I ever told them that Mancers can't meld their gifts and work together. That I was told it was impossible."

"They did not know it was impossible, therefore, they did it." Nika nodded. "What else could you do, if you did not think it impossible?"

"I..." Daanir looked at Tarjiaan, who shrugged. "I... that's a bit like asking a fish to walk."

Tarjiaan snorted. "They do, you know."

"*What*?" Daanir heard his voice crack. "Jiaan!"

"In Sualiman, and I've seen them!" Tarjiaan insisted. "There are fish that walk on land when the water dries up. Short distances, and from one body of water to the next. But I saw them do it, and I thought I'd lost my mind. Ishantar had to explain to me that they do it because there isn't enough of what they need in one pool, so they move to the next. Over time, they changed. They became what they needed to be, in order to survive." He paused. "Huh."

"What?" Nika asked.

"The fish changed over time to survive. Do people do that? Do mages or mancers? Nyssa asked what kind of mancer you are. A new kind? One who can command metal and machine?" He looked at Daanir. "Now, I have a question. You did something. Then you were told it's impossible. Can you still do it?"

Daanir stared at him, his mouth suddenly dry. He looked around, feeling almost panicked, searching for something metal — he heard a series of small pops, and his chair collapsed underneath him.

"Daan!" Tarjiaan bolted to his feet, looking down over the edge of the table. "What happened?"

"I..." Daanir looked around at the pieces of chair. He could see the nails that had once held it together all over the floor. "I think I pulled out all the nails."

"Did you hurt yourself?" Nika asked as she came around the table.

"No, I'm fine." Daanir stood up and looked around at the wreckage. "I haven't done something like this since I was new."

Tarjiaan chuckled. "Well, that shows you still can. Can you put it back together, or should I call the carpenter?"

Daanir grimaced and rubbed the back of his neck. "I... you probably want the carpenter. Metal listens to me. Wood doesn't." He crouched and sent his power chasing out over the floor, watching as the scattered nails collected into a neat pile. He grinned and looked up. "Yeah, metal listens."

"Find something to put those in, and pull up another chair," Tarjiaan said as he sat back down. "The food will be here soon, and you still need to report."

Daanir gave his report as they ate. Tarjiaan let him talk, more than familiar with how one of Daanir's reports could take different flows and eddies, but still end up being complete. He ate slowly, making mental notes, asking questions. When Daanir finished, Tarjiaan leaned back in his chair and drummed his fingers on the table.

"How many?" he asked softly. "How many mancers follow Ilaris? How many people does he have behind him?" He closed his eyes, suddenly tired. "How do we know who to trust?"

It was a rhetorical question, but *Wave Runner* didn't know that. [You can trust me.]

Tarjiaan smiled. "I know that, my dear. And... *Wave Runner*, can you speak to any other above ship?"

[Not until my outside voice is fixed. I can hear, but I can't speak.]

"Huh. That means she's receiving signals, but can't transmit. We must have fixed something and not realized it," Daanir said. "What are you thinking, Jiaan?"

"I'll tell Marikaar to start monitoring for broadcasts. And I'm thinking that once *Wave Runner* can speak to the other ships, she can ask the ships who their captains will follow." Tarjiaan frowned, then shook his head. "No, that won't work. To be close enough for her to speak to them, we'll need to be in range of their guns. Which... that will tell us faster than a conversation who they follow."

"Once we get to the dockyards, we can arrange a fleet-wide broadcast of the recording, and a recording from you," Daanir said. "Theo says that *Dauntless* will escort us. I said that, didn't I?"

"You did," Nika said. "Daan, how much more is there? You need to rest."

Daanir frowned, then shook his head. "Can't think of anything else. My head is full of foam. I need to sleep."

"I have one thing to tell you," Tarjiaan said slowly, "and it may keep you from sleeping." He glanced at Nika, then sighed. "Daan, if you want to stay in the secret passages once we get to the dockyards, I will understand completely. As a matter of fact, it may be better if you do not leave the *Wave Runner* at all."

"I... why?" Daanir looked puzzled. "I was looking forward to seeing Mentiras and Narrick. Why stay onboard?"

"Because of something Theonus told us," Tarjiaan said. "Why Gellan was on his ship."

"He told me about Station Six," Daanir said. Then his face went impossibly pale. "Oh. Is... he's at the dockyards, isn't he? Ishian? He's there?"

"He's there," Tarjiaan replied. "But you don't have to face him."

Daanir looked down. He sat in silence for a moment, then shook his head. "Yes, I do. I need him to see that he didn't break me. That I didn't fail. And I need him to see me with you." All of a sudden, he grinned. "I need to see him shit his pants when he sees you. And sees just how much you look like an older version of Ranji."

Tarjiaan frowned, then remembered telling Daanir and Nika what he knew about Ishian. "Oh, that will be interesting. The first time, at least. We'll be there for some time, repairing all the damage. If it gets to be a problem—"

"I'll either stick to you like a barnacle, or go below to my passages," Daanir said. Then he yawned. "Right. Sleep. I should tell Kaapi I'm back."

[I can tell Kaapi that you are back, and that you are resting. I like Kaapi.]

Daanir looked up. "Have you talked to her yet? Or to Naajir?"

[Not yet. Do you think I will frighten them?]

"Confuse them, maybe. Let me introduce you," Tarjiaan said. He turned and smiled at Nika. "Do you want to tuck in with Daan? You need to rest."

"You need to rest, too. You are still recovering," Nika countered. Then she yawned, and looked so startled that Tarjiaan fought back a laugh. She covered her mouth with one hand.

"I'll rest once we're underway," Tarjiaan said. "If you're still asleep, I'll join you. But you and Daan need to rest now."

Daanir stood up slowly, his hands flat on the tabletop. "When you see Ishantar, tell her that we'll be going over to *Dauntless* tomorrow so that I can introduce them."

"I'll do that. Now go get some sleep!" Tarjiaan tipped his head back for Daanir's kiss as the Mancer went past his chair. Daanir smiled and held his hand out to Nika. She stood up, then came to kiss Tarjiaan before following Daanir into the bedroom. Tarjiaan watched the door close, then sighed and closed his eyes. He was tired, but he had work to do. He touched his coat pocket, checking for the packet of ration biscuits Nika had put there, then stood up. As he headed to the door, he took out his comms earpiece and put it in.

"There. Now you can talk to me no matter where I am," he said as he left the day cabin.

[Thank you,] *Wave Runner* murmured in his ear. [Where are we going first?]

"To introduce you to the apprentice Mancers, I think. And properly to Ishtantar."

[They are in the comms room.]

Tarjiaan nodded, seeing Marikaar coming toward him. "Captain!"

"Marikaar, report." Tarjiaan gestured. "And walk with me."

Marikaar fell in next to him. "Captain, we've been using signal flags to communicate with the *Dauntless*. They're ready to get underway."

"Very good. They'll be escorting us to the dockyards." Tarjiaan tucked his hands behind his back. "Mancer Gellan attempted to incite mutiny, and he is dead. The other mutineers are in custody on the *Dauntless*, and Theonus will deal with them later. Mancer Royal and Mancer Ishantar will be splitting their time between the *Wave Runner* and the *Dauntless* until such time as we can replace their Mancer."

Marikaar nodded. "I'll make certain that one of the submersibles is reserved for them. Will they need a pilot?"

"I don't think they will, but I'll leave it to the Mancer Royal to decide." Tarjiaan looked up at the sails. "Good wind. Do you still think ten days?"

Marikaar looked thoughtful, then nodded. "I'll hold to that, yes."

"The sooner we get underway, the sooner we'll be there. Great Mothers grant that we don't meet with any trouble between here and there," Tarjiaan said, then looked around. Who was singing?

"Captain?"

"Is someone singing?" Tarjiaan turned around, but saw no one. Then he realized what he was hearing, and touched his earpiece. "*Wave Runner*? That's lovely, but distracting."

"Captain, what is it?"

Tarjiaan smiled. "Is your earpiece in? Daanir discovered something new."

Marikaar looked skeptically at Tarjiaan. "I always wear my earpiece. What new tricks has the Mancer discovered now?"

"Introduce yourself, my dear."

Tarjiaan heard *Wave Runner* immediately, [It is very nice to meet you properly, First Mate.]

Marikaar's jaw dropped. He stared at Tarjiaan, then stammered, "I... well, this is a surprise. A good one. Nice to know that the Mancers were telling the truth. And it's nice to meet you, *Wave Runner*."

Tarjiaan smiled. He started walking again, and Marikaar hurried to join him. "When this is all over and done, we'll have to message Quentas and let him know."

[Please?] *Wave Runner* said. [I remember Quentas. He was nice.]

"How far back do you remember, my dear?" Tarjiaan asked as they went below decks and down one of the thankfully wider corridors.

[My first real memory is when we went to the land and stayed there for a long time. But you stayed with me, and kept me company. I didn't know how to talk yet.]

"On land?" Tarjiaan frowned. "Oh! The last time we were in Sualiman! That was four years ago. I apologize for not knowing and not including you."

[But you did! You talked to me, and so did First Mate Quentas and First Mate Marikaar and Ishantar and everyone else! Logiri told me stories. And you played music for me.]

"We raised her up like a human child," Marikaar said softly. "She learned it all organically, the same way a baby would have."

"Interesting," Tarjiaan said. "I wonder how many other ships of the fleet are the same? Other than *Wave Runner* and *Dauntless*?"

"Something to explore once this is done," Marikaar said. "Now, do you need me in comms?"

"No, thank you." Tarjiaan waited until Marikaar had hurried off before opening the door to the comms room. As he stepped inside, he heard Naajir's raised voice, "Try it now!"

"And... is that working?" Kaapi called back. "I don't see anything. Ishantar?"

[I can hear more things! I can hear *Dauntless*, and there is a submersible, but it is very far away.] *Wave Runner* sounded excited in Tarjiaan's ear.

"Tell Marikaar," Tarjiaan murmured.

[I will.]

"Something is working," Tarjiaan called, and saw Kaapi and Naajir pop out from behind equipment. "*Wave Runner* says that she's getting signals."

Naajir grinned. "I thought bypassing that break would work!"

Kaapi looked at him, then at Tarjiaan. "Captain, what do you mean *Wave Runner* says?"

Tarjiaan smiled. "Where's Ishantar?"

"Up in the wiring." Naajir pointed up. He looked up. "Ishantar, the Captain is down here."

"I hear him," Ishantar said. "I am coming." A moment later, she appeared in an open panel. "Might I ask the Prince-Captain's help?"

"How did you even get up there?" Tarjiaan asked, coming to stand under the panel. In his armor, it wasn't too high for him to reach and help Ishantar jump down.

"There was a chair, but once I was up, it was too far to get down," Ishantar answered, laughing. "Now, what is this I hear? *Wave Runner* says she is hearing?"

Tarjiaan looked up. "*Wave Runner*? Say hello."

[Hello, Mancer Ishantar. Thank you for taking care of me. Hello, Mancers Naajir and Kaapi.]

Naajir whipped around toward Kaapi. "You were *serious*?"

Kaapi laughed. "I told you! I told you ships can talk!"

"It takes a special Mancer to hear them," Ishantar said. "I never thought I would. Prince-Captain, was this something the Mancer Royal did?"

"I think perhaps it's something that's happened over time, as our ships grew more advanced," Tarjiaan said. "And it's not just *Wave Runner*, Ishantar. Tomorrow, Daanir is going to take you to meet *Dauntless*." He briefly told them what had happened, and that *Dauntless* would be escorting them.

"Is my papa hurt?" Kaapi asked.

"He's fine, Kaapi. And right now, he's taking a nap." Tarjiaan smiled. "I have a feeling that if he'd tried to avoid resting, Navi would have put him to sleep."

[I like Healer Navi,] Wave Runner said. [He is a Mancer for people.] Kaapi burst into giggles, while Tarjiaan bit his lip to keep from laughing. [Is that funny? Have I made a joke?]

"It was a delightful observation," Tarjiaan answered. "And one that I don't think anyone has thought of before."

"I wasn't laughing at you," Kaapi added. "I promise! I've just never thought of that before, and I like it!"

[Captain explained the difference between laughing at and laughing with to Captain's Lady. I understand. I do not think I have made a joke before.]

"I'm not entirely sure you've made one yet," Naajir said. "We can teach you."

"No pranks, Naji," Tarjiaan said. "You can teach her about humor, but explain why pranks are not acceptable." He looked up again. "I can make you swab the deck if you get into trouble, but I can't make the decks swab themselves."

Lights flickered, and Tarjiaan looked at Ishantar. She shook her head, then coughed.

"Prince-Captain, I think you just made the ship laugh."

Chapter Nine
Rituals

"DOCKYARDS AHOY!"

Tarjiaan smiled at the call, looking out over the water and past the *Dauntless*. He could see the floating dockyards in the distance, sharp against the scarlet-painted sunset. Were they close enough?

[Captain,] *Wave Runner* said, her mechanical voice clear in his earpiece. [The *Dauntless* says that they are in comms range, and asks that the Mancer Royal join them to send the recording. Shall I send for him?]

"Thank you, *Wave Runner*. Please do so." He looked up at the sky again. "Tell him to join me at the helm first."

A few minutes later, Daanir trotted up the stairs. He came to stand next to Tarjiaan, looking at the dockyards.

"*Wave Runner* says I need to head over to *Dauntless*, but you wanted to see me first," he said, not looking at Tarjiaan. "We're close."

"We are," Tarjiaan agreed. "Are you ready?"

"No," Daanir answered. The word was followed by a quick, brittle smile. "But I'm doing it anyway. He tried to break me. He tried to own me. He failed. And he needs to see that he failed."

Tarjiaan kept one hand on the wheel, reaching out to rest his other hand on Daanir's shoulder. "I'm going to enjoy watching him choke on it. And if he tries anything, he'll regret it."

A hint of a true smile. "You'll make him regret it?"

98

"Me?" Tarjiaan laughed. "No, I have a better idea. If he tries to hurt you, I'm giving him to Nika."

Daanir coughed. "You're *what*?"

"Giving him to Nika," Tarjiaan repeated. He squeezed Daanir's shoulder, then put his hand back on the wheel, adjusting their course. "Did you know that Navi was teaching her offensive uses for her healing?"

"I think I suggested it to him, to be honest," Daanir admitted. "I've been going back and forth so much that I missed they started. I'm guessing from your reaction that she's good?"

"She hasn't tested it on a person yet," Tarjiaan answered. "Even though Antivar volunteered to let her try on him. She refuses to hurt someone needlessly."

"Antivar... volunteered?" Daanir whistled. "The man has stones on him."

"He does indeed. Especially since most of what Nika and Navi have been doing has been planning possible... defenses." Tarjiaan chuckled. "Our wife is *terrifying*, Daan."

"Our wife?" Daanir repeated, sounding as if he was tasting the words, rolling them in his mouth to better understand the feel of them. He made a soft, huffing sound. "Huh. Our wife. What does she think of that?"

"She already calls us her favored males, so she's already decided that she's our wife," Tarjiaan said. He looked up at the sky, feeling the immense weight of time. The years seemed to be getting shorter, and today had crept up on him. He wasn't ready. And he wasn't ready for them to see....

Next year. He'd share next year.

"She needs a break from her practice," he said, trying to sound casual. "Why don't you take her with you? Let her tour another ship. And... and it's late. You could bunk there tonight."

"It's not that late," Daanir replied. "Why would we stay? It's not going to take me that long... wait. Do you *want* us to stay? Jiaan, why?"

Tarjiaan took a deep breath and let it out slowly, then looked at Daanir. He'd spent too many years waiting to have this man at his side again to ruin it now. Besides, if he couldn't trust Daan with this, he might as well throw himself over the side. "What's today, Daan?"

"Today?" Daanir repeated the word slowly. "I've lost track. I...." He blinked. "Oh..."

"I'm not going to be fit company for anyone tonight, and I know it. Marikaar knows what to expect tonight. And... I expect this year, things will be rougher than usual. Better for you both to be out of range. Stay on the *Dauntless* tonight."

Daanir walked around the wheel so that he was facing Tarjiaan, his arms folded over his chest. "And do you honestly think that Nika will agree to stay away when you're hurting?" He paused, frowned, then added, "Or that I would agree to stay away when I know you're hurting?"

Tarjiaan looked away, then nodded. "I should have realized that you'd say that. And that you'd react that way. I just... I wasn't ready to share this with you. And I... Daan, the only person who's ever ridden through this storm with me was Logiri."

"So you were going to ride it out alone, rather than letting us support you." Daanir scowled, then pointed one finger at Tarjiaan. "I'm telling our wife."

"Daan!" Tarjiaan stared at him, then started laughing. "Fine. I'll tell her myself. *Wave Runner*—"

[I have asked the Captain's Lady to join you.]

Tarjiaan shook his head. "My ship seems to agree with you, Daan."

"Our ship, and why shouldn't she?" Daanir came back around the wheel, circling behind Tarjiaan and sliding his arms around his waist. "Why do you think any of us would want to see you hurting?"

"Which is why I wanted you to go spend the night with *Dauntless*. You wouldn't have to see me."

"See you do what?" Nika asked as she came up the stairs. "And spending the night on the *Dauntless*? Who, and why?"

Tarjiaan looked over his shoulder at Daanir, who smiled at him. "You said you were going to tell her. So tell her."

Tarjiaan rolled his eyes and turned back to Nika, who looked puzzled. "Nika, I was thinking that perhaps you and Daanir might spend the night on the *Dauntless*, because... well, because I know that tonight is going to be hard for me, and I don't want to accidentally hurt you or Daan."

To his surprise, she nodded. "Wilaanger told me what today was. I had wondered what that might mean. If there was any ritual that you had to commemorate the day, or to honor your father. Why do you want us to leave you?"

"I thought..." Tarjiaan paused, then let the truth come out. "I usually spend the night drunk."

"I thought you did not drink anymore?" Nika said slowly. Then she frowned. "Wait. You said that you only drink on one night a year. This is the night?"

"This is the night. I pour a drink for my father, and for Ranji, and I pour the rest of the bottle into my memories. I wake up the following morning feeling as if I'm made from eggshells, but I don't remember much of the night before." Tarjiaan closed his eyes for a moment, letting the sea wind sooth his nerves.

"No."

Tarjiaan opened his eyes to see Nika had come up next to him. She rested her hand on his arm. "I am not leaving you to suffer alone."

"Told you," Daanir murmured. "For the record, I'm not leaving you either. I'll go get the message sent out, but I'll be back. Don't get started without me, if you can help it." He let Tarjiaan go, stepping up to stand next to him, looking up at the sky. "Which means I should go. Any messages for Theo?"

"Just... tell him that I won't be available until the forenoon watch. Four bells, maybe five."

Daanir nodded. "Right. I'll tell him. And I'll have a report for you when I get back. I'll stay until we get an answer." He turned and met Tarjiaan's eyes. "You do not have to do this alone, Jiaan."

"I wasn't alone before," Tarjiaan protested. "Logiri—"

"Logiri is a true friend," Nika said. "And he is not here. You were going to do this alone because you wanted to spare us your darkness and your pain. But is that burden not something that we especially should share? We love you."

Tarjiaan shifted to put his arm around Nika. "I love you, too. And you're right. I'm just... I'm learning." He hugged her, then sighed. "I'm sorry."

"You're forgiven," Daanir answered. "But for clarity's sake, why are we forgiving you?"

"For trying to close you out." Tarjiaan looked up at the sky. "You should go. Nika, do you want to go with him? I promise I won't do anything until you get back." He looked at her and smiled. "You can practice your piloting."

She laughed. "Before I am too big to fit in the seat?"

"That will be a few months," Tarjiaan said. "You're not even showing yet. I thought you might enjoy getting the practice."

"I will, and thank you." Nika tugged his arm. "Come down here."

Tarjiaan laughed and leaned down, closing his eyes as Nika took his face in her hands and kissed him. As he straightened and recovered his balance, there was another tug on his other arm; he turned and leaned down for Daanir's kiss.

"We'll be back as soon as we can," Daanir said as he steadied Tarjiaan, then let him go. "Don't do anything until we get back. Understand?"

"I promise." Tarjiaan watched them disappear down the stairs, then turned his attention back to the wheel and the waves.

Daanir leaned over the console and studied the comms. "Are we ready?" he asked. Mentally, he kicked himself. He'd already asked that question. He was stalling.

"We're ready," Tybin, the *Dauntless'* comms officer answered. "Captain, comms are open."

Theonus nodded. "Hailing the dockyards. This is the *Dauntless*. Do you hear us?"

A moment later, a voice crackled over the comms. "*We hear you,* Dauntless. *You're not alone.*"

"Affirmative. We are escorting the *Wave Runner*, who is battle damaged and has no comms." Theonus glanced at Daanir. "Request secure communication with your commander. Top priority."

"*Understood,* Dauntless."

Several minutes passed before a voice Daanir recognized came over the comms. "Dauntless, *this is Mentiras.*"

Theonus nodded. "Commander, prepare to receive a secure file."

"*What?* Dauntless, *you know who you have there—*"

"I know exactly who I have here. File incoming..." He looked at Daanir and nodded, and Daanir started the transfer. "Now. Let me know when you receive."

"*File received. This is a recording of... Great Mothers!*"

"Watch the entire thing, Mentiras. Then we'll talk." Theonus made a sharp gesture, and the comms officer nodded.

"Comms closed, Captain."

"Now we wait," Theonus said. He turned to Daanir. "Where did Nika get to?"

"Nyssa is showing her the ship, and I think she offered to help in your infirmary," Daanir answered. "But she's itching to get back. She piloted the entire way here and docked on her own for the first time. She wants to do it again."

Theonus burst out laughing. "She's definitely more than a match for the Sea Prince."

"For both of us," Daanir agreed.

"And it was an arranged match?" Theonus shook his head. "Ikaanaji picked well, may the Mothers sing his name forever." He tapped the comms officer on the shoulder. "Anything, Tybin?'

"I... yes, they're hailing." Tybin worked the controls. "Comms are live."

"*Hailing the* Dauntless, *this is the dockyards.*"

"Dockyards, this is the *Dauntless*. You watched the recording?"

"*I did, and... this is true? But... we were told...*"

"A lie. You were told a lie. Tarjiaan is on board the *Wave Runner*, battered but unbeaten, and very much alive. Mancer Royal Daanir is standing right here with me, and Princess Ysnika is currently touring my ship with my battle companion." He glanced at Daanir. "Oh, and the Sea Prince Naajir is on board the *Wave Runner* as well."

"*I see. Does the* Wave Runner *need a tow ship, or is she capable of docking under her own power.*"

Theonus arched a brow at Daanir, who nodded. "Hello, Mentiras. Good to hear your voice."

"*Well!*" Mentiras laughed. "*You seem to have done well for yourself, Daan. Will your pet ship need a tow?*"

Daanir burst out laughing. "I forgot you called her that. We won't be able to coordinate a tow with our comms down. If you've got a long line, that might work, but otherwise, Tarjiaan can bring us in."

"*Tarjiaan is Taarik's son and no mistake. He can sail a teapot into a high wind and not spill a drop,*" Mentiras said. "*I'll arrange a long line to help for once you're close enough. When do you expect to reach us? Will you dock tonight?*"

"Not tonight, no," Daanir answered. "Midday tomorrow, I expect."

"*Repair berth nine, and I'll get the repair teams ready for you. Will you supervise, Daan? I seem to remember you not wanting to let anyone touch your baby when we built her.*"

"I wouldn't say no to Narrick's help," Daanir answered. "It's going to be a big job, and he knows the *Wave Runner* almost as well as I do."

"*I'll tell him to have his team ready. Dockyards out.*"

Tybin did something on the console, then looked up. "Comms are clear."

Daanir reached out and fumbled for a chair, sagging into it and folding forward over his legs.

"That went well," Theonus said.

"That went too well," Daanir replied, his voice muffled. "They believed it too fast." He sat up to see Theonus frowning at him. "What do you mean?"

"You didn't believe it when you saw it. Not right off. And honestly, I think you just said you believed it because it was Nika and you never could be rude to a lady. You didn't really believe it until you saw Jiaan. Until he told you. Am I right?"

Theonus smiled. "You know me. You're right. And you're right. They shouldn't have believed that so fast."

Daanir looked up at the ceiling. "I'll tell Jiaan we'll need to be on our guard. Hopefully, seeing him will convince them, too."

"I hope so. Now, it's getting on to be late. Will you be bunking here tonight? You're more than welcome."

Daanir shook his head. "Nika wants to pilot, and Jiaan expects us back on board. We need to head back. Thank you for the offer, though."

Theonus nodded. "Of course. *Dauntless*, would you please tell Nyssa to bring Nika to the submersible?"

[*Dauntless* says that the Mancer Royal and the Captain's Lady have left.]

"Thank you, *Wave Runner*." Tarjiaan turned from the rail, where he'd been looking at the distant lights of the dockyards. "No listening to us tonight, my dear. Not unless I call you."

[Yes, Captain.]

Tarjiaan started toward the great cabin, hearing footsteps behind him as he got halfway across the deck.

"How are you doing today?"

Tarjiaan turned toward the voice. "I was wondering why I hadn't seen you today, Wil. I'm... better than I expected to be." He looked around, then gestured to the door to the great cabin. "I'm going in for the night. Come in."

Wilaanger followed him into the day cabin, taking a seat as Tarjiaan turned up the lights. "Are Nika and Daanir back yet?"

"Not yet, but I expect them soon. *Wave Runner* just told me that *Dauntless* told her they were on their way."

Wilaanger snorted. "And that's a sentence I never thought I'd hear. I wonder if *Chimaera* is aware, the way these two are?"

"If she is, I doubt that she's happy," Tarjiaan said as he sat down in his usual chair. He drummed his fingers on his metal leg, then sighed. "But that's a tomorrow problem. Tonight... I will be getting through tonight."

Wilaanger sighed. "The usual way, I assume?"

Tarjiaan frowned. "What do you mean?"

"Do you think I don't know that this is the one night you crawl back into a bottle?" Wilaanger asked. "Your ship's physician does report to me, remember."

Tarjiaan winced. "I didn't think of that. Are you going to lecture me? Because it won't work."

"No, I'm not going to lecture you." Wilaanger looked around, lingering for a long moment on the memorial portrait that Tarjiaan had moved from the bedroom. It rested on the end of the ward table, with two candles and two glasses resting in front of it. A glass bottle with water beading the sides sat next to Tarjiaan's portable writing desk and his sand glass, which rested at his place at the table. "I'm going to ask to share a drink with you when you pour one for your father and brother. And then I'm going to bed. I'll prepare a morning after remedy for you before I do, though."

"I promised Nika and Daan that I wouldn't start before they got back," Tarjiaan said. "So it will have to wait." He paused. "Thank you. For not lecturing."

"You're a man grown, Jiaan. Now, if you were still eighteen? I might lecture. But as I recall, it didn't work then, either."

Tarjiaan laughed. "It did not." He smiled, then admitted, "I did appreciate it, though. That someone cared enough to lecture. It helped."

Wilaanger smiled and reached out to pat Tarjiaan's arm. "I thought it might. It's why I didn't stop, even though all it did was get your back up. You needed someone who would fuss at you, but not smother you." He paused, then grimaced. "That wasn't a good choice of words."

"I know what you meant," Tarjiaan said. "You were letting me find my own way. Find my balance again." He paused and looked up. "*Wave Runner*?"

[They just docked.]

"Thank you, my dear. Remember, no listening unless I call you." He turned back to Wilaanger. "And now I have two people who fuss at me. They refused to stay on the *Dauntless* tonight. I told them I wanted them out of range, because I wasn't certain how tonight would go, and they refused."

"Are you surprised?" Wilaanger asked. "They both love you."

Tarjiaan nodded. "Honestly? I am a little surprised at how... how much they want to be with me. I don't understand it." He paused, then continued, "Daan was betrayed, and we were kept apart for fifteen years. And Nika... we've only been married just over a month. We had maybe a few days of that before I was taken. Part of me wonders how either of them can possibly love me."

"Is it the same part of you that still thinks that Aanaji was right?" Wilaanger asked. Tarjiaan stared at him for a moment, and the physician nodded. "I said it. I meant it. Is the part that thinks they can't possibly love you the same part that still, on some level, thinks you're a monster who should have died at nineteen?" He gestured to the portrait. "With them?"

"I..." Tarjiaan stopped and licked his lips. "I haven't given it any thought. Not like that."

"When have you had the time?" Wilaanger asked. "Between focusing on surviving and then on keeping us all alive, when have you had time to think and not simply react?"

Tarjiaan nodded slowly, looking up at the ceiling. "I'm going to have time to do a lot of thinking, once we make the dockyards. And I think there's going to be a lot of talking."

Wilaanger smiled. "I'm always here for you, Jiaan."

"Thank you, Wil." Tarjiaan sat up as someone knocked on the door. "I know it's you," he called. "Come in!"

Nika was first through the door, with Daanir following her inside. He closed the door behind him, then looked at the table. "You haven't started?"

"No, I said I was going to wait." Tarjiaan smiled. "How did it go?"

Daanir made a face. "I think we need to be careful. I think they believed us too fast. But they're going to be ready for us. Berth nine."

Tarjiaan frowned. "It's not like we have much of a choice." He nodded. "We'll go carefully. Now... it's past sunset. It's time to begin."

Chapter Ten
Remembrance

TARJIAAN LOOKED AT his armor standing quiet on the rack, then turned his wheeled chair toward the door. When he rolled out into the day cabin, Daanir looked startled.

"Jiaan?"

Tarjiaan nodded. "This is part of it. No armor. No walls. No hiding. Just... me." He rolled down to the end of the table where the portrait rested, and picked up a small box of wick lighters. He took one out, struck it against the rough side of the box, and lit the two candles. He watched the flames dance for a moment before he picked up the bottle and filled the two waiting glasses, then set the bottle down and went back to the head of the table — Daanir jumped up and moved his heavy chair out of the way.

"Thank you," Tarjiaan said as he rolled into place. "I forgot to move that." He reached for the bottle, and hesitated. "Cups. I also forgot cups."

"Let me guess. You usually drink from the bottle?" Wilaanger asked. He stood up. "Where are they?"

"Sideboard cabinet."

Wilaanger walked away, coming back a moment later with four cups. "Nika, do you want to drink?"

Nika looked at the bottle. "Is that something I can drink? Will it hurt the baby?"

Wilaanger picked up the bottle and poured a splash into one cup, handing it to Nika. "That's all you get."

Tarjiaan smiled. "Thank you, Wil. I'll pour." He took the bottle and the remaining cups from Wilaanger, filling all three. He put the bottle down, picked up his cup and closed his eyes, trying to gather his thoughts. Then he laughed.

"This is... so strange," he said. He opened his eyes and looked at the portrait across from him. For the moment, that was his entire focus. "But I just saw you. I just talked to you. It's been... twelve days? I talked to you twelve days ago. And yet... here we are again. Another year. I miss you. I think I'll always miss you, but it's... easier, I think. The missing you isn't as raw. Not since I got to say goodbye." He paused, then raised his cup to the portrait, Daanir, Wilaanger and Nika all following his lead. "The Mothers have claimed you as part of their song. May they sing your names forever." He closed his eyes again, and drained his cup. When he opened his eyes again, he watched as Daanir put his own empty cup down.

Wilaanger finished his drink, then nodded and stood up. "I'm going to go make that morning after remedy for you," he said. "And then... I'm going to light a candle for Ika." He clasped Tarjiaan's shoulder. "Thank you for letting me be part of this. Good night."

"Good night," Tarjiaan said, and waited for Wilaanger to leave. He refilled his cup, took another sip, then noticed that Nika had set her own cup down. "Nika?"

"I do not like it," she murmured. "I am sorry. Does it disturb the ritual if I do not drink?"

Tarjiaan reached for her hand, raising it to his lips to kiss her fingers. "It's fine," he assured her. "This... this is my ritual. My remembrance. And just having you here is enough." He paused, then opened his writing desk and took out a sheet of paper, a pen, and ink.

"What's this for?" Daanir asked.

"I'll show you. Then I'll explain." Tarjiaan took a sip from his cup, letting the alcohol burn down his throat before uncapping the ink bottle. He hesitated, then wondered why before he dipped his pen and started to write. Once he set the nib to the page, the words flowed out of the pen as if they'd been stored there — the composition was automatic after so many years. He finished, signed his name and blew on the ink to dry it. Then he turned the sand glass, watching as the grains started to fall to the bottom globe. For a moment, the urge to just burn the page without letting them see was strong, and again, he wondered why.

"I write this letter every year," he said. "And when the sand runs out, I burn it. The only person who has ever seen one of these was Logiri, because one year I passed out before I could burn it. He burned it for me, and he swore never to reveal that he'd seen it." He met Daanir's eyes, then passed him the page.

Daanir frowned, looking down at the page. His eyes widened, and he gasped, "Jiaan!"

"Pass it to Nika," Tarjiaan said. "Then I'll explain."

"I do not read well yet," Nika murmured as she took the page from Daanir. Her lips moved slowly as she read, and her frown deepened. "Ab-di... does this say abdicate? This letter says you are abdicating the crown?"

"It does," Tarjiaan said. He rested his hands on the table, looking down at the ink smudge on his finger. In an hour, that would be the only evidence that he'd written the letter. "And when the sand runs out, I'll burn it. But for one hour, the only people relying on me are my crew. For one hour, I am nothing more than the ship captain I always wanted to be. For one hour, the future of this nation isn't resting on my shoulders. For one hour, the weight is gone, and I can breathe, and I can grieve everything that I've lost. And at the end of the hour, that letter turns to ash, and I take up the burden once more." He looked up. "This year though, it felt... strange. Writing that letter felt different. I almost didn't. Then... once I signed it, I almost burned it before letting you see it." He paused. "I don't think I'll be writing another one."

"I can tell you why," Daanir said softly. He looked across at Nika. "Do you know?"

She looked puzzled for a moment, then nodded. "I think I do."

Tarjiaan looked at her, then back at Daanir. "What am I missing?"

"That you are not bearing the burden alone anymore," Nika said. Tarjiaan turned back to her as she rested her hand on his. "This year, and all the years we have together, we will bear this burden together. You know this, and that is why it is different."

"She's right," Daanir said. He stood up, came around behind Tarjiaan, then leaned down and wrapped his arms around Tarjiaan, his cheek resting against Tarjiaan's. "We're here. We've got you. You're not alone anymore."

Tarjiaan swallowed, the words settling with solemn certainty in his bones. He reached up with his free hand to clasp Daanir's arm. He nodded, hearing the soft, scratchy sound as his beard rubbed against Daanir's, watching as Nika took the letter and stood up. She looked around, then went to the sideboard and took out a metal bowl that she brought back to the table. She held the paper to the candle flame, turning it slowly as it started to burn before dropping it into the bowl.

"Next year, we will have a new ritual," she said, never turning from the fire burning in the bowl. "Next year, we will introduce our child to your father and to your brother, and we will celebrate their lives, not their deaths. And when the children are old enough to understand, we will tell them all the stories about Taarik the Demon Captain and his First Mate, Aaranji, who sailed the seas beyond death to defend the kingdom they loved."

"I like that," Daanir said in Tarjiaan's ear. "We'll sing their names in harmony with the Mothers."

Tarjiaan nodded, but his voice was snagged in a net of years-old unshed tears. He reached out for Nika's hand, pulling her into his arms, into his lap. Feeling her weight against him, Daanir's arms tight around him, he held tight to them both and finally, fully released his grief. He wasn't sure how long he cried, but when he finally could breathe, when his eyes were finally dry, he felt... lighter.

"I think it is time we took you to bed," Nika murmured.

"That sounds like a good idea," Daanir agreed. "You need to rest and sleep this off."

"I'm not drunk," Tarjiaan said, his voice more raspy than usual. He looked at the full cup and the bottle, and the idea of drinking any more turned his stomach. "And... I'm not going to be. I don't want it." He took a deep breath and hugged Nika more tightly to his chest. "I want to do one thing before we go to bed. Daan, would you get something for me?"

"Of course." Daanir kissed his cheek, then straightened. "What do you need?"

Tarjiaan pointed to a long, low cabinet. "My double-neck and my light harp—"

"Oh?" Daanir squeezed his shoulder. "Which one?"

"Which would you prefer?" Tarjiaan asked. He looked at Nika. "Well?"

"We have seen the recording of you playing the double-neck. I would like to see the light harp."

Daanir grinned. "I agree with her. I'll get it." He went to the cabinet and opened the doors, coming back with the oddly angled body of the light harp. Nika watched him, then cocked her head to the side.

"What is that?" she asked. "I thought... a harp that was small, perhaps. One that did not weigh much. But this is nothing like what I thought. There is no pillar. And where are the strings?"

Tarjiaan smiled. "You'll need to move so that I can show you."

Nika mock-scowled. "I have to move?" she teased. Then she kissed Tarjiaan quickly and shifted off of his lap, taking her seat at the table. Tarjiaan took the harp body from Daanir and settled the base on his thigh, leaning the body against his left shoulder. He touched the power stud where the body met the neck, and heard the soft hum as the emitters powered on. One by one, the slender beams of light appeared.

"Oh!" Nika gasped. "The strings are made from light? Then... how do you play?"

"You break the beam," Tarjiaan answered. He plucked one of the strings, and a clear note rang out. "The hardest part of learning how to play is learning how work the strings, because they don't quite behave the same as metal strings." He flexed his fingers, then looked up. "What should I play?"

"Something we haven't heard before?" Daanir suggested, pulling a chair out so he could sit next to Nika. "Something new."

Tarjiaan nodded, focusing on his strings. Unlike a stringed harp, he actually had to watch as he played — there was no tactile feedback from the strings, so he couldn't close his eyes and fall into the music. Which meant he was very aware of being watched as he started to play. He chose something he'd only just written, a song inspired by a sudden storm. It started with sharp, almost frantic notes to mimic the sudden, torrential rains that had drenched everyone on deck, then gradually slowed into the soft, gentle pattern and melody of a rain shower at sea. The higher notes were the raindrops striking the windows in his cabin, and the lower notes were the wind in the sails, with the rise and fall of the melody mimicked that of the waves. The song slowed even more, growing softer, quieter, until the final chord signaled the end of the storm. He rested one hand on the neck, the other on his leg.

"How was that?"

"Rain?" Daanir asked. "I was hearing rain, wasn't I?" He looked at Nika. "Did you hear it?"

"Yes, but I thought I was imagining it," Nika said. "Jiaan, that was wonderful!"

Tarjiaan smiled and ran his free hand over the body of the harp. "Thank you. Do you want something else?"

"*Safe Harbor*. My song," Daanir said, standing and moving behind Nika. He put his hands on her shoulders. "Our song."

"Daanir?" Nika looked up. "No. That is yours. Jiaan can make one for me."

"Until he does, it's ours." Daanir smiled. "I'll share." He leaned down and kissed Nika. "It's ours."

Tarjiaan smiled. "I'll need my double neck."

Daanir came around and took the light harp, putting it back in the cabinet and bringing the lute back to Tarjiaan. Tarjiaan strummed the strings, adjusted the tuning, running through the song in his head as he did. He'd written this song for a small lute, so he'd need to adapt it for the double neck. He strummed the strings once more, then started playing, picking out the melody that he hadn't been able to bring himself to play in fifteen years. He didn't dare look up. If he did, he wouldn't be able to continue. Instead, he took a deep breath and sang words that he thought he'd never sing again:

> "*Go bid the compass true north to neglect*
> *That with assured reliance it did embrace*
> *Go bid the still water cease to reflect,*
> *Go bid the stars their paths no more to trace.*
> *And when these all shall be convinced to do*
> *Then shall I cease, cease to love you.*"

His voice sounded rough to his ears. It wasn't the trained voice of his youth, that was for certain — he was years out of practice, and he could hear it. He was on key, at least, but the rasp seemed more prominent when he sang. But it wasn't unpleasant, either. Just... different.

He could live with different.

He relaxed into the music, and the words came as easily as if he'd only just written them. The song wasn't long — only three verses. Nineteen lines of poetry that he'd agonized over at eighteen, struggling to put into words the feelings he had for his battle companion. He'd been terrified that night, afraid to admit his love, and stunned to find out that his battle companion shared his feelings. Reciprocated them.

It had been his gift on the night Daanir turned eighteen, and it had been their first night together.

He played the final chord and let the strings fall quiet, looking up to see Daanir still standing with his hands on Nika's shoulders. His eyes were closed, and as Tarjiaan watched, Nika reached up and touched his hand. He smiled, taking her hand as he opened his eyes and looked at Tarjiaan.

"I had no idea how much I needed to hear that," he whispered, his voice just barely audible over the creaking of the ship. "I... Jiaan..."

"It was perfect," Nika said. "Jiaan, it was perfect. It was beautiful." She looked up at Daanir. "Go on."

Daanir smiled and raised her hand to his lips, kissing her knuckles. Then he walked around her, coming to stand in front of Tarjiaan. He took the lute from Tarjiaan, turned to set it on the table, then turned back. There was no hesitation, not a hint of doubt as Daanir bent and kissed Tarjiaan, one hand cupping the back of his head, the other locked in the loose cloth of his shirt. Tarjiaan closed his eyes and rested his hands on Daanir's waist. He heard the footstep a moment before Nika touched him, running her hand over his shoulders.

"We should go to bed," she said softly.

Tarjiaan felt Daanir laughing against his lips. "I like that idea," he whispered. "Let's take our husband to bed."

"Our husband?" Tarjiaan repeated, looking up as Daanir straightened.

"Well, if Nika is our wife, doesn't that mean that we're her husbands?" he asked. "Nika?"

"That makes sense," Nika said. "But how does that make you two each other's husbands?"

"Because addition is commutative," Daanir said with a grin.

"I... I do not understand," Nika said. "How does addition come into this?"

Daanir laughed and ran one hand through his hair. "It's... well, math makes more sense to me than people. Certain people excluded, of course." He pointed to Tarjiaan, then to Nika. "You plus you plus me. We add up to three. But when we're together, we're a whole."

Tarjiaan nodded. "I'm following so far. Go on."

Daanir pointed again. "That whole is the sum of three parts. Each of those three parts added together comes to the same sum. So if one plus one plus one equals three, then it doesn't matter which one comes first. We're all together adding to three. Or... or one...." He paused, frowning. "It made sense in my head."

"No, it does make sense," Nika said. "And it is not as complicated as you are making it. We each have promised the others to support and to love each other. To take care of each other. That is marriage. We do not need a ritual or words said to make it so. We know who we are to each other."

Daanir blinked, then nodded. "That's... a much simpler way of putting it."

"It doesn't always have to be complicated, Daan," Tarjiaan said. "Sometimes, it's as simple as one-two-three." He held his hand out. "Let's go to bed."

Tarjiaan woke when he heard distant knocking. It sounded as if someone was at the door to the day cabin, but there wasn't much he could do about it — he was pinned to the mattress, being used as a pillow by both Daanir and Nika. Nika had claimed his left shoulder, while Daanir had his head pillowed on Tarjiaan's stomach. Both of them were still deeply asleep, and Tarjiaan didn't have either the leverage or the inclination to try and move them. Until one or both of them woke, Tarjiaan was going nowhere.

Not that he minded. He felt better than he had in ages. He took a deep breath and closed his eyes, running one hand over Daanir's bare back. He'd told people that he wasn't going to be available until midmorning. He could sleep a little more....

Someone knocked on the bedroom door. Tarjiaan raised his head, glaring at the door, which creaked as it opened. Wilaanger peered around the edge of the door, and his eyes widened when he saw Tarjiaan looking back at him. He withdrew, and the door closed, the lock clicking loud enough to make Daanir jerk.

"Easy," Tarjiaan murmured, running his hand down Daanir's back once more. "It was the door."

"Door?" Daanir croaked. "What..." He raised his head, blinking, clearly not awake. Until he saw Tarjiaan – he smiled and shifted up to kiss him. Tarjiaan sighed and closed his eyes, letting Daanir control the kiss. He heard a sleepy laugh from his left, and Daanir gasped and broke the kiss. Tarjiaan opened his eyes to see that Nika was running her hand over Daanir's ribs.

"Good morning," Tarjiaan said. "Before we get too involved, Wilaanger is out in the day cabin."

"He said he would come this morning and bring a morning after remedy," Nika said.

"And I think he was expecting to find me unconscious," Tarjiaan said. "He looked more than a little surprised to find me awake." He tightened his arms around them. "I don't want to get up yet, but we have work to do."

"Do you want me to wash up and keep Wilaanger company while you wash and dress, and put on your armor?" Nika asked. "I will send for food."

"So long as you remember to eat a ration pack while you wait." Tarjiaan turned so that he was nose to nose with his wife. "I don't want you getting sick."

She smiled and kissed him. "I will eat. And I will eat again once breakfast arrives. Now don't delay." She sat up, kissed Daanir, then slipped from the bed, picking up her clothes before she disappeared into the washroom. Tarjiaan reached up and stroked Daanir's jaw.

"The beard suits you," he murmured. "I should have said it before. I like it. It looks very good."

Daanir chuckled, resting his head on Tarjiaan's chest. "If you keep petting me, we won't get out of this bed," he warned. "And I never thought I'd grow one. Remember when I tried?"

"You gave up after three days. Said the itching was driving you insane."

"I tried after that, but... well...." He shrugged. "And this time... I was distracted enough that I never noticed it." Daanir fell quiet. "The last time I shaved was the morning everything happened. I haven't had a razor or the time since."

Tarjiaan nodding, closing his eyes. "I like it. It looks good on you." He smiled. "So, if I keep petting you, we won't get out of bed? Promise? We can have Nika back—"

"You're the one who said we have work to do." Daanir shifted and sat up. Tarjiaan propped himself up on his elbows.

"I want a day when none of us have to get out of bed," he said. "Just one day!"

The washroom door opened, and Nika stepped out. "One day in bed?" she repeated. "That will have to be before the baby comes. I do not think we will be able to stay the entire day in bed once we have a baby to care for."

"She has a point." Daanir got up, then stretched. He scrubbed his hand over his face. "I need to shave—"

"No."

The answer came from two directions, and Daanir looked startled. "What?"

Tarjiaan shifted and sat up with his back against the headboard. "Did you not just hear me say I like it? It looks good on you. If you don't want to shave, please don't." He grinned. "It's interesting. I've never been kissed by a man with a beard before."

"It is very becoming," Nika added. "Why would you shave it?"

Daanir blinked. "I... you're both serious? You like this?" He gestured to his face. "I..."

"Do you like it?" Nika asked. "When you look in the glass, does it look right?"

Daanir frowned. Then he turned and walked into the washroom. Nika came to perch on the edge of the bed, and they waited for Daanir to come back out. When he did, he looked puzzled.

"I... yes," he said. "I do like it. I mean... it's like Captain Taarik's, and I always thought it was a good look." He smiled slightly. "I'll keep it. I need to learn to take care of it so I don't look unkempt. More than I usually do, anyway."

"I can teach you that," Tarjiaan said. "But now I'm curious. Why were you so ready to shave if you like it?"

Daanir folded his arms over his chest and sighed. "Ishian. He... he didn't like it. And when I told him I didn't want to shave..." He stopped and gestured to his face, running his fingertip over the scar on his jaw. "He shaved me."

Tarjiaan stared at him, for a moment unable to believe his ears. "He... he did *what*?"

Daanir shook his head. "Rather not sail those waters today, if you don't mind?"

Nika got up and went to him, putting her arms around him. "We will not let him hurt you again, Daan."

Daanir put his arm around her. "I know." He grimaced. "Ah... later. I'll tell you later. Once we're away from here."

"Away from him?" Tarjiaan asked. He nodded. "Understood. I want you to consider something, Daan. Do you want him to face justice?"

Daanir shrugged. "I don't know. Maybe. Ask me again once all of the more important things are done."

Tarjiaan held his hand out. "Come here." He waited until Daanir came back to sit down on the bed and took his hand, pulling him closer and holding him against his chest. Nika joined him, once again wrapping her arms around Daanir. Tarjiaan ran his hand over the back of Daanir's neck.

"Mancer mine, there is nothing more important to me than the two of you."

Chapter Eleven
Dockyards

ONCE DAANIR SEEMED more grounded, Nika went out to the day cabin, leaving them to get ready. Tarjiaan shifted onto his chair, and rolled to the washstand in the corner.

"You're not using the washroom?" Daanir asked. "I... oh." Tarjiaan turned to see Daanir looking from him to the door to the washroom. "I... yeah, we'll fix that."

"You had no idea that I was using a rolling chair," Tarjiaan said. "Or that the chair wouldn't fit through the door into the washroom. The washbasin and the privy chair are what I started using on the *Sea Wolf*. It works."

Daanir frowned. "I didn't notice. Which... I should have noticed. I should have put more thought into this. It's late, but I can make this more comfortable," he said, his fingers moving idly. "Easier for you. And for Nika." He looked at Tarjiaan and grinned. "If she is carrying twins, she'll appreciate extra room."

"You're in charge of the refit," Tarjiaan said. "I trust you. Now, let's get ready. Washroom is all yours."

By the time they came out into the day cabin, the table had been set. Wilaanger sat next to Nika, and he turned and smiled as Tarjiaan came closer.

"I apologize for waking you," he said. "I didn't think you'd be conscious, let alone moving. Although I should have realized I was wrong when I came in."

"How?" Daanir asked, taking his place at the table.

Wilaanger reached out and picked up the abandoned bottle from the previous night. "This. It's not empty. And the cup Tarjiaan was using is still full. You barely drank anything last night, did you?"

"The one drink I had when you were here, and I think a sip of the refill," Tarjiaan answered, sitting down and leaning back in his chair. "That was all, and that's all it will be. I won't be doing that again. Nika suggested a new ceremony for next year. One that doesn't involve drowning my memories."

"Shall I put the portrait away?" Nika asked.

"I'll do it," Daanir said. "I don't think you'll be able to reach the hook." He stood up and walked to the end of the table, picking up the portrait. "Why don't you serve? Did you eat?"

"I did eat," Nika answered, turning to speak to Daanir's back as he took the portrait into the bedroom. "I ate some ration biscuits while we waited. Jiaan, what would you like?"

"A little of everything, please. I'm hungry. Wil, will you stay?"

"Thank you. I brought the morning after remedy, but I see you don't need it. And I had a thought I wanted to discuss with you all. You especially, Daanir." He accepted a plate from Nika, and picked up the teapot, filling four cups. Nika passed another plate to Tarjiaan, and he smiled when he saw his favorite smoked fish and rice dish.

"Aranti is making certain I eat. Where she found the supplies for this, I don't know." He took a bite. "It's missing something, but it's still good."

"What did you want to ask, Wil?" Daanir asked, coming around to take his place at the table again. He smiled as Nika handed him a full plate. "Thank you." He took a bite, then mumbled, "Eggs. It's missing the eggs."

"While we're in the dockyards, I think it would be a very good idea if *Wave Runner* stayed silent while we have workmen aboard."

[I heard my name?] *Wave Runner* said. [May I listen?]

"You did hear your name," Wilaanger answered, tipping his head back. "Good morning."

[Good morning, People Mancer.]

Daanir coughed on his mouthful. He wiped his mouth, took a sip of tea, then repeated, "People mancer?"

Tarjiaan smiled as he sipped his tea, watching the play of emotions on Daanir's face. "She hasn't said that in front of you yet?"

"No!" Daanir answered. "My lovely, Wilaanger is a physician. Not a people mancer."

[He is a people mancer,] *Wave Runner* insisted. [And he says I may call him that.]

Daanir blinked. "He says... how long has this been going on?"

Tarjiaan chuckled. "Ten days? It started the day we met *Dauntless*. *Wave Runner* called Navi a people mancer, and I thought it was charming."

"So did I. She called me that when she was introduced to me," Wilaanger agreed. "And I gave her permission to call me that. In truth, I rather like it." He laughed and looked up. "She explained to me that mancers take care of their ships and fix them when they're broken. People mancers do the same for people. Isn't that right?"

[Yes!]

Daanir looked up at the ceiling, looking as if he was going to say something. Then he stopped. He frowned, then nodded. "I... right. I see how that sails." He grinned. "I never thought of it that way."

"It is very charming," Nika said. "*Wave Runner*, am I a people mancer?"

[You are Captain's Lady,] *Wave Runner* answered. [And a people mancer.]

"Back to the original thought," Daanir said. "Why should she stay silent, Wil?" He paused again. "Oh. Wait. I get it. Antivar had the same thought, when we went to *Dauntless* to take her back from Gellan. Our ships, they're like children. They're still young, and we need to protect them. Especially since we don't know what Ilaris would do if he found out that the ships are aware, especially if he has other mancers answering to him. We can't let that word get back to him."

"That's exactly my thought," Wilaanger said. "While we're in drydock, *Wave Runner* shouldn't speak to anyone that she has not been explicitly introduced to and invited to speak with." He looked up. "Do you understand why, my dear?"

[I think so,] Wave Runner said slowly. [You don't want me to talk to people I don't know, because they might try to hurt me the way the bad mancer tried to hurt *Dauntless*.]

"Exactly so," Wilaanger said. "I'm pleased you understand. I don't want you to be hurt."

"*Wave Runner*, I'd like to add to that," Tarjiaan said. "As Wilaanger said, you need to stay quiet while our crew are not on board. But I want you to pay attention to what people are saying around you, and let me or Daanir know. Will you do that?"

[I am to be quiet, and I am to listen. Shall I record?]

"Yes," Tarjiaan said. "And once your comms are repaired, if anything frightens you or if you have any questions, you'll be able to reach us if we're away from the ship."

"We'll get the comms done first," Daanir said. "And I'll stay onboard until they're done." He looked over at Tarjiaan and Nika. "You don't mind, do you? I need to look after my ship."

[Captain's Lady said you are my father. And Kaapi says we are sisters.]

Daanir grinned. "Well, then. That settles it. I need to stay onboard and look after my child." He frowned. "Who's older?"

[We have not yet decided.]

"I don't mind," Tarjiaan added. "I'm assuming you're asking because if you stay, we're all staying?" He arched a brow at Nika, who smiled.

"Of course we will stay with Daanir," she said.

"You don't want to take the royal apartment?" Daanir asked.

"Not without you." Nika sipped her tea and took a bite of her rice. "We are one. We determined that last night."

"We are one," Tarjiaan agreed. "But I think I know why Daan is asking, and it's something you don't know." Tarjiaan glanced at Daanir. "The bath?"

Daanir laughed. "Exactly."

"What about a bath?" Nika asked. She looked at Tarjiaan, then at Daanir. "There is no proper bath on the *Wave Runner*."

"No, but there's one in the royal apartment on the floating dockyards," Daanir answered. He paused, then turned to Tarjiaan. "I just realized something. You never once brought the *Wave Runner* in to the dockyards. Not since I sent her to you. That's a long time to not have any major refits."

Tarjiaan shrugged. "She never needed them. You outdid yourself, Daan. The first major issue we had onboard was the hydroponics, and we were on our way to the dockyards when everything started."

"You built her to your standards, Daan," Wilaanger said. "Do you wonder why she never needed any updates?"

"And the *Sea Wolf* was in for refits right after I took command. She went in again right after Mentiras took her when I took the *Wave Runner*."

"So that's how you know about the royal apartment," Daanir said. He nodded. "Right. We missed each other by... what? A year?"

Tarjiaan reached over and rested his hand on Daanir's arm. "We're together now." He smiled, then turned back to Nika. "Sailing back. Yes, there's a proper bath in the royal apartments at the dockyards. With a large bathtub."

Nika looked thoughtful. "How large? Compared to the one in our quarters on the *Chimaera.*"

Daanir frowned. "I... it might be bigger. I'm not sure."

Nika nodded. "We will find out." Then she smiled. "I am looking forward to a bath, once we are all able to stay together."

"Just don't start renovating the washroom here until we're able to stay there," Tarjiaan said. He looked down at his empty plate and tried to decide if he wanted more.

"There is more of the... what is this?" Nika picked up a bowl and passed it to Tarjiaan. "It is very good, but what is it?"

"It's a Sualimani dish. Spiced rice and smoked fish." Tarjiaan put some more onto his plate. "There's usually eggs and vegetables mixed in as well. I first had it when I lived with your grandmother's court, and Aranti knows I like it." He picked up his fork and speared a piece of fish. "Now, do we have a tow for docking?"

"We have no way to talk to them until the comms are repaired," Daanir answered. "So I refused it. Once we're close enough, we'll have a long line for repair bay nine if we need it."

Tarjiaan nodded. "Then I should finish eating so I can take her in."

"Before you go, I have a tidbit of ancient law for you," Wilaanger said. "It's been ages since I thought of it, and I think you'll find it useful."

"What?" Tarjiaan asked.

"How you're going to explain the three of you," Wilaanger answered. "You have a wife. To openly have a lover... well, the more staid nobles of Meradon might frown on that. But... there's a very old practice that's still in the legal texts. It hasn't been used in an age, but it's still there." He took a deep breath. "I found it when Ika and I were young, when he married Alyaan. When... well, it wasn't something he was willing to do, and he was as surprised as I was that it was even an option."

"Oh," Daanir murmured. "And what is it?"

"Consortage."

Tarjiaan coughed. "Wait. I remember reading about that. It's still legal?"

Nika looked puzzled. "I do not know this word. What is it?"

Tarjiaan turned toward her. "Consortage is... something like what I told you both about the Tyracan queens, where the queen has her favored males, and they're all equal partners. It hasn't been done in Meradon for years. I think... oh, those lessons were years ago. King Enkazar?" He looked at Wilaanger, who nodded.

"You remember your lessons." Wilaanger looked at Daanir. "You should have learned this."

"I might have," Daanir admitted. "But history never really interested me. And Nika doesn't know it at all."

Wilaanger nodded. "It was one of the few times in our history that the royal line passed to the King's own children. He had no siblings. However, his wife was barren. Theirs was a marriage of affection rather than alliance, so rather than put Queen Clymina aside, Enkazar took a consort." Wilaanger gestured to Tarjiaan. "Aamynta was the Tarjiaan's seventh grandmother, and the mother of his maternal line. She's also the reason for the tradition of the conjoined-a in the royal family names."

"Which doesn't explain how I got it," Daanir said. "I'm not royal anything."

Tarjiaan took Daanir's hand. "Royal consort. Which, if you accept, also makes your children officially of the royal line."

Daanir blinked. "I... oh. Kaapi?" He paused. "That... that won't be an issue later, will it? For her and Naji?"

"She'd be a royal adoptee, the same as you are," Tarjiaan said. "They're not related by blood in any way, so there should be no issue if they want something more later."

Daanir grinned. "Then I should go tell her that she'll be Kaapi Meranas before the sun sets today." He stood up, came around the table, and leaned in to kiss Tarjiaan. "That's a yes. I accept."

"Ahoy the ship!"

Tarjiaan nodded at the distant shout. He already knew that the smaller boat had drawn up alongside the *Wave Runner*, had felt it skimming across the surface of the water as a ticklish trail over the back of his hand. He murmured, "Comms," and heard the beep in his ear. "Ready the lines! Strike the sails." He glanced up, watching as the topsails were lowered. He kept his hands on the wheel — even with no sails, the wind could still push a ship off course, even one as large the *Wave Runner*. He could feel the currents as pressure against his hands, and he adjusted as necessary.

"*Captain, lines are secured! They're ready to bring us in,*" Marikaar announced in his ear.

"Proceed." Tarjiaan said. He kept his attention on the tiller, on the rudder, on the movement of the ship, making the slight corrections to keep them on course as the lines were taken in, pulling them into the repair berth waiting for them. He saw Nika coming up the stairs, and nodded at her. She smiled and took her place on his right, not saying anything until the ship jerked slightly.

"What was that?"

"The long line," Tarjiaan answered. "They're drawing us into the berth. If you're interested, you might want to go by the rail."

"I was curious," Nika said. "How do we stop? How do we not hit the dockyards?"

Tarjiaan grinned. "The short answer is practice. But it still happens sometimes. A gust of wind at exactly the wrong moment could do it."

"Then I should let you pay attention." Nika trailed her fingers over his back as she passed behind him, going to the rail. Tarjiaan stole a glance at her, the breeze tugging at her clothes, the excitement writ clear in her face. Then he forced his attention back to his duty. He was *not* going to hit the dock with his wife watching!

The line drew them in slowly, with Tarjiaan adjusting their speed and making sure that they were entering the slip straight on. He heard Marikaar ordering the lines deployed, and tacked so that *Wave Runner* was tugging against the lines, braking their forward momentum just enough that once the lines were moored, the Wave Runner was secure and still. Tarjiaan turned from the wheel to see Nika coming toward him.

"You're going to miss the most interesting part," he said. "Come back to the rail." He took Nika's hand and led her to the stern rail. "Watch."

"What am I watching?" Nika asked. "I... is that a gate? They are locking the ship in?"

"Did you wonder how they were going to work on the ship while it was still afloat?" Tarjiaan asked. The ship shuddered as he finished speaking

"I had not thought about it before now. I did not know enough to ask the question." Nika looked down over the rail. "Is... where is the water going? And what was that? I thought we had stopped. Did we hit the dock?"

"No." Tarjiaan gestured to the starboard side rail. "They've raised a cradle underneath the *Wave Runner* to hold her. And with that gate closed, they can drain the water out of the berth and work as if they were on dry land." He looked over the side and saw a familiar face on the dock. He smiled and waved, and saw the man wave back.

"Is that Mentiras?" Nika asked.

"It is. Let's go find Daan."

It didn't matter where he was or how often he did it — walking down the gangplank onto a dock always felt just slightly *wrong*. Tarjiaan glanced over his shoulder to check that Daanir was on his left, then raised his right hand to his lips so that he could kiss Nika's fingers. "Ready?"

Nika smiled up at him. "I am ready. Shall we?"

Tarjiaan nodded. "Daan, remember your new title and how I'm going to introduce you."

Daanir grinned. "I remember. I like it. And I can't wait for him to hear it. Let's go."

They started down the gangplank. At the bottom, Tarjiaan could see the welcoming committee, with Mentiras at the front.

"See him?" he whispered, knowing Daanir would hear.

"No," Daanir answered. "He's not there."

"Good." Tarjiaan stopped at the bottom of the ramp. "Permission to come aboard, Commander?"

"Granted!" Mentiras laughed and met Tarjiaan as he stepped onto the dock, taking his hand, then giving him an enthusiastic hug. "It's good to see you, my friend!" Mentiras stepped back and looked Tarjiaan up and down. "Oh, you don't look well. Have you been ill? Is Logiri still with you? Isn't he taking care of you?"

Tarjiaan held up his free hand. "We have a lot to catch up on, my friend. But let me give you the pleasant part first. Commander Mentiras, allow me to present you to my wife, the Princess Ysnika."

Mentiras' jaw dropped. "Your... your wife?" He looked at Nika and smiled, bowing deeply. "Ma'am, I am honored. And amazed. I never thought this old sea wolf would settle down."

Nika laughed. "I have heard much about you, Commander. I am pleased to meet you."

"And I believe you know my battle companions, and our royal consort?" Tarjiaan added, watching the shock play over Mentiras' face. "Mancer Royal and Royal Consort, Lord Daanir Meranas."

Mentiras looked at Daanir, then back at Tarjiaan. "That... that string of words is just one long attempt to make me faint, isn't it? Of course I know Daanir!" He looked past Tarjiaan. "Oh, you look good, lad! The beard suits you. Battle companion? You've taken that back up? Good! And you're Mancer Royal now, and you're *consort*? I didn't even know that was a thing you could do! You fell up, my lad, and no mistake!"

Daanir laughed. "I did. I definitely did." He stepped up next to Tarjiaan. "Is Narrick here?"

"He told me that he'd be getting his team ready, and he'll be along shortly," Mentiras said. "He's looking forward to working with you again. I... Tarjiaan, what am I supposed to call you? Given that I've seen that recording?"

"The throne isn't mine yet, Mentiras. For now, you can keep calling me Prince-Captain. Or by my name. You earned that right a long time ago."

Mentiras smiled. "One should never assume. Now, will you be staying in the royal apartments?"

"Once we get the comms back," Tarjiaan answered.

"I want to be in shouting range," Daanir added. "Once the comms are repaired and I can be reached when I'm not onboard, we'll move over."

Mentiras nodded. "I should have realized you'd want to be in the depths of the work. You always did. Now..." He stopped.

"Tarjiaan, who is that?" Tarjiaan turned to look, and saw Naajir and Kaapi at the top of the gangplank. "Did you... it hasn't been *that* long since I last saw you!"

"I... what?" Tarjiaan turned back to Mentiras. "I..."

Nika laughed. "Commander, you are mistaken. That is not Tarjiaan's son," she said, and Tarjiaan stared at her. "That is what he was asking, Jiaan."

Tarjiaan looked back at Mentiras, who laughed. "It is, and thank you, ma'am," Mentiras admitted.

"I... no, Tir. That's Naajir. My nephew. The young lady with him is Daan's daughter and our royal fosterling, Kaapi Meranas."

Mentiras nodded. "Also words I never thought I'd hear. Is she a mancer, too?"

Daanir smiled. "She is." He turned and looked up the gangplank. "Kaap, come down and meet the commander."

Kaapi came slowly down the gangplank, holding tightly to Naajir's hand. At the bottom, she froze. "Papa?" she said softly. "This... this isn't *land*, is it?"

"No, Kaap," Daanir said, going to take her other hand. "The floating dockyards are a really, really big ship. They can move and reposition."

"Would you like to tour our engine room?" Mentiras asked. "You won't believe the size of it! I can arrange a tour."

Kaapi's eyes widened. "I... you can?"

"Of course!" Mentiras smiled. "Your father trained here, lass. Our Mancer is fond of him. And I think he'll like you. He'll be happy to show you around, once we get some of the work done on this poor ship." He looked up at the *Wave Runner.* "Prince-Captain, I think our first order of business is to sit down and go over the contents of that recording. I have... so many questions."

"We'll answer what we can," Tarjiaan said. "Now, my crew will want to take liberty, and I have a rather a lot of Tyracan refugees. One of their ships defected. That won't be a problem, will it?"

"I'll make sure that the word gets out," Mentiras said. "We have rather a lot of refugees ourselves. Make sure you send your refugees out paired with your regular crew. Just to be on the safe side. Some of our people are nervous, and some of the refugees are... tense. I'll talk to your First Mate. Who is... not Quentas, yes?"

"My first mate is Marikaar," Tarjiaan said.

"He's at the top of the ramp," Naajir said. "I'll get him." He darted back up the ramp, and Mentiras laughed.

"That sort of energy is wasted on the young," he said. "Now, Captain, come to my office, and we'll get things squared away."

Tarjiaan turned toward Nika. He saw her eyes widen, and the alarm on her face.

"Daanir—"

Tarjiaan whipped around in time to see that all the color had drained from Daanir's face. He was staring up the dock, toward a handsome older man who was coming toward them. Tarjiaan reached out and took Daanir's arm.

"That's him?" he murmured.

Daanir nodded. "Kaap," he croaked. "Go back onboard. Go with Naji. I'll come get you... later. I'll get you later."

"I... Papa?"

"Go, Kaap. I'll... I'll tell you later."

Kaapi looked at Tarjiaan, who nodded. "I'll take care of him."

"Thank you, Captain Papa," she whispered. Then she ran back up the gangplank. Tarjiaan took Daanir's hand and squeezed his fingers.

"Just say the word and I'll feed him to the sharks," he whispered. That got a grin from Daanir.

"Cruel to the sharks," he whispered back. He squeezed Tarjiaan's hand and smiled slightly.

"Captain!"

Mentiras' warning was a heartbeat too late, as Ishian shoved Tarjiaan out of the way and grabbed Daanir by the arm. "Well, it's been a long time," he growled. "Welcome back, Dani-boy. I've been waiting to get my hands on you again."

Chapter Twelve
Allies

BEFORE TARJIAAN COULD move, Nika did — she wrapped one hand around Ishian's wrist. Tarjiaan had no idea what she did, but Ishian yelped and staggered back, staring at her. Nika snapped something in Imperial, then turned to Daanir, putting her hand on his arm and tugging him gently away from his attacker.

Ishian glared at her, taking one step toward her, his fist raised. Tarjiaan grabbed him by the scruff of the neck and threw him across the dock — he landed solidly at Mentiras' feet, then staggered to his feet. He looked up at Tarjiaan and went pale.

"You will keep your hands off my consort and my wife," Tarjiaan growled.

"You... this is impossible! You're *dead*!" Ishian stammered. "You... they told me you were dead!"

"They were wrong." Tarjiaan looked back at Daanir and Nika. "Nika?"

"He is unharmed," Nika said. "Mentiras, who is this lout? He is one of your men?"

"Ah... no, ma'am." Mentiras walked over to Ishian and slapped him soundly on the back of the head. "You idiot! That's the Queen you've insulted, and the Royal Consort you're manhandling! Are you trying to die?"

Ishian looked past Tarjiaan. "Consort? Wife? I..." He blinked and looked at Tarjiaan again. "Queen? But...you..."

"Jiaan, I think that he thinks you're Ranji," Daanir called. "And I'm fine. Startled, but fine."

"That doesn't mean that he's getting away with putting his hands on the Royal Consort," Tarjiaan said. He looked at Ishian. "You thought I was my brother, hm?"

"You... you're Tarjiaan, aren't you?" Ishian shook his head. "You're the Sea Prince. I... you look like him. Like Aaranji. Enough to fool me." He looked away, then back. "I... did he ever... tell you about me?"

"Oh, he did," Tarjiaan answered, folding his arms over his chest. "I know exactly who you were to my brother. And what you did to my brother. I know exactly why you were exiled to Station Six." He stepped closer and lowered his voice. "And I know what you did to my consort when he was sent to Station Six. So if you value your worthless, cowardly skin, you'll stay as far as possible from him, my wife, and my ship. Is that understood?"

Ishian blanched. Then he stepped back, bumping in to Mentiras and nearly falling. Mentiras steadied him, then stared as Ishian fled the docks.

"I... I think I need to hear more about this," Mentiras said. "There's clearly something I don't know about that one. Shall we go to my office?" He paused. "I don't think I have a chair that will hold you, Jiaan, but you don't look like you should be standing."

"I'm fine, Mentiras," Tarjiaan said. "Let's get this done."

Mentiras left them in his office while he went to fetch Mancer Narrick. It was a small room, and felt smaller once Tarjiaan was inside. At Mentiras' insistence, he took a seat on a long, low cabinet that ran along one wall – the only thing in the office that would support the bulky weight of Tarjiaan in his armor. Nika took the chair facing Mentiras' desk, while Daanir leaned against the wall, shifting slightly from one foot to the other. He shook his hands out, then tipped his head from side to side, stretching his neck.

"Daan, sit down," Nika said.

"Can't sit. Not yet," Daanir answered absently. "Need to... to not sit."

"Worse than you thought it would be?" Tarjiaan asked softly.

Daanir grimaced. "I wasn't expecting him to do something like that in front of everyone," he answered. "I thought... he'd try to get me alone. Or he'd just... circle. I never thought he'd attack in front of everyone." He looked up. "Nika, what did you do?"

Nika turned in her chair. "To the lout who dared to put his hands on one of my men? Burns. Deep ones. They may scar."

Tarjiaan blinked. "Leaving him with a scar in the shape of your hand?"

"Leaving him with a very visible reminder that putting his hands on anyone uninvited has consequences," Nika corrected. She folded her hands in her lap and raised her chin slightly, her expression unreadable. "He is lucky that his wrist was closest. And that his coat was long."

Tarjiaan blinked. "What did his coat...?" Then he realized what she meant, and his voice trailed off. She arched a brow at him, and he coughed, looking at Daanir, who looked as stunned as Tarjiaan felt.

"I... you were right, Jiaan," he croaked. "Our wife is terrifying."

Nika looked startled. "Terrifying?" she repeated. "You called me terrifying?" She looked up at Tarjiaan. "Why?"

Tarjiaan held his hand out to her. She rose and came toward him, and he pulled her closer, until she was standing between his armored legs. "Because, my love, you have discovered that Ysnika, Masthaka's daughter, is braver, fiercer, and much, much stronger than she ever thought she could be. You have discovered that you are a proud Sualimani warrior, and that you have the power to protect the people you love. You understand that you have everything to lose, because you know exactly what it is that you have gained. And since you understand that, and you know what it means and how it feels to be powerless, you will do everything at your disposal to keep the people who you love, and the people who depend on you from ever feeling that way." He raised her hand to his lips and kissed her fingers. "That makes you ruthless in defending yourself and the people you love."

"And that makes me terrifying?" Nika looked thoughtful, then nodded once and smiled. "I think I like being terrifying."

"Honestly?" Tarjiaan pulled her closer. "I like it, too. It's very... exciting."

Nika's brows rose. She laughed, caressing his cheek with one hand. "Do you?" She glanced over her shoulder. "Exciting? Do you agree, Daanir?"

Daanir pushed away from the wall and came to join them, standing behind Nika. He rested one hand on Nika's waist, and the other on Tarjiaan's shoulder, stepping close enough that Nika was pressed between his body and Tarjiaan's. She gasped, then tipped her head back.

"I like this," she whispered. "I think that if this is the reaction that both of you have to me being terrifying, then I shall do my best to always remain so."

Tarjiaan laughed and reached around her to grab Daanir's belt, tugging them both closer. "So long as you're terrifying when you defend our people? You're going to get this reaction for a very long time."

"Agreed," Daanir murmured. Then he looked up. "Incoming." Tarjiaan let his belt go, and he stepped back, offering his hand to Nika. She hesitated, then joined Tarjiaan in sitting on the cabinet. Once she was settled, she reached for Daanir's hand and tugged him closer.

"Come sit with us," she said.

Tarjiaan nodded. "You should be with us. Come and sit." He looked at Nika. "Are you in the middle, or is he?"

"Oh..." Nika frowned. "We will all have to take turns, I suppose. For now, I think Daanir should be in the middle."

"Not that I'm complaining, but why?" Daanir asked as he squeezed between them on the cabinet and put his arms around them both. He smiled as Nika slid her arm around his back and leaned against him. "Not complaining at all."

"Because you need to know that you are safe," Nika answered. "That we will protect you."

"We did it before," Tarjiaan added. "Put you in the middle so you knew you were safe. Remember?"

Daanir laughed. "I remember. I remember thinking you were going to use my guts as bait, because I had no idea that's what you were doing when I woke up."

The door opened, and Mentiras came inside. Behind him was an older man with graying hair, Sualimani dark skin, and sparkling eyes. He smiled broadly when he saw Daanir.

"There's my feral kitten! I didn't believe a blasted word of it. I want you to know that. And now Mentiras is telling me it's all false? And there's proof?"

Daanir burst out laughing, getting up and going to the other man, hugging him tightly. "It's good to see you, Narrick. And I know. If there's only one other person on or over the waves who would deny that bilge, it would be you."

"Feral kitten?" Tarjiaan repeated. He shook his head and laughed. "I... Daan, that suits you so much!" He stood up slowly, and watched at Narrick's eyes widened.

"Oh, Daan," the older mancer breathed. "Here's part of your proof, then. You can't have killed the Sea Prince if he's standing right in front of me. And... this is what you were telling me. About the armor... Prince-Captain, may I take a closer look at your armor? Daan told me about his designs. I've never had the chance to actually see what he was talking about. When it's convenient for you?"

"Of course," Tarjiaan said. "We'll be here until the *Wave Runner* is fully repaired, which I don't anticipate being a small task."

Narrick grimaced and shook his head. "I had a brief look from the docks, and I spoke to Mancer Ishantar. The solar sails alone... that might take weeks." He reached out and ruffled Daanir's hair, a fond smile on his face. "With this one? Perhaps less than weeks. But we'll put her back together, I promise. Now, we have talking to do? And proof?"

"Narrick hasn't seen the recording," Mentiras said. "I thought he should, so we can make certain he is fully informed." He gestured to the desk and the monitor. "Shall we?"

Tarjiaan sat back down on the cabinet, and this time, Nika took her place on his right, while Daanir perched on his left. He wasn't certain why, until Mentiras dimmed the lights and started playing the recording. Then he understood — in the dim light, he reached for Nika's hand, felt Daanir's firm grip on his shoulder, anchoring him in the now.

Finally, it was over, and Mentiras raised the light level once more. He looked at Tarjiaan, blinked, then stood up. He went to a cabinet in the corner and came back with a bottle and several glasses.

"I... I don't drink," Tarjiaan stammered as Mentiras offered him a glass.

"Did you think I'd forget that?" Mentiras asked, filling another glass and taking a sip. "It's not alcoholic. It's fermented seaweed tea. It is an acquired taste, though. You might like it. My wife makes it."

Tarjiaan blinked, staring at his former first mate. "Wife? I missed that!"

Mentiras looked startled. "You never got the message? I invited you!" He frowned. "I sent several messages, come to think of it. Because you told me about Daanir, and he was here and... well, pining is the only thing I can call it."

"I think I can tell you why Tarjiaan never got the messages," Daanir said softly. "The same reason he never got mine. Ilaris was keeping us apart."

"I see." Mentiras cleared his throat. "Actually, I don't, but you'll explain. And Jiaan, you know Tyva. Except that when you knew her, she was Tyvvin."

"Tyvvin? Our cook on the *Sea Wolf*? I had no idea you two were paired!" Tarjiaan looked at Mentiras, then shook his head. "I'm sorry, Tir. I'd have been here for you both if I'd known."

"And that seems like the perfect opening. Let's talk. Tell me what that recording didn't, and what you want us to do." Mentiras gestured to the monitor as he took a seat at his desk. Narrick took the other chair.

Tarjiaan sipped the surprisingly good, slightly fizzy tea and started recounting everything he knew. All his plans. What they'd done and what they'd seen. And where they were going from here.

"That recording needs to get out to the kingdom. Which will be difficult, with Ilaris controlling the comms system." Tarjiaan set his now-empty glass aside. "That's very good, Tir. Tell Tyva I like it."

"I'll tell her." Mentiras frowned slightly, drumming his fingers on the tabletop. "Narrick, what do you think?"

"With regards to the message?" Narrick looked distant, nodding with a slow and gentle rhythm. "I could do it. I know the codes. We have the repeater here, and we can manage to shunt enough power into it to push an emergency broadcast on all channels and all frequencies. But we'd only be able to do it once. Once they change the codes at the main transmitter, we'll be locked out." He scratched the back of his neck. "It'll be a risk. We're not exactly maneuverable if he sends an attack force against us. But how many will follow him, once the truth gets out?"

"No idea. But we'll manage," Mentiras said. "Our King needs us, and we need to rally behind his flagship. Once she's repaired, that is." He turned back to Tarjiaan. "What are your orders, your Majesty?"

"You don't have to call me that, Tir," Tarjiaan said. "I told you. I'm not king yet. Not until the throne is mine."

Mentiras looked at him. "I've been thinking about that since you told me on the dock, and I think you're wrong. And since you ordered me a long time ago to correct you when you got things wrong, I'm going to keep on doing it." He pointed one finger at him. "You *are* the king, and the throne has been yours since that bastard murdered Ikaanaji. You not only hold the throne, you *are* the throne. That ugly replica in the royal belowship? That's just a chair. So get used to being called Your Majesty." He paused, then grinned. "Your Majesty."

"And if you want," Narrick drawled, "we can even find a fancy chair for you."

Tarjiaan stared at him, then started laughing. "I don't need a fancy chair," he finally said. "If you could even find one that would fit me. Tir, I've known you a long time. You helped me learn who I was as a captain. Do I have to order you to call me by name?"

Mentiras looked thoughtful, nodding his head slightly. Then he shrugged. "Only if you think you need the practice in ordering people around," he answered with a grin. "Now, how do we want to do this?"

"Theonus offered to carry word to any other above ship, but Ilaris has ordered all support pods reassigned. And apparently he's shuffled mancers around, putting people loyal to him in place," Tarjiaan said.

"He's more than shuffled the mancers. He's recalled every single one of us," Narrick said. "My orders to report to the royal belowship are in my workshop, but I'm delaying as much as I can."

"When did that happen?" Daanir asked.

Narrick shrugged. "Ten days? Maybe? I can find out. Is it important?"

"I don't know," Tarjiaan said. "Regardless, we're run the risk of a mancer who answers to Ilaris distorting the message, or keeping it from being received. We have to be ready to act when that message goes out."

"Which means we have to focus on the repairs," Daanir added. "And keep the fact that we're here away from general channels. Which... don't you have to report in on who is in for repairs?"

"Leave that to me," Mentiras said. "I can make it so that no one will know *Wave Runner* is here without coming and looking for themselves." He paused. "You were going to order Great Migration. Should we move? I'd hate to do that. We're the closest safe place for some of the refugees—"

Daanir frowned. "You said something about that before. What refugees?"

Mentiras frowned slightly, then his jaw dropped. "Oh, you don't know. And why would you? You haven't had comms..." He paused, clearly collecting his thoughts. "It's been... a month, maybe more. What we're being told is that there's war on land. Civil war, and it's not been pretty. Our sentry ships keep finding small crafts, some of them barely seaworthy, and all of them overloaded with desperate people running for their lives and hoping that the Sea Prince will welcome them."

Tarjiaan blinked in shock. "I... I wonder how they knew to ask that," he said. "We heard from the ship that turned to our side that they're told there are no survivors when an Imperial ship meets the *Wave Runner*. Who is telling them that the Sea Prince welcomes refugees?"

"Maybe the news came from the Sualimani?" Daanir suggested.

"I don't know," Mentiras said. "No one's told me how they know Meradon welcomes refugees, but what they did tell us that that the Empire is falling to bits under its own weight. The Lestalti people have risen up against the Emperor in the name of the crown prince. The Sualimani are allied to them, in the name of Queen Ysnia's daughter, who was the prince's wife. Which... I didn't know the prince was married. But they tell us that the Emperor has gone mad, that the crown prince has vanished, and rumor has it that he was killed—"

"He is not dead," Nika said. "His wife's name was Masthaka, and the Emperor murdered her." She looked at Tarjiaan, who nodded. She smiled slightly and looked back at Mentiras. "She was my mother."

Mentiras looked at Tarjiaan. "You left that part out!"

"I did, and I apologize." He looked at Nika. "Do you want to tell them, or should I?"

"If you would?" Nika laced her fingers into his, and he saw how tired she was. He nodded and put his arm around her, hearing her soft sigh as she rested her head against him.

"Nika and her brother Navi are the grandchildren of the Sualimani queen, and she is the last daughter of the Tyracan royal line," Tarjiaan explained. "She is the rightfully born queen of Tyraca. And the last we saw, their father was alive and onboard the *Chimaera*. He told us that he escaped the palace and married Masthaka, who renamed him Rathsafa. The Emperor brought him back to the palace in chains. Rathsafa thought his wife and children dead, until he discovered Masthaka and Nika in the harem. When he tried to free them, the Emperor executed Masthaka as punishment." He realized something, and looked down at Nika. "I just realized. He doesn't know that we found Navi."

Nika smiled slightly. "I hope we will be able to introduce them." She sighed. "My father told us that he learned that the Emperor was going to have him put to death, and was going to take me as his wife—"

"His own granddaughter?" Narrick gasped. "That's vile!"

Tarjiaan nodded. "And the rest you know. My uncle arranged a marriage for me, thinking that the Emperor was willing to make peace. But it was all a ploy by Rathsafa to get his daughter to safety. And it all went wrong. Ilaris betrayed us, and handed me over to an Imperial mage." Daanir took his hand, and he rubbed his mancer's knuckles with his thumb. "I spent twenty-three days as a prisoner of the Imperial navy, until Daanir and Nika masterminded a plan to rescue me and save the *Wave Runner.*"

"With the help of an Imperial ship that swore to Meradon and the Sea Prince," Daanir added. "Good thing, too. I wouldn't be here if not for them."

Nika nodded. "My brother Navi was an Imperial healing slave. He is a gifted healer, and without him, we would have not been able to save Daanir's life when the... what was that weapon called?"

"The rail-cannon," Daanir answered. "It exploded."

Narrick gasped aloud. "It... it *what*?"

Daanir sighed. "Don't say it."

Narrick didn't listen. "I told you that weapon wasn't ready! I *told* you!"

Tarjiaan looked at Daanir. "Sensitive, you called it. Daan, you didn't give me a prototype, did you?"

"No! It was sensitive. But it was as ready as it could be." Daanir dropped Tarjiaan's hand and folded his arms over his chest. "It unbalanced easily, yes. But having one meant that the Imperial

Navy wouldn't ever have anything to counter it, and... it was me trying to keep you safe at a distance. Remember, I thought you didn't want me anymore." He let his hands fall. "Narrick, it blew up because I had to force a connection to get the shot that saved us all." He sniffed. "It wasn't a bad weapon. It just... was sensitive. The next model will be better."

"Do we need a next model?" Nika asked. "Do you propose taking that on land?"

Daanir's brows rose. "I... maybe? Smaller, handheld... no. It goes off balance too easily. I don't think... maybe."

"Why would we need it on land?" Narrick asked. "Your Majesty, what are you thinking?"

"There is no longer an Imperial navy," Nika answered. "They were all destroyed in the last battle, during the storm. Any battles from this point will be on land. And if there is already battle on land, then... Jiaan, there is an end in sight, is there not?" She looked up at him. "There is a possibility that the Emperor may fall before we ever reach land."

Tarjiaan considered it, then nodded slowly. "Possibly. But we're not there yet, and what happens on land is not my concern. Not yet. Right now, our fight is closer to home. Once we have Meradon secure, then we can sail to Sualiman and see if we're needed for the next fight."

"I'm sorry, but did you say that there's no navy left?" Mentiras asked. "Blessed Mothers beneath the waves, is that true?"

Tarjiaan nodded. "So far as we know. Tir, I'll have to introduce you to the most promising young officer I've ever had the pleasure to welcome as a refugee. His name is Antivar. He told us that there aren't any new ships being built. The Empire doesn't have the resources. So everything that they had was on the waves, and is now at the bottom of the sea." He leaned forward, resting his hands on his metal knees. "Right now, my focus is on repairs, and on learning things. And I should meet with the refugees. Unless you think that will alarm them?"

"No, I think it's a good idea," Mentiras answered. "What do you need to learn, Jiaan?"

Tarjiaan smiled. "Tir, is there anyone living here who knows anything about Reckoning?"

Chapter Thirteen
Reckoning

"RECKONING?" MENTIRAS frowned. "That's... funny you should mention that." He tapped his fingers on the tabletop. "One of the refugee ships came in with someone... well, I think the kindest thing I've heard anyone call Kyraath is 'that crazy old barnacle.'"

"One of the refugees?" Daanir asked. "Is he Lestalti? Sualimani?

Mentiras shook his head. "Meradonese. Kyraath told us that his people stayed behind when the kingdom went to sea. He's from the Delta, which explains a lot about him right there."

Tarjiaan chuckled. "I remember my father telling me that his people came from that area, and that Delta folk were a different breed," he said. "So why is this funny?"

"Because he's a Reckoner," Mentiras said. "Or the best blasted faker I've ever seen. He brought the refugee ships in with faulty navigation systems and no charts. He told me he doesn't need systems or charts, that Mother Ocean tells him where he needs to go. Now tell me that's not a Reckoner." He picked up his own neglected cup and drank. "He's... I wouldn't say he's mean. I've seen him with the dock kittens and children, and he's as gentle with them as a Great Mother. Magnificent storyteller — the children adore him. But he doesn't have any patience for adults." He grinned. "And he purely hates Ishian. Which... Daan, I need that story now, if you please? I didn't push you when you were stationed here before, and maybe I should have. Tell me what he's done."

Daanir's hand in Tarjiaan's shook, and he coughed. "I..."

"Do you want us to leave or stay?" Tarjiaan asked softly. "What will help?"

Daanir turned and met his eyes. He took a deep breath and squeezed Tarjiaan's hand. "Stay. I... if I don't... I need to say it. But if I stop, I won't start again and I...." He stopped talking as Nika got up, walked past him, and sat down on his other side. She took his hand.

"Go ahead," she said. "We are here. You are safe."

Daanir nodded and closed his eyes. "They drugged me to get me away from the *Chimaera*. I didn't want to go. I knew I needed training, but... I never wanted to leave Jiaan. My place was with him. But... they took me away. And when I woke up on Station Six, I was in Ishian's quarters. He told me I was his. And... for the next six years, I was..." He stopped again. Shook his head. "He told me no one else was ever going to want me. That all people were ever going to see was the man who failed Meradon, the battle companion who failed to keep his prince safe. That I was lucky to have him. More like that. Things I sometimes still hear in my nightmares. Between him and Gellan, they came closer to breaking me than I like to remember. And..." He paused again. "I told Nika this. And Narrick, you know this. But when Ishian told me he was going to have me stationed at Six permanently, I forged transfer orders and smuggled my way out."

"I knew the minute you handed them to me. They weren't a very good forgery," Narrick said. "All I knew was that I had this frightened, feral kitten with emotional scars more visible than the one on his face, who was running from something he wasn't willing to tell me. It didn't matter what was chasing him, though. I wasn't going to let him go back to whatever it was that hurt him that badly."

"Because you adopt every motherless kitten and seabird and orphaned child in the dockyards," Mentiras interjected. Narrick smiled.

"That was uncalled for, no matter how true it is. But then my feral kitten showed me what he could do, and I wasn't ever going to let that talent out of my sight. I called in every favor I had to get Falian to let me keep Daanir here." He smiled. "It was worth it. It was so very worth it. I'm proud of you, my boy."

Daanir smiled slightly. "Thank you. I... this was him." He touched his jaw. "I was trying to grow a beard, and he didn't like it, so...."

Mentiras whistled softly. "I need to hear this plain, Daanir, and I apologize. But did Ishian force you?"

Daanir nodded, closing his eyes. "I... yes. He did. Forced, assaulted, tortured... do I have to say more?"

"No, you don't," Mentiras said gently. He reached out and tapped a button. "Chief Rothga!"

"*Commander?*"

"I need you to find Commander Ishian and show him to his new quarters in the brig."

"*Oh, and it's not even my natal day! You're too good to me. Rothga out.*"

Daanir looked stunned. "I... you're arresting him? But... it was years ago! I... I didn't think anything could be done!"

"Things like that don't just go away after a year, Daan. Or several years. There's no expiration date on doing the right thing," Mentiras replied. "Is there, your Majesty?"

"There is not," Tarjiaan said, smiling. "He can warm the brig, and he can answer for what he's done. To you, and eventually, he'll answer to Ranji."

"Your brother?" Narrick asked. "What about him?"

"Ishian was my brother's battle companion," Tarjiaan said. "He abandoned his position in the middle of a fight, almost got Aaranji killed, and was suspected of attempting to defect to the Empire. He was court-martialed, and the only reason he wasn't executed was that Ranji asked for clemency. He wasn't stationed at Six. He was exiled there."

"I don't think any of us knew that." Mentiras said. "He just showed up here with the Station Six Mancer, and told us that the station was overrun. Given the state of the sub he was piloting? It wasn't too hard to believe, but we never got a clear answer out of either of them as to what happened."

"I doubt the station was overrun," Daanir said. "As badly as it was mismanaged when I was there? And as much as I had to work to keep it running? It probably failed catastrophically, and Ishian and Gellan ran for it and abandoned the people stationed there."

"What about Gellan?" Narrick asked. "He had a hand in abusing Daanir. But he was reassigned."

"You don't need to worry about him. He's dead," Tarjiaan answered. "He was assigned to the *Dauntless*, attempted to mutiny, and was killed. The rest of the mutineers are still in the brig on the *Dauntless*. Theonus tells me that they insist that they don't know anything about where Gellan's orders were coming from."

"We can guess...." Mentiras started. Tarjiaan shook his head.

"Guessing won't give us facts, Tir. I need to know for certain if Gellan was getting his orders from Ilaris, or if there's someone else out there we don't know about." He rubbed his forehead, fighting back a yawn. "I think the thing I'm most looking forward to in the immediate future is being able to rest and truly recover. I think the last really good night's sleep I had was...."

"On the *Chimaera*?" Daanir suggested.

"I never got a good night of sleep on the *Chimaera*," Tarjiaan answered. "You saw my nightmares. That was a normal night. No, my last real night of sleep was..." He paused, thinking back. "A few days before I was summoned to the *Chimaera*."

"Twenty-three days a prisoner," Mentiras said. "You're lucky you came out of that sane, Jiaan." He glanced at his monitor. "I'll order the royal apartments opened. Even if you don't stay there, the sitting room should be available to you for meetings."

"And the bath?" Nika murmured. Daanir snorted.

"Yeah, the bath. We all need one." He leaned into Tarjiaan's side. "Are we starting today? Or are we resting today?"

"I think..."

"We are resting today. And bathing. And having a good meal," Nika said.

Tarjiaan laughed. "Yes, Healer."

Mentiras chuckled. "Give us an hour to get the apartment ready."

Tarjiaan stood up. "Is the Admiral still in residence?"

Narrick laughed. "Of course he is! Well, his grandson is."

"I look forward to meeting him, then." Tarjiaan stood up, turning to offer a hand to his wife and his consort. When he turned back, Narrick has also gotten to his feet.

"And I'll walk back to the *Wave Runner* with you."

They left Mentiras' office, and Daanir looked around. "I... this feels so strange."

"What does?" Narrick asked. He looked around. "I don't see anything."

"That's just it," Daanir replied. "He's not there. He's not hiding in the shadows. Not even in my imagination. Not anymore. He's in the brig. Well, heading for the brig." He stopped, looked around once more, then smiled. "I'm free. I don't have to worry about him ever again."

Nika took his hand. "It's a wondrous feeling, is it not? To be free."

Daanir looked at her, then laughed and put his arm around her. "You understand, don't you? Yes. It's like... there's a weight I didn't even know was there, and now it's gone."

Tarjiaan watched them, smiling. "Thank you," he said softly to Narrick, "for taking care of him. For taking him in."

"He should never have been there," Narrick replied in the same soft voice. "I knew that even though I never knew why. Now I understand. And seeing you all together? I *understand*." He grinned. "You three together just might change the direction of the tides, just because you're bored and want the excitement."

Tarjiaan chuckled and started walking again, his heavy footsteps ringing on the deck as they headed toward the *Wave Runner*. "Nothing quite so drastic. Not yet, anyway."

"Jiaan?" Daanir called as he and Nika followed. "Who's the Admiral? I didn't know there was one in Meradon."

Tarjiaan looked back over his shoulder. "Narrick, you didn't introduce him to the Admiral when he was here?"

Narrick frowned, then shook his head. "I never did. I can't believe I never did! That's... Daan, I apologize. And I'll have to apologize to him, because that's a horrible dereliction of duty. All dockyard officers are supposed to meet the Admiral."

"Well, I wasn't an officer when I left, so I suppose that makes sense." Daanir and Nika came up on Tarjiaan's other side. "Do you mind if I go on ahead? I should let Kaapi know I'm fine." He paused. "I hope she didn't see any of that. It would upset her."

"Who is Kaapi?" Narrick asked.

Daanir grinned. "Narrick, I have to introduce you to my daughter. Who is also my apprentice. She'll be working with us." He sniffed. "It's funny. I think the one good thing Ilaris ever did for me was tell me that I needed an assistant, and bring Kaapi into my life."

Tarjiaan nodded, but he noticed the speculative look on Nika's face. "What is it, Nika?"

"Daanir, I do not think he did that to do a good thing, or for your benefit. Or for Kaapi's," she said slowly. "I think he was acting in his own interest." She looked up at him. "He brought Kaapi to you so that he would have a way to control you. He did not bring her to simply be your assistant. He brought her to be a hostage, in case he could not control you otherwise."

Daanir coughed. "I..." He stopped, covering his mouth with one hand. Then he nodded. "I... Mothers below, that's terrifying. She... she's a child. He could have controlled her—"

Tarjiaan crossed to stand in front of Daanir and rested his hands on Daanir's shoulders. "She's safe, Daan," he said, meeting Daanir's eyes. "Ilaris will never get near your daughter again."

Daanir nodded. Then he smiled. "Our daughter," he corrected. "I heard her call you Papa. Captain Papa." He took a deep breath and looked up the gangplank, and his smile widened. Tarjiaan looked and saw a pair of silhouettes, dark against the bright blue sky. "They're watching us."

"Then let's go aboard and let them see you're safe." Tarjiaan paused. "You trust Narrick?" he asked in a low voice.

"Completely," Daanir answered. "Why... oh? Are you thinking that we should introduce him?"

"The thought did occur," Tarjiaan answered. "It will probably make repairs easier if she can tell him where things are bothering her and what changes happen when you both are working." He looked up the gangplank again. "Give it a day or two of work. Then decide."

They walked up the ramp to the deck, and Tarjiaan stepped out of the way, standing next to Naajir as Kaapi launched at speed and hit Daanir hard enough to drive him back a few steps. He laughed and hugged her tightly. "I'm fine, Kaap."

"You weren't fine!" she wailed. "That man... who is he? Why did he grab you like that?" She looked around and scowled at Tarjiaan. "And you didn't stop him!"

"Kaapi, don't yell at the Captain. He and Nika both stopped him," Daanir said, turning the girl to look at him. "I'll explain. But who he is isn't important. He's in the brig now, and going to stay there."

Kaapi frowned. "He hurt you," she said. "Not today. Before."

Daanir nodded. "He did. But I got away from him. And he won't hurt me again. Commander Mentiras and Mancer Narrick aren't going to let him."

Kaapi frowned. "Are you sure?"

Daanir took a deep breath. Then he nodded. "As sure as I can be. But if it will help settle your heart, I'm sure the Captain can assign a guard for us when we leave the ship."

"Will Antivar be enough of a guard to help you feel safe?" Tarjiaan asked. Kaapi looked up at him, her eyes wide. She nodded.

"I like Antivar," she answered.

Daanir grinned and looked at Nika. "He's marrying Navi, isn't he?"

"He is," Nika answered. "Why?"

"Because that makes him your uncle, Kaap," Daanir said. He paused. "We'll need to tell him that, so we don't confuse him when we see him next. But Antivar and Navi are your uncles now."

"Oh!" Kaapi grinned. She stepped back and looked Daanir up and down. "Are you sure you're not hurt?"

"Startled. Not hurt. And if I had so much as a scratch, Nika would put it right."

"Of course I would," Nika said. She joined them, putting one arm around Kaapi. "The only reason Tarjiaan did not take that lout's head off is that I was closer, and I was in the way."

"What did you do, Mama?" Kaapi asked. "You did something. I saw it. But I couldn't tell what."

"I burned his wrist," Nika answered. "He will have a scar in the shape of my hand for the rest of his hopefully very short life."

"Aunt Nika!" Naajir gasped. "You didn't!"

"I did," Nika replied. "And I would do it again in a heartbeat for any of you." She smiled. "Shall we go and find Antivar and let him know that he is an uncle?"

"Daan, why don't you go with them? Then you and Kaapi can take Narrick on a tour, show him the extent of the damage?" Tarjiaan suggested. "I need to meet with Marikaar and Thistintal so we can arrange for leave for the crew."

"I heard my name?" Marikaar said as he joined them. "Arranging leave?"

"Yes," Tarjiaan said. "If you'll send for Istin?"

"And I'll comm our clerk," Narrick said. "Tell her to get herself up here to help with arrangements. By your leave, Captain?"

Tarjiaan was seated at the day cabin table with Marikaar on his right and Thistintal on his left when someone knocked on the day cabin door. He looked up from the crew lists. "Come in!"

The door opened, and a young woman peered around the edge. "Prince-Captain? I am Ilenwy, Commander Mentiras' clerk. I was told you needed me to help arrange lodging and leave?"

"We do, and thank you." Tarjiaan gestured to the table. "Come in and sit."

She smiled and came inside, closing the door behind her. She barely looked older than Kaapi, and was about as tall. She had a satchel over one shoulder, which she placed on the table as she sat down next to Marikaar, and from which she pulled a flat wooden box. Tarjiaan watched as she opened the box, took out a ledger, a bottle of ink, a pen and several small pegs. The pegs went into holes in the edges of the box lid, turning it into a writing slope. She flipped open her ledger, uncapped the ink bottle, and picked up her pen.

"It's a pleasure to be here," she said. "The Commander didn't tell me who else I would be meeting with today. May I be introduced?"

"Of course," Tarjiaan said. He gestured to Marikaar. "This is Marikaar, my first mate, Across from you is Thistintal, the first mate from the Imperial ship. We call him Istin, and he's been acting as second mate on the *Wave Runner* since we took them on board."

Ilenwy nodded. "Yes, the Commander tells me that you have the equivalent of two ships' worth of crew. One of ours, and an Imp vessel—"

"It's actually more like the crew of three Imperial ships," Istin added. "We lost two ships when we attacked the *Wave Runner* and lost."

Ilenwy's brows rose. "I see. How many crew do you have in total?" she asked, looking down at her ledger.

"In total, or from each ship?" Marikaar asked.

"Both," Ilenwy answered.

"From our ship, we're at two hundred and eighty-one," Marikaar answered.

"And from the Imperial ship, we have four hundred and seventy-nine." Istin completed the answer.

She wrote down the number, then looked up. "How large were your ships?"

Istin laughed. "About half the size of the *Wave Runner* here. We were tight."

"You must have been packed in like fish." She frowned. "You're still packed in like fish. Arranged sleeping berths in the holds, I gather?" Marikaar nodded, and she smiled. "And have you resupplied your Imps? Or are they still wearing their own uniforms?"

Marikaar frowned. "We haven't had enough in spare anything to outfit all of them. Why?"

She nodded, looking back at her ledger and turning pages. "I thought that might be the case. Will they have an issue with staying on the *Wave Runner* until we have a chance to get them all outfitted?" She looked up again. "We have the space for them, but having that many Imp uniforms in quarters will make the refugees nervous. And nervous people make rash decisions."

Marikaar frowned. "I hate to single them out, though. They fought alongside us, turned on their own people to help save our Prince-Captain and get us out alive. They're more loyal than some people born to the waves, and that's the honest truth."

"Thank you, Marikaar," Istin said. "We've had some of the *Wave Runner*'s crew share things like shirts and socks, but we understand that things are uncomfortable, especially when your crew isn't used to things like having a hot berth for weeks on end. How long would it take to resupply all of us, and get everyone into a Meradonese uniform?"

Ilenwy looked down at her ledger, turning pages and nodded slowly. "I think... I'll have to talk to the purser, see what we have on hand in ready-made, and what we'll need to make. If I had to guess, we're looking at seven to ten days, at the very least. But the purser will know for certain."

"That's a fair answer," Istin said, "and if we have to wait until we won't frighten people before we can take leave, then we can be patient. Although, if you have a bathhouse out there, I personally can't promise to be patient for long!"

Tarjiaan chuckled. "I understand that feeling. And we can send people out with escorts," he offered.

"That's a kind offer, Captain, but there are twice as many of us as there are of your men. Who will be escorting whom? We can wait onboard until it's safe for us to go... it's not really ashore, is it?" Istin folded his hands on the table. "There is one thing, though. Would it be too much to ask that you not call us Imps?" he asked, his voice level. "I know that when the Captain does it, or the Mancer or Marikaar, they're talking about those on land. Not us. But, Ilenwy, you're talking about us, and I would hope for more... well, more courtesy than that."

Chapter Fourteen
Delta

ILENWY LOOKED STARTLED. "I... I didn't mean..."

Istin shook his head. "You don't know our history. Every man that was crammed into our ship was a conscript, sent to sea to die because we dared to speak against the Emperor. They sent us out to die, and we all thought we were dead when we ran up against the Butcher of Meradon. Who turned out to be a man who treated us with more respect and courtesy than our own commanders ever did, and who sent us on our way with supplies and good wishes. When our captain came to us and told us that the Prince-Captain was being held, and that we might be able to help him in return, every man of us agreed to turn traitor to the Empire and risk our lives for a hope of a better tomorrow." He paused, and Tarjiaan took a moment to look at Ilenwy. Her face was red. Istin sighed and continued, "I understand that I can't ask that of the everyday people who live in the dockyards. Or the refugees. There's a lot of anger there, and it's warranted. There's a lot of anger among my folk, too."

"At us?" Tarjiaan asked.

"Oh, no!" Istin laughed, his face lighting up. "Never at you, Captain!" You've treated us as equals when you never had to. Sun and Sand know you had no reason to do so, but you did, and we honor that. No, the anger on our side is at the Emperor, same as you. Especially now when we're seeing what a real ruler can be." He smiled at Tarjiaan, then turned back to face Marikaar and Ilenwy. "We came from a country that's caused all of us a lot of pain. I know that. But my men? We're doing better. Trying to, anyway. And it would help us feel as if we had a part of a new something if you didn't exclude us by calling us the same name as the ones who are still trying to tear it all down."

Tarjiaan coughed, and Istin turned to look at him. "Istin, what were you before they sent you off to sea?" he asked.

Istin grinned. "I was a teacher, Captain. The people in power objected to me teaching the truth of how the Empire came to be, and I was shipped out with the first batch of conscripts. That was... three years back?" He paused. "No. Four. Lost this my first year." He reached up and tapped his cheek, right underneath his eyepatch. "Now, I'm constantly amazed I'm still alive."

Marikaar shook his head. "Why am I not surprised you were a teacher? Ishantar told me that you were going through her books."

"Istin, once this is settled, we need to talk," Tarjiaan said. "My nephew needs a tutor—"

"And the Mancer's daughter, too?" Istin asked. "Those two are inseparable. And two are as easy to teach as one."

"And possibly one more, if we have the time."

Tarjiaan turned, surprised. He hadn't heard the door open, but Nika stood just inside, her hand still on the latch. "I didn't hear you come in!"

She smiled and came the rest of the way over to the table, holding one hand up when Marikaar and Istin both started to rise. "No, please. You do not need to stand. I will not be staying long. I heard most of what you said, Thistintal, and I agree. We cannot be one when some are treated as other." She turned to Tarjiaan. "Jiaan, Antivar has agreed to act as Daanir's guard when he goes ashore, but there is a... complication."

"Complication?" Tarjiaan frowned, then realized what it might be. "Navi wants to go with him?"

"He insists on it," Nika confirmed. "And will not hear otherwise. Will you speak to him?"

"Healer Navi? He's as stubborn as the day is long," Istin said. "Always has been, as long as I've known him. And a good thing, too. The Mancer wouldn't be here if not."

"True, and I'm grateful for that every moment of every day," Tarjiaan said. "Nika, I'll talk to him, but he's a man grown, and he knows his own mind. It's his risk to take, and... I think he's trying to protect you and me as well." He reached for Nika's hand, tugging her closer. "Navi knows what Daan means to us. He's not just going to protect his man. He's going to protect ours."

"I wonder," Ilenwy said, sounding timid. "You have Sualimani healers? Do you think we could... borrow them? Our physicians are incredibly backed up with all the refugees."

"We have two physicians and two Sualimani healers on board," Tarjiaan answered. "And before I say yes or no to that request, I'd like to hear your response to Istin. Because if I don't like your answer, then Prince-Healer Ysnavin and Queen-Healer Ysnika, both of them late of the Empire, will be staying on board, where they'll be safe."

"I..." Ilenwy stammered. She coughed, then sighed. "I hadn't realized I was doing it," she admitted. "And I apologize. Maybe I should go be the one to go back to school. That was... ignorant."

"Don't you worry about it. Ignorance can be fixed," Istin said. "Simple ignorance, anyway. When you don't know any better, you can always learn. It's the willful ignorance that's harder to fix. If you know better, but don't care? That's a problem." He smiled. "You want to learn, so we'll do fine, Ilenwy. We'll do just fine." He turned so that he could look at Nika. "And if you want lessons, my lady, we can certainly arrange a time when one of your men is available—"

"Istin, you're in Meradon now," Marikaar said, and Tarjiaan got the sense that this conversation had happened before. "Our women don't need minding."

Istin groaned. "I forgot. Again. I'll get it, eventually." He smiled up at Nika. "I apologize, my lady. But... well, you know...."

"I do understand," Nika said. She rested one hand on Tarjiaan's shoulder. "And I am learning, too. It does feel strange, to be able to come and go as I please, and spend time with anyone I wish to speak with." She laughed. "What was it that you said? Simple ignorance?"

Istin chuckled. "And I walked squarely into that, with my eye open." He leaned back in his chair. "Captain, I'll speak to Commander Antivar, but I don't think our men will take much persuasion. We don't want to cause trouble, so we can wait until we're outfitted. Just... if we could arrange trips to that bathhouse? I'm tired of feeling like something that crawled out of the bilge!"

Tarjiaan leaned back in his chair and wished for a cup of tea. Nika had gone back to the infirmary to help Wilaanger while Tarjiaan finished his meeting. Ilenwy left with the crew lists and the schedule for escorted rotations to the bathhouse, and promised to bring back as many tailors as she could muster to start outfitting the former Imperial crew, as well as a list of assigned quarters for once the crew could leave the ship. Marikaar and Istin were off informing the crew of the reason for the delay in leave. Hopefully, it wouldn't cause any friction between Tarjiaan's crew and Antivar's. The delay in leave would delay some of the more intensive repairs, but there was no way to help that.

"*Wave Runner*?"

[Yes, Captain?]

"Has Daanir introduced you to Narrick yet?" He tipped his head back.

[Not yet, Captain. They are still working. Narrick has made some interesting observations about the extent of the damage. I think some of the words were rude, though.] Wave Runner paused. [First Mate Marikaar is coming back with two men I do not know.]

"Thank you for the warning. Listening only, my dear." There was no answer, and a moment later, there was a knock on the door. "Come in!"

Marikaar came inside, followed by Mentiras and an older man who looked as if he was crafted of old ivory, aged wood, and wrinkles. "Captain, the Commander told me that he'd promised you an introduction?" Marikaar said.

"Introduction?" Tarjiaan frowned, then remembered. "Oh, yes! You would be... Kyraath?" Tarjiaan stood up; the older man looked him up and down. He seemed puzzled, and Tarjiaan assumed it was because of his armor.

He was wrong.

"You have the look of the Delta in you," Kyraath said. "I... wait. Oh, yes. I know your kin. Knew your kin."

Mentiras coughed. "Kyraath? You know the Captain? You didn't say anything about that?"

Kyraath looked at him. "Not what I said. I've never seen the Captain before." He nodded toward Tarjiaan. "Captain, your da was Taarik, weren't he?"

"Yes," Tarjiaan said, stunned. He gestured to the table. "Please, sit down. I can send for something—"

"Thank you, Captain, but tisn't necessary." Kyraath sat down and looked around. "Nice ship. Good lines. Handles well?"

Tarjiaan smiled. "The *Wave Runner* is the finest ship I've ever sailed. I'd be honored to take you for a tour once we have a chance to talk." He took his seat, waited until Mentiras and Kyraath were seated.

"Captain, tea?" Marikaar asked. "And... see what Aranti has on hand?"

"Thank you, Marikaar. I was just thinking I'd like some tea," Tarjiaan replied. Marikaar bowed his head and left, closing the door behind him. Once he was gone, Tarjiaan tried to order his thoughts.

"I don't know where to begin," he said. "I wanted to talk to you about Reckoning. They said my father was a Reckoner—"

"He was," Kyraath interjected. "Well, he might have been. His da definitely was."

Tarjiaan paused. "That's... more about my father's father than I ever knew," he said. "I had no idea that my father's family were Reckoners, and I seem to be coming into that magic. I can tell what's around us, even under the surface. I felt a waterspout spiral up as if it was winding around my arm. Tides and eddies push against me, and other ships are like a fingernail tracing over my skin." He watched as Kyraath nodded. "This is all normal for you, isn't it?"

"Completely. And it's not a surprise you're coming into it. The sea is in your blood, and she calls to her own." He cocked his head to the side. "And you look like a clubbed seal. You had no notion about any of this? Your da didn't tell you? About his people, or about the sea calling your blood?"

Tarjiaan shook his head. "I know next to nothing of what my father's life was before the war. He said something about coming from the Delta, but that was all. He might have told my brother and sister more, but no one told me anything."

"Oh. Oh, yes," Kyraath said softly, nodding. "I mind it. I doubt he said much. Your da, he didn't leave with good words between him and his da. I mind it well." He sniffed. "Never you mind it.

There's none left in the Delta of your kin. Not that you knew them to mourn them. But your grandda... yeah, I can see him in you." He paused, then nodded. "What do you want to know?"

"First, I want to know about Reckoning. Everything I know says that it's a magic of the royal line, and that it died out years ago. But you said my father might have been a Reckoner, and my grandfather definitely was one. And... if it's something that's from the Delta, then it's not of the royal line, is it?"

Kyraath nodded. "Could have been both. The Delta is where Meradon was born. We all of us came from the Delta, once. The power comes from the Delta, from the place where Meradon was born from the heart of the sea." He smiled. "Does your royal kin tell that story?"

"My father told that story. And my mother sang it," Tarjiaan answered.

"Good. That's a good thing. It's important to know where we come from. Gives us an anchor against the storms in life." Kyraath nodded again. "Now, in the Delta, like calls to like, so we keep the power in the blood. Your royal kin... it's been an age since they came from the Delta, so that sea call isn't as strong."

Tarjiaan nodded slowly. "That makes sense. My father being Delta born means that the power is back in the royal blood. Or at least, it's in me."

"And you're wanting to learn how to use it, hm?" Kyraath asked.

"I do Is that something you can teach me?" Tarjiaan asked. "We'll be in the dockyards for... well, I'm not even certain. That last storm—"

"Turn your head?" Kyraath interrupted. "Let me see your pride."

"Kyraath, don't be rude!" Mentiras chided.

"It's fine, Tir." Tarjiaan turned his head, letting Kyraath see his earrings.

"Two gold? That's all?"

"I'm due a third, from that last ship-killer storm." Tarjiaan turned back to face him. "My father had fourteen gold."

"He definitely came into his power, then," Kyraath said. "And you're coming into it, if you came through that storm." He paused, drumming his fingers on the table. "It's... not an easy thing to teach," he said at length. "What the sea says to one of us, she don't always say to all. It's..." He paused, then snorted. "Hard to explain. I can't teach you what I do, but I can tell you what I know."

Tarjiaan nodded. "I understand. I didn't know that it was quite that personal. I'd appreciate anything you can tell me." He paused, then leaned forward and rested his arms on the table. "About Reckoning, and about my father."

Kyraath arched a brow. "You're certain you want to know?"

Tarjiaan nodded. "Kyraath, I could tell you my bloodline on my mother's side back to the founding of Meradon. On my father's side, my bloodline stops with him. He never spoke of his family. As far as I knew, he didn't have one. You said that he fought with his father?"

Kyraath looked distant. "The Delta... it's not like other places that were in Meradon. I've heard of them — towns and cities, where people lived all together on top of each other. The Delta isn't like that. Never was like that. Most people live in family rafts, and if they come together, it's in groups so small that they don't have a name other than their motherline. We fished, and we farmed in the tidal flats, and hunted crabs and shellfish in the delta. Our ways... we ebbed and flowed with the tides, and were just as regular. But not your da. His father wanted him to settle down and follow the current, but Taarik, he wanted more. He wanted the horizon. They fought like two bull seals. Then... I don't know which of them said the words. Likely he said something that set Taarik on edge. I weren't there, and no one ever told me. But between one night and the next, Taarik was gone. He took his skiff and he left." He shifted in his chair, then turned to look as the door opened. Marikaar came back in, followed by Aranti with a wheeled cart.

"Captain, if you'd told me you were hosting, I'd have had this ready," she chided.

"If I'd known I was hosting, I would have," Tarjiaan said with a laugh. "Thank you, Aranti. I can serve."

She sniffed. "Captain, that didn't work with Logiri and it's not going to work with me." She set the teacups on the table and picked up the teapot. Once the cups were filled, she set the pot down, then placed a covered plate on the table. "I went to the quartermaster in the dockyards to arrange for supplies. They had some Sualimani citrus biscuits, and I thought Her Majesty might like them," she said. "Will she be joining you?"

"She's helping with the infirmary inventory," Tarjiaan answered. "If you'd set some aside for her? Or send some to the infirmary for the physicians and the healers? I think they'd appreciate it."

"That Healer Navi needs feeding," Aranti said with a nod. "He's a sweet boy. I'll send them a plate and some tea."

"Thank you, Aranti."

She smiled, bowed slightly, then left. Tarjiaan waited for Mentiras and Kyraath to help themselves before taking a biscuit.

"So, my father and his father argued, and my father left the Delta," he said as he broke the biscuit in half and ate a piece. "How old was he?"

"Ah..." Kyraath growled softly. "Not yet a man by our count. Sixteen, or thereabouts. It's been so long that I forget."

"Father was sixty-nine when he died," Tarjiaan said slowly. "He was nineteen when he saved my mother's life during the Flight to the Ships." He frowned. "He was a child himself when he left the Delta."

Kyraath shrugged. "We come up early in the Delta. And don't tell me you didn't come up early out here. You've been at war since before you were born."

Tarjiaan chuckled. "Truth." He sipped his tea, then shook his head. "I wish I'd known this truth. I wonder if my sister knows any of this." He grimaced. "I hope I get a chance to ask her."

"You'll have to give that wish to the seafoam, and see if the Mothers answer," Mentiras said, knocking his knuckles on the table. Tarjiaan smiled.

"Kyraath, would you like that tour?" he asked. "You can tell me what you know as we go."

Daanir slid out from underneath a console and sat up, looking at Narrick. "So, you see what we're working with?"

"Or not working with," Narrick said, standing up. He leaned against the nonfunctional console and sighed. "Daan, we'll be at this for weeks."

"Weeks isn't bad," Daanir said, folding his legs and resting his forearms on his knees. "I was honestly expecting months, especially with that mast and the solar sails. But... can you keep us safe that long? Jiaan needs to recover." He looked around. "We all need to recover. It's been... rough."

"And it's not likely to get any easier," Narrick said with a nod. "I understand. And I think we can keep you all safe. Mentiras has ideas, and I'll make them happen. And we'll keep Ishian under lock and key until you're gone." He frowned and looked around. "Where'd your girl go?"

"Off to find Naji, I think," Daanir answered.

"Why didn't you ever tell me?" Narrick asked, his voice low. "I'd have *done* something. I'd have helped."

Daanir looked up at him, at the concern in the older man's face. "I'd just escaped from what amounted to six years of torture, at the hands of people who should have been helping me. Teaching me. I had no idea if I could trust you, because I trusted them."

"And by the time you knew...."

"I'd convinced myself it was too late. That there was no point." Daanir shrugged and got up, dusting his trousers off. "So, we need to get comms online first."

"I'm actually thinking of working parallel," Narrick said. "Getting a team on the mast and the sails, while you and I focus on the electronics, and a hydroponics team gets to work refitting your farm."

"Nimas will appreciate that," Daanir said. "Jiaan says he can grow root vegetables. I'm not sure I believe that."

Narrick laughed. "I don't think your captain is capable of telling that sort of lie." He paused. "Consort, hm? I didn't realize that was a thing."

"I don't think any of us knew." Daanir looked around. "I think we're done here, unless we want to get started with anything."

"Unless we're ripping out these consoles, there's nothing to start. Where's your workroom? We'll get a battle plan started. Make some lists. If you didn't know, then how did it happen?"

Daanir gestured, and they left the comms room, walking side by side. "It's not my workroom. It's Ishantar's. She's officially the mancer assigned to the *Wave Runner*. But she's allowing me to use it while I'm onboard."

Narrick made a soft huffing sound. "Having a pair of mancers onboard usually ends up in arguments," he said slowly. "If not explosions. We tend to be solitary. How are things working with two mancers?"

"Ishantar and I get on fine, and we're splitting two ships between us." Daanir led Narrick belowdecks, and down to the large workroom he was currently sharing with Ishantar. She was, to Daanir's eyes, unusually tidy for a mancer. Every drawer and cabinet was labeled, and every tool had a place. It did make it easier to find things, but Daanir always felt as if he was encroaching into a strange country when he needed to work here. He waved one arm as they entered, taking in the entire space.

"This is Ishantar's workroom," he said. "I'm not sure where she is at the moment."

"When I met her earlier, she said something about needing to check on the *Dauntless,*" Narrick said, looking around. "She may have gone off to where they're berthed." He looked at Daanir. "She's... very neat, isn't she?"

"She says it's a Sualimani trait," Daanir answered. "Now, you said we need lists?"

"Just something to give me an idea of the scale." Narrick pulled a stool over to the worktable. "Comms, the mast, the solar sails, hydroponics, and what else?"

Daanir opened a drawer and took out paper, ink and pens, bringing them to the worktable. He sat across from Narrick, and they made lists — everything they'd mentioned. The loading mechanisms for the gun houses. Power for the force cannons.

"Wait, why the washroom in the great cabin?" Narrick asked when he saw it on Daanir's list. "Did they damage that? How?"

"No damage. It just needs to be refurbished," Daanir answered. "Tarjiaan uses a wheeled chair when he's not wearing his armor, and it doesn't fit through the door." He looked up. "I didn't know about the chair when I designed the great cabin. I left plenty of room for the armor, and didn't think at all about what he'd need if he wasn't wearing it."

Narrick nodded. "Well, we're thinking of it now. Do some research, see what else he'll need." He looked around. "You did amazing work on this ship. I don't think there's a finer ship in the fleet." He met Daanir's eyes, smiled, and nodded. "I should have said this a long time ago, Daan. I'm proud of you."

Daanir felt his throat tighten and his face grow hot. "I..." he stammered. "Thank you. That... that means a lot."

Narrick smiled. "You're welcome, son. Now, let's get a schedule set for this work."

Chapter Fifteen
Tripod

IT HAD BEEN YEARS SINCE Tarjiaan had last walked through the dockyards, and he noticed what appeared to be new construction along the route to the officer's quarters and the royal apartment.

"Building out?" he asked.

Mentiras smiled. "Had to," he answered. "We've doubled the crew since I took over, increased the work areas. It takes a full two hours to walk from one end of the dockyards to the other now."

"And this is where the crew will be living while the ship is repaired?" Tarjiaan looked over his shoulder to see Antivar and Navi, who were walking side-by-side behind him and Nika. After they toured the royal apartments, they would meet Wilaanger and Chel at the refugee barracks. Then Tarjiaan would leave the others in the infirmary and go back to the *Wave Runner.*

"That block of barracks there," Mentiras answered, pointing. "And the one behind it."

"You have that many empty beds?" Nika asked. "With all the refugees?"

"The refugee barracks are on the other side of the dockyards, ma'am," Mentiras answered. "And the infirmary is halfway between."

"So we will have to walk two hours to see the refugees?" Nika looked up at Tarjiaan. "That is a very long walk for you."

"I'm fine, Nika," Tarjiaan said. "And if I know Mentiras, he won't have us walking."

"I'll be taking you around in my personal skiff," Mentiras said. "There's a small dock behind the royal apartments, and I asked Tyva to bring the skiff around and leave it there." He smiled. "She wants to know if you'll dine with us tonight, Captain."

Tarjiaan looked at Nika, who nodded. "Thank you, Tir. We accept. Just tell us when and where."

Mentiras gestured to a door that bore the royal Kraken seal. "I thought that if you said yes, we'd dine here. There's more than enough room. If that's acceptable?"

"That's fine, Tir. We'll just need to let Daanir know, so he knows to join us."

"I'll message Narrick. If I know mancers, they're probably already up to their elbows in parts and grease."

"We should have Naajir and Kaapi with us as well," Nika said.

"Your heir and your fosterling? I'll tell Narrick," Mentiras said. He stopped outside the door. "I know you won't be staying here until the *Wave Runner*'s comms are repaired, but everything in here has been prepared for occupancy. No supplies, though — we have no way of knowing what exactly you'll need, or what you have. So you'll have to give me a list."

"The top item on that list is that Nika and Daanir will need clothes," Tarjiaan said. "I have uniforms on board, but the only part of Daan's uniform that survived the rail cannon exploding was his coat."

Mentiras nodded. "I'll send for the quartermaster, see what we have, and what can be altered. We'll get that taken care of."

"Thank you, Commander," Nika said. "Will we also meet the Admiral tonight?"

"I think he's here already, actually." He opened the door and stepped out of the way. "Your Highness."

Tarjiaan took Nika's hand and led her into the royal apartments. The rooms smelled unoccupied — citrus and polishing wax and incense and nothing else. That would change once they moved in. Movement caught his eye, and he turned to see an enormous fluffy cat strolling out of another room. "There he is. Nika, this is the Admiral."

"A cat?" Nika gasped. "The Admiral is a cat?" She joined Tarjiaan, taking his hand. "I have never seen one so large!"

"He's a Meradonese forest cat. They like the sea, and most ships have at least one. There's been an Admiral in residence on the floating dockyards since Meradon came to the sea." Tarjiaan crouched, steadying himself with one hand on a table while he offered his other hand to the cat to sniff, getting a head bump in return. He chuckled, stroking the soft silver and black banded fur. "This is... the eleventh Admiral, I think? Tir?"

"Thirteenth, and he's the son of the Admiral from when I took over command, and the grandson of the one that claimed your coat as a bed when we were here on the *Sea Wolf*."

Tarjiaan laughed. "Logiri never did get all the fur off that coat," he said. "The *Marauder* never had a cat. They made Father sneeze. I'm glad I don't have that problem."

Mentiras nodded. "Tarjiaan, does the *Wave Runner* have a ship's cat? I asked Narrick, and he said that she didn't leave here with one, because there wasn't a litter when the ship launched."

Tarjiaan looked up. "We still don't, actually. Mostly because of horrible timing — every time we meet with a ship with a breeding pair, they've just placed their last litter."

"The Admiral's Lady just had a litter. They'll probably be ready to sail the same time your repairs are done," Mentiras said. He clicked his tongue at the Admiral, who left Tarjiaan to wind around Mentiras' legs, meowing loudly. Mentiras picked him up, cradling him like a baby. "My lady, do you like cats?"

"I do, but as I said, I have never seen one this large." Nika stepped closer. "May I?"

"Offer him the backs of your fingers. Let him get your scent." Mentiras turned so that Nika could better reach. "Then you can scratch him under his chin. He loves that."

Tarjiaan stood up as Nika started petting the Admiral; his purring was loud enough to fill the room. "We could have one of the kittens?" he asked, coming over to join Nika.

"I would like that," Nika murmured, not looking at him. She was focused on the cat, smiling softly as the purring got louder. Tarjiaan put his arm around Nika's shoulders, enjoying her pleasure, watching as Navi came closer. He smiled at the healer and stepped back, letting Navi get close enough to offer his fingers to the cat.

"If you like, I can bring you over to meet them," Mentiras said. "We'll see if any of them take to you. Forest cats are... particular about their person. They tolerate a crew, but they'll bond with one person for their entire lives." He trilled at the Admiral, who twisted his neck to look at him and trilled back.

"Are you his person?" Nika asked.

"No. The Admiral is very friendly for a forest cat, and he knows I almost always have a treat for him. But the person he absolutely adores is Tyva. If she were here, he'd be all over her, and ignoring the rest of us." He bent, put the Admiral down, and gestured. "Let me introduce you to the kittens, then I'll take you over to meet the refugees." He led them out of the royal apartments; the Admiral, Tarjiaan noticed, followed at Nika's heels.

"Does a forest cat have more than one person?" Antivar asked, coming up on Tarjiaan's other side. "He seems to be taken with the Queen."

"They usually don't. I think he just has excellent taste," Tarjiaan said. "Tir, where are we going?"

"Just here," Mentiras answered, opening a door and gesturing them inside. "The Lady and her litter are in our quarters. Admiral, tripping people isn't polite!" he chided as Admiral stepped into Navi's way.

The room was comfortably shabby — a couch that had seen better days, a rug that had clearly been abused by generations of cats. Tarjiaan could hear a chorus of kitten complaints as a door opened and a tall woman came out.

"Tir?" she said. Then she saw Tarjiaan and smiled. "Prince-Captain!"

"Tyva," Tarjiaan smiled as his former ship cook. "It's good to see you. Congratulations. Married life suits you. You look wonderful."

"Thank you," she replied. "You look...." She paused. Frowned. "Captain..."

"I know," Tarjiaan said, laughing. "I look like chum. It's been... well, Tir will fill you in on the details. It's been rough." He turned, holding his hand out to Nika. She joined him, and Tarjiaan put his arm around her. "Tyva, I want you to meet my wife. Nika, Tyva was our cook on the *Sea Wolf*."

"Captain!" Tyva gasped. "You're married? How wonderful!" She laughed. "Nika, it's lovely to meet you. I hope you and the Captain are happy together."

Nika looked up at Tarjiaan. "We are, and I think we will be. Thank you, Tyva."

Tarjiaan turned to see Antivar and Navi near the wall. "And let me introduce Nika's brother Navi, and his intended Antivar."

Tyva smiled. "Oh, you're both new to Meradon, aren't you? You have that look."

"There's a look?" Antivar asked. "And... yes, we are."

Mentiras laughed. "The look of someone who isn't quite sure just what they've gotten themselves into, and don't know yet if we're going to help you or eat you. That look." He turned to his wife. "Tyva, the *Wave Runner* doesn't have a cat." Tyva blinked.

"Oh, that won't do," she said. "We just happen to have a surfeit. Lady throws large litters — eight this time." She went back to the closed door and opened it, letting out a clamoring sea of fur and complaints, tails held high as ship masts. Nika made a sound very much like a squeak and sat down on the carpet, where she was immediately surrounded by kittens. Tarjiaan moved off to the side, standing near Mentiras.

"Go on," Antivar murmured, nudging Navi. "Go play with the kittens."

Navi grinned and joined Nika on the floor, and Antivar joined Tarjiaan and Mentiras.

"I know Naajir and Kaapi have never seen cats before," Tarjiaan said. "Ship cats don't do well in the belowships. Has Navi ever seen one?"

"He has, but he's never played with cats before," Antivar said. "This is new for him."

"Never played with a cat?" Mentiras repeated, sounding strangled. "How?"

Antivar grinned as Navi laughed. "Until a few weeks ago, Navi was a healing slave on a warship. He's never known anything else."

"Oh, the poor child," Tyva murmured. "Is that why he's so scarred?" She folded her arms over her chest. "He's free now. And if one of the kittens chooses him... well, he'll have his first pet."

"I hope neither of you sneeze," Tarjiaan murmured. Antivar laughed again, and went to go kneel next to Navi, who was petting the kitten that he had cradled against his chest.

"I think one of the kittens has already made his choice," Mentiras said softly. "I... Tripod, what are you doing out here?"

Tarjiaan heard a yowl, and looked down to see a cat at his feet. This wasn't a kitten — from its size, it was about a year old, with a smooth coat of many colors completely unlike the fluffy forest cats. It yowled again, then jumped, and Tarjiaan scrambled to catch the cat before the animal could set its claws into his coat and the skin underneath.

"I apologize, Captain," Mentiras said. "This is Tripod. He was born on the *Endurance*, and placed with us... well, you see why."

"I see," Tarjiaan said. The reason for his name was clear — Tripod was missing his right front leg. "What happened to him?"

"The ship physician said it was a birth injury." He reached out and scratched Tripod's ears. "We're not sure of his bloodline — the *Endurance's* queen went missing when they were last in Sualiman, and she came back gravid. Tripod was runt of the litter, and no one thought he was going to survive. He doesn't seem to have any trouble getting around, but the *Endurance's* captain didn't think that he was suitable to be a ship cat."

Tarjiaan shifted the cat in his arms and started scratching him behind the ears, smiling as he started purring. He already knew in his bones that he'd been chosen, that there was no way he was leaving without this cat. "I think Tripod disagrees," he said. "I think he's decided he's not only going to be a ship's cat, he's going to be the captain's cat." He stopped scratching, and Tripod twisted and reached up with his front paw, catching Tarjiaan's sleeve and dragging his hand back down. "Oh, I see! You're already letting me know you're in charge?"

"Are you sure, Captain?" Tyva asked. "It's no bother at all if he stays with us."

"I think it will bother him." He looked at Tripod. "Won't it?"

"Jiaan?" Nika came over to him, a purring ball of fur in her arms. "Who is that?"

"This is Tripod, and he's chosen me." Tarjiaan shifted the cat again, and Tripod decided that being cradled was no longer what he wanted. He clambered up Tarjiaan's chest and perched on his shoulder, digging his claws through the cloth. Tarjiaan winced and reached for the cat, only to have his hand batted away.

"And he has decided that is his perch," Nika added, laughing. She looked down at the kitten she was holding. "This one fell asleep as I was holding her."

"That means she wants you, my lady," Tyva said. "You've been chosen."

"And Tarjiaan has been chosen as well." She looked up at Tripod. "Will they be friends, do you think?"

"Tripod knows all of the kittens, and the Admiral and the Lady both allow him to take care of them. So it shouldn't be an issue," Tyva said. "Now, this little one isn't old enough to leave her mother, so you'll have to come and spend time with her." She looked over at where Navi and Antivar were sitting with another kitten. "And your brother and his man can come to visit their little one, too." She smiled at Tarjiaan. "However, I don't think we'll get Tripod away from you with a prybar."

Tripod chirped his agreement.

Once Navi could be convinced to leave his kitten behind, Mentiras led them down to the skiff, casting off and taking them around the dockyards. He pointed out various places of interest, but Tarjiaan doubted that Nika or Navi heard a word of it — the two sat side by side, talking in low, excited voices. Antivar watched them, a fond smile on his face. Tarjiaan was fairly certain it matched the one he wore.

"You haven't heard a word I've said, have you?" Mentiras asked. "You've got cat fever."

Tarjiaan laughed. "I just might," he said. "Father told us about how important ship cats were, but he could never have one on the *Marauder*. And as much as I liked him, Tempest never really warmed to me. Remember? Willeck was his person, and I think the only reason he lived as long as he did was that he wanted to be certain I was taking care of Willeck's ship."

"I've no doubt you're right. I've missed Tempest for years."

"Tempest?" Antivar asked. He glanced back at Navi and Nika. "I don't think I'm going to get a word out of him that doesn't involve the kitten for the rest of the day. Who was Tempest?"

"Our ship cat on the *Sea Wolf*," Tarjiaan answered. "He was old when I took command of the ship, and he had opinions about his new captain. His previous captain died in a storm, and Tempest never forgave me for not being him."

"How old is old for a ship cat?" Antivar asked.

"Tempest was twenty-five when Tarjiaan became captain," Mentiras answered. "He'd been on that ship longer than most of the crew, and when he died, the ship just wasn't the same."

"He was older than I was," Tarjiaan added. He reached up and stroked Tripod, who was draped around his shoulders. "When I was introduced to him, he hissed at me. I was worried he'd never accept me."

"And did he?" Antivar asked.

"I'd been captain just short of a year when I woke up to find him sharing my pillow," Tarjiaan said. "It was the first time I'd ever heard him purr. I think he was telling me that he approved of me." He paused, listening to Tripod's soft purring. "A few days later, he didn't wake up." He looked out over the water. "Where are we going, Tir?"

"Just there," Mentiras answered, angling the skiff toward the dock.

As they left the skiff, Nika came and took Tarjiaan's hand. He ran his thumb over her knuckles, hearing Navi behind them, talking about his kitten, his broken phrasing even more fractured by his excitement.

"Navi is very excited," he murmured.

"He is," Nika agreed. "I think that being invited to befriend a kitten is truly making him realize that he is free, and that he is safe. He's never had a pet before. He told me that there was a ship cat on his first ship, but he was never allowed to befriend her, and he was punished if he tried."

"What about you?" Tarjiaan asked. "Have you ever had a pet?"

"No. There were pets in the women's quarters, but they belonged to the favorites. I was not allowed. I was never allowed to have anything of my own before I came here." Nika smiled up at him. "Thank you."

Tarjiaan returned her smile. "You are very welcome. Have you decided on a name for the kitten yet?"

"Not yet," she answered. "She is very delicate, and very small. And she's very soft. I think... Gossamer, perhaps. But I am not certain if that is the right name."

"You'll find her name," Tarjiaan said. "Once you spend more time with her. Now, are you ready to meet the refugees?"

"Are you?" she countered. "You have had a very long day, and you're still not recovered. You need to eat and rest."

"I'm fine for the moment, and I'll eat and rest once I get back to the *Wave Runner*." Tarjiaan took a deep breath and drew himself up, then reached up and stroked the cat's soft fur. "Shall we, my queen?"

She smiled. "Yes, my king."

Mentiras led them into a large building, passing down a corridor into a comfortable, well-lit communal space full of people. Tarjiaan saw children playing in a corner, watched over by older women who were sharing tea. There were men playing cards, and someone was playing a chitarra. The music stopped, and silence fell as people noticed them.

"Commander?" an older man said as he came forward. His accent showed his Imperial background, but he didn't look like any of the naval officers or sailors that Tarjiaan had ever seen. This man was broad-boned, and if he'd been well fed would have been solidly built. His broad hands were callused and scarred. He had laugh lines around his eyes, and wrinkles that spoke of years of smiles. "Is there something we can help with?" He glanced at Tarjiaan, then looked back to Mentiras. "Is something amiss?"

Mentiras smiled. "No, Tommen, there's nothing wrong. We have the flagship in drydock for repairs, and the Sea King and his queen wanted to meet with your people."

Tommen paled. "The... the king?" He looked at Tarjiaan again. "I..."

"I wanted to welcome you to Meradon," Tarjiaan said. He smiled, kept his hands at his sides, kept his voice low and nonthreatening. "And see what you needed. And possibly hear some of what is happening on land. If you're willing to talk?"

Tommen swallowed and looked over his shoulder. When he did, a small girl ran up to him, taking his hand.

"Grandy, he has a cat!" she exclaimed, pointing.

Tarjiaan chuckled. "I do," he said. He went to one knee and lifted Tripod off his shoulder, cradling the cat in his arms. "This is Tripod. Would you like to meet him?"

She nodded, her eyes wide, and came forward, offering her hand to Tripod to sniff. The cat sniffed her fingers, then bumped her hand with his head.

"I had a cat," she said gravely as she petted Tripod. "But he ran away when we had to get on the boat to come here. Grandy said it wasn't safe to go find him."

"What was his name?" Tarjiaan asked.

"Ember. He was all orange all over. Mama said he didn't have but a single brain cell, and it was loose, so every time he shook his head, it bounced all over the place."

Tarjiaan burst out laughing. "I like that description," he said. "I've known people like that."

She giggled. "Were they very silly? Ember was very silly." She smiled. "Can I take Tripod and show my friends? If I bring him right back?"

"That's up to Tripod," Tarjiaan said. He reached up and scratched the cat's ears. "Will you behave?" he asked. Tripod chirped, then jumped down and rubbed up against the little girl's legs. She scooped him up and carried him away, and Tarjiaan got back to his feet.

"I didn't ask her name," he said. "And... Grandy? You're her grandfather?"

Tommen nodded, his eyes wide. "And that's the most she's spoken to anyone since we got here," he said, sounding stunned. "You... you're really the King?"

Tarjiaan held his hand out. "There's a traitor in the royal belowship who would say otherwise, but yes. I am the King. My name is Tarjiaan, and this is my wife, Ysnika."

"Your Majesty, it's an honor." Tommen nodded. "And it's hardly fitting for me to keep a king standing. Come and sit, and we'll talk."

Chapter Sixteen
Refugees

THE SITTING AREA WHERE Tommen led them was in the middle of the space, where everyone could see them. Tarjiaan took Nika's hand and led her to the padded chairs, and waited until she was seated before he took his own seat. It creaked alarmingly under him, and he looked down for a moment before standing.

"Is there a more robust chair?" he asked. "Tir?"

"I should have thought of that," Mentiras said. "I'll send for a metal one. It won't be long."

"Thank you." Tarjiaan turned to see Tommen standing next to his own chair. "Tommen, you don't have to wait. Please, sit. Furniture... well, furniture for me has to be reinforced." He looked down, mentally arguing with himself. Against his old habits. He didn't know this man. He had no reason to trust him... and Tommen had no reason to trust Tarjiaan. Unless he was given one. And Tarjiaan had no reason to hide anymore. "The armor isn't only for protection. It's so that I can walk."

Tommen blinked. "I... oh. How... that's rude. I shouldn't ask that."

"In battle, against an Imperial machine—"

"An Executioner," Nika supplied, and Tommen blanched.

"You're the one who found the fault?" he whispered. "And you survived. That... no wonder they call you the Invincible!"

"Not just me, but yes. However, it cost me my right leg mid-thigh, and my left just above the knee," Tarjiaan said. He felt a hand slip into his, and Nika squeezed his fingers.

"And this lets you walk?" Tommen let out a long sigh. "Oh, I wish... my son lost his leg in a farming accident. Something like this... if... if there was peace, could this knowledge be shared?"

"Of course!" Tarjiaan said. "Is your son here? Did he make it out?" He looked over to where a group of children were laughing, playing with a piece of paper tied to a string for Tripod to chase. "Your granddaughter's father?"

"Yes... and no." Tommen took his seat and folded his hands. "My son Zyan was... is Syrzi's father, but he's not here. We're not sure...." He paused, then shook his head. "Not all the boats that left shore made it here. My son and his wife... we don't know..."

Tarjiaan turned immediately to Mentiras, who nodded. "We've had rescue vessels out since the first refugee craft reached us. We're still looking."

"After that last storm... I'm keeping a good face for my granddaughter, but I don't think they're still out there," Tommen said softly.

"If they're out there, we'll find them," Mentiras said. "We'll keep looking. They could have ended up back on shore for all we know." He turned. "Here's the chair. And tea."

A moment later, Tarjiaan was sitting, and Mentiras poured tea and handed the cups around. Tarjiaan took a sip, then smiled. "They call me the Invincible, hm? I haven't heard that one. I thought I'd heard all of them, especially once Antivar there explained why I was called the Butcher."

Tommen's jaw dropped. "Antivar? You... is his full name Girantivar?"

"Yes. You know him?" Nika asked.

Tarjiaan turned, looking around, finally saw Antivar and Navi near the door. "Antivar! Come here!"

Antivar looked startled, and trotted over, Navi on his heels. "Captain?" he said as he reached them. He bowed, then asked, "Was there something you needed?"

Tarjiaan gestured to Tommen. "The gentleman knew your name. Your full name."

Antivar turned and frowned slightly. "I... I'm sorry. Have we met, Uncle? If we have, I can't recall it. I apologize—"

"You don't know your uncle?" Mentiras interjected.

"Polite," Navi said with a laugh. "Proper. Honored elder."

"Oh?" Tarjiaan said. "Thank you, Navi. I didn't know that, and I don't recall hearing it among the refugees on the *Wave Runner*."

Antivar smiled. "You might not have. The only person old enough to warrant calling them "uncle" is Healer Wilaanger, and I would not be so familiar to a healer without invitation." He turned back to Tommen. "Have we met?"

"No, but I've heard all about you. Never thought I'd meet you. Your mother—"

Antivar's smile faded. "Oh... you knew my mother."

"Son, I know your mother. She's... where is she? Excuse me." He looked around, then raised his voice. "Reeshi!" He stood up and walked away.

All the color drained from Antivar's face; he swayed, and Tarjiaan jumped up to steady him. Antivar stared at him with wide eyes.

"They told me she was dead!" he whispered, his voice harsh. Navi put his arm around him, and Antivar hugged him close. "The ship mage told me she died!"

"Lies," Navi said. "Always lies."

Antivar nodded, then stood up straighter. "Mam?" he croaked. Tarjiaan turned to see Tommen coming back with an older woman. She was fussing at him.

"— I told you! I have something on the stove, and it'll burn if I don't watch it. I...." Her voice trailed off, and she stopped walking, covering her mouth with her hands. She shook her head, and her voice was just barely audible. "Ivar?"

"Mam..."

She burst into tears, and Antivar burst into a run, catching her in a tight embrace before he, too, started crying. Navi stepped forward, and Nika caught his arm.

"Give them a moment," she said. "Let them have each other."

Tommen stepped back, then joined Tarjiaan and Nika. "I... what did I do?"

"Antivar was told that his mother died," Tarjiaan said. "That was why he defected to Meradon. The first time I asked him to stay, he refused because he had to think of his mother and what they might do to her if he didn't come back."

"Which... he had good reason. When the ship didn't come back when it was supposed to, her village smuggled her out before the Emperor's men could take her. They got her out of Tyraca and down the Salten River into Lestalt. She ended up with us." He smiled. "She wasn't the first we took in. She settled in our village, fit right in. She told me about her boy, and that he never came back from sea," Tommen said. "That's why I was so surprised when you introduced him." He folded his arms over his chest, looked back, and sighed. Tarjiaan studied him for a moment, then smiled.

"So... have you asked her?"

Tommen grinned. "Clear as glass, am I? We started keeping company just before the world fell in. My son and his wife like her. Syrzi adores her. And... I think we all know life is too short to not grab what's good with both hands and hold on." He paused, then frowned slightly. "You... don't think he'll object, do you?"

"No," Navi answered. "Make happy?"

Tommen looked puzzled. "If you're asking if I'll make her happy, that's a promise. If you're saying he wants her to be happy, then... well, that's also a promise. And we haven't been introduced?"

Navi looked at Tarjiaan, his eyes wide. Tarjiaan reached out and rested one hand on Navi's shoulder. "Prince-Healer Ysnavin is my wife's brother," he said. "And he and Antivar are betrothed."

"Betrothed?" Tommen blinked. "That's allowed in Meradon?"

"It is," Tarjiaan replied.

Tommen nodded slowly. "I... see," he murmured. He rubbed one finger up and down the bridge of his nose, then gestured to the chairs. "Sit. We can talk until they're ready to join us."

Tarjiaan turned and gestured for Navi to sit. Navi scowled, then rolled his eyes when Nika took his hand and tugged him down into a chair.

"Sit," she said. "He is fine, and he will call you when he is ready."

"He told me that she knows about you," Tarjiaan added. "And that she had no objections."

Navi looked startled. "Told you that?"

"He did. I think... oh, I think it was the night after the Wave, when he stayed awake to help me stay awake." Tarjiaan resettled in his chair. "I still owe both of you an earring," he added.

"When you have time," Nika said. "And are rested and recovered."

"Before we leave, then," Tarjiaan said, and turned back to Tommen. "If you can tell me, I have so many questions. Why are you all here? We heard something about famines, and Mentiras said there was war on land. What happened?"

Tommen sipped his own tea and nodded. "The spark that started the fire was the news that the Prince had vanished. Rumor said that the Emperor went mad. He's getting old, and his mind and body are failing. Tales tell that he's been trying to find the secrets to immortality, putting his mages to the question, and killing those who push back. He's said to have murdered his own son and heir, sacrificed him, and him the last link to our queen." He grimaced. "I'm Lestalti, born the same year our queen married the bastard that murdered her. We know our Prince. Nadarish was raised among us. He's one of us, and we hoped he'd rise against his father when he escaped to Sualiman. Then they brought him back, and... well, we never stopped hoping that he'd try again. But now he's gone, and the Lestalti people are rising up in his name. The Emperor is putting down the resistance, and he don't care who he tramples to do it."

"He is not dead," Nika said. "At least, he was not when we last saw him, on the royal belowship." She paused, then sat a little taller. "And if he is now dead, then Ilaris will answer to me."

Tarjiaan turned to her, studied the steel he'd always known lay beneath the surface. He smiled. "First claim is mine, love. But I wouldn't mind your help."

She rested her hand on his. "Thank you."

Tarjiaan turned back to see Tommen staring at them. "I... he's alive?" the older man stammered. "You saw him?"

Tarjiaan nodded. "He uses the name Rathsafa, and he came to us under... not exactly false pretenses, but certainly not under official ones. We thought it was an alliance, a marriage that would bring peace and allow the people of Meradon to go back to our lands. But when he reached us, once Nika and I were wed, he revealed his real name, and his plan — he had allies among the Lestalti people, and among the Sualimani. He wanted Meradon to join him in overthrowing the Emperor once and for all. If we hadn't been betrayed from within, I think that alliance would have gone forward. I think it was the chance of that happening that forced Ilaris' hand." He took a deep breath. "The following morning, Ilaris murdered my uncle, and gave me as a prisoner to the Imperial priest who had accompanied Rathsafa."

"How did you escape?"

Tarjiaan turned. He hadn't realized that they had an audience, but a group of men and women had surrounded them, all of them listening intently. "I was rescued," he answered. "By my wife and our consort. They took back control of the *Wave Runner* — the flagship — and we used the storm to defeat the Imperial fleet. From what we understand, there is no longer an Imperial fleet." He looked around. "Once we are able to secure the throne, we will join the fight to finally end this war."

"My lady?" Tommen asked. "You... who...?" He stopped, looked from her to Navi. "A marriage alliance. That means..."

"Rathsafa is our father," Nika answered. "We were taken from him, and our mother murdered at the Emperor's command. Part of his plan was getting me out of the Palace before the Emperor..." She paused and shook her head. "He did not know that Navi lives. He thought I was all he had left, and he risked everything to save me from a horrible fate, and bring me to someone who he hoped would protect me."

"You're his daughter," a woman said. "That means..."

"I am the last daughter of the Tyracan royal line," Nika finished. "I know. And I am the oldest child of the rightfully born Lastalti king."

"And Queen of Meradon," Tarjiaan added.

"And that is the only title I wish," Nika said with a smile. "But when this war is finally over, when all of the Sisters are free again, then we will worry about who will rule where." She smiled at Navi. "Lestalt could be yours?"

Navi snorted. "Cats fly first." He grinned and poked her shoulder. "You better."

Nika caught his hand. "You are just as good. You are a far better healer than I am. And that is what will be needed when the fighting is over. Healers, to sooth old wounds and make things better." She paused. "And perhaps by then there will be an heir or two?"

Tarjiaan chuckled. "Perhaps." He turned back to Tommen, who was sitting in stunned silence. "Tommen? I've overwhelmed you, haven't I?"

"I... I don't even know what to think first," Tommen admitted. "That our Prince lives. That he was making alliances to try and end this insanity. That he has children." He glanced over his shoulder. "And that one of them may very well be my new son's husband. This is... much more than I expected today to bring!" He paused, then sighed. "Your Majesty, what else can I tell you?"

Before Tarjiaan could answer, Antivar joined them, leading his mother by the hand. "Captain," he said, his voice rough. "I... I want to introduce you to my mother."

"Antivar, I would be honored." Tarjiaan stood up. "My lady—"

"You call me Reeshi, son," Reeshi interrupted. "I'm no lady."

"Mam, he's the king..." Antivar protested, looking horrified. "He... I..."

"Antivar, it's fine," Tarjiaan said. "Reeshi, I'm honored to meet you. Antivar told me about you, and I'm very happy that you're safe and alive. And here."

"I could say the same. Thank you for saving my boy." She smiled up at Antivar. "And I'm told I have another son to welcome?" Reeshi asked. "But you're not him. He'd have told me if he'd caught a king."

Tarjiaan laughed. "No, ma'am."

"Actually, he is another son, in a way," Tommen corrected. "Reeshi, the queen is sister to your boy's man."

Reeshi's eyes widened. "Is that so?" She looked back at Tarjiaan, tipping her head back. "Well, you never need to stand on a box to get something off a shelf, now do you?" Antivar gasped and stammered, but Tommen spoke first, saying something in Lestalti, too fast for Tarjiaan to follow. Reeshi blinked and covered her mouth with her hands. "Oh..."

"You didn't know," Tarjiaan said gently. The jibe hadn't caused so much as a ripple in his emotions, and he wondered why. He smiled and shook his head. He'd figure it out later. "I'm not upset. Reeshi, you had no way to know. And honestly, I think one of the first things Nika said to me before our wedding was 'you're so tall!'" He looked back at Nika. "Wasn't it?"

"I had only seen you seated before the ceremony," Nika answered. "I did not see you in your armor until just before the ceremony." She frowned slightly, then laughed. "It seems so long ago!"

Tarjiaan held his hand out to her, and when she'd taken his, he bent to kiss her fingers. When he turned back to Reeshi, she still looked upset.

"I still shouldn't have said it," she insisted. "It... it wasn't polite. I shouldn't speak that way to the King."

Tarjiaan paused. Then he smiled when he realized the real reason why this wasn't bothering him. "You didn't treat me as a king, Reeshi. You treated me as a son. And... I welcome it." She looked skeptical, and he nodded. "Truly, I do. Reeshi, my mother died when I was so small I barely remember her." He squeezed her hand, and bent so that he could better meet her eyes. "I've never had someone mother me."

Reeshi looked horrified. "You... but... how? You were heir to the throne! Who *raised* you? Where was your father?"

"When my mother died, I was the sixth prince, with four older cousins and an older brother. And my father was a commoner and a sea captain. I was too young to join him, so I went to the crèche — it's where our war orphans live until they're old enough to stand alone or serve above the waves. I joined my father when I was ten."

"That's no way to raise a child," she said. "I understand why, though. There were plenty of orphans on both sides."

"Wait until you meet our consort," Tarjiaan said. "He's almost as tall as I am, and he doesn't wear armor."

"Your... consort?" Reeshi repeated. "They do things differently in Meradon." She looked over her shoulder. "You still have to bring a pretty girl into the house."

"Once I meet her, Mam," Antivar answered. "You still haven't met Navi."

"I haven't." She turned back, looking past Tarjiaan to Nika and Navi. She smiled and held her hands out. "You're Navi, aren't you?"

"Yes," Navi said slowly. He fidgeted, biting his lip as he looked back at Nika. She took his hand, and he smiled slightly and drew himself up, looking back at Reeshi. "I... not talk... good." He paused, then took a deep breath. "Honor to... meet..."

"Oh, my dear," Reeshi murmured, and stepped close enough to Navi to take his face in her hands. "Ivar told me. You protected him, and they hurt you for it. I promise you that no one is going to hurt my boys anymore."

Navi gaped at her. "Your boy?"

Reeshi nodded. "You're my boy. Just as much as Ivar is my boy." She held her arms open, then enveloped Navi in a tight embrace, stroking his back as he started crying.

"Captain?" Antivar asked, coming up next to Tarjiaan.

Tarjiaan looked at him. "I think I can guess what you're going to ask."

Antivar grinned. "If you think I'm going to ask when we can hold the wedding, you're right. But I had another question, too." He bit his lip, then said, "I'm marrying your wife's brother. And my mother is mothering you. So does that make us brothers now?" He paused, then grimaced. "That wasn't too forward, was it?"

Tarjiaan swallowed, feeling a lump in his throat. "No, it wasn't," he answered. "And... I would like that."

"You don't think your brother will mind, do you? I truly don't want to raise the ire of the Demon Captain's first mate."

Tarjiaan laughed. "I think Ranji would like you. And I think he'd welcome you with open arms."

"Good." Antivar nodded. "That's good. Now... Captain, my brother, sit down before you fall down."

Chapter Seventeen
Maintenance

TARJIAAN WATCHED AS Tyva guided the skiff away from the dock, then looked up at the *Wave Runner*, admiring the view. He rarely got to see his ship from this angle, rarely got to appreciate her sleek lines and her grace. There were already craftsmen working in the pit. He assumed they were doing the usual maintenance tasks that should have happened had the ship actually made it to the dockyards when they were supposed to. He didn't think there was any battle damage below the waterline, but he'd make certain to ask Daanir when he had the chance.

"So," he said, turning his head slightly and feeling the soft brush of fur, "this is your new home. Want to explore?" He started walking, feeling Tripod shifting on his shoulder. The cat had resumed his perch shortly before they had left the refugees, and Tarjiaan had a data disk in his pocket that contained a recording of everything he and Tommen had discussed. Tonight, he'd call a meeting of his officers and share the information. No... no, it would have to be tomorrow. They had the dinner tonight. And if he wanted to be awake for the entire dinner, he'd need to take a nap now. He made his way up the gangplank and stopped at the top, seeing the rush and scurry of craftsmen and sailors all around the deck.

"Uncle!"

Tarjiaan followed the sound of Naajir's voice, smiling when he saw Naji and Kaapi coming through the crowd with Istin following them.

"Have you started your lessons already?" he asked as they reached him. "Istin, I hadn't thought you'd start yet."

"Not so much starting the lessons as seeing where we'll be starting," Istin answered. "I asked them to talk, so I could see where things lay." He smiled. "I think we're all going to enjoy this. A good student is a fine thing, and a pair of them is better. Now where did this little one come from?" He reached out and offered his fingers to Tripod, who bumped his head on Istin's hand. "He's a friendly one."

"His name is Tripod, and he's decided he's mine," Tarjiaan answered. "Naji, Kaapi, neither of you has ever met a cat before, have you?"

"That's a cat?" Kaapi asked. "I... do they all have three legs?"

"No, Tripod is special." Tarjiaan coaxed Tripod down into his arms. "Come closer. You saw what Istin did? That's how you introduce yourself."

Naajir stepped forward first, holding his hand out for Tripod to sniff. He gingerly stroked Tripod's head, then smiled. "He's soft. And... what's the noise he's making? He sounds like an engine."

"He's purring," Tarjiaan said. "That means he's happy."

Kaapi stepped closer, her hands tucked behind her back. "He has sharp teeth. Tearing teeth. He eats meat?"

"He does," Tarjiaan said. "And if you're gentle with him, he won't bite you. Do you want to try?"

"Ah... not yet." Kaapi blushed. "I..."

"Take your time," Istin said. "New things can be scary. Even when they're smaller than you are."

"His teeth are so pointy!" Kaapi repeated. Tarjiaan smiled and shifted Tripod so that the cat was lying along his arm.

"Naji, you and Kaapi will be joining us for dinner in the royal apartments. Mentiras has offered to pick us up in his skiff well in advance, so we can use the bathing room in the apartments to get ready." He looked around. "Have either of you seen Daanir?"

"He and Mancer Narrick and Mancer Ishantar are in the comms room," Naajir answered. "I thought we might go back to help them. But if we're going to have a special dinner, we should go and talk to Marikaar and see about proper clothes." He held his hand out to Kaapi. "Come on, Kaap."

The two children hurried off, and Tarjiaan looked around at the flurry of activity on the deck. "How long has this been going on?"

"They all arrived not long after you left," Istin answered. "The tailors are here, too. That Ilenwy came back with lists and a whole army of people with measuring sticks and cords." He smiled. "I should go let them get my measure. Captain, by your leave?"

"Go on, Istin. And thank you." He turned away and started through the crowd and went belowdecks, heading toward the comms room. As he got closer, he could hear raised voices through the open door.

No, only one raised voice. Daanir. Giving orders.

"I said just rip it out! I meant it! That thing isn't even good for ballast anymore." He walked past the open door, not noticing Tarjiaan standing outside. "Take that side down to the bare metal. It all needs replacing."

Tarjiaan hesitated, then walked away, going back above and heading to the great cabin. He knew better than to bother Daanir when he was in the throes of his work. He'd come back later. Or better yet, he'd let *Wave Runner* tell Daanir that he was looking for him. He let himself into the great cabin, bending to put Tripod down. The cat bounded off to explore as Tarjiaan stood up again.

"*Wave Runner?*"

[Captain,] *Wave Runner* replied. [I have a ship cat?]

"We have one ship cat now, and possibly another on the way. One seems to have chosen Nika. This is Tripod, and he chose me." Tarjiaan went into the bedroom, and checked to make sure his chair was where he'd left it — locked in place next to the armor rack. He turned to see that Tripod had followed him, and was sniffing around the wheels of the chair. "Do we still have internal comms?"

[Yes, Captain.]

"If you would please tell Marikaar that Mentiras is sending supplies for Tripod?"

Silence, then *Wave Runner* responded, [First Mate is very happy that we have a ship cat, and will bring any supplies as soon as they are available. He would like to meet the cat at your convenience.]

"Thank you. Now, if you could whisper in Daanir's ear and let him know that I'm onboard? No hurry on that, though. I promised Nika I would rest, and I might be asleep by the time he gets free."

[I will tell him when he is available.]

Tarjiaan smiled and took off his coat, hanging it up before he stepped back into the armor rack, aligning brackets and locking them in place, then lowering rails to help him transfer. He triggered the release; the armor hissing open sent Tripod scurrying to hide underneath a cabinet.

Tarjiaan moved into his chair, unlocked it, and rolled over to the cabinet. "Tripod, come out. It's fine." No cat, and Tarjiaan sighed and rolled back toward the bed. He shifted onto the bed and unbuttoned his shirt before lying down.

He was dimly aware of the cat joining him on the bed just before he fell asleep.

Daanir looked around the now-empty comms room and nodded. "Good."

"This is good?" Narrick asked. He leaned against the wall. "You've gone from having broken comms to no comms at all."

"And now we can replace them with comms that actually work, and are better than the ones we got rid of." Daanir grinned. "Yes, this is good. We can start putting the new ones in place tomorrow. I—"

[Daanir, the Captain is onboard. He says to tell you that there is no rush. He is resting.]

Daanir paused, letting *Wave Runner's* mechanical voice fade away, realizing that it took whatever he was going to say with it. "I... lost the line on that thought," he finished, letting his voice trail off.

Narrick just smiled. "You've been working yourself ragged. You need to rest. And there's a dinner tonight, isn't there?"

"Is there?" Daanir frowned, trying to remember. "I don't know. Maybe?"

"I think there is. So go and take a nap. No falling asleep in the soup. It'll upset Tyva."

Daanir grinned. "Fine. No upsetting the person who could poison the soup." He looked around. "How soon do you think we can get the comms in and online?"

Narrick frowned, scratching his chin. "We have everything on your *in a perfect world* list, so... two days? Maybe three?"

"That soon?" Daanir grinned. "You know, I've missed working with someone. I loved Riguaarin, but he was in his cups a lot nearing the end, because nothing else would control his pain."

Narrick winced. "He was a good man. It was a shame to see him failing that way."

Daanir nodded. "It was. And because of that, I've been pretty much working alone since I left here. Training Kaapi is wonderful, but she's not an equal. Yet."

"She's talented, your girl. She'll be a strong mancer when she hits her growth." Narrick smiled. "We could talk like this for hours, and that's not letting you rest. Off with you. I'll go put in the orders, and we'll talk about timetables at dinner. I should know more about the mast by then."

Daanir nodded. "I'll walk you off, then."

"You can walk me to the top of the gangplank," Narrick corrected. "Your guard isn't here. And I don't trust Ishian to stay put, no matter what Mentiras says."

Daanir went cold. "You think he'll get out?"

Narrick nodded slowly. "The man is charismatic. People follow him. And he has friends in the dockyards who either won't believe stories about his past, or who don't care. You go nowhere without a guard, or me. Or both." He reached out and rested his hand on Daanir's shoulder. "I'm not letting him get his hands on you again, my boy."

Daanir closed his eyes and swallowed, then nodded. "Thank you. This... it means a lot to me."

Narrick squeezed his shoulder, then let him go. "You mean a lot to me. Now, walk me to the gangplank, then go take a nap!"

Narrick waved from the bottom of the gangplank, and Daanir waved back, then wandered across the deck. He'd always think of Taarik as the closest he'd ever had to a father, but Narrick was a close second. He chuckled — why did the father figures in his life have rhyming names? Was there a pattern to it? Did his actual father have a rhyming name? He had no idea. Nor did it matter, but it was funny to think about. He'd have to tell Tarjiaan.

The great cabin was quiet and dim when he entered, and the door to the bedroom partially ajar. That was strange — the door closed automatically to make sure it didn't slam into anything when they were at sea. Was it broken? He rested his hand on the wall and examined the mechanism. The auto-close was turned off.

[*I turned it off,*] Wave Runner whispered in his mind without his asking. [*So that Tripod could get in and out.*]

Tripod? Daanir opened the door and entered the bedroom, moving quietly. Tarjiaan was lying on his back, one arm thrown over his head in limp abandon. His other arm was outstretched, and there was a furry pillow resting by his hand. A furry pillow that raised its head and yawned, showing off sharp teeth and brilliant green eyes.

"Oh," Daanir whispered. "You must be Tripod." He walked over and offered the cat his fingers, then scratched the smooth, soft fur. "Welcome to the ship." He looked at Tarjiaan, then started taking off his coat, trying to decide how he was going to crawl into bed without waking him. He sat down to take his boots off, and the chair creaked; Tarjiaan jerked slightly and raised his head.

"Wha... Daan?"

"Sorry," Daanir said. "I was going to join you."

"I'll shift," Tarjiaan said, his voice rough and full of sleep. He rolled onto his side, then smiled. "Oh, you came out? I thought I felt you jump up." He stroked the cat, then shifted closer to him, leaving a wider slice of mattress for Daanir.

"Where did he come from?" Daanir asked as he stretched out behind Tarjiaan, pressing up against his back. He reached over and petted the cat, then caught his breath when Tripod rolled over and batted at his hand. "Oh! Is that why he's called Tripod?"

"He came from the *Endurance*, and apparently their queen went wandering and came back with a rogue litter," Tarjiaan said. "He was born like this, and they didn't think he'd make for a good ship cat. He picked me when Mentiras took us to meet the Admiral."

Daanir frowned slightly. "Jiaan, is the Admiral a *cat*?"

Tarjiaan looked over his shoulder. "You didn't know? He's the thirteenth Admiral. And Nika and Navi were both chosen by two of his kittens. Once they're old enough, they'll move on board."

"I knew there were ship cats in the dockyards, but I had no idea of their names. Some of them would wander in and out of the workrooms. Most of the time it was too noisy for them, though. They didn't like it."

"The sound of the armor opening scared Tripod." Tarjiaan petted the cat again, chuckling as the cat attacked his hand. "Easy, there. No teeth." He laughed again, then looked back at Daanir. "Kaapi is scared of him."

"Kaapi hasn't ever seen a cat before," Daanir said. "So I understand why. I was the same way when we were on the *Vagabond* that one time with Ilijiaan. Remember? She'll warm up to him. I don't think he'll give her a choice." He tightened his arm around Tarjiaan. "Are you awake?"

Tarjiaan looked back over his shoulder. "Why?"

"Wondering if I should put you back to sleep." Daanir stretched up and kissed Tarjiaan, shifting so that Tarjiaan could roll onto his back. "If you're interested?"

Tarjiaan smiled. "Oh, I find you very interesting." He tugged on Daanir's shirt. "Come down here."

Tarjiaan woke slowly, resting on Daanir's chest, reveling in his warmth, in his presence, listening to the lazy heartbeat underneath his ear. The mancer was asleep, one hand on Tarjiaan's back, possessive and protective even in sleep. Tarjiaan yawned, closing his eyes again. More sleep would be good... and the door hinges in the other room squeaked. He smiled as the door opened and Nika peeked inside. She noticed him looking at her and came to sit on the edge of the bed.

"Did you sleep?" she asked softly.

"I did," Tarjiaan answered, reaching for her hand. "Come here."

She pulled her hand out of his and stood up, but only for long enough to take off her shoes, coat and skirt. Wearing only her blouse, she climbed back onto the bed and curled up against Daanir, who didn't move.

"Where is Tripod?" she asked, gently stroking Tarjiaan's shoulder.

"He was here, but... I think we frightened him." Tarjiaan raised his head and looked around. "He found the cabinet has enough room underneath to hide. He might be there."

Nika nodded, resting her head on Daanir's shoulder. The mancer jerked, his breath catching as he looked up. He smiled and put his other arm around Nika.

"When did you get here?" he croaked.

"Just now," Nika answered. "And Jiaan told me to join you. This is nice, just being together." She smiled. "Although I think I missed some of it?"

"Should we have waited?" Daanir asked. "I didn't think—"

"Daan, she's teasing," Tarjiaan said.

"I am," Nika added. "I do not mind. I was busy. I do not expect you to deny yourselves because I am elsewhere. There will be other times." She grinned. "There is a very large bath, I am told?"

Tarjiaan chuckled. "Large enough for all of us to share," he agreed. "You can show Daan what you showed me."

"Oh?" Nika ran her hand down Daanir's chest and belly, and Tarjiaan felt him shiver. "Do you think he will like that?"

"What are you showing me?" Daanir asked. "What will I like?"

"You will find out," Nika said. "Once we are in the royal apartments. Which... when do we need to go?"

"Mentiras is going to come and get us, and... I have no idea how long we've been asleep." Tarjiaan shifted, rolling onto his side and propping himself up with one elbow. "*Wave Runner?* What time is it?"

[Afternoon watch, six bells,] *Wave Runner* answered.

"Mentiras will be around to get us at seven bells, and supper is four bells on the first half watch" Tarjiaan said. "We need to get up and pack clothes to take to the apartment. And..." He frowned. "I'll need to bring my chair. I can't bathe in the armor."

"How many chairs do you have?" Daanir asked. "If you only have the one, we should see if we can find another one for the apartment."

"I only have the one at the moment," Tarjiaan answered. "There's another one, but it was being repaired. The caning on the seatback split." He frowned, then sighed. "And the carpenter who works with caning was on leave in the belowships because his wife just had a baby. So I'm not certain where the chair is. Ishantar might know."

"When she gets back from the *Dauntless*, I'll ask her and we'll see if we can find it. There has to be someone in the dockyards who knows caning." Daanir sat up. "I'll ask Narrick. He should know. What do you need me to pack for you, and where's something to carry it in?"

"Are the children joining us?" Nika asked.

"Yes," Tarjiaan looked up again. "And Antivar and Navi. *Wave Runner,* will you remind Naji and Kaapi that they're to pack up the nicest clothes that they have and meet us on deck as soon as they are ready, and that we're leaving at seven bells. Then relay the same message to Antivar and Healer Navi." He turned to Daanir. "There should be a basket in the wardrobe, and I'll need a uniform. Pack two of anything of mine that will fit you. Which... I think limits you to borrowing my shirts and coats. You can't wear my trousers." He frowned as he sat up. "Nika, what are you going to wear?"

"I have the uniform that I wore today, and the clothes that the other women on the ship gifted to me," Nika answered. "I am not certain what of that is appropriate for this dinner?"

"We're all going to need to speak to the tailors," Tarjiaan said. "I'll ask Mentiras or his wife to see if they can find something for you while we bathe." He looked around. "Daan, what did you do with my clothes?"

Chapter Eighteen
Preparations

IT WASN'T THE FIRST time Tarjiaan had sat down to dine with the officers of another ship, but this time felt very different. He checked his appearance in the mirror, wondering what Logiri would think. He'd probably be appalled at the sight of Tarjiaan's choppy, too-short hair. But that wasn't it.

Someone knocked at the bedroom door, and a young-sounding voice called from the other side, "Your Majesty? I have clothes for Her Majesty."

That was it. This would be his first time sitting at the head of the table as king. He glanced at the bathing room door, but there was no sign of Daanir or Nika, so he went and answered the knock. The young woman on the other side was carrying a large basket, and she looked up and blushed as she realized who had answered. She was as fair as Daanir, and probably a head taller than Nika, with more generous curves and a sweet smile.

"Your Majesty," she repeated, and bobbed a slight curtsy. "I... Commander Mentiras sent me to help Her Majesty prepare, if she'd like the help? Or if you need any help? He says that your valet isn't in attendance, and he thought that I might be of use to you and your wife and your consort."

"Come in." Tarjiaan stepped back to allow her into the room. "Her Majesty is still in the bathing room, as is the Lord Consort. You can put that down, and I'll see if either of them need help."

"Thank you, Your Majesty."

He smiled. "You can relax. What's your name?"

"Oona, Your Majesty."

Tarjiaan nodded, going to the bathing room door. "Nika?" he called. "There are clothes here for you. And someone to help us prepare."

"Thank you!" Nika called back. "We are almost finished. I will call for her when I am ready."

Tarjiaan turned to see Oona standing close enough to hear. She curtsied again, then looked him up and down. "I... may I ask a question, Sire?"

"Of course."

"Did you cut your hair with a knife?" She blushed scarlet when she finished speaking. "I apologize. That was rude. It's just... you look so... untidy."

Tarjiaan smiled. "My valet would agree with you. No, I didn't cut it. It was cut while I was a prisoner, and I haven't had the time to do anything about it. Or, to be honest, cared that much. The people who are around me know what happened."

"I apologize, Sire," Oona repeated. "I didn't know. I... may I take care of it, while I'm waiting to help Her Majesty? I know how. I was a body servant to Captain Elsider on the *Gallivant*."

"Oh? If you served Elsider, you clearly know what you're doing. I don't think I've ever seen him with a hair out of place." Tarjiaan looked around. "I would appreciate your help, Oona. Tell me what you need me to do."

She smiled, showing off dimpled cheeks. "I'll need to fetch the right tools. If there's a chair where you're comfortable sitting, could you pull it to the center of the room? And take off your coat, please?"

She was quick — by the time Tarjiaan had moved the chair and hung his coat up, Oona was back. She was carrying a smaller basket, and had a long cloth over one arm. She looked at the chair, then turned it slightly.

"Better light?" Tarjiaan asked.

"A better angle for the light," she answered. "You don't wear a surcoat? I think you're the first I've met who doesn't."

"They don't lay right over the armor." Tarjiaan brushed one hand down the front of his short and over the topmost edge of the armor. "And most are too long to wear under the armor – they get caught in the mechanism. I've had some tailored, but I've never been happy with the cut, so I just don't wear them."

"I see." She studied him for a moment. "Let's begin. If you'll take a seat?"

Tarjiaan sat down, and Oona shook out the cloth, revealing a cape that she draped around him. She took a comb out of the basket and started combing his hair. He closed his eyes and relaxed, listening to her alternate disgusted grumbling with tuneless humming as she worked. By the time the bathing room door opened, there was a fine dusting of hair on the cape, and she'd stopped grumbling. The scissors stopped for a moment.

"Lord Consort?" she said. "If you'd like to be next, I can trim your beard."

Tarjiaan opened his eyes to see Daanir, completely dressed, but with his coat hanging open. He looked startled. "I... I don't want to shave—"

"Trim, not shave." The scissors started again. "Just tidying it up and making it more even."

"It's what I was going to show you how to do," Tarjiaan added. "Oona, how are we?"

"We're just about done. I've evened things out," she answered, "But it'll need to be done again once it grows out more." She combed his hair once more, then dusted off the back of his neck with another cloth. "Let me take the cape and shake it out, and then I'll see to the Lord Consort. Unless Her Majesty needs me?"

Daanir chuckled. "Her Majesty says that she's thinks she'll be clean after one more long, hot soak. So you have time. What do I need to do?"

"Take off your coat, then come sit down." Oona took away the cape, and Tarjiaan stood up, letting Daanir take his place. Once she was back, she draped the cape around Daanir, then picked up the scissors. Daanir flinched.

"Lord Consort?" Oona said.

"I... go slow?" he said weakly. "The last time I had something sharp that close to my face..."

"The scar here?" Oona asked. "I understand. I'll tell you everything I'm going to do before I do it. Right now, I'm going to see what's needed." She held up a comb.

"You're going to comb my *face*?"

"Trust me. How long do you want your beard to be when I'm done?"

Daanir frowned, then looked at Tarjiaan. "Like Jiaan's."

"Short and tidy. Of course. Now just relax."

Tarjiaan leaned against the desk and watched as Oona slowly and carefully narrated every part of trimming Daanir's beard and hair. Daanir slowly relaxed under her ministrations, started asking questions. When he started making jokes, Tarjiaan excused himself and knocked on the bathing room door.

"May I come in?"

"Please!"

He opened the door and entered, closing it behind him. Nika was still in the bath, a deep tub that had easily accommodated all three of them. He walked around to the far side, avoiding puddles as he made his way to a chair.

"Is your hair shorter?" she asked as he walked around.

"The servant who came to help you trimmed it. She's working on Daan's beard now," he answered. "Is the bath to your liking, my queen?" he asked as he sat down.

"It looks very nice. And yes, very much so," Nika answered. She turned, resting her arms the lip of the tub. "It is not as nice as the one in our rooms on the *Chimaera*, but it is lovely to have the room to have both of you with me. Is there a way to have something like this on the *Wave Runner*?"

"That is a question for your other husband," Tarjiaan said, making her laugh. He smiled, then realized something. "By this time next year, we may be living in a palace somewhere. In Meradon, maybe? Or in Tyraca."

Nika frowned. "What happens to *Wave Runner* when we have to live on land, Jiaan?"

Tarjiaan blinked. "I... I don't know. I never thought about it." He leaned back, folding his arms over his chest. "I never thought I would live on land. I never thought it would be possible. Now... it's not only possible, it's likely. And... I don't know what to do with a fleet of ships that might all be aware, and that won't have a purpose once the war is over."

"There will be those who do not want to go on land," Nika said slowly. "Or who cannot, like Nimas. They can remain at sea, can they not?"

Tarjiaan nodded, staring at the wall opposite, not really seeing it. "I... yes. We could continue to have Meradon below the waves. I just... I hadn't considered who would take the *Wave Runner* once she wasn't mine anymore." He shook his head. "When you're not certain if you'll see tomorrow, you don't tend to think that far in advance."

"It is time to start thinking past tomorrow, Nika said. "And it is time for me to get out. I am wrinkling."

Tarjiaan reached out and picked up a drying sheet, holding it open as Nika climbed out of the bath. She let him wrap the cloth around her, smiling as he started to rub her dry.

"I enjoyed watching you two," he said softly.

"Did it surprise you?" she asked. "That you like to watch."

"It did. I never knew that about myself." Tarjiaan put his arms around Nika, pulling her closer. "And you enjoyed me watching. I could tell."

She laughed and kissed him. "I did enjoy it. But we do not have time for me to show you how much. There is a maid?"

"Her name is Oona, and she was a body servant to one of the most fastidious captains I've ever met."

Nika nodded. "If you will send her in once she is finished with Daanir?"

Tarjiaan smiled. "Of course, my queen." He kissed her, then let her move away before standing up and leaving the bathing room. Outside, Oona was taking the cape from around Daanir's neck.

"Once you're ready, Oona, Nika is ready for you."

"Of course," Oona said. "Let me shake this out and pack these tools up. Then I'll go and help Her Majesty—"

"Who will probably insist on you calling her Nika," Daanir said.

"I'll let her tell me that." Oona left the room. When she came back, Antivar and Navi were with her. "Your Majesty? I have... we haven't been introduced. I'm sorry."

"Oona, this is Prince-Healer Ysnavin, and his intended, Commander Girantivar," Tarjiaan said. "The Commander is Lord Meranas' guard, and Prince-Healer Ysnavin is Her Majesty's brother."

"Oh!" Oona turned slightly pink. "I apologize. I didn't know." She tipped her head to the side. "You'll be after Her Majesty, then?"

"After..." Antivar repeated. "For what?"

"Getting ready for dinner," Oona answered. "Making you presentable."

Antivar looked down at himself. "I... am I not? This is what I had, and Istin tried his best to get it ready...."

"Look fine," Navi said, resting his hand on Antivar's arm. "Look nice."

"You do," Oona said. "And I apologize if I made you think you didn't." She gestured with one hand, making a twirling motion. "Turn?"

Antivar looked completely mystified, but he turned in a circle. "Like this? Now what?"

"Now... once I'm done with helping the Queen, there are a few things that I can do to adjust your coat, and to tidy up your hair. If you want me to? I should have asked that first. For both of you?"

Navi sniffed. "Put a bow on a fish."

Oona arched a brow. "You are considerably better looking than a fish, Your Highness."

"She's right," Antivar murmured. "Once the Queen is ready, we'll see if there's time."

"I'll make certain that there is," Oona said. She picked up the large basket and disappeared into the bathing room.

"This is... strange," Antivar said. "It's more than I expected. I don't want to embarrass you, Captain."

"You won't," Tarjiaan said. "And if you have questions about anything, ask Daanir, or Wilaanger."

Antivar nodded. "I will ask. I didn't think that a simple dinner would be so different, but this is not what I'm used to. But then, I wasn't a very high-ranking officer before. I didn't go to many formal dinners." He looked at the door to the bathing room. "The lady... what was her name?"

"Oona?" Daanir asked. "She's very good. Very calming."

"She's very pretty," Antivar added. Navi snorted.

"Mother says pretty girl?" he asked. He glanced at the door. "Perhaps."

"Maybe you should get to know her first?" Daanir asked. "Before you start making plans?"

"We have time." Antivar smiled. "Who else will be in attendance tonight?"

"Commander Mentiras and his wife," Tarjiaan answered. "Mancer Narrick. Wilaanger and Chel. Captain Theonus and Nyssa. Naajir and Kaapi, and I should check on them." He paused. "I don't know who else. But when we got here, I looked in the dining room and the table was fully set, with more chairs than I thought there would be." He looked around. "Has anyone seen Tripod?"

Antivar gestured toward the door. "With the children, last I saw him. They're out in the sitting room. I wouldn't be surprised if they both come to the table covered in hair."

"Both?" Daanir asked. He grinned. "I should check on them. I'll be back." He picked up his coat and left the bedroom, and Tarjiaan stepped in front of the mirror again. His hair looked neater. Logiri would probably still fuss over it, but it would be a much shorter fuss than before Oona had done something.

"I forgot my good earrings," Tarjiaan said. Then he frowned. "No, those are still on the *Chimaera*. This will have to do." He looked at Antivar in the glass. "Do Imperial men wear earrings?"

"Not usually," Antivar answered. "I've been trying to decide if I want to have one, since you said I'm owed one for the storm."

"Take your time," Tarjiaan said. "There's no hurry." He turned as the bathing room door opened and Nika came out. She wore a high-necked gown of gold-shot green that fit close in the bodice, and flared out into a full skirt. "Nika, that's lovely!"

She smiled and turned in place, making the skirt flare. "It is so very pretty!" she said. "I was so surprised when Oona showed me. I was not expecting anything this fine!"

"The Commander said that there was a wardrobe for the royal apartment, things that were stored here in case there was a visit. I had a vague idea of Her Majesty's measurements, and I hoped this would fit." Oona grinned. "I'm pleased I guessed right!"

"How?" Nika asked. "You knew my measurements? How?"

"Lady Tyva," Oona answered. "She's got a very good eye for this sort of thing." She turned to Navi and Antivar. "Now, your Highness? Do you want to go first?"

Once Antivar and Navi were done, Tarjiaan led Nika out into the sitting room. He wasn't prepared for Kaapi's reaction.

"Mama, you're beautiful!" The girl jumped up and rushed over to them, then stopped. "I... I'll get you messy. I have hair on me, because Tripod was sitting on me, and... you're so pretty!" She looked up at Daanir, who had followed her over. "Papa, will I be able to dress like that someday?"

"Do you want to dress like this now?" Oona asked.

Kaapi immediately turned to Daanir. "Papa? May I?"

"Is there time?" Daanir asked.

Oona grinned. "I'll make time." She held her hand out. "Let's go."

Daanir patted Kaapi on the shoulder. "Go on. Have fun."

Kaapi laughed, hugged him, then left with Oona. Naajir watched as they left, then carried Tripod over to Tarjiaan.

"She decided she wanted to try petting him," he said. "Then he curled up in her lap and started buzzing. Now she wants one of her own."

"That's not surprising." Tarjiaan took Tripod, laughing as the cat clambered up his chest and onto his shoulder. "You can see the whole room from up there, hm?"

"You do look wonderful, Aunt Nika," Naajir added. "I... I think I've seen that dress before. In a picture." He frowned. "Yes, I have. My mother wore it."

"Your mother was here?" Tarjiaan looked Daanir. "When?"

"Long enough ago that she fit into a dress Nika can wear now," Daanir answered. "So she was shorter. Mentiras might have an idea as to how long ago. There will be records."

Nika looked down at herself, smoothing the front of her dress. "She must have looked stunning. This color would suit her wonderfully."

"She would have." Tarjiaan nodded slowly. "I never realized Aanaji was above the waves. She never said anything about that." He frowned. "Then again, we never really talked. I was too young, and then..." His voice trailed off when he realized everything that came after *and then*.

"And then," Daanir agreed. "You never really talked to your sister at all, have you?"

"I don't think I have. Hopefully, I get the chance to remedy that," Tarjiaan said. "Naji, are you ready? This is your first time standing as the Sea Prince."

"Don't remind me," Naajir said with a weak smile. "I'm feeling very unmoored about this. I don't want to be heir. I know I'm not the right person to be your heir. But I'm all you have for now."

"Naajir, you would make a wonderful heir," Nika said. "You only need the proper training, and we will make certain that you have it. Istin is going to start your lessons, and Marikaar will find someone to teach you to fight."

"About that... Uncle, I'm years behind. I barely know how to fight, and I don't have a battle companion. And I'm not likely to have one anytime soon, am I? There's no one to train with me but Kaapi."

Tarjiaan nodded. "We'll sail that current when we get there," he said. "I haven't had a moment to spare to think about it. But I promise, we'll get you paired off." He looked up, saw the question in Antivar's face. "It's required for Meradon's princes to be battle trained, and to have a battle companion. Naji should have started training at ten."

"But it isn't required for the princesses?" Nika asked. "Did Aanaji have one?"

Tarjiaan heard Daanir snort, and fought back a smile. "No," he answered. "From what I understand, Aanaji refused the offer of weapons training. At volume, to hear Ranji tell the story. But there have been fighting women in the royal family. And fighting queens. But I don't think any of the women had battle companions the way the men do."

Nika looked puzzled. "Why not?"

"I honestly don't know," Tarjiaan admitted. "I never thought about it, and never thought to ask. We can ask Wilaanger. He might have an idea. But that might need deeper study into the archives, so it's a question that will have to be answered later." He paused, studied Nika, then smiled. "You want to learn to fight."

Nika raised her chin. "I hear about how my mother's people are warriors. About how the women rule. And I will be queen. Of Meradon, possibly of Tyraca. I should learn how to defend my people, how to lead them. How to give orders in battle, and what orders to give. I know none of this." She looked at Daanir and smiled. "I know how to shoot, at least. Even though I have not yet shot at anything."

"You've done very well for not knowing," Daanir said. "Using the sub to get close to the Imp ship so I could blow a hole in the side was brilliant."

"Thank you," Nika said. "But that was desperation. I need to know what to do. I need to learn."

"Then you will learn," Tarjiaan said, nodding. "I'll teach you myself. And we can have Ishantar teach you Sualimani fighting styles." He paused. "After the baby comes. I'm not risking you or them. Acceptable?"

Nika frowned. "May I at least learn to shoot properly? Just in case it is needful?"

"That's not a bad idea, Jiaan," Daanir said.

Tarjiaan nodded. "I agree. I'll talk to Mentiras. There has to be somewhere on the dockyards for drill—"

"There's a salle, and I know where." Daanir sighed and smiled sadly. "Just because I didn't think I was a battle companion anymore didn't mean I didn't keep training. It was something to do, and something that kept me away from Ishian. And I think it kept me sane on Station Six. I kept it up here. The main reason that I'm out of practice is because I went below. Riguaarin kept me too busy to get to the salle."

Tarjiaan nodded. "You'll have to tell me where. You can't be in two places at once, and I know you want to be with the *Wave Runner*."

"I still need to train," Daanir said. "I'll make time to do both, once the comms are in. Which... Narrick says a few days. They have everything on hand." He smiled, no doubt at the look on Tarjiaan's face, because his next words were, "That was my reaction. I thought it would take ages. But we stripped the room to the walls today, and tomorrow we'll start rebuilding. And he says he'll have a timeline on the mast tonight."

"Would I be allowed to train as well?" Antivar asked. "Because if I can, then I can help with Prince Naajir's training. We're closer in size, and I think in reach." He glanced at Daanir. "And if Daanir will be onboard the *Wave Runner* to rebuild, then I can slip away for an hour or two."

"That sounds something very close to a plan," Tarjiaan said. "We'll finalize it over dinner. Was that the door?"

Chapter Nineteen

Dinner

WILAANGER AND CHEL were the first to arrive. Chel looked at Nika and clapped her hands in delight.

"Oh, that looks splendid on you! Who chose that?"

"We have a maid... no. What did you call her, Jiaan?" She looked up at Tarjiaan.

"Oona is a body-servant. Her role would be something between a maid and what Logiri does for me."

Nika nodded. "And... you said she served a fastidious captain. A man?" She glanced at the door to the bedroom. "In the Empire, a woman who served a man that closely would be expected to serve in all manners. But that is not the way in Meradon."

Tarjiaan nodded. "No, that wouldn't have been expected of her."

"And the captain would be... thought less of," Wilaanger added. "For dallying with a subordinate. It's considered a breach of decorum — a captain doesn't look for bed partners among their crew."

"It might still happen, but only if they both agreed," Chel said. "And they'd be discreet about it."

Nika frowned. "But Theonus and Nyssa? Are they not married?"

"Theonus and Nyssa were battle companions before he became a captain," Tarjiaan said. "Which means she's not a subordinate. She's considered the equivalent rank."

Nika turned and looked at Daanir. "How does that work when you are battle companion to a king?"

"Ask Wil," Daanir answered. "I'm still new at this."

Wilaanger laughed. "It's a special case," he answered. "If you consider rank as a set of stairs, once Ika took the throne, he was on the topmost step. I was a step below, as was his wife. That was also true of the Heir. But in all other cases, a battle companion is raised to the rank of their partner. So Daanir should have been considered a royal fosterling and a prince long before he was actually adopted."

"I wasn't ever a prince!" Daanir protested. "I'm still not!"

"Wil, Father never told us that," Tarjiaan said. "Should he have?"

"Your trainer should have," Wilaanger answered. "Your father was a commoner. He didn't have a battle companion, and he probably didn't know the traditions. But your trainer should have."

Daanir frowned and shook his head. "I don't remember being told any of that. Jiaan?"

"No." Tarjiaan looked at Daanir and grinned. "So. Prince Daanir?"

Daanir coughed. "No. Don't even start that. It's weird." He shook his head. "Lord is bad enough, and I earned that. Prince? That's like putting shoes on a fish." He glanced at the door. "Let Kaapi be a princess, though. She'll make a good one."

As he spoke, the door opened, and Oona came out, followed by a young lady in a blue gown. It took Tarjiaan a moment to realize that he was seeing Kaapi — her messy brown hair had been pulled back into a sleek hairstyle that let ringlets tumble over her shoulders. Her belowship-pale complexion had been warmed by cosmetics, and the jewel-tone gown set off the jewel-blue of her eyes.

Daanir stared at his daughter, then walked over and bowed, holding his hand out to her as he rose. "My lady, will you give me the honor of escorting you?"

Kaapi blushed. "Papa!"

Daanir just smiled. "You look beautiful, Kaap. Oona, thank you."

"It was my pleasure, Lord Meranas." Oona smiled. "And Lady Kaapi is a delight to work with."

"I'm not a lady," Kaapi protested.

"You are," Tarjiaan said. "As a royal fosterling, you are." He noticed Navi moving toward Naajir, and only then noticed that his nephew was staring. Navi sidled up next to the boy, leaned in close, and whispered something that Tarjiaan just barely heard.

"Breathe!"

Naajir jerked, turning to stare at Navi, then blushed. Navi laughed and hugged him, then went back to Antivar's side. The door opened, and Tyva and Mentiras came in. Tyva smiled, then looked around.

"Oh," she murmured. "The serving crew isn't here yet. If you'll excuse me?" She hurried out, and Mentiras shook his head as he joined them.

"She's been fussing about this dinner all afternoon," he said. "She wants it to be perfect. She's got a crew to serve at the table tonight, and they should have been here already." He smiled. "Your Majesty, you look lovely. That dress suits you."

"Tir, Naajir says that he's seen a picture of my sister wearing this dress," Tarjiaan said. "When was she here?"

"I don't think I've ever met your sister, Jiaan," Mentiras answered. "So not while I've been here. I'll check the logs." He looked around. "We're expecting Captain Theonus and Lady

Nyssa, and I asked Tommen to join us, and he'll be bringing Reeshi. Oh, and Narrick will be here if he can tear himself away from his requisitions. Are we repairing or rebuilding that ship of yours, Daanir?"

The rest of the guests arrived as Daanir outlined his plans for the *Wave Runner*. Narrick joined in the discussion, which continued once they had reached the table. Young men and women in neat uniforms circled the table, filling glasses, serving food. Tarjiaan sat at the head of the table, relaxing as the ebb and flow of conversation settled into familiar, familial eddies. On his right, Nika reached out and rested her hand on his.

"How are you feeling?" she asked softly.

"I'm fine," he answered. "This is... this is good. This is what a family dinner should be." He smiled as one of the servers offered him a platter of crusted fish. "And Tyva seems to have made every one of my favorite foods."

Nika nodded, then looked up. "Tyva, is there anything with milk?"

Tyva frowned. "Ah... no. All of our milk stores are long gone. Why?"

"Because Kaapi cannot have milk," Nika answered. "And I do not want to spoil her evening."

Kaapi was seated next to Daanir, on Tarjiaan's left. She smiled. "Thank you, Mama."

Tyva nodded. "Well, that's a happy accident, then. If we'd had milk, I would have used it in several of these dishes." She nodded. "I'll make a note of that, so I know for the future. Although I have no idea when we'll be getting fresh milk. Our hydroponics are maintaining, as are the fowl, but milk? We haven't had that for days."

"What happened to the support pods that serve the dockyards?" Tarjiaan asked. He frowned and looked at Theonus, who sat halfway down the table on the left. "The same as the fleet support pods?"

Theonus nodded. "I'd wager pearls on it. How do you control a fighting force?"

"Use their bellies," Tarjiaan grimaced. "Which means we'll have to move fast once the broadcast goes out."

The energy in the room shifted into something more serious, moving from a relaxed family dinner into a meeting of Tarjiaan's chief — and only — advisors. Narrick cleared his throat. "I've done some planning, based on the tour I had with Daanir today, and my own assessments. We can have the comms replaced in two days, and we can work on the hydroponics at the same time. Once those are both done, and your men are quartered in the barracks, then I can move those teams into working on the repairs to the gun houses and the loading mechanisms. I'll have a better idea how long that will take once we get things taken apart in there, but from what Daan showed me, we're looking at probably at least seven days for those repairs. Possibly ten." He paused, then nodded. "We're lucky in that I think we have everything we need on hand."

"Even the mast and the solar sails?" Daanir gasped.

"The *Destiny* requisitioned replacements months ago," Narrick answered. "But she never made it in for refit." He paused again. "With all the work that needs doing, we're looking at possibly thirty days, give or take five to ten."

"That soon?" Tarjiaan felt a surge of surprise and relief. "I'd thought it would take longer. And we'll do the broadcast when?"

"Once the *Wave Runner* is ready to sail," Mentiras said. "Partly so that you can get clear before they have a chance to move on us, partly so we can sweep once more for refugees before we move to get clear."

Tarjiaan nodded, sitting back as a servant placed a full cup of tea in front of him. He nodded his thanks, picked it up, and took a sip. "That gives us enough time to make plans on how we're going to do something about a usurper in a belowship that we can't reach." He sipped the tea again. "Tyva, this blend is very nice."

"Thank you," Tyva smiled. "I hoped you'd like it. It's a new blend. I'll make certain Aranti has some for you."

Daanir waited for a servant to fill his teacup, then took a sip. "Given enough mancers, we might be able to bring the *Chimaera* to the surface."

"What do you mean, enough mancers?" Narrick asked. "How would that work?"

Daanir shrugged. "We have a month to figure out how to make it work. I think we can do it. So if we bring together enough allies, we might be able to bring the *Chimaera* up from the surface. Or at the very least, from a submersible."

"The *Chimaera* has no guns," Wilaanger said. "You'd be able to get close. You might even be able to get onboard."

"But could you do any of this without risking the hostages?" Tarjiaan asked. "I'm not willing to put any of their lives at risk. Not unless there's no other way to end this." He looked around the table. "My sister. Chel's husband. Nika and Navi's father. My closest friend."

"This is another of the hard choices, is it not?" Nika asked. Tarjiaan nodded.

"It is, and it's one that I want to avoid having to make." He sipped his tea and sighed. "Partly because I don't want to have the blood of all of the hostages on my hands. And partly because it's too easy — if I destroy the *Chimaera* and all aboard, then Ilaris will become a hero in the eyes of anyone who followed him and who believed his lies." He sighed. "He has to be taken alive, and his lies revealed to the entire kingdom."

"And even then, those who follow him may not believe them," Tommen said. "That's the way in the Empire. There's always those who think the Emperor is a fine and just ruler, never mind the trail of bodies he's left in his wake."

"They're also always the ones who have the most to lose," Reeshi added. "The officials and the priests. The nobles who live on the Emperor's leavings. They want what they want, and never mind the rest of us. There will be those in Meradon, too, I suppose?"

"That's a discussion we've had," Daanir said. "About how food supplies have been diverted from where they're supposed to go." He pointed at Kaapi. "That's why we didn't know Kaapi couldn't have milk until she came to me. She'd never had it before."

"Wait, what was this?" Tarjiaan asked. "You mentioned something about food being diverted, but not in depth, and I forgot to ask for more information. All I know for certain is that it's something that makes Nika want to upend the fleet. When was there a full discussion, and where was I?"

"Ah..." Daanir stammered. "You... weren't with us."

Tarjiaan frowned, then nodded. "Ah. I see. Please fill in the gaps later?"

"We will," Nika said. "As you said, I cannot upend the fleet until this is resolved and the throne secure. There is time."

Tarjiaan smiled and took her hand. "There is. Now, repairs will take roughly thirty to forty days? How do we stand on leave for our men, and for our new crew?"

"Ilenwy reported that they've started work on outfitting the crew that needs it. We can start moving your men out to the barracks and off the ship by late tomorrow, I think."

"That's very quick," Wilaanger said. "We have a lot of men who need to be clothed."

"And we have a lot of pre-made garments that just need to be tailored," Tyva countered. "We keep a good stock, because you never know what's going to be needed or how much."

"Granted, we don't have as much as we usually do," Mentiras added.

"On account of my folk, I warrant?" Tommen asked. He and Reeshi sat at the foot of the table, next to Tyva, and across from Theonus and Nyssa. "I'm glad of it. It helped us to settle in."

"Speaking of settling," Tarjiaan said. "The *Wave Runner* is at three times her normal capacity. We're going to have to reassign some of them, and I don't have a support pod."

"How many again? Ilenwy told me, but I can't remember."

"Four hundred and seventy-nine," Antivar answered. "Counting me and Navi."

Mentiras nodded slowly. "Tyva, we can handle that many, can't we?"

"It won't be that many, I don't think," Antivar said. "I know my men. They'll follow the Captain who gave us a chance into battle against the south wind itself, if he asked them to."

"Which, I won't be doing that," Tarjiaan said. Antivar grinned.

"We know. That's part of why we'll follow you. You won't throw our lives away for sport. I'll talk to them, see who is willing to stay back and act as a relief force and guard for the dockyards. If you're worried about possible retaliation after the message goes out, then you should have a guard." He paused, looking thoughtful. "I may talk to Istin about staying and commanding that guard."

"Do that, if you will," Mentiras said. "Then let me know final numbers and we'll get them set in more permanent housing. The barracks are comfortable, but... well, they're barracks."

Antivar laughed. "You've never been aboard an Imperial warship, then? Sharing a bunk with two other people is more comfort than we saw from the moment the *Sea Witch* set sail. Even as an officer. I promise, you won't hear a single complaint from any of my men who stay."

"Mentiras, you're going to need physicians, aren't you?" Wilaanger said. "The afternoon we spent in your infirmary seems to show that you're horribly understaffed."

Mentiras nodded. "We've added the equivalent of a ship on leave to our population, without adding in the usual support from that ship's crew. We could use another physician or two."

Tarjiaan frowned slightly. "What are you thinking, Wil?"

"That I might stay," Wilaanger answered. "I'm an old man, Jiaan. The front line isn't a place for me. Not anymore. I'll stay here and work with the refugees, and leave battlefield healing to the younger, stronger, and much more powerful healers you'll be keeping with you." He shrugged. "It's a thought. I might not. But it might be better if I do."

"We can certainly discuss it," Tarjiaan said, trying to keep his voice level. He hadn't considered leaving any of his family behind when the *Wave Runner* left the dockyards. But Wilaanger made a good point. He glanced at Nika. Perhaps....

"No," Nika murmured. "I will not stay."

Tarjiaan stared at her. "You can hear me thinking now?"

She laughed. "No! It was plain on your face. You were thinking of having me stay with Wilaanger. And I will not. My place is on your right." Before Tarjiaan could protest, she reached up and touched his lips with one finger. "I am staying."

"Nika, you know what he's worrying about," Daanir said.

"I know. He worries for the baby." Nika trailed her fingers over Tarjiaan's cheek, stroking his beard. "And I worry for you both. I will not be left behind."

"I... pardon me, but... baby?" Mentiras stammered. "Your Majesty? Are you certain? You're welcome to stay with us."

"I am certain," Nika said. She smiled, turning in her chair. "Tyva, when will the kittens be old enough to come to the *Wave Runner*?"

Tyva smiled. "Another few weeks. You'll need to come visit with them every day, so that they get used to you, and you learn what they need. And... well, now that I know you're pregnant, I'll have different instructions for you than I will for Prince Ysnavin."

"Please," Navi said. "Just Navi." He frowned slightly and turned to Antivar, saying something in Imperial. Antivar smiled.

"Fancy."

"Ah." Navi turned back to Tyva. "Not fancy. Not yet. Later fancy. Now, just Navi."

"That sounds like a wonderful idea," Narrick said. "We can all be fancy later."

The mood in the dining room lightened as conversation shifted back to lighter things. Tarjiaan leaned back in his chair, finishing his tea. Now that he'd eaten, he felt deeply tired. He hadn't had enough sleep, or long enough time to recover.

"Mentiras," he said, and his voice sounded odd to his ears. Was he slurring? "I'll want to visit Owain, if he's still in the dockyards?"

Mentiras looked at him oddly. "Jiaan, are you all right?"

Tarjiaan smiled. "Tired. Just... tired." He blinked, then jerked in surprise as Navi jumped to his feet, his chair clattering to the ground. He ran up the table and grabbed Tarjiaan's hand in one hand, then pressed his other hand to Tarjiaan's chest.

"Water," Navi snapped. "Must drink now!"

Movement. Raised voices. Tarjiaan heard Nika, telling him to drink. Someone was holding a cup to his lips, but his eyelids were too heavy, and he was so tired...

"Daan, get him out of the armor! We need to move him!" Wilaanger snapped.

Daanir nodded, shocked and terrified all at the same time. He reached out and touched Tarjiaan's leg, watching as the armor released.

"Take him to the bedroom," Mentiras said. "Theonus—"

"Daan, you take his left," Theonus said, coming up the table. "I'll get his right. Tell me where we're going."

"This way." Nika stepped back as Daanir and Theonus lifted Tarjiaan out of his armor and carried him out of the dining room and back to the bedroom. Inside, Oona looked up in shock.

"What happened?" she gasped.

Daanir didn't answer. He didn't know. Navi answered for him. "Poison."

Daanir almost dropped Tarjiaan. "You're sure?"

"Yes," Navi said. "Down. Need to work."

Carefully, Daanir and Theonus moved Tarjiaan onto the bed. They stepped back, letting Navi in. He knelt on the bed and put his hand on Tarjiaan's chest.

"Out," Navi said without turning. "Nika stay. Wil stay. Chel stay. All other, out."

"What about Tripod?" Kaapi asked. Daanir turned to see that she had the cat in her arms. Navi looked up. He nodded.

"Tripod stay."

Chapter Twenty
Aftermath

DAANIR PACED ACROSS the sitting room, looking at the closed bedroom door every time he had to turn.

"Daan, you're going to exhaust yourself. Sit down," Theonus said. He and Nyssa had stayed when the others had left. To support Daan, Theonus had said. He'd keep an eye on things here while the others did what was needed elsewhere, and he'd act as their guard while Antivar went with Mentiras to take all of the servants into custody. He was leaning against the outer door, his arms folded over his chest, the expression on his face hard and cold. "Sit."

"Can't sit," Daanir said. He stopped walking and looked at the door again. "How long has it been?"

"Since you asked last? Not even five minutes. Since they closed the door? Half an hour? Maybe?" Nyssa answered. She sat on the couch, her arms around Naajir and Kaapi. Kaapi was still in her finery, but was sitting as if she were in her usual clothes — shoes off, her knees pulled to her chest, and her hair falling down around her face and shoulders. Her cosmetics were smeared with tears. Naajir's face was expressionless, but his eyes were angry and cold.

"What happens when they find out who did this?" he asked.

"First they have to find out who—"

"The girl who served the tea," Naajir snapped. "She poured from a pot for us. But she gave Uncle a full cup. I saw it. I thought it was strange."

"Did you tell Antivar?" Daanir asked.

"And the Commander," Naajir answered. "They said they'd find her. And find out why. I just want to know what happens next. She tried to kill the king. What's the punishment?"

Nyssa took a deep breath. "It's not pretty. Are you sure you want to know?" She looked up at Daanir. He let out a long breath and nodded.

"You can tell them. They'll see it when we get Ilaris, after all."

Nyssa grimaced. "I'm not sure where it is on the dockyards, but there's something called a Sentence Ring. I'm told that on land, it was in a cove underneath the Palace. When someone is convicted of a high crime, like murder or treason, they're taken to the cove and chained to the ring. Then they're left there for Mother Ocean to claim when the tide came in."

Naajir stared at her. "I... really?"

"Really," Nyssa answered. "And I can't even remember when they last sent someone to the Great Mothers that way."

"I don't think it's happened since Meradon left land," Theonus said. "At least, I've never heard of it being done. But there's a Sentence Ring on the outside of every belowship. If they had to use it, the belowship would surface. The prisoner would be taken out to the ring and chained there. Then... the belowship returns to the deep." He paused. "It's quicker than how they'd do it on land. But I can't say either of them is merciful."

"Good," Naajir said, wrapping his arms around himself. "It shouldn't be merciful. They tried to kill Uncle Jiaan."

Daanir knew that he should say something. Should try to convince Naajir he was wrong. That he shouldn't wish that on anyone, no matter what. But there was no way he could say the words, not when he wholeheartedly agreed with the boy. He started pacing again, only to stop when the bedroom door opened.

Wilaanger and Chel walked out, closing the door behind them. Chel looked asleep on her feet, and Wilaanger looked tired and drawn. For a moment, Daanir's world felt as if it was cracking. He saw Theonus straighten...

"Easy," Wilaanger said. "It's fine. He'll be fine. He's asleep now, and it wouldn't surprise me if Nika and Navi both were as well. They fought the Mothers for him." He leaned against the wall and looked around. "Where's Antivar?"

It took Daanir a moment to find his voice. He coughed, then stammered, "He... he went with Mentiras. They went to go find all the servants. Someone knows something, and they're going to find out who is behind this."

"What was it?" Theonus asked. "It was something in the tea. We've figured that much. Well, Prince Naajir figured that out — he noticed that they gave Tarjiaan a full cup, but that the rest of us were served from a teapot."

Wilaanger nodded. "And did you tell that to Mentiras?"

Naajir nodded. "I told him and Antivar. They said they'd find her."

Theonus turned to Wilaanger. "So... what was it?"

Wilaanger shook his head. "Navi told me, but it's something neither of us have ever heard of. He says that it's from the Empire. Which raises the question of how it got here."

"With one of the refugees?" Daanir said. He grimaced. "That's the most likely vector. But it's also the obvious one."

"Which means it's not likely to be that," Theonus said. "Someone is playing at misdirection, and probably isn't happy that there are so many refugees in the dockyards. They know that the first place anyone will look for an Imperial poison is at a former Imperial."

"And thereby will catch two fish with a single net," Daanir said. "We need to tell Mentiras."

"You're right," Nyssa said. "I can go. At the very least, I should go and let them know that Tarjiaan will survive." She stood up and smiled. "Captain?"

Theonus stepped away from the door. "Be careful out there, love."

She smiled and kissed them, then left. Theonus locked the door after he and leaned against it. "So, now what?"

"Now, we wait. Wait for Tarjiaan to wake, and wait for Mentiras and Antivar to find something." Wilaanger gestured to the door. "Daan, you should go in. He'll want to see you when he wakes up."

Daanir took a step toward the door, then stopped and looked at the couch. Naajir smiled.

"Would you mind if we went to the *Dauntless* with Captain Theonus?" he asked. "We haven't met her yet."

Theonus chuckled. "You're a bit old for me to say I'm babyminding," he teased. "I don't mind, Daan. Ishantar was still onboard when we came for dinner, so they can come with me, and go back to the *Wave Runner* with her when she leaves."

Daanir nodded slowly and turned to Naajir and Kaapi. "Is that what you want to do? You could wait here with me. Play with Tripod. Poke around and pick your rooms. This is where we'll be staying while they work on the *Wave Runner*, after all."

Naajir looked at Kaapi, who shrugged. "Whatever we do, I want to change first," she said. "This... I like being pretty. But it's not practical."

"It's not practical, but we should keep things like this for special occasions," Daanir said.

"Like your dress uniform?" Kaapi asked.

"Exactly. And you looked beautiful, Kaap."

She smiled. "Thank you, Papa. Oona says that she can teach me to do my hair and to do cosmetics, and help me pick things out. She says that it might be a good thing for me to learn, in case there is something special I need to do because I'm part of the royal house." Kaapi stood up, brushing down her skirts, then looked at the closed door and frowned. "My clothes are in the bedroom."

"I'll get them," Daanir said. He opened the door and slipped inside, moving as quietly as he could. Tarjiaan was lying in the middle of the wide bed, one hand resting on his stomach. Tripod was curled on his chest, purring loudly enough that Daanir could hear him. Nika lay on her side next to him, one hand on Tarjiaan's arm. And Navi was curled in a large chair, a blanket spilling off his legs. Daanir stopped long enough to replace Navi's blanket and put another one over Nika, then went and collected Kaapi's clothes. When he came back out, Wilaanger and Theonus were alone in the sitting room.

"Chel went to lie down, and the children went to look at the other bedrooms," Theonus said before Daanir could ask where the others had gone. "How are you doing?"

Daanir shook his head. "I've been trying not to think. If I think, I'll go insane. How close was it, Wil?"

Wilaanger sat down and rubbed his face with one hand. "Closer than I'd like to think about," he admitted. "This... I think he came closer to dying today than he did when the Imps had him."

Daanir whistled softly. "What was it?"

"Ask Navi," Wilaanger answered. "I've never heard of it. But he knew it. He said that he's dealt with it before. It's a favorite for getting rid of a rival, because it's near undetectable, and it doesn't change the taste whatever its in." He paused and shook his head. "Mothers below, I'm tired."

"Go back to the *Wave Runner*, Wil," Daanir said. "Get some rest."

Wilaanger smiled. "You're an optimist to think I can get back to the ship as tired as I am. I'll find a bed in here. There are enough of them. You'll be all right to watch over them?"

Daanir nodded. "I'm awake. And I'm not sleeping until he wakes up, and until there's another someone here to guard." He looked down at himself. "Except I'm unarmed. Not even a saber. Once Theo leaves, if I need to stop someone, I'm going to have to use the metal in the room."

Wilaanger reached into his coat and took out a small force pistol, offering it to Daanir, who stared at him in surprise.

"I never noticed you were carrying," he said, taking the pistol.

"That's rather the point, isn't it?" Wilaanger answered. He slowly got to his feet and held his hand out. "Give me the bundle. I'll give it to Kaapi so she can change." He took the clothes from Daanir and headed down the corridor. A moment later, Naajir came into the sitting room.

"We've picked our rooms," he said. "And Kaapi is changing." He paused and looked down the corridor. "May I ask a question?"

"Of course," Daanir replied.

"I... Kaapi looked so different. But... it was just clothes and face paint!" He paused, then shook his head. "I don't understand why she looked so different."

Theonus chuckled. "May I answer?" he asked Daanir.

"Please," Daanir replied. "Because I have no idea."

Theonus nodded. "Naajir, you've seen Kaapi every day for... what? Months?" He waited until Naajir nodded, then smiled. "You're used to her. This forced you to look at her again, and really see her." He chuckled. "The first time I saw Nyssa dressed formally, I couldn't stop staring. It was like I'd never seen her before."

"That was it!" Naajir agreed. "It was like she was a different person. But still Kaapi." He paused. "I don't understand it."

"You will," Theonus said. "And don't rush it. You have time."
He looked past Naajir. "Ready, Kaapi?"

Kaapi came out of the corridor, dressed in her regular clothes,
her face washed and her hair combed and pulled back into a tail.
She smiled. "I'm ready. Papa, be careful."

"I'll be careful. You mind Ishantar and the Captain." Daanir
walked them to the door and let them out, then locked the door
and let out a long breath. Nothing to do now but wait.

It was the buzzing that woke Tarjiaan — what was that noise?
And there was a weight on his chest... he blinked and opened his
eyes, wondering for a moment where he was. Where his armor was.
He raised his head, and the question about the noise answered by
raising his own head and meowing. Tarjiaan smiled and reached up
to pet Tripod, looking around. He was on the bed on the bedroom
of the royal apartment. Nika was asleep next to him, and Navi was
in a chair, covered by a blanket, also asleep. Tarjiaan frowned and
looked around. His coat was gone, and he was still in his shirt and
trousers. And he had no memory of how he got here. Where was
his chair? Or his armor?

Across the room, Navi jerked, sitting up and opening his eyes.
He blinked, saw Tarjiaan looking at him, and smiled, letting the
blanket slide to the floor as he got up.

"Better?" he asked in a low voice, coming to sit on the side of
the bed. He held his hand out, and Tarjiaan took it, laying back
down.

"I feel fine," he answered. "Tired. Did something happen?" He
turned to look at Navi, who raised one finger, cocking his head to
the side. Tarjiaan closed his eyes and took a deep breath, wondering
what Navi was looking for. He didn't feel sick.

"Better," Navi said. "Wait. Fetch Daanir." He got up and went to the door, opening it and looking out. "Daanir. Come."

Daanir appeared in the doorway, and his obvious tension vanished when he saw Tarjiaan. "You're awake."

"Fine. Is fine," Navi said. He looked out again. "Ivar?"

"Hasn't come back yet," Daanir answered. "And Wilaanger is asleep."

"Good." Navi looked back at the bed and chuckled. "Nika asleep still."

"I'll wake her," Daanir said. "Go get some rest. The second room on the right is available, and close enough that if we need you, you'll hear. I'll tell Antivar you're there if he comes back before you wake up."

Navi smiled. "Thank you." He left, and Daanir closed the door behind him before coming to join Tarjiaan on the bed.

"How do you feel?"

"Confused," Tarjiaan answered. "What happened?"

Daanir took his hand and ran his thumb over Tarjiaan's fingers, not looking up. "We're not sure who is responsible. Not yet. But someone poisoned your cup. Navi recognized it. Wil says it's something he's dealt with before, so he knew what to do." His hand in Tarjiaan's shook. "But he said it was close."

"There wasn't a poison sniffer in the dining room?" Tarjiaan asked.

Daanir blinked. "I... I never thought to look!" He frowned, his eyes closing halfway. "I... yes, there is. And it seems to be working. Maybe... Wil said he'd never heard of it. Maybe the sniffer didn't recognize it because it's not something we see here in Meradon. Navi knew it because it was an Imperial thing."

"He does good work. I feel fine," Tarjiaan said. "Just tired." He rested his hand on Tripod and sighed. "This is twice someone has slipped something into my tea. I don't think I'm going to drink tea ever again." He took a deep breath, thinking about the dinner, about the full teacup that should have been a warning. "Logiri would have slapped me," he said. "For taking a cup that was just presented to me, that I didn't watch being filled. He taught me better than that."

"He taught you?"

Tarjiaan turned and smiled at Nika, who was on her side, propped up on one elbow. "I'm sorry," he said. "For frightening you both. Yes, he did. After the last assassination attempt. He wanted me to know what to look for, how to protect myself if he wasn't with me. I let my guard down, and he's never going to let me hear the end of it. He warned me to be careful, to not take a drink if I didn't see it made, and to not rely on poison sniffers."

"You survived," Nika said. "I think he will forgive you the lapse." She leaned over and kissed him. "It is a very good thing that Navi recognized what was happening, and that he has dealt with this before."

"I'll have to thank him..." Tarjiaan closed his eyes, thinking back to lessons with Logiri. "Ah... what was it? The poison. Did Navi tell you?"

"Navi didn't tell me, and Wil said he'd never heard of it," Daanir answered.

"I think..." Nika paused, sitting up and reached out to stroke Tripod. "It was tears of something."

"Tears?" Tarjiaan repeated. "Tears of the Sunset?"

"Yes, that was it."

"Navi beat Tears of the Sunset." Tarjiaan rubbed one hand over his face. "That's an Antar poison. Logiri told me about that one. He said that it was impossible to detect, not even by sniffer. And it's impossible to save someone once they've had a fatal dose. Which means that Navi is a stronger healer than anyone suspected. And possibly, that Logiri's plan worked."

"What plan?" Nika asked.

Tarjiaan shifted, and Tripod slipped off his chest with a squeak and an indignant look. Tarjiaan chuckled and pushed himself up to a seated position, his back against the headboard. "That's better. This bed is too soft. My back hurts. Now, Logiri's plan. When he was teaching me how to protect myself against his family, he was also teaching me about his family. The Antar build up resistance to their poisons, little by little over years of training. He started to do that with me, for my protection, but when his initial supply ran out, he couldn't get more."

"Wait," Daanir said. "Are you saying he was poisoning you? And you knew?"

"He called it inoculation, and it was with Chel's full knowledge and supervision." Tarjiaan coaxed Tripod into his lap. Petting the cat, he looked around the room. "Where's my armor?"

"In the dining room," Daanir answered. "Theo and I carried you in here. The armor is still sitting at your place at the table."

Tarjiaan smiled. "Well, at least it's comfortable. Tell me what's happening now."

Nika nodded, shifting around on the bed until she was sitting on Tarjiaan's left, pressed against his side. Tarjiaan put his arm around her, then turned to Daanir and held out his other hand. Daanir smiled and took the place on Tarjiaan's right.

"We're reversed," he said as Tarjiaan pulled him closer. "Nika, I'm in your spot."

She giggled. "Is it very strange?"

Daanir laughed. "I'll suffer through it. Now, let me see. Mentiras and Antivar have gone to question the servants, and Nyssa went after them to tell them you were going to be fine. Naajir and Kaapi went to the *Dauntless* with Theo, and will be going back to the *Wave Runner* with Ishantar. Tyva walked Tommen and

Reeshi back to the refugee barracks." He paused, idly reaching out to pet the cat. "I can't think what else."

Tarjiaan nodded. "Any idea what Tir is thinking? Who might have done this?"

"I'm not sure about Mentiras," Daanir answered, "but Theo thinks that it can't be any of the refugees. It's too obvious. He thinks it's someone looking to take you down, and hurt as many refugees as possible while doing it."

Tarjiaan closed his eyes, picturing the people he'd met among the refugees. "I doubt there are any Antar men in the refugee barracks," he said slowly. "They're Imperial nobles. Tyracan by birth. I think almost everyone in the barracks is Lestalti."

"Then how did someone get Antar poison?" Nika asked.

"The same way you'd get anything else you wanted but couldn't get legally — smuggling," Tarjiaan replied. "But this... this means that someone is smuggling from the Empire, from Imperial nobles directly connected to the Emperor. What would they be trading that the Empire would want?"

Daanir grimaced. "Information."

"Exactly." Tarjiaan took a deep breath. "Daan, bring my armor in? I need to get up."

"What happened to waiting until you were cleared?" Daanir asked as he got off the bed.

"I'm not entirely certain that we have the time."

Chapter Twenty-One
Recovery

BY THE TIME TARJIAAN was back in his armor and had washed up, there was someone knocking at the apartment's main door.

"Wait here," Daanir said, taking a pistol out of his coat. He left the bedroom, closing the door behind him. Tarjiaan put his coat back on and started buttoning it, listening. There were no raised voices. No sounds of pistol fire. The bedroom door opened, and Daanir peered inside. "Mentiras is here."

Tarjiaan offered Nika his hand and they left the bedroom together; as soon as Mentiras saw them, he visibly relaxed.

"Your Majesty," he said, bowing slightly. "Praise the Mothers. Where's that healer? I owe him a wealth of thanks."

"You gave him a kitten," Tarjiaan replied. "I think he'll consider that thanks enough."

"It's not nearly enough," Mentiras said. "How are you? Really?"

Tarjiaan smiled. "I'm fine, Tir. What did you find?" He gestured to the couch. "Sit. I want to hear all of this."

"There isn't much," Mentiras said as he took a seat. "We brought in all of the servants we could find, but the girl who gave you the cup has vanished. Antivar is with Rothga, searching her quarters. They questioned the others, and every single one of them swears that they know nothing, and all of them are ready and willing to swear fealty." He sighed and rubbed his hands together.

"And, on my way here, I got a message from Marikaar. Apparently, a team that no one authorized got onboard the *Wave Runner*."

"What?" Daanir blurted.

"They didn't get far," Mentiras assured them. He frowned slightly and shook his head. "Funny thing — they ended up trapped in an empty passage. The blast doors malfunctioned, Marikaar said. He said that he found them when alarms went off, but he didn't say why the alarms went off in the first place."

Tarjiaan fought to keep a straight face. "We'll have to look into that," he said, and saw Daanir bite his lip. Mentiras looked at him, then arched a brow.

"I'm missing something, and I can tell. But it's clearly something you're not ready to tell me, so I'll let it pass." Mentiras grinned. "For now. But... Daanir, Narrick told me that he mentioned something to you about Ishian's friends?"

"Oh, no," Daanir groaned. "The tech team, or the assassin?"

"Possibly the tech team. We're not sure yet. Possibly the assassin, too." Mentiras shrugged. "We'll find out when Rothga gets done with her quarters."

"Where would Ishian have gotten a poison used by Imperial assassins?" Nika asked. "How would he have that sort of access?"

Tarjiaan swallowed. "I think I know," he said softly. "There were rumors... I want to talk to him."

"What?" Daanir gasped. "Jiaan!"

Tarjiaan met his eyes. "Aaranji told me that when Ishian betrayed him, there was talk about him defecting to the Empire, but there was never any proof. That's why Ranji pled clemency for him. But if he was trying to go to the Empire, he may still have contacts."

"Are you saying he's been an Imperial plant? All these years?"

"I'm saying it's possible. And with him exiled out in Station Six, who would ever notice?" Tarjiaan shook his head. "I need to know."

"I'll arrange for guards," Mentiras said. "Tomorrow?"

"As soon as you can," Tarjiaan said. "We need to know soonest so we can close the breach. If Ishian is selling information to the Empire, then there's a possibility that Ilaris already knows we're here. Or he'll find out soon." He turned to Mentiras. "Have Ishian's quarters been searched?"

Mentiras frowned. Then he took an earpiece from his coat pocket and slipped it into his ear. "Rothga? When you're done searching the girl's quarters, go toss Ishian's. Let me know what you find. What? Oh... thank you." He took the earpiece out and sighed. "They found the girl."

"I don't like the sound of that," Tarjiaan said. "Is she dead?"

"From what Rothga says, she may be before the night is over," Mentiras answered. "It appears that when she was caught... she finished your tea. She's in the infirmary."

"In the... where is Navi?" Nika asked. "If we can save her, she can tell us why."

"Navi's asleep. Second room on the left," Daanir answered. He turned toward the corridor. "Navi!"

Tarjiaan heard a thump, then the door opened and Navi appeared as if launched from a cannon. He was rumpled, barefoot, and looked as if he'd been sound asleep five breaths ago. "What?"

"I will explain as we go," Nika said, holding her hand out. "Commander, will you take us?"

"Your Majesty?" Mentiras stammered.

"Go, Tir. Daanir and I will go back to the *Wave Runner*. Meet us there."

Nika turned on him. "You will not!" she snapped. "You will not go anywhere when you nearly died two hours ago! You will wait here!"

"Or I can have Tyva bring the skiff around," Mentiras offered. "I'll comm her as we go."

"Nika, we'll wait for the skiff," Tarjiaan said. He crossed to her, leaned down and kissed her. "I promise. Now go. We'll see you back at the *Wave Runner*. Tir, keep watch on them."

"I'll take care of them," Mentiras promised. "And I'll comm Tyva now." He led them out of the apartment. Tarjiaan closed his eyes and took a deep breath, trying to order his thoughts. He went to sit on the couch, and heard another door open.

"I heard shouting?" Wilaanger said as he came into the sitting room. "What happened?"

"They found the girl who poisoned Tarjiaan," Daanir answered. "But she tried to kill herself when she was caught. Nika and Navi have gone to see if they can save her."

Wilaanger blinked. "I... how long ago did they leave?"

"They just left," Tarjiaan answered.

Wilaanger nodded. "I know where the infirmary is. I'll catch them before they get too far. How are you?"

"I'm fine," Tarjiaan said. "Go save a life."

Wilaanger grinned. "Chel is still here?"

"She hasn't come out," Daanir answered. "I'll tell her where you've gone."

"And keep her with you," Wilaanger added. "Just in case." He went back to the bedroom, then hurried through the sitting room and out. Tarjiaan rubbed his forehead and sighed.

"What are you thinking?" Daanir asked.

"Not entirely certain, to be honest," he answered. "What was that about Ishian's friends?"

"Narrick says that Ishian is charismatic, and that he has friends on the station who either won't believe he'd done the things he's done, or who won't care," Daanir answered. "And those may be the people behind this." He paused, then grinned. "Looks like *Wave Runner* can take care of herself?"

Tarjiaan laughed. "I was trying so hard not to laugh!"

Daanir nodded. "I know. I saw. I'll have to tell her I'm proud of her." He leaned against the wall and tipped his head back. "You're certain you're fine?"

"I'm fine, Daan." Tarjiaan rose and stood in front of Daanir, resting his hands on the wall on either side of Daanir's shoulders. "I promise. I'm fine."

"You could have been not fine," Daanir murmured, resting his hands on Tarjiaan's chest. "Getting to you was too easy."

"I let my guard down," Tarjiaan said. "It won't happen again." He stroked Daanir's beard, running his fingers over the line of the mancer's jaw. "I won't frighten you like that again."

Daanir snorted. "Going to find new and better ways?"

"I could try being boring," Tarjiaan countered.

"I can't see you ever being boring."

Chel woke up just as Tyva arrived with the skiff. Tyva fussed over Tarjiaan while they waited for Chel to get ready, then she took them down to the skiff. As she cast off, Tarjiaan remembered the question he'd asked hours before.

"Tyva, is Owain the carpenter still in the dockyards?"

"He's retired, but yes," she answered. "He still makes instruments and teaches music, but he's not working in the yards. Not unless there's something that needs his artistry." She glanced at them. "New instrument?"

"I need to replace my chitarra," Tarjiaan answered. "And my nephew is a musician. So I wanted to gift him with something. I thought I'd take him to meet one of my teachers."

"Owain was your teacher?" Tyva asked as the skiff slid through the water. Tarjiaan could see the *Wave Runner* in the distance as they came around the side of the dockyards. "I don't think I knew that."

"It's been years, but yes."

"Wait, " Daanir gasped. "Owain, our music teacher from the *Marauder*? I remember he requested the transfer. He's still here?"

"You didn't know?" Tarjiaan asked. "I last saw him the last time we were in drydock, before you were here. But with how long you were here, you never worked with him?"

Daanir shook his head. "Narrick handled working with other craftsmen. When I wasn't actively working on the docks, I stayed in the workrooms, or in my quarters. I kept my head down. And when work started on *Wave Runner*, I didn't work with the higher-level craftsmen." He grinned. "The ones I got were higher level when I was done with them, though. I didn't let them skimp on their work."

Tarjiaan laughed. "You should come with me when take Naji to meet him. He asked me about you when I was here last."

Daanir looked puzzled. "But he never came and found me when I was here. I wonder if he didn't know? But... the mancer rosters are posted. How could he not know?"

Tyva glanced back at them. "Perhaps he thought there was another Daanir?" she suggested. "Or... well, this is Owain we're talking about. He's very... focused. I doubt he could tell you the names of anyone outside the carpenter's shed."

Tarjiaan nodded. "He was always like that. When we go to see him, come with us."

Daanir shrugged. "It depends on what work needs doing. I might be up to my elbows in something, and getting *Wave Runner* back on the water is my first priority."

"I understand." Tarjiaan heard Tripod chirp and chitter on his shoulder, felt the cat's tail lashing against his back. He turned, trying to see what had caught the cat's attention. "What do you see?"

"Birds," Tyva answered, pointing to a small flock of birds on the railings they were passing. "Tripod loves birds. He'd make such a fuss over them when he saw them out the windows."

"How do you have birds?" Chel asked. "We're so far from land."

"I asked the same questions when we first came here," Tyva said with a laugh. "It was the first time I'd ever seen birds that weren't game birds on a farm ship. And they tell me that sometimes, you get birds that stowaway on ships from closer to land. Or that are blown far off course by a storm. They settled here with us." She drew the skiff up to a dock and secured it. "Go and rest, Captain. And if I haven't said it yet, I'm so sorry that dinner was ruined."

"It wasn't, Tyva," Tarjiaan said. He stood up and smiled at her. "I enjoyed everything you made. And I do still want that tea."

"Thought you weren't drinking tea anymore," Daanir muttered.

"I can make my own tea," Tarjiaan answered. "Come on. I want to talk to Marikaar."

Marikaar met them at the top of the gangplank. "Prince-Captain," he said. "We've heard something was amiss?"

Tarjiaan blinked. "From who?"

"The children and Ishantar arrived from the *Dauntless* not long ago. Naajir was fairly close-lipped, but Kaapi said something happened."

"I'll tell you once we're private," Tarjiaan said. "We heard that something happened here? And that our girl can defend herself?"

Marikaar grinned. "She can. Shall we talk in the day cabin?" He smiled and nodded and Daanir and Chel, then looked past them. "Where's the Lady?"

"In the infirmary with Navi and Wilaanger," Tarjiaan answered. "That's part of what we'll be talking about."

"I'll meet you there," Daanir said. "I want to check on Kaap."
He ran his fingers over Tarjiaan's back before walking away.

"Captain, do you need me?" Chel asked.

"I don't think so," he answered.

She nodded. "Then I'm going to go and check on the infirmary.
None of our physicians are onboard, and if there was work going
on, there's the possibility for injuries. I should check on things
there." She bowed her head slightly, then walked away, and
Marikaar fell in next to Tarjiaan as they walked to the day cabin.
Tarjiaan coaxed Tripod off his shoulder and sat down, cradling the
cat in one arm.

"What happened?" Marikaar asked, sitting down.

"Logiri is going to be angry," Tarjiaan answered. Marikaar
blanched.

"Assassination attempt?" he breathed. "How close?"

Tarjiaan leaned back in his chair and took a deep breath.
"Logiri is going to be *very* angry."

"Tarjiaan!"

Tarjiaan grinned, letting Tripod jump down the floor. "Oh,
now that's a tone I never hear from you. I'm fine. And Navi is a
much stronger healer than any of us realized."

"Thank the Mothers for that," Marikaar said. "And... you're
fine?"

"Tired, but fine. The girl who did it tried to kill herself when
she was caught, and is in the infirmary. That's why Nika and Navi
and Wil are there now. Trying to save her life, and trying to get
answers. There are a few theories, but no one truly knows why. And
until we do know why, we're keeping things quiet."

"Because?"

"Because she used an Antar poison, and if it gets out that
someone tried to kill me using an Imperial poison, the refugees will
be targeted. I'm not letting that happen."

Marikaar nodded. "My news seems almost boring by comparison." He glanced upwards. "Are you listening?"

[I am always listening. Captain, are you certain you're well?]

Tarjiaan smiled. "I'm fine, my dear. And I heard that you defended yourself. I'm proud of you."

A long pause. Then *Wave Runner* said, in a very small voice, [You are proud of me? I did a good thing?]

"You did a very good thing, and I'm sure Marikaar told you that?" Tarjiaan looked at Marikaar, who nodded.

"I did tell her, and I told her that you and the Mancer Royal would be very pleased with how she handed them."

[You told me to listen and record, so I did that. I listened and I recorded them, and I heard them talking about their orders to find and destroy my central core. So when they were in the passage, I closed the blast doors on both sides. I thought about evacuating the air, but I decided you would want to talk to them.]

Tarjiaan looked at Marikaar, who looked shocked, "I appreciate that, *Wave Runner*," he said. "I do want to talk to them. I also want to hear the recording."

[Now?]

"Ah... not at this moment," Tarjiaan answered. "Thank you, *Wave Runner*. Have you told Daanir any of this?"

[Yes, and he is examining me, making certain that there was no damage. But I am fine. As you are fine. Someone tried to hurt the both of us tonight. I do not like that.]

Tarjiaan nodded. "I'm not happy about that, either. But we'll find the answers. And Narrick told us over dinner that your comms will be replaced within the next two days. So you'll be able to talk to *Dauntless*, or to us when we're out in the dockyards."

[Thank you!] *Wave Runner* sounded relieved. Tarjiaan glanced at Marikaar, who frowned.

"What's wrong, *Wave Runner*?" Marikaar asked.

[I know I am to be quiet when there are people who are not mine onboard, because we want to be safe. But it's lonely. I can't talk to anyone, because there's always someone around them that I don't know.]

Marikaar sighed. "I'm sorry. I always have my earpiece in. You can talk to me. You do know that, don't you? If I can't talk back immediately, I will as soon as I can."

[Thank you. I miss when it was just our people, and I could talk to whoever I like.]

Tarjiaan nodded. "I understand. We're all having to be more... careful. And more formal. But it's better when it's just us, isn't it?"

[Speaking of just us, the Captain's Lady and the People Mancers have just come onboard.]

"Thank you, *Wave Runner*." Tarjiaan sighed, "Now to find out who's trying to kill me and why."

The door opened, and Nika looked inside. She smiled when she saw them, coming the rest of the way in. Behind her, Navi and Wilaanger followed.

"How do you feel?" Nika asked. Tarjiaan held his hand out to her, drawing her close to his side.

"I'm fine. Tired, but I've been tired for days. Not looking forward to telling Logiri about this. Now, sit and tell me. What did you learn?" He paused. "Did she survive?"

Nika took her place at Tarjiaan's right, while Navi and Wilaanger moved to other, empty seats. Navi sighed and tipped his head back. "Alive," he answered. "Sick. Not awake."

"Mentiras has assigned guards to keep watch over her," Wilaanger added. "We should be able to talk to her in the morning."

Tarjiaan nodded. "And did the search find anything? Is Antivar back?"

Navi shook his head. "No. Soon."

"Navi, go to bed," Nika said. "Antivar will be here soon, and we will send him to join you. You are going to fall asleep sitting there."

Navi smiled. "Slept in worse," he said. He stood up, came around the table to kiss Nika's cheek, then bowed his head to Tarjiaan.

"My brother, you don't need to bow to me," Tarjiaan said. "Go to bed." He waited until Navi left before turning back to Wilaanger and Nika. "Daanir is examining *Wave Runner*. Who defended herself tonight — an unauthorized work crew attempted to reach her central core."

Wilaanger coughed. "I... does this mean that Ilaris has people in the dockyards?"

Tarjiaan shrugged. "Honestly, I'd be more surprised if he didn't," he replied. "I think that we may not move to the royal apartments once the comms are ready. At least, not immediately. Not until we have to."

"That makes sense," Nika said. "If anyone asks, it is because the royal apartments do not have what you need to be comfortable. It is the truth, after all. No one will be the wiser."

Tarjiaan took her hand. "That's very true," he agreed. "Now, the children came back with Ishantar, and Chel is in the infirmary. Once Antivar comes on board, the entire family will be accounted for." He rubbed his thumb over her fingers idly. "The work crew is in the brig. I should speak to them."

"What is a brig?" Nika asked.

"Ah... the shipboard prison?" Wilaanger answered. "And if you're going to go speak to them, go armed and do not go alone."

Tarjiaan sniffed. "Are you going to tell me how to button my coat next?" he asked. "I wasn't planning on going alone. Since Antivar isn't available, I was going to ask Istin to go with me. And Daan."

"Not me?" Nika asked.

"No," Tarjiaan answered. "I am not taking my pregnant wife anywhere near people who recently tried to destroy our ship. I will tell you what they say when I come back." He stood up. "Better to get it done now, I suppose. *Wave Runner*, let Marikaar know I'm going to speak to the prisoners. Is Istin available?"

[First Mate asks that you wait for him. And Second Mate Thistintal is not onboard. However, Girantivar has just arrived.]

"Thank you, my dear." Tarjiaan went into the bedroom and opened a cabinet, belting on his pistol and his saber. When he came back out, Marikaar had just come into the day cabin.

"Captain, you're wanting to question them?" Marikaar said. "I'll come with you."

"Thank you, Marikaar. Where's Istin?"

Marikaar grinned. "That young clerk of Mentiras' invited him to dine. The way she was eyeing him, though? There might be more than supper being eaten."

"Marikaar!" Wilaanger gasped. "The queen—"

"Has heard worse," Nika said. "I hope they have a pleasant night. It is good that someone will."

Tarjiaan nodded. "*Wave Runner*, tell Daanir I'll want him to join us, and ask Antivar if he is able to as well."

"If I am able to do what?"

Tarjiaan turned and smiled, seeing Antivar standing in the open door. "I didn't realize you were there. You've had a long evening. Are you able to come with us and question prisoners?"

"We have prisoners?" Antivar looked stunned. "Why?"

"I'll tell you as we go," Tarjiaan said. He turned to Nika, leaned down and kissed her. "I'll be back as soon as I can."

"Be careful."

Chapter Twenty-Two

Interrogation

DAANIR OPENED HIS EYES and tipped his head back against the wall. "Looks like you're fine, sweetheart. You did a good job protecting yourself."

[Thank you,] *Wave Runner* answered. [The Captain has asked that you join him in questioning the prisoners.]

"Now?" Daanir asked.

[Yes. He has prepared his weapons, and First Mate and Girantivar are with him.]

Daanir nodded. "Then I'd better get moving." He got up from the floor and dusted off his trousers. "Let me know if anything untoward happens. And keep the recording you made of that crew ready for me. I think we'll want it." He left the central core room and trotted down the long corridor, passing crewmen going from duty stations off to their beds, and those coming on duty to replace them. Several of them nodded. Smiled. Waved. All of them got out of his way. He came up into the air, slowing to a walk, panting slightly.

"Winded? A battle companion, winded?"

He glanced over his shoulder and grinned. "Working in the machines works different muscles, Ishantar. You know that."

"Perhaps," she said with a shrug, falling in next to him as he started walking. "But working in the machines is not an excuse to not be in fighting form. You need to practice."

Daanir nodded. "I said something like that when all this started, when I took up being Jiaan's battle companion again. That was the day before our world was upended, and I haven't had a chance to start yet. Are you offering to practice with me? And where are Naji and Kaap?"

"The children said something about studies. And no, I am not offering to practice," Ishantar answered. "And not because I do not want to help you. I have seen the Captain fight, and if you fight as he does, our styles will not fit well together. No, I need to speak to you, as the Mancer Royal."

"Right now?" Daanir stopped and turned to look at her. "Tarjiaan sent for me. Do you need me now?"

"I should also speak to him." Ishantar paused, looking around. "I have been thinking. And I am not needed here. Not while you are here. The *Dauntless* needs a mancer."

"Oh," Daanir murmured. "I... yes. We need to discuss this with Tarjiaan. I don't want you feeling as if I'm pushing you out of your place."

She smiled. "You are not. I know you are not. Daanir, you infused every rivet and bolt of this ship with your love for her captain, and it shows. This ship, it was always meant to be yours. I have enjoyed serving here, and I love the *Wave Runner* dearly. But she was never mine. She never spoke to me, but the moment you came aboard, she welcomed you. She is yours and I've simply been taking care of her for you."

Daanir nodded. "I understand that feeling. I felt that way about the *Chimaera*." He looked around. "It's late enough and I have enough to do that I think this talk won't happen until tomorrow."

"I was not thinking we would have it now," Ishantar said. "I just wanted to let you know that I needed to have the conversation.

Where are you going?" She looked at him intently, then frowned. "You are very serious. Is something wrong?"

"Jiaan is going to question the fake work crew that tried to reach the central core room."

"The what?" Ishantar grabbed his arm. "What happened?"

"You didn't know?" Daanir asked. When she shook her head, he sighed. "Of course. You were with *Dauntless*. Come with me."

Tarjiaan walked out of the day cabin to see Daanir coming towards him with Ishantar in his wake.

"*Wave Runner* said you needed me when you went question the prisoners. I assume that means you want me on your left?" Daanir asked.

"Naturally," Tarjiaan answered.

Daanir smiled. "Officially on your left, I mean. Armed. Let me get my weapons. Don't move." He headed into the cabin.

"Captain," Ishantar said, drawing Tarjiaan's attention. "I missed something? Someone attacked the ship?"

"They tried to. They came on board as a work crew, and attempted to access the central core," Tarjiaan answered. "*Wave Runner* defended herself, and left them alive for questioning."

"Which is where you are going now."

Tarjiaan nodded. "Do you want to come with us?"

Ishantar looked thoughtful, then shook her head, her braids swaying. "No. I would be in the way, and no help to you at all. Captain, I will want to speak to you tomorrow, if I may?"

"Tomorrow?" Tarjiaan studied her. Ishantar seemed unusually nervous — she'd never been one to fidget, and yet, she was shifting from foot to foot, her hands seemingly unable to stay still. "Is something wrong?" he asked. "Did something happen on... oh." He paused, looking out over the dockyards to where he could just see the *Dauntless* moored. "Are you going to ask me to transfer you, Mancer Ishantar?"

She smiled. "You're a very good guesser."

"I know you," he replied. "And you never need to be nervous with me, Ishantar. We'll talk tomorrow. You, me, Daanir and *Wave Runner*. I want to hear your reasoning. For something like this... you've been thinking about it for an age. It's not a snap decision. You don't make snap decisions." He glanced back to see Daanir come out of the cabin, wearing the pistol and saber he'd claimed from the armory. "Tomorrow, Ishantar. Two bells after dawn. We'll talk while we eat."

"Thank you, Captain. I'll go look in on the work done today. Not that I think it needs looking at, but it gives me something to do." She bowed, then turned and walked away.

"She tell you?" Daanir asked. "Why she wants to talk?"

"I guessed, and she confirmed. We'll talk tomorrow over breakfast." He took a deep breath. "I hate this. Ready?" He glanced at Daanir, who nodded. "Marikaar, let's go." He followed his First Mate, hearing Daanir falling in behind him on his left. Antivar followed behind them as they headed belowdecks, going down into the lowest decks. Tarjiaan could feel the walls closing in around him as they entered the brig, and for a moment, regretted not having the prisoners brought to him.

"Jiaan? Your shoulders are up in your ears," Daanir murmured.

"It's close down here." Tarjiaan tried to relax, but somehow, that only made it worse. He could feel the sweat running down his back. Daanir rested his hand on Tarjiaan's shoulder.

"Breathe," he murmured. "The walls aren't moving. There's air. You're fine. You can get out if you need to get out."

Tarjiaan nodded, feeling the weight of Daanir's hand like an anchor, holding him moored against the incoming tide of panic. "I'll be fine. Desensitization starts now, I suppose."

Daanir laughed. "It'll be easier tomorrow. By this rate, you'll be running through the passages by the time we leave."

Tarjiaan smiled, and felt more of the tension fade. Marikaar looked back at them.

"Captain, would you prefer me to bring them on deck?"

"I'm here already," Tarjiaan said. "Let's get this done."

Marikaar nodded. "Here." He gestured, then tapped the lock panel on a door. The solid door slid away, revealing bars and the interior of a featureless room containing four men. "On your feet, you lot!" Marikaar barked. "His Majesty wants to talk to you." Marikaar looked at Tarjiaan. "From left to right," he said. "Galtri, Vemmin, Atelan, and Hargin."

Tarjiaan stepped closer to the bars, looking at the four men. Atelan looked vaguely familiar, but the others were strangers. "Your plans were overheard," he said. "You came onboard my ship with the intent of damaging or destroying her central core. Do you have anything to say for yourselves before I pass judgment?"

"Overheard?" Galtri sputtered. "We didn't say anything to overhear! We're just another repair crew!"

"Play the recording," Daanir said to the air. The speaker in the cell ceiling crackled to life — the voice on the recording sounded very much like Galtri, who turned pale at the sound.

"*All we have to do is set the device in the core, and it's done,*" the recording said. "*He said it was that easy. All systems burned out, and possibly some little explosions. Unlikely to scuttle the whole ship, but enough to keep them here.*"

"Nothing to overhear, you say?" Tarjiaan asked, watching as the man flushed so red that Tarjiaan wondered if he'd faint. "Would you care to change your story?"

"I... Captain—"

"Who sent you, and how did you intend to access the core?" Tarjiaan interrupted.

"The device we were given was supposed to open the door," Vemmin blurted. "Get in, open the door, drop the box inside, get out. That was all." The other men glared at him, and he shrugged. "No reason to hide it. They have us."

"Who gave you the box?" Tarjiaan asked.

"And where is it?" Daanir added.

"I have it," Marikaar answered. "It's secure. I was saving it for you to examine, Lord Mancer."

"That's the Mad Mancer?" Hargin whispered. "He don't look mad."

Tarjiaan glanced at Daanir, who snorted. "Hardly mad. Angry, maybe. You tried to hurt my ship."

"Our ship," Tarjiaan murmured. Daanir snorted again, this time clearly amused.

"Why are you calling the Mancer Royal the Mad Mancer?" Marikaar asked.

"Because he went mad and killed..." Galtri started, and his voice tapered off as he looked at Tarjiaan. "Oh."

"Oh," Tarjiaan repeated. "You believed the lie that Daanir went mad and murdered me, my uncle, and the Physician Royal." He held his arms out. "And, yet, here I am, alive and in front of you. The Physician Royal is alive."

"But... we were told... the Sea Prince was killed, and there was someone pretending..." Galtri asked.

"He's not a pretender. That's Tarjiaan. That's the Sea Prince," Atelan said. "We were lied to, you said? I see it now."

"You were," Tarjiaan said with a nod. "Have we met? You look familiar."

"I was a crèche brat," Atelan answered. "In the royal crèche. You left a year before I was adopted out to the maintenance and engineering crew. But you didn't change much. I know you." He turned to Galtri. "He's the Sea Prince, and we were lied to."

Galtri stared at him for a moment, then looked at Tarjiaan. "Then... what about the king? Is he alive, too?"

"Sadly, no," Tarjiaan answered. "My uncle was murdered by the same person who spread all the lies about Daanir, and who gave me to the Empire as a prisoner. It was Daanir and my wife who saved my life." Tarjiaan folded his arms over his chest, trying to ignore the encroaching walls. "Was it Ilaris who sent that device to you?"

"I..." Galtri frowned. "Ilaris? The Lord Chamberlain? No, Captain." He paused. Frowned. "Your Majesty?"

"Captain is fine for right now," Tarjiaan answered. "Where did you get the box?"

"Galtri, tell him," Vemmin urged. "We're already fucked. Maybe we can be a little less fucked."

Galtri nodded. "Fine. Right. We're part of the regular work crews, the lot of us. And... this older man came to us maybe a month ago? I don't mind his name, but he came to us and told us that we had to act in service to the crown. That the Mancer who killed the king and the Sea Prince was on this ship, and that if it came to the dockyards, we needed to act. That he had someone he was controlling who was pretending to be the Sea Prince, and they were going to take over the dockyards and rise up against the Princess Regent. Said that she was holding the throne for her son, the Sea Prince's heir. On account that he was too young. He's only... how old did he say? I forget—"

"Fourteen," Tarjiaan filled in. "And he's here with us. He escaped from the *Chimaera* with my wife, the Physician Royal and the Mancer Royal." He frowned. "That's the same thing that Theonus was told," he added. "That's the official story, I imagine. Never mind that we have proof otherwise."

"And that man, he gave you the box?" Daanir asked. He held his hands apart. "The box is about so big? Magnets on the bottom, but nothing else? No marks or anything?"

All four men looked surprised. "You know what it is?" Galtri asked. "He wouldn't tell us. Just said it would stop... well... stop you."

"Daan?" Tarjiaan said. "What is it?"

"Shall I go and get it, Lord Mancer?" Marikaar added.

"No," Daanir answered. "I know what it is. Well, I know what I think it is. And I know who gave it to you. And it wouldn't stop me. But it would have hurt the ship." He turned toward the bars. "Mancer Gellan gave you the box right after he got to the dockyards, didn't he? Or just before he left?"

"Gellan! That was his name!" Galtri said. "Who is he?"

"Was," Daanir corrected. "He's dead. And he was a mancer, and a traitor who led a mutiny on the *Dauntless*." He sighed. "That box... the one he used on *Dauntless* must not have worked properly. Or we got to it before it could do any real damage. I'm not sure if it matters which."

"Marikaar," Tarjiaan said. "Message Mentiras and tell him that we have four of his workmen in custody and I'm remanding them to him for discipline. This isn't treason. They've been misled, and I'm not going to fault them for it. And tell him I want Ishian questioned for any involvement. He was too close to Gellan for my liking."

"Ishian would be better off as ballast," Atelan grumbled. "I took a belaying pin to him when he wouldn't stop pestering my wife."

"You didn't hit him hard enough," Daanir muttered, and Atelan grinned.

"I heard that."

"You were meant to." Daanir turned to Tarjiaan. "This lot aren't dangerous, I don't think."

"I agree," Tarjiaan said. "Misguided, as I said. I think we'll see more of that until we get the truth out there. Ah... Marikaar, share the recording with them before you hand them over to Mentiras.

I want them to understand how badly they were used." He turned. "Antivar, once they've seen the recording, see them escorted to station security."

"Yes, Captain." Antivar bowed slightly.

Tarjiaan smiled. "Then go to bed. Your man is waiting for you."

Antivar grinned. "Yes, Captain. If I may, how are you feeling? I haven't seen you since they carried you out."

"Carried you... Captain?" Atelan sounded truly concerned. "Are you well?"

Tarjiaan looked at Daanir, who frowned slightly, then nodded. "Go ahead. Can't hurt."

"True," Tarjiaan agreed. "Tonight, there was a dinner in the royal apartments, organized by Commander Mentiras and his wife. And one of the servants tried to poison me. If not for a young Sualimani healer familiar with Imperial poisons, I wouldn't be standing here."

"Captain!" Atelan gasped. "And... you're sure you're fine?"

"Tired," Tarjiaan admitted. "I wasn't entirely recovered from twenty-three days spent as an Imperial prisoner, so now... this is a setback. Nothing more." He paused, then shook his head. The walls were too close, the air too heavy.

And Marikaar too observant. "I've got this, Captain," he said. "Go above, and take your own advice. Go to bed."

Tarjiaan smiled, turning back to the cell. "Thank you for being honest. If you have any questions, or think of anything else we should know, please tell the Commander."

"Thank you, Captain... your Majesty," Galtri replied, and the others murmured their agreement. Daanir rested his hand on Tarjiaan's back, and they started back up the corridor.

"That went better than I thought it would," Daanir said. "I don't think they're related to the servant, do you?"

"I doubt it," Tarjiaan answered, not paying complete attention to Daanir. They weren't moving nearly fast enough for him, and he picked up the pace slightly. "I think the young woman is more likely just as misguided, but the source is different. If she'd been working for Ilaris, she'd be more likely to have tried to poison you."

"Oh, now that's happy and cheerful," Daanir scoffed. "I'll be having lovely dreams off that thought."

Tarjiaan laughed. "Good. Your nightmares and mine can keep each other company. Let's get above. I'm strangling."

Daanir watched as Tarjiaan relaxed the moment they walked out under the dark sky – he took a deep breath, then let it out slowly.

"I don't think I'm ever going to be able to be in a below-ship again, Daan," he said. "I'm not sure I can. I couldn't breathe."

"You were breathing. You were fine," Daanir said, taking Tarjiaan's hand. He squeezed Tarjiaan's fingers gently. "You did it. This was the first step. To be honest, you did better than I thought you would."

Tarjiaan snorted, walking over to the rail and resting his hands on it. "It feels strange how still we are," he said. "Have you ever been on land, Daan?"

Daanir joined him, resting his forearms on the rail. "Never. My whole life has been belowships, above ships, stations and the dockyard. I've never even seen land." He looked out at the lights of the dockyards. "You said something about being sick?"

Tarjiaan nodded. "For the first few days, yes. The healers said it was something to do with my ears and how I was used to being in constant motion, so it confused my balance. I'm not sure what ears had to do with it, but I didn't argue." He chuckled. "I was too sick to argue. It's going to be interesting for our people. Some of them are like you. They've never even seen land, let alone set foot on it."

"We'll have some who don't want to come back to land, no matter that's been the goal the entire time," Daanir said. "And some who can't adapt to land. But the ships will be there, and they'll be able to stay onboard. We'll still have Meradon below the waves, and we'll still rule the seas." He took a deep breath. "It's hard to imagine a life without the war. I don't know how to live with peace."

"I know. But I want to learn. I want my children to have that. Our children should never have to fear the things that we did. They should never have to worry about attacks making them orphans, or leaving them crippled. I don't want them to even be able to consider that. I want that to be a story we tell them, something that happened a long, long time ago."

"I like that idea," Daanir said. "Let the way we grew up be history, and that's all."

Tarjiaan nodded. "But if we want to get there, first we need to finish here. Which means we need to keep this ship safe." He took his earpiece out of his pocket and put it in. "Marikaar."

"*Captain?*"

"Post guards overnight. No one onboard except for crew, no one approaching the ship on the docks."

"*I'll get that arranged as soon as I'm done with his lot. Go to bed, Captain.*"

"I heard that." Daanir took Tarjiaan's arm. "Come on. To bed with you."

The day cabin was quiet and dim, the lights turned down. Tarjiaan glanced at Daanir, who shrugged.

"Nika probably went to bed," he said softly. "It's been a long day."

"It has been," Tarjiaan agreed. He led the way to the inner door and the bedroom, stepping out of the way so that Daanir could follow him in. Inside, Nika was sitting up in the bed, a book open in her lap, her head bowed. Tripod was pressed up against her leg, curled into a circle.

"Looks like she tried to wait for us."

"She has a habit of doing that," Tarjiaan said. He was smiling, a soft, fond look. "This is how I found her after that drink with Uncle the night of our wedding. It's how I found out she knows how to read."

Daanir nodded. "It seems like so long ago."

"I think we were all different people then," Tarjiaan replied, going to the armor rack. Daanir started getting undressed as Tarjiaan clipped the armor in place and triggered the release; as the armor hissed open, Tripod jerked awake, scrambling to his feet, his back arched. Nika blinked, shaking her head.

"Tripod? What... oh!" She smiled when she saw Daanir, then turned to look at Tarjiaan as he moved from armor to chair. "I did not hear you come in. What did you find?"

"That there are a quite a few gullible people in the dockyards, and Gellan was almost certainly working with Ilaris," Daanir answered, tugging his shirt over his head. "The crew who tried to get to the central core here had the same kind of device that Gellan used on *Dauntless*."

Nika nodded. "What is to be done with them?"

"I've given them back to Mentiras," Tarjiaan answered. "They weren't traitors. They were tools being fed the wrong information. Marikaar is showing them the disc from the *Chimaera*, and sending them back. Now we need to wait for the girl to wake up, and see if she's the same."

"That's a tomorrow problem," Daanir said. "For now, it's time for bed."

"She is no longer a problem," Nika said. "Rothga came to tell us. The girl choked on her own vomit, and they could not save her. We will have no answers from her."

Tarjiaan rolled his chair over to the bed. "Do you think we'd have gotten any answers from her?"

Nika looked thoughtful, then shook her head. "I doubt it, but Rothga may have a theory. She said that they found messages from Ishian in her quarters, and some possessions that they recognized as his. And there was female clothing of her size in Ishian's quarters."

"A lover?" Daanir stretched out on the bed next to Nika. "Someone who blamed Jiaan for Ishian getting arrested? But that doesn't make a lot of sense. He didn't order it. Mentiras did. And it was all because of me, so why poison Jiaan?"

Tarjiaan transferred to the bed and laid down, smiling as Tripod climbed up onto his chest. He reached up to pet the cat and listened to him start to purr. It was soothing, and he fought back a yawn. "Someone will question Ishian and then we'll know. Someone who isn't one of us."

"You do not want to know?" Nika asked. She lay down and rested her head on Tarjiaan's shoulder. On her other side, Daanir rolled toward her, curling against her back and putting his arm over both of them.

"I want to know," Tarjiaan answered. "I'm just not taking on the responsibility of finding out. He's Mentiras' prisoner. Therefore, he's Mentiras' problem. We'll find out when we find out, and not a moment before."

"And until then?" Daanir asked.

"We rest," Tarjiaan answered. "And heal. All of us."

Chapter Twenty-Three
Artifice

TARJIAAN STOOD ON THE docks and looked up at the new solar sails that had only just been completed the day before. For the first time in a long time, *Wave Runner* looked whole, and he hadn't realized how much he'd missed that.

"She looks very fine, don't she?"

Tarjiaan smiled. He'd spent part of every day that they'd been in the dockyards with Kyraath, trying to learn to use his new abilities. Over the past month, he'd grown fond of the old man, who occasionally reminded him of his own father. "She does, Kyraath. She does."

"You'll be leaving soon, then?" Kyraath asked. "Following the *Dauntless*? You've got a traitor to catch, and an Emperor to overthrow."

"We're almost done with everything we needed to do in drydock. Repairs are finished. So are the upgrades. I've gotten an earring for everyone who wanted one and was owed one for the storm. We'll be sending out the broadcast tonight," Tarjiaan said. "And we'll be calling in the fleet. Which mean we'll be leaving in a day or two. There are a few things I need to finish before we go, though. Things I've been meaning to do, but have gotten pushed to the side for one reason or another." He gestured toward the gangplank, and they started walking together. "The most important to me is that I promised my nephew that I'd introduce him to my music teacher while we were at the dockyards. Owain served as a carpenter here, and he's a fine luthier. Naajir needs an instrument of his own, but between my duties, his mancery studies and his lessons, we haven't had time." He looked up at the high clouds. "At least we've finished moving our things back to the ship. The royal apartments are nice, but I'm ready for my own bed."

Kyraath nodded slowly. "I understand that. Mother Ocean, she calls me, but this place? It's not mine. I'm a Delta man, and the tidal flats are more my home than the deep sea." He waved one arm. "I can't get used to so much horizon."

Tarjiaan chuckled. "I felt the opposite the entire year I spent in the Sualimani court. But I do understand. Hopefully, you and the others will be able to go home when we're done."

Kyraath nodded. He looked out over the water, then smiled. "Tell me what you're feeling."

Tarjiaan paused and thought about it. The question was familiar after a month of Kyraath's tutelage. "There's a pod of Great Mothers there," he said, pointing. "And dolphins on the other side of the dockyard."

"You can feel the dolphins?" Kyraath asked. "That's a good range. How many?"

"Mothers or dolphins?" Tarjiaan asked.

Kyraath grinned. "Both."

Tarjiaan grimaced. Splitting his focus to get that fine of an answer hadn't been going well. "There are... seven Mothers. One calf. And the dolphins... they move so fast. Twelve, I think."

"Good. Very good." Kyraath nodded his approval. "And how stands the weather?"

Tarjiaan looked at him. "You know I haven't been at all accurate with weather."

"You'll get better with practice. Well?"

Tarjiaan sighed and closed his eyes, focusing his power on the air around them, testing pressures and winds and vapor, trying to translate that into something more than his first answer, which was "we'll probably have some sort of weather."

Kyraath had not been amused at that answer.

This time, though... he recognized the feel to the air. "Storm," he murmured. "I... I don't think it'll hit us. I don't think the wind is right. But there's a storm out there." He opened his eyes and turned, looking out over the water. Not a cloud to be seen. "I can't see it, but I can feel it."

"So can I," Kyraath said. "Looks like you're a stormwitch, and not a weatherseer. Couldn't really tell before. But now... not a bad skill to have."

"Stormwitch?" Tarjiaan repeated. "You didn't tell me there were differences."

"Because I weren't going to set you up to claim one or the other. I needed to see what you could do." Kyraath nodded once. "Your da was a stormwitch. But his da was a weatherseer."

"Explains why my father had fourteen gold."

"It does," Kyraath agreed. "It does. Now, where are you off to? Music things? Without the cat?"

"I know better than to take a cat into Owain's workshop. Which is where we're going once I find Naajir." Tarjiaan looked up the gangplank. "He and Kaapi left the residence this morning after we ate. They didn't say where they were going, but I know they came to the ship, and I suspect they're with Daanir and Narrick."

Kyraath took his arm. "You're letting them run about untended? After what happened? And your lady, where is she?"

Tarjiaan looked at him and laughed. "Do you think I'm a fool? Since the *Wave Runner's* comms were replaced, we've had eyes on the children anytime they're in the dockyards. The same can be said for me, for Daanir, for Nika, and for everyone else in the royal circle. Even you, old man. So I knew the children are here, and Nika and Navi are both at the infirmary, helping the dockyard physicians." He carefully didn't mention *whose* eyes — Daanir had made the choice to keep *Wave Runner's* awareness a secret known only to her crew. "If anyone so much as sneezes at any of them in the wrong key, we'll know. And there's the added benefit that the children have a lot of honorary aunts and uncles on the dockyards."

"They are popular," Kyraath agreed. "Especially since Tommen started taking them around to help with the other Lestalti folks. They've been raised right, the pair of them. It's good that you're keeping an eye on them."

"To be honest, I'm starting to wonder if it's unnecessary," Tarjiaan admitted. "There's been nothing since that girl made the attempt on me."

"They ever find out why?" Kyraath asked as they started up the gangplank. "I never did hear."

"Rothga told us that she was apparently Ishian's lover, and attacked me to try and get revenge on Daanir. Which Ishian denies, even though the girl left proof in her quarters. He also denies any knowledge of the poison or how she got it. He blamed the refugees, which we were expecting, and which we warned Tommen about. He and his people cooperated completely with a search, and there's no evidence that any of them brought it in."

"Which means... what?"

"Well, all the we can say for certain is that they aren't involved. Anything more will need a confession from Ishian, and he isn't talking. Not to Rothga, and not to me. So he sits in the brig, and Mentiras will deal with him after we're away." At the top of the gangplank, Tarjiaan stepped to the side and looked around, taking his earpiece out of his pocket and putting it on.

[Good morning, Captain,] *Wave Runner* said in his ear.

"Good morning," he replied. "Location of Naajir and Kaapi? In the workshop?"

[Yes.] There was a long pause before *Wave Runner* continued, [and they told me to ask you not to go below. They are in the middle of working. Do you need them?]

"Please tell Naajir that I'm making good on a promise, if he is available to join me. I want to do this before the broadcast, just in case we have to leave quickly."

[He will be with you shortly.]

Tarjiaan nodded and turned back to Kyraath. "He's on his way. So what about you, Kyraath? You're welcome to come with us when we leave, but I'll understand if you want to stay on the dockyards."

"I hain't made up my mind yet," Kyraath answered. "Been thinking of asking if I could stow away, seeing as you still need teaching. But at the same time, that just takes me further away from the Delta. I'm feeling that I need to find a way back home."

"Once it's safe—"

Kyraath snorted. "I challenge any Imp to last a day in the Delta. It's the safest place on land... if you know what you're about." He grinned and nodded. "There they are. Those two are inseparable, aren't they?"

Tarjiaan turned and saw Naajir and Kaapi coming toward them. "They are." He smiled as they came within earshot. "Am I allowed to know what's going in in the workrooms?"

"No," Naajir answered, and laughed. "And that's not from me. That's from Uncle Daan. There's something we need to do?"

"I owe you an instrument, and I want to make certain I can fulfill my promise before we leave." Tarjiaan grinned at the stunned look on Naajir's face. "Did you think I forgot?"

"I'm the one who forgot!" Naajir admitted. "I... we're going now?"

"I'm not certain how much time we'll have once the broadcast goes out," Tarjiaan said. "We may have to leave very quickly. So now is the best time."

"And possibly the only time," Naajir added. "Kaap, do you want to come with us?"

Her nose wrinkled as she frowned. "I... I should stay and help Papa."

"Is Narrick not here?" Tarjiaan asked.

"No, he said that he's pretty much finished, so he's got some other things he needed to do in the dockyards," Kaapi answered. "We're working on something else. I think Papa is going to have dinner with Mancer Narrick after the broadcast. I don't think he expects us to have to leave immediately."

Tarjiaan nodded. "I hope I'm wrong about that. When I see Nika, I'll tell her that we'll be alone for dinner. Unless Daan has already told her."

"We haven't seen Aunt Nika since breakfast," Naajir said. "How are we going? Where are we going?"

"In reverse order? We're going to the carpenters sheds, and we're walking. It isn't far. Kaap, tell your father where we'll be for me?"

She smiled. "I'll tell him. I can't wait to see what you get, Naji." She turned and headed back the way they'd come. Naajir looked down at himself.

"Am I presentable?" he asked. "I can go change."

"You're fine, Naji," Tarjiaan assured him. "Owain never was one for ceremony. Let's go."

Kyraath followed them down the gangplank, then left them as they set out across the dockyards. Tarjiaan took a deep breath and tried to banish his growing nerves as they headed into the maze of workshops, metal shops and storerooms. His stomach felt as though there were fish swimming circles in it. Tonight he would face his people... and he would see what came of it.

"What will the broadcast be?" Naajir asked. "I mean... what do I do?"

"You'll stand next to your aunt, and you'll be seen. That's all," Tarjiaan answered. "Now, you will need to dress for that, but Tyva arranged for a formal uniform for you."

"Is that why she needed my measure?" Naajir asked. "I was wondering. No one explained." He tucked his hands behind his back. "Uncle, what happens next?"

"That depends on the reaction to the broadcast tonight," Tarjiaan answered. "We'll either have a fleet coming to ally themselves to us, or we'll have a fleet coming to try and kill us. In the first case, we'll lay a plan to go and deal with Ilaris. In the second... we'll make a run for Sualiman. Queen Ysnia will take us in, I'm certain." He paused, thinking of Logiri. Of Aanaji. "I hope it won't come to that. But I can't swear that it won't, so the plans are laid."

Naajir nodded. "Land... I don't know. I don't know if I actually believe that there is land."

Tarjiaan laughed. "I think at your age, I felt the same way. Then I lived there for a year. It was... odd." Tarjiaan pointed. "That's where we're going."

Their destination was a house that seemed out of place among the workshops and storage areas of the dockyards. Owain insisting on living near his shop, and the previous commander of the dockyards had just given in and accommodated him. Tarjiaan stopped at the door and knocked, hearing nothing from inside.

"Is he home?" Naajir asked softly.

"I don't know," Tarjiaan answered. He was about to knock again when he heard someone inside.

"I hear you!" The door opened, and a familiar, wizened old man stood inside. He looked Tarjiaan up and down, then up again.

"Jiaan?" he croaked. Then he smiled. "I heard you were in. Was wondering if you'd come and see me. Come in!" He stepped back, then looked past Tarjiaan. "And... who is this?"

"Master Owain, this is my nephew, Naajir," Tarjiaan said. "He's a musician, too, and I promised him an instrument of his own."

"Well!" Owain laughed. "That would make you... Aanaji's boy, yes?"

Naajir blinked. "Yes, sir."

"Come in! Come in! Tell me, lad, what do you play?" Owain led them into the house, which Tarjiaan knew was deeper than it looked — Owain's workshop was visible through a door on the far side of the room.

"I play flute, viol, small lute and light-harp," Naajir answered. "I only just started light-harp. And I want to learn double neck, but my hands aren't big enough yet."

Owain nodded, then stepped back, clearly studying the boy. Tarjiaan remembered being the subject of that intense gaze, and knew what Owain was going to say next. "Hold your arms out."

Naajir nodded, then stretched his arms out to the sides. Owain walked around him, then took one of his hands. "Spread your fingers." He studied Naajir's hands, then nodded again. "Two years. Maybe three. But you'll have the span for it. No calluses. Why?"

"When my mother and I were recalled from the *Allegiant* to the *Chimaera*, we left everything behind. All of my instruments, all my recordings. They're all still on the *Allegiant,* and none of them were ever new." He smiled shyly. "I've never had a new instrument before."

"You can learn just as well on an old instrument," Owain said. "What are you looking for today? I don't have flutes, mind. That wasn't ever an instrument I made. But viol? Small lute? Those I have. And what about you, Jiaan?"

"My small lute was lost on the *Marauder*, and my chitarra was smashed in a storm. I was hoping to replace at least the chitarra," Tarjiaan admitted, and braced himself for the verbal storm he was expecting. Owain arched a brow at him, and his smile faded.

"Smashed in a storm?" Owain repeated, and folded his arms over his chest. Almost automatically, Tarjiaan tucked his hands behind his back and lowered his head. Owain burst out laughing. "Oh, stop that!" he chided. "You're not ten anymore. I'm not going to dress you down. And that's not like you, my boy. So what happened?"

Tarjiaan relaxed. "I'm not entirely certain," he answered. "I put her away in the cabinet, same as my other instruments. I closed the cabinet and locked it, but when I got back to the day cabin, the cabinet door was open and my chitarra was in pieces. It was a rough storm, but only the chitarra fell out."

"The storm winds wanted that chitarra, then," Owain said. "Come to the back. Both of you." He turned and led the way into the workshop, which smelled of wood shavings, resin, lacquer and glue. One wall was all racks of tools, and storage frames full of various woods, all ready to be remade into instruments. The workbench stood in the center of the room, underneath lights that were currently off. On the wall opposite the tools was another door, and Owain opened it and gestured for them to enter.

"If you take something down," he said as they walked through the door, "put it on the table and leave it for me to put away."

Tarjiaan nodded, letting Naajir go first into the room so that he could see his nephew's reaction. Naajir took four steps in and stopped, staring, his mouth hanging open.

"I... I've never seen so many!"

Owain chuckled and followed Tarjiaan into the showroom. "I've been making them a long time, lad. Now, viols are there. Small lutes are here, and chitarras are there."

Naajir turned to look at Tarjiaan. "What can I pick?"

"What do you want?" Tarjiaan asked in response. "What's your favorite?"

Naajir smiled. "Viol."

Owain gestured towards the instruments. "Be my guest."

Naajir walked toward the racks of viols, studying each of them without touching them. Owain joined Tarjiaan in watching him.

"He reminds me of you at that age," the old man murmured. "Is he good?"

"I haven't heard him yet," Tarjiaan admitted. "He told me that my sister encouraged him to follow in my footsteps."

"You haven't put an instrument in his hands to hear him?" Owain sniffed. "Really, Jiaan!"

"Owain, in the past two months, I've almost died twice. I've been a little distracted."

Owain turned to look at him. "Twice? I heard about the girl here. The one who had her head turned by that piece of garbage from Station Six. When else?"

"When I was an Imperial prisoner," Tarjiaan answered. "If it weren't for my wife and my battle companion, I wouldn't be here now."

"Battle companion. Where is Daanir? He's with you again, I know. And I know he was stationed here for a time. Never did find out why."

"Daan is on the *Wave Runner*, and doing something that I'm not allowed to know," Tarjiaan answered. "As to why he was here, it's a long story. But he's with me again, and that's what is important. He was curious, though. Wondering why you never seemed to meet when he was stationed here."

Owain snorted. "Because anyone outside the mancer sheds who even looked sideways at that boy got sent off with more than a warning, and I'm too blasted old to wrangle with Narrick."

"What does that mean?" Tarjiaan looked over at Naajir, who had taken one of the viols down. The boy was focused on the instrument, but Tarjiaan lowered his voice anyway. "Owain, what do you mean?"

"You ever seen a ship cat queen with only one kit? That was Narrick with Daanir," Owain shrugged. "I told him I knew the boy from the *Marauder*, but it didn't make any difference. No one outside the mancer sheds was allowed near him."

"That's... I wonder if Daan knew?" Tarjiaan considered it — knowing that Daanir had escaped near imprisonment on Station Six, he could understand Narrick wanting to protect him. But this seemed excessive. "I'll ask him when I see him."

"And tell him to come see me," Owain said, then raised his voice, "Bows are in the drawer under the rack, lad."

Naajir looked at them and smiled, then took a bow from the drawer. He set the viol down, rosined the bow, then picked the viol up and tucked it under his chin, drawing the bow across the strings. His smile broadened as he started playing, and Tarjiaan fought back a smile.

"That's one of yours, isn't it?" Owain whispered.

"It is, and I don't know if he knows that," Tarjiaan answered.

"Go on and pick a chitarra. Join him."

Tarjiaan went to the instrument racks and studied the chitarras, listening as Naajir played. He had a good touch, and Tarjiaan was fairly certain that this arrangement was new — had Naajir arranged the song for viol? He'd have to ask. He noticed one chitarra on a low rack and bent to pick it up — a beautiful instrument of pale blond wood, with inlays of some darker wood in near crimson red. He leaned against a cabinet and carefully tuned it, then played a single note that rang through the room like a bell.

"Ah, that one. She's got a big voice for a chitarra," Owain said. "She's taking a liking to you?"

"I think she is," Tarjiaan answered.

"Then bring them up to the sitting room, so we can hear them together. I'll get out my hammers."

"You play hammers?" Naajir asked. "My mother showed me, but I didn't have a chance to start learning them."

"Aanaji plays hammers?" Tarjiaan asked. He followed them out to the sitting room. "I had no idea."

"She's good. And she's fast," Naajir answered. "It's fun to watch her. What should we play?"

"Do you know *Sailing Homeward*?" Owain asked, setting the string board of his instrument against his legs and picking up the hammers. "Your grandmother wrote that one."

"I know it," Naajir answered.

"Good. Very good. Jiaan, you start."

Chapter Twenty-Four
Summoning

NAAJIR SPENT THE REST of the day in such a good mood that it could almost be described as giddy. He thanked Owain four times, thanked Tarjiaan five, and talked all the way back to the *Wave Runner.*

"That was a nice technique," Tarjiaan said when Naajir finally stopped to breathe at the top of the gangplank. "Tucking the viol into your arm so you could sing. Did you think of that?"

"Mama did, and my vocal teacher was amused by it, so we tried it." Naajir hugged the viol case to his chest. "I want to go show Kaapi. May I be excused?"

"Go on. But don't be long. We have to go to the residence to get ready for the broadcast." He watched the boy run off, and turned toward the day cabin. He didn't bother to put his earpiece on — he could talk freely to *Wave Runner* once he was inside. He opened the door and saw Nika at the table, her back to the door, looking down at something in her hands. She turned in her chair as the door opened, dropping what looked like a bundle of green and gold cords. Underneath her chair, Tripod immediately pounced on them, dragging them away.

"Jiaan!" she said. "I was not expecting you."

"I wasn't expecting you to be here, either," Tarjiaan said. "I thought you and Navi were going to be at the infirmary all day."

281

"I came back to take a nap, and I wanted to work on... something." She looked down at the bundle, then sighed. "I wanted it to be a surprise."

"Considering I don't know what you're doing, it still is." He set the chitarra case on the table and went after the cat, rescuing the bundle from him. "Tripod, go play with Gossamer." He brought the cords back to the table and gave them to Nika. "It's still a surprise. Unless you want to tell me."

She took down at the bundle, then carefully smoothed it out on the tabletop, revealing an unfinished knotted band perhaps three fingers wide. Tarjiaan immediately recognized the knotting pattern.

"A martial collar? Nika, you're making a collar for me?" He dragged his chair closer and sat down. He was grinning like a fool and he knew it, but it didn't matter. The only person who mattered was his wife. "That... I didn't think you'd make one for me!"

"You like it?" She smiled shyly. "I asked Ishantar to show me how to make one. And it is a cuff, not a collar. You said that a collar might undermine your authority with your men."

"My love, I will happily wear whatever you give me," Tarjiaan said. "May I look closer?"

She nodded and handed the band to him. "Ishantar said that you would wear it on your left wrist."

Tarjiaan nodded, running his fingers over the intricate knots. "This is beautiful. I can't wear to wear it." He smiled and handed it back to her. "Thank you."

She smoothed it out on the table again. "I will make one for Daanir as well, but I am not certain of the colors."

"May I help choose? And do I have to wait until his is done?"

She smiled. "Yes, please. And yes. I do not want to spoil the surprise for him by giving you one first. You will get it on the same day, and you must keep the surprise." She pointed at him. "Promise!"

Tarjiaan nodded. "I promise." He reached out and caught her hand, kissing her fingers, then her palm. She ran her nails over his beard, making him shiver.

"We do not have time, do we?" she murmured.

"Unfortunately, no."

She sighed and rolled the unfinished cuff up, tucking it away into a pouch. "Will you show me your new chitarra?"

He smiled and got up, going around the table to open the case. He took the chitarra out and brought it back to his chair, sitting down and gently strumming the strings. She reached out and ran her finger over the wood, as gently as when she stroked the head of her kitten.

"Is it hard to learn to play?" she asked.

"No, but it does take time," Tarjiaan answered. "Do you want to learn?"

Nika nodded, then frowned. "I do not know when we will have the time for me to learn. But I do want to." She folded her hands in her lap. "Did Naajir find an instrument to his liking?"

"He did, and I'm certain you'll hear all about it at supper. Which, by the by, Daanir will be taking with Narrick," Tarjiaan answered. He got up and untuned the chitarra, then put it away in its case. The case went into the cabinet, and he checked the lock as he closed the door. He turned back and held out his hand. "Shall we?"

Exactly as he'd expected, Naajir spent the entire trip to the residence talking about his new viol and playing with Tarjiaan and Owain and how he hoped to learn hammers once he mastered light harp. Tarjiaan listened with only half his attention as the skiff slid through the water.

"You might as well already be in Sualiman," Daanir said, sitting down next to Tarjiaan. "Fretting over the broadcast? It'll be fine."

"No, thinking about something Owain said," Tarjiaan answered. "He knew you were here in the dockyards. He says Narrick wouldn't let him see you."

"He said... what?" Daanir frowned. "That... that's strange. Why would he say that?"

Tarjiaan shook his head. "From what Owain said, Narrick wouldn't let anyone outside the mancer sheds anywhere near you."

Daanir's frown deepened. "That's... maybe it was to protect me? Remember, he suspected—"

"I don't know, Daan." Tarjiaan closed his eyes. "It'll be fine, you said."

Daanir took his hand. "It will be fine. We'll get that broadcast out tonight, and what happens next happens."

Tarjiaan nodded, opening his eyes and watching as Tyva guided the skiff up to the slip. "I'm glad we're back to the *Wave Runner*. And Daan, that bathing room is excessive!"

"It is not!" Daanir protested. "You needed the room for your chair. And... well..." He smiled and glanced over at Nika. "We all like having a large tub."

"We do," Nika agreed, turning toward them and smiling. "I do like the new bath, Daanir."

"You're outnumbered, Jiaan," Daanir teased. "Now stop worrying. Things will work out just fine." He paused. "Do I have to be in the broadcast?"

"Yes. You need to be at my shoulder, to show that Ilaris is lying about everything. And you're going to be acknowledged as our consort tonight before the entire kingdom."

Daanir ran his fingers through his hair, laughing. "I hadn't thought about that. My turn to be nervous?"

Tarjiaan squeezed his other hand. "We've been through worse. We're still here."

"We are. Which means we need to talk to the kingdom tonight."

"I need to talk to the kingdom tonight. You need to stand there and look good." Tarjiaan grinned at him. "Want to trade?"

"No!" Daanir laughed. "No, this is all on you, Your Majesty." He raised Tarjiaan's hand to his lips and kissed it. "But we'll be here to help."

They had decided on the sitting room of the royal apartments for the backdrop of the broadcast, and the room was full of recording equipment and things that Tarjiaan wasn't entirely certain of. They didn't look like the recorders he was used to, but he'd never done something on this scale before. He also didn't have time to ask questions — Narrick shooed them away to get ready, telling them that they would proceed as soon as everyone was prepared.

Now, Tarjiaan stood in front of the mirror in the bedroom, missing Logiri as he checked the fit of his coat. It was oddly jarring to see the royal gold Kraken badge on his breast, the extra braid and trim at his throat and cuffs.

"You are going to break the glass if you keep scowling that way."

Tarjiaan blinked and looked at Nika's reflection. "I didn't realize that I was."

"You are. What is it?"

"This." He touched the Kraken. "The Sea Prince doesn't wear the Kraken, and I haven't yet gotten my mind around the fact that this is mine now. That all this gold is mine now."

"It is much more ornate than your coat when we married, or for the dinner," Nika said, coming up to stand next to him. She wore a formal uniform, but her ornamentation was all gray pearls and silver. "And this is nothing that I have seen anyone wear."

"That's because Meradon hasn't had a queen since before I was born," Tarjiaan answered. He looked at himself in the mirror again. Oona had worked her magic once more, and he actually looked presentable. Logiri would have approved...

"You are scowling again."

Tarjiaan sighed and turned away from the mirror. "Missing Logiri. All of this? He'd have loved it. The pageantry and being able to make a fuss over me? He loved that, and he never got to do it very often. Oona is good, but..."

"But she is not Logiri." Nika took his hand. "I understand." She turned as the bathing room door opened and Daanir came out, his shirt hanging open and untucked. He looked at them and whistled.

"Oh, you both look wonderful!" he said. "The Queen's pearls... I've seen pictures. They look good on you, Nika."

"Thank you."

"You should hurry up," Tarjiaan added.

"I will go and see if Naajir is ready," Nika said. She tipped her head back, and Tarjiaan recognized the invitation, leaning down and kissing her. She smiled, went to collect a kiss from Daanir, then left the room.

Daanir sat down and pulled on his newly-polished boots, then rose, buttoning his shirt and tucking it in, buttoning his trousers and pulling up his braces, then putting on his surcoat. He picked up his coat and took Tarjiaan's place at the mirror, fastening buttons and cinching his belt. He reached up and touched the Mancer Royal badge, then walked over to where his sheathed saber rested on the bed. He picked it up, clipped it to his belt, then drew himself up and looked at Tarjiaan.

"Your Majesty, shall we?"

Tarjiaan walked out of the bedroom first, and Daanir fell in next to him as they entered the sitting room. Narrick was standing with his back to them, looking over one of the pieces of equipment. Mentiras was facing them, and looked up as they came in. His eyes widened, and he bowed.

"Your Majesty."

Narrick looked over his shoulder, then straightened, turning to face them and bowing as deeply as Mentiras had. "I apologize," he said. "I didn't hear you come out."

"Apology accepted," Tarjiaan said. "And I told you, Tir. You don't have to call me Your Majesty. I need some people around me who remember who I am when I'm not behind the Kraken."

Mentiras smiled. "Of course, Jiaan. We're almost ready for you. And if you don't mind me saying so, but Her Majesty looks very fine."

"Thank you, Commander," Nika said as she came back into the sitting room. Naajir followed her, looking uncomfortable in his uniform.

"Naji?" Daanir said. "What's wrong?"

"Nervous," Naajir said. "This is... the most official thing I've ever done."

"All you need to do is stand next to your aunt and let yourself be seen," Tarjiaan said. "I'm the one doing all the talking today."

"Are you ready?" Narrick asked. He gestured to a chair set up in the center of the room. "That's where you'll be."

Tarjiaan nodded and sat down, looking over his shoulder as the others arranged themselves around him — Daanir on his left, Nika and Naajir on his right. He took a deep breath and turned to face forward.

"Do you have notes?" Narrick asked. Behind him, Daanir snorted.

"Notes? Jiaan doesn't need notes."

"I'm fine," Tarjiaan said. "And he's right. I don't need notes." He settled himself in the chair, took a deep breath, and forced himself to relax. "I'm ready whenever you are."

Narrick arched a brow, nodded, and turned to the machines. "All right. Do you see the green card on the top of the monitor? That's where you need to look. I'll start the recording in five... four... three... two... one!"

Tarjiaan focused on the green card and counted to five before beginning. "People of Meradon, hear me. I am Tarjiaan, son of Taarik and his wife, the Princess Aajinisa. I come before you today accompanied by my wife, the Princess Ysnika, by my battle companion, the Mancer Royal Daanir Meranas, and by my heir, Prince Naajir. You have likely heard reports of my death at the hands of the Mancer Royal. You have likely heard reports that he went mad and murdered me, along with my uncle, our beloved Sea King Ikaanaji, and the Physician Royal Wilaanger. And yet, here I am, alive and well, and with the Mancer Royal on my left where my battle companion belongs. Unfortunately, while I am alive and well, the reports of my uncle's death are true. He was not, however, murdered by my battle companion. People of Meradon, my uncle the king was betrayed and murdered by the Lord Chamberlain, Ilaris Meranas. Ilaris poisoned my uncle and drugged me, handing me over to an Imperial ship as their prisoner. If not for the efforts of my wife, my battle companion, and the crew of the *Wave Runner*, I would not be here to bring you this truth." He paused and looked up at Nika, who had rested her hand on his shoulder. Then he turned his attention back to the green card. "I do not ask you to take my word for this. There is proof, a recording that was smuggled out of the royal belowship at great risk. I have seen this recording, and I warn you that it is disturbing." The monitor on which the green card was resting lit up, and the recording started to play once more. Tarjiaan sat silent as he watched, as he listened to his sister's confession, and as the screen went dark, he took another deep breath and resumed his speech.

"I do not know if my sister still lives. I know that she risked everything to make certain that this recording and her son reached a safe harbor. I know that Ilaris is a traitor to the crown and to the people of Meradon. And I know that I must now take up the Kraken, a duty I did not expect to fall to me for many years." He paused, reaching up to touch the Kraken badge. "People of Meradon, as the Sea King, I summon to join me all ships who are true to Meradon and who believe in the great promise that we would one day walk the shores of our ancestral home. We will remove the traitors from our waters, and restore peace to Meradon below the waves. And once loyalties are assured, we will join forces with Sualiman and Lestalt and finally take back our homeland. My people, the Empire is falling. The Imperial Navy is no more, and there is war on land. The time to retake Meradon is at hand." He slowly got to his feet. "My people, when first my uncle Ikaanaji led our kingdom to safety and established Meradon below the waves, he swore to the Great Mothers that we would once more walk on land, that Meradon would once more spread from the Delta to the desert, and from the mountains to the seas. He died with that promise unfulfilled. Today, I take up the Kraken, and I take up that sacred promise. The time to strike is now, my people. But first... we must clean the rot from our own ship." He held his hand out to Nika, bringing her forward and putting his arm around her shoulders. He paused, looked at Nika, then looked back at the green card. "The people of Meradon are, in truth, the Heart of the Sea. I know we have been living with war for so very long. For some of us, it is all we have ever known, and we thought that it was all we ever would know. We have held the promise of peace close for a long time. Now, however, we can see the end. Peace is there, and if you believe as I do that we can win it, if you would follow us, find us at the coordinates attached to this message. Proceed at your top speed, and if you encounter the *Chimaera*, do not engage. There may still be hostages onboard. One of those hostages is my sister, the Princess Aanaji, and another is the rightfully born King of Lestalt, who is my wife's father." He looked at Nika again, then smiled, suddenly both more tired and more hopeful than he'd been in a long time. "Safe journey to all of you, and may the Great Mothers protect us all. Good night."

Silence, until Narrick finally spoke. "Got it. Please tell me that you did not just pull that speech entirely out of the air?"

"Of course not!" Tarjiaan protested, sitting back down. "I thought about it beforehand."

Daanir snickered. "Now ask him how long beforehand he thought about it."

Narrick frowned slightly. "What? All right. How long?"

Tarjiaan grinned. "I started when I put my coat on, and finished when I sat down."

Narrick groaned and shook his head. "Right. Fine. Daan, stay and help me with sending this out. Then I promised you supper." He looked around and smiled. "Naajir, would you like to help? You've got a good touch."

Naajir looked startled. "I... may I?" He turned to Tarjiaan. "Uncle, may I stay?"

Tarjiaan smiled. "If you'd like. I'll tell Kaapi where you are."

Naajir frowned slightly. "I don't want her mad at me because I'm working here and she isn't. Maybe I should go back."

"We can send for her," Narrick suggested. "If that's fine with you, Daanir?"

"Of course," Daanir said. "I'll comm the ship while we get that broadcast sent. Now, we're not using the repeater? We're focusing it through the *Wave Runner's* comms?"

"The new comms are the most advanced ones we have, currently," Narrick answered. "And I added amplification that makes them stronger than the repeater—"

"I was wondering why you did that...."

The conversation got more technical, and Tarjiaan led Nika back into the bedroom, sitting down on the bed and groaning.

"That went very well," Nika said. "You really did not plan that in advance?"

"I had an idea of what I wanted to say, but no more than that," Tarjiaan answered. "I'll comm Tyva for the skiff once we're changed. Then..." He reached out and took Nika's hand, tugging her closer. "What would you say to a quiet night in bed? Just you, me and the cats?"

She smiled. "That sounds lovely."

By the time they had washed up and changed, the sitting room was empty. Tarjiaan looked around, surprised. "He left without saying goodbye."

"I imagine he will be quite contrite when he comes in later," Nika said. "We took longer than I thought... unless that's him?" She added as someone knocked on the door.

The door opened, and Tyva came in, followed by Rothga. They both looked worried. "Your Majesty, we've had some excitement," Tyva said. "I want to get you back to your ship as soon as possible."

"Tyva, what's wrong?" Tarjiaan asked.

"We're not certain how, but somehow, Ishian's escaped the brig. We're searching for him now. He can't have gotten far." She looked past them. "Where's the Mancer Royal?"

"He's having supper with Mancer Narrick tonight, and Prince Naajir is with them. Kaapi is supposed to join them." Tarjiaan pulled his earpiece out of his pocket. "*Wave Runner*, do you hear me?"

[I hear you, Captain.]

"Is Kaapi still on board?"

[She just left with Girantivar, Captain. Mancer Narrick sent a skiff to pick them up. Is there something wrong?]

"Possibly. Monitor the station signals and wait for further orders." He took out his earpiece and put it away. "Kaapi's on her way, and she has an escort."

"Then let's get you back to the ship." Tyva gestured, taking them down to the skiff. Rothga saw them off, then hurried away from the dock as they cast off. Tarjiaan frowned, then put his earpiece back in.

"*Wave Runner*, let Daanir know what's happening," he said.

[Right away, Captain.]

"Your Majesty, the speech was wonderful," Tyva said. "We all watched it." She waved at another skiff, and Tarjiaan heard a familiar voice. He laughed and waved back at Kaapi and Antivar.

"Have a good evening!" he called, before turning his attention back to Tyva. "The broadcast went out?" He looked around, then wondered why. It wasn't as if the fleet was going to just appear! "How soon do you think we'll hear any response?"

"We've already heard from the *Dauntless*, from the *Gallivant*, and from the *Endeavor*." Tyva smiled. "All three have sworn to follow the King, and are heading for our location. And only one of them knew ahead of time."

"That's good," Tarjiaan said. He yawned and looked up at the darkening sky. "Supper and sleep, I think. Before things get even more interesting."

The waters were calm, and they disembarked near the *Wave Runner* and walked up the gangplank to find a quiet ship and Marikaar waiting for them.

"They'll come," Marikaar said, looking satisfied. "They'll definitely come."

"There are three underway already."

"Good!" Marikaar smiled, then nodded. "Go to bed, Captain. You're looking done in. I'll ask Aranti to bring around something for you."

"Thank you, Marikaar."

The day cabin was dark and quiet, and Tarjiaan lit lamps while Nika went through the bathing room. He sat down in his chair and yawned, tipping his head back. Supper and sleep was the plan, but maybe sleep and then supper would be a better order...?

An alarm jolted him to startled awareness, and he jumped to his feet. "Report!"

It wasn't Marikaar who answered. It was *Wave Runner.*

[Captain, I can no longer find Daanir or Naajir on the ship. The cameras in and around Mancer Narrick's quarters have all gone dark. But I heard a commotion, and a gunshot... and Kaapi. I heard Kaapi scream. I have alerted station security.] A terrifying heartbeat later. [Captain, a submersible has just left the station. Mentiras is hailing.]

"Put him through!"

"*Your Majesty,*" Mentiras voice came through the speaker on the ceiling. Tarjiaan tipped his head back, noticing that Nika stood in the doorway, her eyes wide. "*Tommen just commed. He and Reeshi have Kaapi. She's safe, but she's scared. They're not getting anything coherent out of her, so I'm bringing them all to the Wave Runner. I know she was going to Narrick's so I sent a team.....*" He paused. "*Security is reporting there's a man down at Narrick's quarters. They're bringing him to the infirmary.*"

"I will meet them there. Send for Navi," Nika said. "Jiaan, wait here for Kaapi. She needs one of us to be here for her." She ran from the room. Tarjiaan swallowed.

"Keep me informed, Mentiras."

Chapter Twenty-Five
Captive

DAANIR WOKE SLOWLY, feeling as if his head was going to split open. His jaw hurt, and it was hard to breathe. Nothing felt right...

Because he couldn't feel anything but himself. The machines were gone.

"He's waking up."

"That was quick. Be ready to dose him again." Familiar voice. Who...?

The thought was interrupted by a familiar, sinister laugh. "Oh, he's not going anywhere. Don't forget — I have experience in restraining him."

Daanir recognized the voice — Ishian! He jerked, felt the straps binding him in place; he panicked, suddenly eleven years younger, trapped and alone and at Ishian's mercy. He heard Ishian laugh again, and finally remembered to open his eyes. Ishian was standing over him. Older Ishian, and Daanir snapped back to the present. He looked around, trying to get a sense of place, trying to find the machines that he could hear around him but couldn't seem to reach. He pushed harder, and felt the unmistakable nausea and headache. Limiter. They had put a limiter on him. He was trapped inside his own head.

Where was he?

Submersible. They were on a submersible. And... he went cold. Naajir was lying on the couch, his eyes closed, bound and gagged. What did Ishian want with Naajir?

Then he remembered that he'd heard another voice. There was someone at the controls, piloting the submersible. Someone who shouldn't have been here, who should never have been here.

Narrick turned his chair to face them. "Ishian, I told you to leave him alone."

Ishian sniffed. "And I told you that I want another chance at him before they execute him. That was the price."

"Not. Here." Narrick's voice was clipped. "Once we get to the *Chimaera*. Now sit down and leave him be. They're hailing us."

Ishian grumbled and walked away, leaving Daanir alone with his racing thoughts. The invitation hadn't been unusual — they'd done it so many times when he'd been stationed here. He remembered taking Naji and going to Narrick's quarters, that Kaapi and Antivar were coming to meet them. Going inside. Narrick had poured drinks for them. What had been in the drink? He wasn't sure, but it had hit hard and fast. He remembered Kaapi and Antivar arriving. Antivar trying to sound the alarm. He remembered the shot. He remembered Antivar falling backwards. He remembered the blood.

He remembered hearing Kaapi scream.

Daanir's stomach turned. Where was his daughter? He couldn't turn far enough. He couldn't see. He looked to the side, saw Naajir's eyes were open. The boy looked terrified. There was no way to talk to him, to ask him what he'd seen. No way to know what had happened to his daughter.

A solid thump. Machines whirred and hissed, and the engines faded away to nothing. Narrick stood up and walked past the seats, heading toward the hatch. As soon as he was gone, Ishian was back, wrapping his hand around Daanir's throat and squeezing.

"When I'm done with you," he growled, "you'll be begging them to execute you."

"Ishian!" Narrick's voice was sharp, echoing through the submersible. Ishian straightened, then jerked as the shot rang out, deafeningly loud in the small space. Daanir heard Naajir's muffled scream, but couldn't look away from the charred, red ruin that had been Ishian's chest. The man staggered back, then fell with a solid, final thud.

Narrick walked back into view, the force pistol still in his hand. He looked down at the body, kicked his leg, then spat.

"Was that necessary?" Daanir jumped at the sound of Ilaris' voice from somewhere behind him.

"Yes, it was," Narrick answered. "The man was vile. A useful tool, but vile." He turned. "I've held up my end of the bargain."

"Have you?" Ilaris asked. "I see the traitor and the boy. Where is the girl? I told you to bring her or bring me proof that she's dead."

"The girl is unimportant."

"That is not what I ordered," Ilaris snapped. "Where is the girl? Is she dead?"

"I told you that I would not kill a child," Narrick answered. He glanced at Daanir, who sagged in relief. Kaapi was alive. That... that was good. "The girl was left behind, and is of no importance," Narrick continued. "She's barely trained as it is."

"I gave you an order, Mancer," Ilaris said.

"And I told you no," Narrick said. "Like it or not, Ilaris, you need me. You need a Mancer at your side to control the other mancers." He reached down and grabbed the Mancer Royal badge, ripping it from Daanir's coat. "This should have been mine. Falian promised it to me. I should have been Mancer Royal after him, not that pathetic drunkard." He glanced at Daanir, then added, "It would have gone to you after, Daan. I always meant for you to follow me." He turned back to Ilaris. "It's mine now. That was what you promised."

"I did promise that," Ilaris replied, and his tone made Daanir want to run and hide. Another shot rang out, and Daanir flinched as blood splattered his face. Narrick looked almost surprised as he fell. "But I've decided that mancers are more trouble than they're worth," Ilaris finished. "Guards, take the prince to his mother, and bring the traitor to the brig. He will be executed as soon as we can surface."

Daanir heard footsteps, and guards walked into view. Two of them helped Naajir to his feet and marched him away. Two more unfastened the straps binding Daanir in place and dragged him to his feet, considerably less gentle than how the others had treated Naajir. He didn't fight them, letting them take him out of the submersible and through the corridors he thought he'd never see again.

There was nothing he could do, except pray that Tarjiaan would be able to find them in time.

Naajir tried struggling, but one of the guards grabbed him by the scruff of the neck and shook him, the same way he'd seen Tripod shake one of his knotted rag toys.

"Behave," the guard chided. Naajir scowled at him, and the man laughed. The other guard stopped outside a door and tapped the call signal. The door opened, and Naajir saw his mother — her eyes widened and she stepped out into the corridor.

"The Lord Protector has rescued your son, your Highness," the guard said. "He is to stay with you and behave himself."

"I... of course," Aanaji said. She put her hand on Naajir's shoulder, seemingly ignoring the fact that her son had been presented to her as a prisoner. "If we may be excused?" she added. "I'm certain you have other, more important duties."

Both men bowed, and Aanaji put her arm around Naajir's shoulders and led him into their quarters. The door slid closed behind them, and she turned and hugged him tightly.

"He's coming," she whispered. "We will talk once he is gone." She pulled back and smiled, gently unfastening the gag and tossing it aside. "Look at you," she murmured. "It hasn't been that long, and you've grown. And... an earring? You sailed through a storm?"

Naajir nodded. "Mama, I..." Her eyes widened, and the door slid open. Naajir turned to see Ilaris standing in the doorway.

"Well, the young prince had returned to his mother's loving arms," he said. "Aanaji, I would have a word with your son."

Aanaji rested her hand on Naajir's shoulder. "He's listening."

"And not answering," Naajir added. "I'm not telling you anything."

Ilaris chuckled. "Is that any way to speak to your father, boy?" he asked. Naajir stared at him, shocked that Ilaris would say it aloud, remembering too late that he wasn't supposed to know. But Ilaris didn't seem to notice that the surprise was misplaced. "Yes, boy. I am your father, and you will show me the proper respect. Now, tell me. What do you know of the pretender's plans?"

Naajir stared at him. "I haven't been here. Why would I know your plans?" The words fell out of his mouth before he could stop them, and from the look on Ilaris' face, they were not what the man expected. His eyes narrowed, and Naajir felt... pushing. He shivered and shook his head.

"Tell me," Ilaris repeated. "I want to know their plans."

"I don't know any plans," Naajir insisted. The pushing got harder, making the inside of Naajir's head itch. He grimaced, closing his eyes. "I don't know anything!"

"You will tell me!" Naajir's collar tightened as Ilaris grabbed his shirt, and Naajir squeaked as the man pulled him closer. Istin's lessons took over, and he lashed out, kicking Ilaris in the knee — Ilaris howled in pain and staggered backwards, catching himself on a chair before he fell. He glared at Naajir as he straightened, then limped forward.

"Ilaris—" Aanaji stepped between them. "He doesn't understand. Let me—"

Ilaris lashed out, slapping Aanaji and knocking her out of his path.

"Leave her alone!" Naajir barreled into Ilaris, knocking him back and kicking him again. Before he could get out of reach, Ilaris struck back, his fist catching Naajir in the jaw, snapping his head back; he stumbled and fell, automatically curling into a ball. Ilaris stood over him, breathing hard, rubbing his hand.

"Woman, control your brat," he snarled, before limping out of the room. Naajir didn't move, watching the door. His jaw throbbed in pain, and he tasted blood.

"Naji." His mother crawled over to him. "Let me see." He helped him to sit up, then moved behind him and untied his wrists. As soon as he could move, Naajir threw his arms around his mother and hugged her tightly. She kissed his forehead and hugged him back. "Let me get a cold compress."

"Mama—"

She shook her head and nodded slightly toward a corner of the room. Naajir fought the urge to turn, instead reaching out with mancery and finding the camera that hadn't been there before. He ducked his head, nodding slightly as he slowly got to his feet.

"Sit on the couch," Aanaji said, and left the room. When she came back, she was carrying a medical compress. She sat down next to him, tapped the button to activate it, and pressed the now-cold pad to his face. As she leaned closer, she whispered, "Mute the microphones and the camera."

He nodded, setting the camera on a loop to show the previous two minutes, and turning the speakers off completely. "Done."

"Did you find him?" Aanaji asked. "Is Tarjiaan alive?"

"Yes, and he's ready to fight back. You didn't see the broadcast?" Naajir asked. "Mama, the entire kingdom knows what Ilaris did. They've all seen the disc. Narrick..." he stopped, closing his eyes. "Narrick betrayed us. But... he and Daanir boosted the signal to get the broadcast out to every ship in the fleet, above and below the waves. Loyal ships are going to be converging on the dockyards." He glanced at the camera. "Mama, Ilaris can't control me, and he can't control Uncle Jiaan or Uncle Daan—"

"Uncle Daan?" Aanaji repeated. Then she waved one hand. "Not important. Go on. We don't have much time."

Naajir nodded. "Daanir thinks that Ilaris can't control someone more powerful than he is. He can't control a trained mancer, or a Reckoner. Or a healer."

"Reckoners? That's a myth."

"Uncle Jiaan is a Reckoner. And Aunt Nika is a Sualimani healer."

"Is she? I'd never have expected that. Then... well, then, they're safe if it comes to a fight," Aanaji said. "I... I'm trying. But I'm not trained. It is getting... easier, though. He's losing control. It's been happening more and more often. I think I know why now — he's losing support, and he's losing control."

"Mama, he's going to order us to surface, and he's going to have Uncle Daan executed," Naajir said. "Can we stop him?"

Aanaji pressed her hands together and tapped her fingers against her lips. "I... I think I can distract him. And I think you can delay him," she said. She got up, went to a panel on the wall, slid it open, and did something that Naajir couldn't see. Then she came back. "In a few minutes, someone is going to come and fetch you. You'll be safe with him. Do what you can, and I'll do what I can to distract Ilaris."

Naajir looked at the door. "What? But... Mama, if I'm gone, he'll hurt you."

She smiled softly. "I know. But if we can do this... then he'll pay. We just have to delay him until Tarjiaan can reach us."

"What about Daanir?" Naajir asked.

"Do what you can," she repeated. She hugged him tightly and kissed his cheek. "I love you. Start the cameras back up, and the speakers."

Naajir nodded, looking down at his hands. "They're on," he murmured. She patted his hand.

"You should get something to eat, and get some rest. We don't have a servant, so you'll have to go to the galley," she said, standing up. "I'm going to lie down. Behave yourself, Naji."

"Yes, Mama," Naajir replied, looking up to watch as Aanaji went into her room and closed the door. He stood up, brushing his hands down his chest before going toward the door. It slid open as he approached, and he recognized the man in black waiting outside.

Logiri.

He pressed one finger to his lips and gestured for Naajir to follow. Naajir looked back once, then hurried out of the room.

It didn't surprise Naajir that Logiri led him to the maintenance passages. It made sense as a place to hide. But he wasn't expecting the other man waiting for them.

"Lord Rathsafa," Naajir gasped. "You're safe!"

Rathsafa grimaced. "Define safe," he replied. Naajir grinned.

"Not dead, and not a prisoner. We didn't know if you were even alive," he explained. "I'm glad to see you are."

"And your uncle?" Logiri asked. "Is Tarjiaan alive?"

"Yes," Naajir answered. "Do you want the entire story, and can it wait until we see if we can free Daanir?"

"The Mancer Royal is here?" Logiri looked stunned. "How?"

"The same way they got me," Naajir answered. "And it can wait. Ilaris said we were going to surface so that Daanir can be executed. We can't let that happen. I need to get to the ballast pumps, and we need to get Daanir out of the brig."

"Which is more important?" Rathsafa asked.

"Ah..." Naajir turned the choices over, examined them from every angle. "Both?"

Rathsafa and Logiri looked at each other. "Do you remember how to get to the engines?" Logiri asked.

"I'll find them. I'm certain the Prince can help me."

"I'm certain that the Prince will have to help you," Logiri said with a wry grin. "You're hopeless with directions, Nadar."

"You don't have to call me by the title," Naajir said. "I'm Naajir. Or Naji. And I can find the engines."

"Then do what you need to do, while I see if I can free the Mancer." Logiri touched Rathsafa's arm, then vanished down another passage. Naajir looked up at Rathsafa, who nodded.

"This way. I think."

Daanir tried to ignore the guards outside the cell. His arms and jaw ached, and his head was pounding. Not being able to touch the machines around him was making him feel sick. He pressed himself into the corner of the cell farthest from the bars and closed his eyes.

How long? It was a question that covered too many possibilities.

How long could a mancer last in a limiter?

How long before he went mad?

How long before Jiaan found them?

How long before he died?

He didn't have an answer to any of them. Outside he heard one of the guards laugh. "Hey, Mancer. You alive in there? You're not allowed to die until we kill you." When Daanir didn't respond, he laughed again. "Not much longer before we surface. You better enjoy breathing while you can."

Daanir ignored his words, but he couldn't ignore the wet-sounding thump. The shout. The heavier thump. He opened his eyes to see both of the guards on the ground in growing pools of blood. A single black-clad figure stood over them, a pair of bloody knives in their gloved hands. The figure was masked and hooded, and Daanir had no idea who it was. They leaned down, wiped the blades on the guards' coats, then sheathed them and turned toward the bars. Daanir stumbled to his feet, torn between keeping as much distance as possible between himself and the bars, and rushing towards the possibility of help. The figure touched the bars, examined the lock, then shook their head.

"Lord Mancer, we don't have time."

Daanir recognized the voice, and whimpered. Help. Real help. He rushed to the bars as the figure lowered their mask. Logiri smiled.

"Can you kneel? I can't reach that gag."

Daanir nodded, going to his knees and turning his back. The strap of the gag loosened, the mouthpiece falling to the floor when he spat it out. He winced, hearing his jaw popping and creaking as he opened and closed his mouth.

"Stay down," Logiri said. "I... how do I unfasten this?"

"The limiter? There's a catch, and a lock." Daanir winced as the wide collar around his neck tightened slightly as Logiri worked. "How are you still free?"

"I'm very good at what I do, Lord Mancer, and I will make that bastard pay for what he did to Tarjiaan. I just haven't been able to get to him yet. He has too many guards."

"Jiaan is alive," Daanir said. "We rescued him. He's coming."

"So says the young prince," Logiri said. He snarled a curse in Tyracan. "I can't get this unfastened!"

"Can you get my hands free? Or unlock the bars?" Daanir asked. "I..." An alarm started to blare. "Oh, fuck. Get out of here!"

Logiri looked up. "I can't leave you!"

Daanir turned, looking at Logiri. "Naji is with you? And... what about Rathsafa?"

"Both of them are —"

"Don't tell me where you're hiding!" Daanir snapped. "You have to keep them safe. Jiaan is coming." He tried to see down the corridor. "Tell Rathsafa we found his son. Tell him that he's going to be a grandfather. Now get out of here!"

Logiri hesitated, then shook his head. He pulled his mask back up. "I'm sorry!" he called. Then he ran. Daanir stepped back, moving further into the cell, watching as guards came running up. One of them dropped to one knee next to the bodies, then looked at Daanir.

"Did you do this?" he demanded.

"No, but I'd love for you to tell me just how you think I did," Daanir answered.

"Who did?"

Daanir shook his head. "They were masked. They ran off when the alarm went off."

Another guard joined them. "No one in the corridor. And the security cameras are offline."

Off in the distance, they heard more alarms. They weren't security alarms — these were the piercing claxons of a system failure. The guards looked at each other, then ran off, and Daanir returned to his place at the rear of the cell.

Nothing he could do but wait.

Chapter Twenty-Six
Mischief

NAAJIR OPENED HIS EYES and stepped back, studying the pumps. "Those aren't going to work again without a lot of repairs," he said. "That should keep us from surfacing."

"Then let's get back out of sight." Rathsafa flinched as alarms started to scream. "What are those?"

"The pump alarms," Naajir answered. He touched the access panel, opening the door to the maintenance passages. "Let's go. They'll be coming to see why the alarms are sounding."

Rathsafa led them into the passages, hurrying back the way they'd come, pausing at every intersection.

"I really am very poor at direction," he said, sound apologetic. "I always have been."

"Left at the next turning," Naajir said. "I can lead."

"It would be better if you did." Rathsafa laughed, turning left. "I would get lost on the way to the market, and there was only one path! I wore a bracelet that Masthaka made for me, to tell me which way was left. They took it from me when I was taken back to the Palace. Now... I just have to remember which wrist had the bracelet."

"That's clever," Naajir said. He smiled. "And you don't have to apologize. Your brain works differently. That's all. Turn right here."

"Nadar!" Logiri came running toward them. "We need to go deeper. I was nearly caught."

"You?" Rathsafa gasped. "How?"

"I'm not certain," Logiri sighed. "But I couldn't get him out. I couldn't get the collar unfastened in time, which meant I couldn't get the cell door open. I don't think I will have another chance." He looked up. "The alarms?"

"The pumps are disabled," Naajir answered. "They're going to need a mancer to make them work again, and I don't think they have one."

Both adults stared at him, but it was Logiri who spoke, "Boy, they have a mancer. He's in the brig. They just need find what incentive will make him do the work, and I'm afraid I know what they'll leverage." He glanced at Rathsafa. "We need to message the lady."

"The lady?" Naajir realized who they were talking about. "My mother?"

"We've been trying to convince her that she needs to hide," Rathsafa answered as they started moving again, following Logiri. "She's been doing what she can to stop or damage Ilaris' plans, so she keeps refusing."

"She will not listen when we tell her that he no longer cares about her," Logiri added. "We've heard him. He thinks of her as a necessary irritation, but he's tired of her. If he can use her to make the Mancer Royal do his bidding, he will."

Naajir stopped walking and closed his eyes, reaching for the camera in his mother's suite. It took him a moment to find the feed, but when he did, he nearly fell.

The room had been destroyed — furnishings and artwork strewn all over. His mother was nowhere to be seen. He opened his eyes, leaned back against the wall, and slid down to sit on the floor.

"They have her." He looked up at Logiri and Rathsafa. "What do we do?"

Logiri took a deep breath, frowned, and walked a short distance down the corridor. Rathsafa held up a hand when Naajir start to say something.

"Let him think," he murmured. He held his hand out and helped Naajir to his feet. "You'll need to eat. If mancery is anything like magery, you'll need to eat something soon. We have... lemon tea biscuits, I think. They're very good."

"Ration biscuits," Naajir said, and smiled. "Aunt Nika likes them. Which is good, because they're the only things that will settle her stomach."

"Settle her..." Rathsafa looked blank. Then his jaw dropped. "I... is my daughter with child?"

"The Mancer Royal asked me to tell you, Nadar," Logiri said. "He also said to tell you that they found your son."

Rathsafa sat down hard in the middle of the corridor. "My... my son? They found my son?" He turned to look at Naajir, who nodded.

"Uncle Navi. He's a healer. He's a very good healer. He saved Uncle Daan's life, and Uncle Jiaan's." He paused. "Aunt Nika is a healer, too. Did you know that?"

"I... no," Rathsafa said, shaking his head. "I... they take after their mother. She was a strong healer. I... a grandchild. Gir, a grandchild!"

Logiri looked at him, then smiled. "We'll get out of here, Nadar. You'll see them again. But now... we have work to do. Let's go."

Daanir was dozing when the guards burst into his cell and grabbed him, dragging him to his feet and out into the corridor. For a moment, he was certain that they had surfaced, that were taking him to the deck and the Sentence Ring. But they didn't take the turn that would led up to the deck, instead heading deeper into the *Chimaera*. They passed his quarters. His workroom. Turned again.

Why were they heading to the engine room?

He was wrong — the engine room wasn't their destination. The pump room was, and Ilaris was there waiting.

"What did you do?" Ilaris demanded.

Daanir blinked. "I... you know exactly where I've been, and you know I can't do anything while there's a limiter locked around my throat. So what do you think I did, and how exactly do you think I did it?"

Ilaris glared at him, then pointed at the pumps. "Fix this!"

Daanir took a step forward, then looked at Ilaris. "First, I can't do anything with my hands tied. Or while wearing a limiter. And if you want me focused enough to not make this worse, I'll need to eat." He looked at the pumps again. He couldn't see anything wrong, but it might have been internal. But something else wasn't right. He turned to Ilaris again. "Why are you asking me to fix this, anyway? You're asking me to make it possible for you to execute me. I'd just as soon blow the ship to bits and save Jiaan the trouble of executing you."

Ilaris smiled. "You wouldn't. I know you, Mancer. You care about people. There are still innocents on this ship—"

"Hostages, you mean."

Ilaris shrugged. "Call them what you will. If you destroy this ship to kill me, you'll go to the Mothers with their blood on your hands."

"Might be a risk I'm willing to take," Daanir snapped. He looked at the pumps again, suddenly cold. "You don't have another mancer on this ship, do you? I'm it."

"Indeed. You are, as you say... it." Ilaris sniffed. "Mancers are far too much trouble to be worth keeping."

Daanir stared at him. "I... Narrick told us that you recalled all of the mancers. What did you do with them, Ilaris?" he asked, his voice low. "Where are my mancers?" Ilaris didn't answer, and Daanir forgot his hands were bound, forgot everything but the sudden rush of fury. He lunged at Ilaris, struggling against the guards who grabbed him as he shouted, "*Where are my mancers?*"

Ilaris just laughed at him. "There are no mancers," he answered. "Mancery has been outlawed in Meradon, an unfortunate result of the Mancer Royal murdering the King and the Sea Prince. Truly, it's very sad. The Emperor very kindly agreed to deal with them for me." He paused, then pointed at the quiet machine. "Now, you will repair the pumps—"

"No." Daanir relaxed, stepping back. "I will not."

"I won't repeat myself again. You will repair the pumps, or there will be consequence."

"No." Daanir grinned. "I won't repeat myself again."

Ilaris rolled his eyes, then turned. "Bring her in!"

"Bring... bring who?" Daanir turned and stared, certain that they were going to bring Kaapi in. But instead, the guards dragged Aanaji into the room. She looked rumpled and tired, and there was a dark bruise on her face. "Who hit you?"

"I did," Ilaris answered. "And if you do not get to work, I will do considerably worse."

"Ilaris?" Aanaji frowned in confusion. "What are you talking about? What am I doing here?"

"You, my dear, are incentive," Ilaris said. He went to Aanaji, brushing her hair back out of her face. "I have no further use for you," he continued. "You failed me."

"I didn't!" Aanaji gasped. "I was good!"

"You failed to control your brother. You failed to kill him. You failed to give me a suitable heir. And you no longer amuse me, Aanaji." He glanced back at Daanir.

Daanir never saw where the knife came from. He blinked, and Ilaris had a blade pressed against Aanaji's cheek. "Now, Mancer, this is your last chance," he said. "You will repair the pumps—"

Daanir met Aanaji's eyes. How had he never noticed how much her eyes were like Jiaan's? They were wide and frightened now. He licked his lips and shook his head.

"No," he repeated. "I will not—" Aanaji's scream echoed in the pump room, and the sight of the blood running down her face made Daanir's stomach twist in ways that blood had never done before. "Leave her alone!"

Ilaris glanced at him. "Are you going to get to work?" He shifted the blade to Aanaji's ear. "She doesn't need two—"

"Stop it!" Daanir closed his eyes, knowing he'd lost. "I... if you want me to work, leave her alone."

"Good boy," Ilaris crooned. He stepped back, and Aanaji sagged and burst into tears. "Take her away. Untie the mancer and bring him some ration biscuits. Do not remove the limiter."

"I thought you wanted this fixed," Daanir said, watching as Aanaji was led from the room.

"You think I'm an idiot," Ilaris said. "You know how to use your hands. Get to work." He turned and left, and more guards marched into the room. One of them came and cut the straps binding Daanir's arms — he stretched, wincing as his muscles protested after being bound for so long.

"Ration biscuits. Water. And... do I get to use the head?" He looked around and sighed. "I've got work to do."

The pumps still weren't working, but Daanir had a better idea of how to fix them by the time the guards took pity on him and let him stop. One of them had him by the arm, and Daanir wasn't certain if it was because he was being escorted, or because he was being steered to keep him from walking into walls. They pushed him into the cell, and he was four steps in before he realized he wasn't alone. He blinked, blinked again, feeling as if he was swaying on his feet.

"Aanaji?"

She was sitting in the rear corner of the cell, her head down on her raised knees. She looked up at his voice, sniffled, then lowered her head again. All at once, Daanir was awake. He turned back to the bars.

"Water? Please?" he asked. "And... something to clean that wound?"

The guard looked past him, hesitated, then looked at his partner. They stepped away, whispering together, then the first one said, "I'll see what I can do."

"Don't put yourself at risk for us," Daanir replied. "Thank you."

The guard smiled slightly, and the pair walked away. Daanir took his coat off and went to Aanaji's side, draping it over her shoulders.

"Let me see," he said gently, sitting down next to her and folding his hands in front of him. "Let me see how bad it is."

"I'm sorry." Her voice was muffled in her arms. "I... I couldn't stop him."

"I know," Daanir said, keeping his voice quiet. Hopefully, the speakers wouldn't pick it up. "We all know. No one blames you, and you did what you could to help us. And you did help us. You got us the information we needed, and you got the children out. You let us get away, and we saved Jiaan. He's coming. Now let me see how badly he hurt you?"

"This is nothing," she answered, raising her head and meeting his eyes. "After so many years and so much blood? This is nothing. I'm sorry I screamed. I wasn't ready."

Daanir smiled. "You don't have anything to apologize for. Now, may I touch you?"

She blinked, clearly caught off guard by the question. "I... what?"

"I know what he's done to you, and I understand. I'm not going to touch you without your leave. But I need to take a closer look," Daanir paused, then added, "If you don't want me touching you, just turn your head so I can see better."

She looked puzzled, but turned and tipped her head so that he could better see the long cut along her cheekbone. It wasn't deep, and head wounds always bled a flood, so Daanir didn't think it was too bad.

"It doesn't look terrible," he said. "If they bring us water, we can clean it, see how deep it is. And maybe they'll even bring medical supplies and I can do something more with it. I don't think it will scar." He snorted. "If it does, we'll match. Just... yours will be higher." She looked at him, and he turned his head and traced the line of his scar underneath his beard. "Mine is here. Now, granted, you can't hide yours like I can hide mine. Although that might be interesting..."

As he'd hoped, she giggled, a weak, wet sound. "You're ridiculous."

"I'm decorative, though. That counts for something." Daanir leaned closer and whispered, "Did you do the damage to the pumps?"

"No," she answered. "I could have, but I never even thought of it. And I wouldn't know how to do it properly. It had to be Naji."

"How much training have you had?"

"None," she whispered back. "I watched every mancer I could when we were on the *Allegiant*, but... that's not the same."

Daanir fought the urge to nod. "Right. I'm going to talk you through securing the cell so we can talk. Ready?"

"I... yes."

Daanir closed his eyes, thinking about the steps that he took for granted. "Right. First, we're going to kill the audio. There should be four microphones in here — one in each corner. Can you feel them?"

Aanaji licked her lips, then murmured, "There are five. There's one in the ceiling." She paused. "Are they supposed to bubble?"

Daanir grinned. "I hear them as fizzing. Yes. You're quick. Now, do you know what I mean when I say you have to cancel out the sound we're making?"

She looked at him. "Sound cancellation? Yes, but... oh! Oh, I see." She frowned slightly, then nodded. "I think I did it."

"Good. Now the cameras. Again, there should be four. What do you hear?"

She smiled slightly. "They hiss. Loop them? That's what Naji did to our cameras."

"Yes," Daanir said. "He's a smart boy. They'll come to find out what's wrong with the cameras before they'll come look at why they can't hear us."

"Done."

Daanir sighed and slumped slightly. "When we get out of this, I'm training you."

Her eyes widened. "You... you are?"

"Yes. You're quick, and you have a good touch. And... you didn't hear him, did you?" He closed his eyes and took a deep breath. "We're it. You, me, Naji, Kaapi and Ishantar. We're all the mancers that are left."

She went ashen. "What?"

He nodded. "He told me before he brought you in. That's why he needed me to do the work. There's no other mancer on board, and there are no other mancers anywhere. He killed Narrick—"

The wash of anger and grief stole his voice, and he swallowed hard, unable to continue. To his surprise, Aanaji took his hand.

"Don't break," she murmured. "I need you."

Despite himself, he smiled. "Never thought I'd hear you say that. But then, I never really knew you, did I? I just said that to Jiaan recently. He never really knew you, either. He wants to."

"After everything I've done?"

"He knows it wasn't you. He knows it was Ilaris, using you. He's going to bone Ilaris like a fish—"

"I want to watch," Aanaji blurted. Then she blushed as Daanir stared at her.

"Oh, I cannot wait to see Jiaan's face when you say things like that. He's going to love it," Daanir said. "Right. Let's see if I can give you a weapon. We'll have to make this fast, because the guards will hopefully be coming back with water. Did Naji ever play with blocks when he was small?" When Aanaji nodded, Daanir smiled. "Good. I want you to take the image of building a wall of blocks around yourself. Imagine it — tall and strong and solid, and keeping out anything you don't want let in. Imagine it rooted down into the bottom of the sea, solid enough that it's not going anywhere. Got it?"

"And this will do... what?"

"Once you get the knack of it, it will keep Ilaris from taking over your mind." He nodded at her skeptical look. "He can't control someone stronger than he is. That's why he never got me, and why he couldn't control Jiaan—"

"Naji said that Tarjiaan is a Reckoner. But that's a myth—"

"It's not a myth," Daanir answered. "He is, and so was your father. He's learning to use it. He's going to find us, Aanaji."

"Will he get here before you fix the pumps?" she asked. Then she paused and looked up. "Daanir, Ilaris showed me something. He has a bracelet made of hair. He wears it all the time now, and he says it's Tarjiaan's hair. That if Tarjiaan comes for him, he'll be able to use it to control him."

Daanir stared at her in horror. "We thought the hair was lost with the Imp ship," he murmured. "When we rescued him, all his hair was cut short. We thought it happened after he was above the waves. We never even considered that it happened here."

"What do we do?"

Daanir shook his head. "For right now? Put the cameras and microphones back, and practice that wall." He tipped his head back against the wall.

"You... you asked me if you could touch me. You knew what happened to me, you said. And you said you understood." She paused. "I... I shouldn't ask this."

"Yes," Daanir answered, not looking at her, staring at the ceiling. "When Ilaris sent me to Station Six. I was there for four years before I forged orders to get away from there. And Narrick..." He stopped again. "He saved me. Fought for me. Trained me. And then... he sold me to Ilaris for the Mancer Royal badge. I... I thought of him as something like a father. Loved him. And he betrayed us."

"Station Six," Aanaji repeated. "I... why do I know that?"

He looked at her, and said one word: "Ishian."

Her jaw dropped. "Ishian? Ranji's Ishian? Oh, Daanir!"

Daanir took a deep breath. "He's dead. He'll never hurt anyone again. He's Ranji's problem now—"

"What do you mean?"

Daanir chuckled. "The Imps have a story they tell about the Demon Captain and his First Mate, who sail the seas in their ship the *Marauder*, hunting Imperial ships. Nika told Jiaan about it when they got married, when she found out that the Demon Captain was Captain Taarik. And... it's not a story."

"That's not funny!"

"I'm not trying to be funny," Daanir said. "I promise you. I saw it. I spoke to them. Ranji said to tell you that he doesn't blame you, and you need to stop blaming yourself. And he's still wearing that red armor!"

"I..." Aanaji stared at him for a moment, then started laughing. "I remember that armor! It was awful!"

Daanir grinned. "Captain Taarik hated it. But Ranji wore it anyway. And... I don't know if they're still out there. They said that their duty was done once the Imp fleet was destroyed. They disappeared like sea foam. So... I don't know. But they were there. We all saw them. And Jiaan sang the Farewell."

Aanaji shuddered. "Good. That... that's good." She looked quizzically at him. "I'm not certain I believe you."

"Sometimes, I'm not sure I believe me." Daanir sighed. "To circle back, I understand that you might not want to be touched because it took me years before I was ready. And I didn't share my bed with anyone until I was with Jiaan again."

"Are you?" Aanaji asked. "I... another question I shouldn't ask. But... I like Nika."

"Nika practically shoved us back together. We're a set now, the three of us. She calls us her favored males, and Jiaan says she's our wife. He's invoked consortage—"

Aanaji burst out laughing. "Oh, that's archaic! Where did he find that?"

"Wilaanger reminded him."

"Good. That's good," Aanaji said. "Ranji said you were the best thing that had ever happened to Tarjiaan. And... I'm so sorry for the role I played in separating you both."

Daanir smiled. "Apology returned unopened. You have nothing to apologize for. It wasn't you. It was Ilaris, and he's going to pay." He glanced up as he heard voices coming toward them. "I hope that's the guard coming back. We'll get that cut cleaned up. Then I need to sleep."

Chapter Twenty-Seven
Contaminant

"TARJIAAN, YOU NEED to rest."

Tarjiaan looked up from the charts scattered across the table. "I can't, Wil. I have to find them. Kyraath says I should be able to use reckoning to do this, but he can't tell me how. Says that it's different for every Reckoner. He tried, and he can't do it. I tried his way, and it didn't work. I need to figure this out, and I need to do it quickly." He looked past Wilaanger, seeing Nika and Navi in the door. "How's Antivar?"

"He's as bad a patient as you are," Wilaanger said, laughing. "Which I did not think was possible. He wants to be out of bed right now. He wants to help. His mother is with him, and Tommen. They're taking turns keeping him in bed."

"When you go back, tell him that he has helped. He told us that it wasn't just Ishian. That Narrick betrayed us, and that they were going to the *Chimaera*." Tarjiaan looked down at the charts and sighed. "I'm running out of time."

"Jiaan?" Navi came up next to the table. "This. Why?"

Tarjiaan frowned slightly. "What am I doing?"

Navi nodded. "Yes."

Tarjiaan gestured to the charts. "Kyraath says that I should be able to find the *Chimaera* — the belowship where they've taken Daanir and Naji. I should be able to use reckoning to find them.

But I don't know enough about what I'm doing to know how to do it, and he says that he isn't strong enough to do it."

Navi nodded slowly, studying the charts. "Tried what?"

"Kyraath showed me how he does it, using a pendulum. But neither of us could find anything that way." Tarjiaan frowned, thinking back over everything he'd tried. "I tried using the charts as... as a representation of the sea, and searching that way, but I could even find the ships that I know are there doing it that way." He sighed. "I can feel the ships all around the dockyards, and the belowships under the surface. But I know they're there. I'm trying to find something when I don't know where to look."

"Pebble in pearls," Navi murmured. He frowned slightly, then looked up. "Look for wrong?"

"I... I don't understand."

Navi growled slightly and closed his eyes, clearly trying to order his thoughts. "Sea... is alive. Yes?" He opened his eyes and looked at Tarjiaan. "Yes? Like... a body?" He reached out and tapped Tarjiaan's arm. "Yes?"

Tarjiaan nodded slowly. "Yes."

"Belowship is not. Yes?" He touched the chart. "Is wrong. Is... con... contaminant?" He glanced at Wilaanger. "Yes?"

Wilaanger frowned slightly, then breathed out slowly. "Oh... oh, I think I understand."

"Care to throw me a line?" Tarjiaan asked. "I'm drifting."

"Navi, correct me if I'm misunderstanding," Wilaanger said. "What he's proposing is that you filter the sea, the way a Great Mother filters her food. It's how he saved you from the poison — he filtered it out of your body. You're going to send your power through the sea as a filter, and you're going to find the thing that shouldn't be there."

"Yes!" Navi crowed.

"Will that not take days?" Nika asked. "The sea is so very big."

"No, it won't," Tarjiaan said, hope rising like the tide. "It won't, because they can't be that far away. You know a submersible only has a limited amount of air, and I doubt they'd risk surfacing and having Daanir or Naji possibly take over the sub. So the *Chimaera* had to be close enough for them to reach without surfacing and being seen." He studied the charts, judging distances and the best speed of a submersible. Would the *Chimaera* move away once they had the prisoners? Possibly, so take that into account. He narrowed his eyes, increased his range, then looked up. "I think... I need to see the sea." He pushed off the table and headed for the door, hearing the others following him as he ran up to the prow and looked out over the sea, then let his barely-trained power flow out past the dockyards and into the midnight-dark deep. He could hear the harmonies of the Great Mothers, feel them moving through the water in unbothered pods. But something ahead of him felt... wrong. He pushed harder, and tasted metal and blood, surrounding a silent splinter that cut through the water like a knife blade.

He snapped back to himself and gasped. "Found them!" he wheezed. "I found them." He turned, catching himself on the rail as a wave of vertigo washed over him.

"Jiaan?" Nika caught his arm. "Oh, you need something to eat."

"I'll eat at the helm," he answered. "We need to set sail. The fleet needs to move." He took a step... and went to one knee as his balance failed him.

"You'll eat, and properly chart the course," Wilaanger said. Tarjiaan looked up to see the group surrounding him — Wilaanger, Nika and Navi. Kaapi, Marikaar, Istin and Kyraath. Kyraath was nodding.

"What did you do?" the older Reckoner asked. "What worked?"

"Food first," Navi said, his voice firm. "Talk after."

Tarjiaan nodded. "Come with me. But first... Marikaar, set course for two points off the port bow, then dead ahead. About..." He paused, then nodded. "Half a day at our top speed. Alert the fleet. Tell them that we're going, but they're to maintain their position at the dockyards and wait further instructions. We're moving out."

Tarjiaan explained around bites, keeping the distant sense of the *Chimaera* in the back of his mind the entire time. Now that he knew it was there, it was as real to him as any of the ships of the fleet. Kyraath watched him with an odd intensity, nodding slowly until Tarjiaan finished.

"You've come into your own," he said. "There's not a Reckoner ever come out of the Delta that would argue that. And not a one, I think, who could have found something at that distance." He frowned slightly, then shook his head. "Still can't find it, myself. So what do we do when we get there?"

"I can go talk to the *Chimaera*," Kaapi said, her voice quiet and firm. "The way Papa talked to the *Wave Runner*. If someone will take me in the submersible. I can get us in." She folded her hands on the table, serious in ways that she'd never been before. It felt as if she'd aged years in the hours since Narrick's attack. "I'm the only Mancer you have, and... I know the *Chimaera*."

"Is she aware?" Tarjiaan asked.

Kaapi's face screwed up slightly. "Almost?" she said slowly, drawing the word out. "It's like... when you're asleep, and you know you have to wake up, but you really don't want to? Like that. She's just on the other side of waking up. I just didn't realize that's what it was that I was feeling when I first got there."

"Jiaan," Nika said, sounding as if she was still testing the depth of her next word. "You told me that the ship cats picked their

person. The way Tripod and Gossamer and Fancy chose us. Yes?"
She looked around. "Do you think that the ships pick their
mancers the way ship cats pick their people?"

Tarjiaan looked at her. "That... sounds very much like the
reason that Ishantar gave for wanting to leave the *Wave Runner*.
She said that as much as she loves this ship, she's always known
that *Wave Runner* wasn't hers. I don't know. But... Kaapi, this is
dangerous, and you're not fully trained—"

"And my father had no training at all when he saved Meradon,"
Kaapi replied. "I'm the only mancer you have. If... if Uncle Antivar
and Uncle Navi and... oh, I don't know who else. If they come with
me, I should be safe enough. And once we're in, I can make the ship
do whatever I want."

"Like surface," Wilaanger murmured. "But... Tarjiaan, I hate to
ask this question, but how are you going to board?"

"I've been asking myself that same question, and I don't have an
answer," Tarjiaan said. "I can't fit into the corridors of a belowship."

"We have... what was it? Half a day?" Istin waited until Tarjiaan
nodded to finish. "We have half a day to answer the question."

"Sleepytime," Navi blurted. Nika looked at him and smiled.

"Oh, of course," she said. "If Kaapi can get into the *Chimaera*,
she can put something into their air systems."

"Sleeping gas," Wilaanger said. "That's not a bad idea. Put them
to sleep, have the ship spill her ballast and surface, and flush the air
once she's above. We can sweep the entire belowship and release the
hostages before anyone wakes up."

Tarjiaan nodded. "We'll call that the if plan. If we can't come
up with anything else. I do not want Kaapi within reach of Ilaris.
Now, do we have any other ideas?"

"Can they tell we're coming?" Istin asked. "Does your
technology let your ships below the surface see what's happening
up here?"

"Yes and no," Wilaanger answered. "They have to be looking. Right now, they think that we don't know where they are."

"But they might look," Tarjiaan said. "We can't assume that we'll get through undetected. Unless..." He looked up. "*Wave Runner*?"

[Yes, Captain?]

"We're about a half day from the *Chimaera*. How soon will you be able to contact her systems? And... would you be able to use the *Chimaera's* systems to speak to a mancer onboard?"

[I can reach them now, Captain.]

Tarjiaan glanced at Nika, saw the shock in her face. He was certain her expression matched his own. "You can?"

[The new comms systems are very powerful,] *Wave Runner* answered. [They are far better than the ones I had before, and Mancer Narrick never removed the extra amplification that was installed for the broadcast. Shall I attempt to contact?]

"Yes," Tarjiaan answered. "Access all security functions and files. Let us know what we're facing. How many crew, how many guards. How many prisoners and how are they being held?"

[Shall I attempt to contact Daanir or Naajir?] Wave Runner asked.

"I doubt they'd be able to hold Daanir if they didn't have him locked in a limiter," Tarjiaan answered. "See if you can reach Naajir. If not, try and reach Aanaji. We suspect she's a mancer, too, but she's unlikely to be trained."

[I do not know Aanaji,] Wave Runner said. [Will she listen to me?]

"I certainly hope so." Without thinking, Tarjiaan reached for Nika's hand; she squeezed his fingers tightly.

[I am in. And... files are fragmentary. There are gaps in recordings, and there are files that have been deleted entirely. I am recovering those. I... this was Naajir's work, most of it. There are some fragments that I do not recognize the mancer signature."

"That must be Aanaji," Tarjiaan said. "Now, how many crew?"

[Total crew... fifty-three. Total guards... twenty. And... Captain, I cannot reach Naajir. There is one mancer, and the signature matches those fragments. No other mancers on board. Oh... Captain, you will want a monitor.]

Marikaar stood up and went to a cabinet, taking out a monitor and setting it up on the table. "Go ahead, *Wave Runner*."

[There is no sound on this recording,] *Wave Runner* said. The monitor lit up, showing the interior of a submersible from the vantage point of the pilot seat. Tarjiaan could see the entire passenger compartment. Naajir, bound and gagged, lying on a couch. Daanir, bound to a chair. Ishian, leaning over a clearly-terrified Daanir, one hand around the mancer's throat. And Narrick, standing at the rear of the submersible, a force pistol in his hand. His mouth moved. Ishian straightened, and Tarjiaan saw the flash of the shot a heartbeat before Ishian staggered backwards and fell. Narrick came forward, and behind him, Ilaris walked into view. There was an obvious argument, and Narrick tore the Mancer Royal badge from Daanir's coat, brandishing it at Ilaris. Ilaris didn't react, and the look on his face never changed as he drew a pistol and shot Narrick at point-blank range.

"Mothers Below," Wilaanger breathed.

"I don't understand." Tarjiaan leaned back in his chair, rubbing one hand over his face. "He saved Daanir from Ishian, years ago. He fostered Daanir's talent, trained him. And... he handed Daanir over to Ilaris for... for what? A piece of metal?" He shook his head. "What else do you have for us, *Wave Runner*?"

The monitor dimmed, then brightened again. [This is right now,] *Wave Runner* said, as the image of a room appeared. Tarjiaan peered closer, but couldn't tell what the room was. He did see

Daanir, though. The mancer was working under the supervision of a pair of guards.

"Those are the ballast pumps," Kaapi said.

[They are damaged,] *Wave Runner* reported. [From the recordings, they intend to surface and execute Daanir, but the pumps are damaged. So they make him repair them, and when they take him back to the brig, Naajir damages the pumps again.]

"Stalling for time," Marikaar murmured. "They know we're coming."

"They don't have Naajir locked away?" Wilaanger asked.

[No. He has been in the mancer passages with Logiri and... I believe the other man is Lord Rathsafa. I cannot reach Naajir. He may be asleep.]

"Then try to reach Aanaji. Tell her that we're coming," Tarjiaan said. "And tell her that if she can get into the security systems, she needs to hide the fact that there's a ship approaching."

[I will try to reach her.]

Daanir sat back on his heels, watching the pump motors purr and churn, knowing it meant his death.

"Fixed?" the guard asked from behind him.

Daanir didn't turn. "Yes. We'll see if it stays that way."

The guard hesitated, then rested his hand on Daanir's shoulder. "For what it's worth, I'm sorry."

Daanir looked up. "You don't have to follow him," he said in a low voice. "You can stop him."

The guard looked at his partner, then shook his head. "We thought about it. But... we're two, and there are eighteen other guards who will happily feed us to the fish if we turn. And Ilaris keeps the key to that limiter on a chain around his neck." He sighed. "Let's get you back to the cell. Then I'll get something for you to eat."

Daanir nodded and stood up. There was a sudden, desperate urge to attack, to steal their weapons, to try and take Ilaris down himself. To end this right now. But... they were right. He was one man, against guards who didn't care that Ilaris was a traitor. He'd never get close. He let the guards lead him back to the brig, trying not to think about what would happen next. There were almost back to the brig when he realized that there were more guards in the corridor than he'd seen before.

"What's happening?" he whispered. "There's never been this many guards here."

"I don't know."

They came around the corner, and Daanir stopped. Ilaris and his guards were standing in front of the cell, and Aanaji wasn't the only person inside. There were more guards inside with her, and three bodies on the ground. The one closest to the door was clearly Naajir. All three were clearly bound, their hands chained behind their backs. From Aanaji's posture, she was bound as well, and two guards had their pistols trained on her.

Ilaris turned toward them. "Are the pumps operational?"

The guards hesitated, then one of them stepped forward. "They are, sir."

"Good." Ilaris gestured, and two of his guards closed on Daanir, grabbing him and wrestling his arms back before he could fight back. Not that he dared — if he raised a hand against them, Aanaji would pay for it. He felt manacles closing around his wrists before he was shoved into the cell with the others. Now he could see that the other two were Logiri and Rathsafa, and that Naajir had a limiter around his neck.

"Surprised to see your accomplices?" Ilaris asked. "They amused me, for a time. The boy especially. You're a credible teacher,

Mancer, to have taught him so much in so short a time. But I'm through with games." He stepped back and touched the earpiece he wore. "The pumps are functional. Take us to the surface." He turned to look at the two guards who had accompanied Daanir to and from the pump room. "Now, for the pair of you. Were you aware that I was listening? I heard every word. Every conversation. Every admission of treason." He turned and walked away, calling, "Kill them," over his shoulder.

"No," Daanir breathed. "Ilaris, leave them alone!" But his voice was drowned out by the echoing gunfire. The guards followed Ilaris away, leaving the bodies behind.

Daanir backed away from the cell bars until his back was against the wall, then closed his eyes and slid down. He heard soft footsteps, the quiet susurration of cloth against the cell wall, and Aanaji's shoulder pressed against his.

"I'm sorry," she murmured. "I... what do we do now?"

Daanir shook his head. "I don't know. I—" He felt Aanaji jerk, and looked at her, seeing a look of shock on her face. "What is it?"

"I..." She closed her eyes, then blinked. "The audio is muted. I... Daanir, there's a voice... I... how do I know if I'm going mad?"

Daanir snorted. "You become a mancer. What voice? Does it have a name?"

Aanaji frowned slightly. "I... *Wave Runner.* I... am I hearing my brother's ship?"

Daanir stared at her, then smiled, wanting to laugh out loud. "You're a stronger mancer than you give yourself credit for. And yes. She's aware. And if you're hearing them, she's close. Tell her what's happening. Tell her they need to hurry."

There was a long pause, then Aanaji nodded. "She says she's in the systems. She knows. She sees us." Another pause. "She says to tell you that her sister is safe. Sister?"

"She means Kaapi. They decided between them that they're sisters." Daanir let out a sigh. "What do they need from us? From you. I'm not good for anything at the moment."

"You're decorative," Aanaji murmured. "That counts for something."

"Aanaji!" Daanir blurted, and she laughed.

"You're too easy to tease," she said. "*Wave Runner* says that we'll need to keep the sensors from showing that they're coming. How do I do that?"

Daanir studied his husband's sister for a moment, then smiled. "I'm going to have so much fun training you," he said. "Right. Ask *Wave Runner* to tell everyone that I love them all, and let's get to work."

Chapter Twenty-Eight
Surface

"THE PUMPS ARE WORKING," Tarjiaan repeated. "How much time do we have?" He looked at the charts. "Not enough. Not nearly enough. We're not close enough to stop them, or to attack. And if they see ships when they bring the prisoners out to the Sentence ring, they'll kill them immediately. We can't get close. We can't get a launch there before they dive. I..."

"What about a submersible?" Kaapi asked. "Can we get a submersible there in time? Because I can destroy the pumps once they're on the surface. That will give us time."

Tarjiaan stared at his foster daughter. "Kaapi, this is dangerous—"

"I know," she interrupted. "Papa-Captain, it's always been dangerous. That's why I was a crèche baby. Because it's dangerous, and because people die. But isn't that why we're fighting? So it stops being dangerous, and no one else has to die?"

Wilaanger covered his mouth with one hand, but Tarjiaan heard him clearly, "Out of the mouths of minnows."

Kaapi scowled at him. "Just because I'm young doesn't mean I'm ignorant. And we're wasting time. If we're going to save their lives, this may be the only way."

"She's right," Marikaar said. "I hate to send her, but she's the only mancer we have, and she was trained by the best there ever was. I'll roust up Antivar and send him with her. It'll keep him from

330

trying to be part of anything he isn't up to yet. Captain, by your leave?"

Tarjiaan closed his eyes and nodded. "Kaapi, come here." Kaapi got out of her chair and came around the table. Tarjiaan took her hands and looked into her eyes. "Once you're in place, let us know so I can get the launches in the water. We'll have to move fast, and there's no room for mistakes. I hate that I have to ask this of you. But you're right. There is no choice. So promise me that you will take no unwarranted risks, and that you will not push yourself. Losing you would destroy him... and me. Do you understand?"

She nodded, tears welling up. "I understand, Papa-Captain. And I'll do it. I'll bring them back."

"Bring yourself back, too. Promise me that, Kaap."

She smiled. "You haven't called me that yet. Thank you." She drew her hands from his, then threw her arms around his neck and hugged him tightly. "I love you. I'll be back."

"I love you, too. And I'm holding you to that." He smiled as she stood up. "Don't make me send your grandfather after you."

Her eyes widened. "You mean the scary ghost grandfather?"

He nodded. "I mean the scary ghost grandfather."

"I promise!" She went around the table and hugged Nika, then turned to Marikaar. "First Mate?"

"Captain, by your leave?"

"Granted." Tarjiaan waited until they were gone before scrubbing his hand over his face. "If anything happens to her, he'll murder me. Twice."

[I will monitor them,] *Wave Runner* said. [And keep you informed.]

"Thank you," Tarjiaan said. He turned to the others at the table. "Once she disables the pumps, we'll need to move fast," he said. "We won't have much time. I can pinpoint where the *Chimaera* will surface, but we'll need to be alongside and in her shadow before they get on the deck, or they'll see us. Prepare the launches, and assemble strike teams. Istin, I think your men will be better suited to this sort of combat than mine?"

"Of course, Captain," Istin bowed. "Permission to go assemble teams? I've seen your launches. How many of them? And... teams of eight under a launch command?"

"Yes. There are four launches and plan for me leading one of those teams."

Istin blinked. "Ah... Captain, not to be rude, but will the launch carry your weight? Those metal breeches aren't exactly light."

Tarjiaan heard someone snort with laughter, and had to bite his lip to keep from joining them. "The launches are reinforced to carry my weight, Istin," he said. "I won't sink."

Istin looked at him with an odd expression. "You won't swim, either. Not if you fall in. Those are just trouser-shaped anchors, and you'll do the rock stroke straight to the bottom."

Someone behind him was definitely laughing. Tarjiaan suspected it was Kyraath, but he wasn't going to turn and look. "Daanir planned for that, Istin. I promise. You're not going to have to dive in after me."

Istin looked past Tarjiaan, and his lips pressed together hard. He nodded, and in a choked voice answered, "Understood, Captain."

"Go on, before you strangle," Tarjiaan said. Istin barely made it out of the day cabin before his laughter was clearly audible. Once the door closed, Tarjiaan turned to see Kyraath, leaning against the wall, one hand over his mouth. He shook his head.

"I apologize," he wheezed. "Truly."

"Accepted." Tarjiaan turned back. "Wil, get the infirmary ready for anything. Nika, Navi—" He frowned. "Where did Navi go?"

[He is on the submersible with Kaapi and Antivar,] *Wave Runner* answered. [Lorithi is piloting. At their top speed, it will take them twenty-five minutes to reach the *Chimaera*.]

"We're that close?" Wilaanger asked. "Nika, let's go get ready. *Wave Runner*, tell Chel to meet us in the infirmary, please?" He stood up and headed for the door. Nika rose, but didn't leave Tarjiaan's side. He reached for her hand and pulled her closer.

"I'll bring him back," he said softly.

"You both need to come back," she said, and leaned in to kiss him, wrapping her arms around his neck and holding on tightly. "You have to bring them all back."

Tarjiaan hugged her close, kissed her again, then let her go. "I'll bring them home," he said as he stood up. "Marikaar?"

The speaker overhead crackled. "*Captain, the submersible is away.*"

"Then all hands, beat to quarters and prepare for battle. All guns at the ready. Issue earpieces to the launch teams, and let's get in the water."

Daanir didn't need to be able to feel the machines to know when they'd reached the surface. He could smell when the air circulators started giving off sea air.

"How are they?" he asked. Aanaji looked up from where she was kneeling next to Naajir.

"They're waking up," she answered. "Can you tell? The engines have cut off. We're stopped."

Daanir nodded. "I know. I can smell it." He took a deep breath. "Anything?"

She shook her head, then looked up at the ceiling. "Nothing. I don't know..." She shifted awkwardly onto her hip. "Are we going to die, Daanir?"

"You can call me Daan, and I don't know." Daanir tipped his head back and closed his eyes. "I hope not," he said in a low voice. "I've never held a baby before."

"What?" Aanaji asked. Then she caught her breath and shifted around until she could get to her feet. She came over to sit next to him and whispered, "Daan? Is Nika pregnant?"

Daanir looked at her and nodded. "Two months."

Aanaji looked up again, horror on her face. "Do you think they heard?"

Daanir looked up, then shook his head. "The reception isn't that good. And they're probably all busy getting ready to kill us. So I don't think so... Naji?"

Across from him, Naajir groaned and rolled onto his side, trying to move his arms. He whimpered, and Aanaji moved, rolling onto her knees, then getting up and going to her son.

"Naji," she said gently. "Can you hear me?"

"Mama?" Naajir coughed, shook his head, then looked around. "What... where are we? Daanir?"

"He knew you were in the passages," Daanir said. "Apparently, the two of us were entertainment."

Naajir groaned. "I tried... I tried to be careful." He looked at Logiri and Rathsafa. "Are they all right?"

"They're waking up slowly." Aanaji closed her eyes. "They're coming."

Daanir nodded. "You did fine, Naji. But he probably knew where all of you were from the start. It's a belowship. There aren't that many places to hide." He shifted and got to his feet, moving toward the bars. He could hear footsteps coming closer.

"Lord Mancer?" Daanir looked over his shoulder to see that Logiri was sitting up. The man looked ill, and Daanir winced.

"Logiri? What's wrong?"

"The gas..." Logiri grimaced and shook his head. "It is not sitting well with me."

Daanir went to him and crouched, studying him. "How bad is it?"

"I will be fine," Logiri answered. He glanced at the bars. "For however long we have left."

Daanir rose and went back to the bars. The footsteps were closer. "I have one more card I can play."

"What?" Aanaji asked.

"A gamble on what Ilaris doesn't know," Daanir answered. "Rathsafa, are you with us?"

Rathsafa didn't move, and Logiri sighed. "Nadar, you have to get on your feet," he said, reaching out with one foot to nudge Rathsafa's leg. "Up. If I can, you can."

"You did not ask if I wanted to," Rathsafa grumbled. He rolled onto his knees and folded forward, his forehead nearly touching the floor. "Gir, will the Sand Queen find us here?"

Logiri sighed. "We're not dying here, Nadar. Now get up."

"Who's the Sand Queen?" Naajir asked.

"The Tyracan goddess of death," Aanaji answered. She blushed slightly when Daanir arched a brow at her. "I may not be the musician that my mother was, or that Tarjiaan and my son are. But I know the stories that make the songs."

"We'll talk more about that later," Daanir said. "All of you, get to the back of the cell. And... if it comes to it, don't fight them. Don't give them a reason to kill you out of hand because you're more trouble than you're worth to them. Remember, Jiaan is coming." He looked back out, and saw the guards come around the corner. He counted them as they appeared — fifteen guards, followed by Ilaris. All at once, Daanir realized that he hadn't seen anyone else. Where were the others, the servants, or the cooks? Adalia, or Kaapi's tutors? The engineering crew who worked under him? He hadn't seen anyone but Ilaris and his guards, and that was frankly terrifying, given how easily Ilaris seemed to kill anyone he no longer needed. Or, Daanir realized, who could tell the truth about what happened on the *Chimaera*.

"Since you're going to kill us anyway," he called as Ilaris got closer, "answer a question. Where is everyone? I haven't seen any crew at all. It can't be just you and the guards. Where is everyone?"

Ilaris smiled. "Still with the questions?" he asked with a laugh.

Daanir shrugged, trying not to wince at the strain it put on his already-aching shoulders. "You don't ask, you don't learn."

Ilaris rolled his eyes, and shook his head, turning away and walking back the way he'd come. "I no longer have to entertain your curiosity. Take them."

Time to play his card. "You realize you're going to be murdering the King of Lastalt," Daanir called.

Ilaris stopped walking. "What did you say?"

"I said that if you do this, you'll be killing the King of Lastalt," Daanir repeated. "There's war on land. The people of Lestalt have risen up in the name of their rightful king, they have Sualiman on their side, and the Empire is falling apart."

Ilaris turned to look at him. "What do you mean? You're saying that our fake emissary is the King of Lestalt? And you expect me to believe that?"

"You need to believe it, because it's true. Rathsafa Nadarish, son of the Lestalti Queen Tishaya, has been acknowledged by the people of Lastalt as their rightfully born king. And his people want him back. They went to war with the Empire because of a rumor that he was dead. And the Empire is about to fall, Ilaris. Think about that." Daanir met Ilaris' eyes. "You want Meradon. You want the throne. If you ever want to be able to set foot on land and hold the Coral Throne the way your father did, you'll rethink this.

Because if it gets out that you're the one who killed the Lestalti king? His people will tear you into bits too small to use as bait."

Ilaris sniffed. "The people will believe what I tell them. And I will tell them that the Mad Mancer returned to finish the job, and that he murdered the Princess Royal and the young Sea Prince while they were meeting with the Lestalti king. Very tragic."

"The people already know the truth," Daanir replied, surprised his voice was as even as it sounded. That he wasn't shaking. "They know who you are, and they know what you did. They've seen the recordings showing you murdering Ikaanaji and giving Tarjiaan over to the Imps. They've seen Tarjiaan alive and well and wearing the Kraken. They've seen me standing on Tarjiaan's left as his battle companion, with Nika wearing the Queen's pearls on his right, and Naajir at her side. They've heard him take on the mantle of the Sea King, they know that the time is now to move to retake Meradon. The entire fleet is converging on him." He studied Ilaris for a moment. "And you didn't know that. Any of that. How did you not know? The broadcast went out before Narrick betrayed us."

Ilaris stared at him. "What broadcast?"

"I just told you what broadcast," Daanir said slowly. "Narrick set it up to transmit to the entire fleet. Whatever allies you think you might have had have abandoned you. Whatever advantage you think you had is gone. Everyone knows that you are a traitor, a rapist, and a murderer, and the King is coming for you."

For a moment, Ilaris looked horrified. Then he composed himself and shook his head. "Let him come," he said, waving one hand dismissively. "We'll be long gone, and he won't even find your corpses. Take them to the deck and chain them to the rings. I will follow."

The guards seemed surprised that there was no resistance, but that didn't mean they were at all gentle. Daanir was shoved more than once, and he heard someone crying behind him. When he tried to look, he was shoved again, hard enough to drive him to his knees. He got up and kept going, until he was out in the air. In the distance, he could see sails.

Too far in the distance — the *Wave Runner* wasn't close enough. They'd never reach the *Chimaera* in time.

They were going to die here.

Numb, Daanir let the guards manhandle him into position, kneeling with his back to the ring, a chain running from his bound wrists to the deck. Aanaji was chained on his right, and Rathsafa on his left. The guards backed away, then turned and headed back toward the hatch.

"I'm sorry," Daanir said softly. "I thought they'd get to us in time."

"They're coming," Aanaji replied. "We can see them. I...." She stopped, her body tensing. "Daan... the pumps just... stopped." He turned to look at her, but she had her head bowed, her eyes closed. "I... I don't know what you call it, but... I think something... exploded?"

"Ex..." Daanir straightened. "Kaapi. But..." Ilaris came out, and Daanir bit his lip. He couldn't give it away. Couldn't risk... whatever was happening outside the belowship. But *how*?

"By the authority of the Coral Throne, and for the good of Meradon," Ilaris intoned, sounding almost bored with the official proclamation, "I declare all of you to be traitors, and sentence you to death." He looked past them, to the distant sails. "I hope he has a good viewing glass," he added. "That's the only way he'll ever see you again." He turned and walked back to the hatch, the guards following him in. The hatch closed with a solid, resounding thump.

Tarjiaan heard the thump of the hatch closing, and murmured into the comms, "On my mark... three... two... one... go! Get them free!"

The launches were tethered to the service ladders that ran up both sides of the belowship, fore and aft. Tarjiaan was the last man from his launch to take the ladder, the most dangerous part of this mission for him — his metal feet had little traction on the wet metal rungs, and he had no sensory feedback on how he was placing them. So the other launch crews were already on the deck by the time he was to the top of the ladder. Istin was crouched next to the kneeling group, cutters in his hand, working to free Aanaji.

"Easy, ma'am," he crooned. "I've got you. Just a moment... what are these chains made of? Sun and Sand, got it! Right. You next, Naji-boy."

"Jiaan!" Tarjiaan heard Daanir's voice, but didn't dare react — if he fell apart now, they were dead.

"Guard the hatch!" he ordered. "If anyone comes through that door, drop them. But Ilaris is mine. Submersible, report!"

"*We're on our way back to the* Wave Runner, *Papa-Captain*," Kaapi said in his ear. "*That pump is going to have to be replaced. Is my papa safe?*"

He smiled. "Good girl. And not yet. We'll be away and safe shortly." He turned and looked around. "Istin, report!"

"Going to take me longer than I thought!" Istin called back. "This metal is... stronger than I thought it would be. Festus, you guard the lady! Get her to the launch!" The crewman bowed and took Aanaji's arm, leading her toward the aft ladders.

"Jiaan!" Daanir shouted again. "Listen to me!"

Tarjiaan started to turn, but the hatch slammed open, guards pouring out.

"Hand to hand!" Jiaan shouted. "Don't shoot unless you have no choice!" He saw Ilaris in the hatch and drew his saber. "Ilaris!"

"Jiaan, no!" Daanir shouted. "Jiaan, he has your hair!"

Daanir's words didn't make sense at first. Then Ilaris smiled and pointed at him, and Tarjiaan felt every muscle freeze. He couldn't move, couldn't speak. It was hard to breathe.

"Enough of this!" Ilaris shouted. "Stand down, or I'll kill him where he stands!" He looked around as the fighting stopped. As Tarjiaan's men slowly lowered their weapons. Tarjiaan could hear Daanir cursing, hear chains rattling, but couldn't turn to see what was happening. Couldn't do anything but watch the man coming toward him, a satisfied smirk on his face.

"Well, so this is how the great Sea Prince meets his end," Ilaris said with a laugh. He held his hand up, showing the braided bracelet than encircled his wrist. "Bound by his own hair." He reached out and took the saber from Tarjiaan's hand, tossing to onto the deck behind him. "I suppose I should be grateful. Now I get to kill you properly." He looked past Tarjiaan, "I'll have to sink that ship. It's too much of a symbol. And once I take care of your little Imperial whore, all the loose ends will be cut." He paused. "Although perhaps I'll let her live until she whelps. She is a pretty little thing, and I will need an heir—" Tarjiaan went cold. How did Ilaris know? He struggled against the magic bonds, but couldn't even make a sound. Ilaris pointed at him again. "Time to die."

Tarjiaan heard Daanir shouting. Heard Logiri and Naajir. But it felt as if it was at a distance, as the sky above and the sea below turned a uniform gray, narrowing to a pinpoint of clear vision through which he could see only Ilaris, laughing at him. He couldn't hear the laughter. Then he saw Aanaji, a bare blade in her hands, running toward them, her eyes wide and wild. She didn't slow, didn't stop.

Not until she'd driven the entire length of the long blade into Ilaris' unprotected back.

The magic holding Tarjiaan vanished, and he staggered back and fell hard, gasping for air as the world snapped back to crystal clarity. Ilaris fell to his knees, blood staining his chest, his lips. He raised his hand and pointed at Tarjiaan, then toppled over and didn't move. As he fell, Aanaji stepped back and sank to the deck, staring and silent.

"Stand down," Tarjiaan said. He didn't have to shout — there wasn't a sound other than the wind. Ilaris' guards didn't need to be told twice — weapons hit the deck, and Tarjiaan's crew slowly circulated, picking them up and piling them away from the new prisoners. The question of what do with them was something Tarjiaan would have to deal with, but first... he slowly got to his feet and looked around, saw crewmen leading Logiri and Rathsafa toward the launches. Istin was kneeling next to Daanir, swearing in a steady stream of profanity.

"Got it!" Istin crowed. "Easy, Daanir."

Daanir winced as he moved his arms, then slowly got to his feet, staggering toward Tarjiaan. He reached out and touched Tarjiaan's chest. "Are you hurt?"

"No," Tarjiaan answered. "I... no. I'm fine."

Daanir nodded. "I knew you'd come for us," he said softly. "I... I'll be with you in a moment." He moved past Tarjiaan, toward where Aanaji was still sitting on the deck, staring at Ilaris' body. Before he reached her, he turned back, looking up at Tarjiaan. "We need Nika. And Chel. Now, Jiaan."

"What?" Tarjiaan asked. "Why?"

Daanir didn't answer, going to one knee next to Aanaji. "Aanaji?" His voice was quiet. Gentle, but Aanaji still flinched, and Tarjiaan realized why Daanir had asked specifically for the women. "Aanaji, it's over. You did it. You stopped him. You saved us all. You saved yourself. He's dead."

Aanaji turned and stared at him. Then his words must have registered, because she crumpled, sobbing. She didn't resist as Daanir gathered her in his arms.

"Uncle?" Naajir stopped next to Tarjiaan. "Should I... what do we do?"

"Let Daan take care of her." Tarjiaan reached up and touched his earpiece. "Marikaar, the submersible will be back shortly. I need them to turn around immediately and bring Nika and Chel to the *Chimaera.*"

"*Understood, Captain. Is it over?*"

"It's over, Marikaar. He's dead." Tarjiaan took a deep breath. "The traitor is dead."

Chapter Twenty-Nine
Composure

THE *Wave Runner* finally drew alongside the *Chimaera*, and launches went back and forth, bringing a skeleton crew to man the *Chimaera*. Ilaris' guards were taken to the brig, to the same cell where Naajir said they had been held. Tarjiaan sent Logiri and Rathsafa to the *Wave Runner*, but Naajir refused to leave him.

"Stubborn," Istin chided with a smile. "That collar. You and Daanir have them, but no one else did. What does it do?"

"It's a limiter. It keeps me from using mancery," Naajir answered. "I've had a headache for hours now."

Istin pulled his cutters out of his pocket. "Let's take care of that, then."

"Uncle Daan is still wearing one," Naajir said, turning so that Istin could work. "He's been wearing one since they took us. I don't know how he hasn't lost his mind yet."

"He'd be the first one to tell you that he lost his mind a long time ago," Tarjiaan said. "Marikaar, report?"

His earpiece crackled. "*Captain, it's a good thing you're not seeing this,*" Marikaar replied. "*You'd want to kill him again. Twice. This poor crew. The ones were weren't needed to run the ship were locked away and are half-starved. I've got Chel's husband here, but... there are people missing. Names on the crew lists that no one can say what happened to them. I'll be questioning those guards, and I'll be sending the remaining crew to the* Wave Runner *for medical attention. But we've got the ship under control, and... well, we're stuck on the surface. Mancer Kaapi did a fine job on the ballast pumps, but now they'll need to be replaced."*

"I'm putting you in command, Marikaar. Choose your crew as you see fit, and take the *Chimaera* to the floating dockyards for refit. Also, once you question those guards, I'll want a report."

"Captain!" Marikaar sounded stunned. *"I... thank you, Captain. I'll inform you as to who I chose, and I'll have that report for you soonest. And... the Mancer Royal is escorting the Princess and the healers to the submersible. He asks that you return to the* Wave Runner, *and he'll meet you there."*

"Thank you, Captain," Tarjiaan said, smiling as he heard Marikaar sputter. He tapped his earpiece and turned to Naajir. "Let's go back to the *Wave Runner.* There's nothing else we can do here, and Daanir and the healers are bringing your mother to the *Wave Runner.* Marikaar has it under control, and we'll meet them at the dockyards."

Naajir nodded, but was quiet the entire way back to the *Wave Runner.* He followed Tarjiaan back to the day cabin, sank into a chair and stared at the floor. Tarjiaan let him be, taking off his weapons and his chest armor, cleaning them, and putting them away, all while keeping an eye on the boy. When he returned to the table, he found that he wasn't the only one minding Naajir — Gossamer was sitting in Naajir's lap, purring loudly enough to hear across the room, while Tripod circled the chair, yowling. Tarjiaan sat down in his usual chair, reaching down and picking up Tripod, catching the cat mid-yowl and making Naajir smile slightly.

"Do you want to talk?" Tarjiaan asked, cradling Tripod in one arm. "Or do you just want company while you think?"

Naajir frowned slightly. "I... I'm not sure what I want," he said. "He... he admitted he was my father. He told me he was." Naajir's frown deepened. "Everyone knows, don't they? We sent the recording out to everyone. They all know what he did to her."

Tarjiaan nodded. "They all know that he abused her trust. That he assaulted her. That it was not her fault."

"And that I'm here because of it," Naajir finished, his voice quiet. "That I shouldn't have ever been born."

Tarjiaan took a deep breath, picking his words as carefully as he could, knowing that the wrong word would shatter his nephew beyond repair. "Naji, your mother said you were the best thing that ever happened to her. She loves you." He reached across and rested his hand on Naajir's arm. "I love you. You're a fine young man, and I'm so proud to have you as part of my family."

Naajir nodded. "Thank you. But... now I'm even more certain that I shouldn't be your heir. I mean... even if everyone believes that my mother wasn't at fault, my father was still a traitor to the crown and a murderer. I can't take the throne. No one will follow me."

"We sailed this course, Naji. I'll honor your choice. You explained your reasoning, and I understand." Tarjiaan squeezed his arm and sat back, laughing as Tripod scaled his chest and perched on his shoulder. "You're going to get too big for that, Tripod."

Naajir smiled. "That won't make him stop. Not if you let him keep doing it. He wants to be there."

Tarjiaan nodded. "And what do you want, Naji? How can I help? I already know that you'll be abdicating your position once the baby comes. What else?"

Naajir leaned back in his chair, looking at the ceiling, trying to find the answers there. "I... I want to be a mancer—"

"You are a mancer, Naji," Tarjiaan said. "Daanir has already named you an apprentice. What else?"

Naajir smiled. "He did, didn't he? And... and it wasn't just a pat on the head, like some of my tutors did. Daan believes in me." He looked at Tarjiaan. "You believe in me. Kaapi... He blushed, and Tarjiaan smiled.

"Ah. You're not old enough, Naji."

"I know!" Naajir grimaced. "It's four more years. And we've both got training to do. And growing to do. And we might not want that in four years. I know that, too." He sighed and looked around. "I don't know how much of it is that she treats me like an equal, not like a trophy. She's been my friend since she found me on the *Chimaera*, and she's never cared that I was the heir's heir. I know that might change, but for now? Kaapi and I are... something." He shrugged. "Someday, I'd like to have someone to stand with me, the way you have Aunt Nika and Uncle Daan. I'd like a ship like the *Wave Runner*, one that looks to me. I'd like to have my music, and my mancery. And... I don't know if I want to live on land."

"I imagine a lot of people your age are going to have that same reaction," Tarjiaan said. "There are going to be those who can't make the change back, or who won't. And we'll manage. Daan said it best — once we're on land, we'll still have Meradon below the waves, and we will still rule the seas. So if a ship is in your future, then a ship is what you'll have." He looked up. "Perhaps... this ship? Once I'm crowned, I'll have to rule from the Palace. *Wave Runner* is going to need someone to take care of her. Someone who loves the royal flagship the way she needs to be loved."

"You're serious?" Naajir's voice cracked.

"If that's what you want." Tarjiaan smiled. "Does that help?"

Naajir nodded, leaning forward and setting the kitten on the floor. "I think it does. Do you think my mother will want to see me?"

"I think you should ask your aunt that," Tarjiaan answered. "*Wave Runner*? Where is Nika?"

[The Captain's Lady is in the infirmary, with People Mancer Chel and... the lady with them? I do not know how to call her?]

"That's Aanaji, *Wave Runner,*" Tarjiaan answered. "You were speaking with her."

[Oh! I did not realize. She's not speaking to me now. Her mind is closed.]

"When she's ready, she'll talk to you," Tarjiaan said. He paused, wondering if she'd ever be ready to talk to him. "And I think that the same goes for you, Naji. When your mother is ready to talk to you, she'll let you know." He looked up as someone knocked on the door. "Come in!"

The door opened, and Daanir came inside. Everything about him looked... slumped. Tarjiaan looked at his throat, which was bare. Daanir noticed and smiled.

"Istin was waiting for me when the submersible docked," he said. "Naji, when you're ready, your mother wants to see you." He paused. "She's... a little fragile right now."

Naajir nodded. "I understand. I won't push." He stood up and turned to Tarjiaan, who held his arms open. Naajir stepped into the embrace, holding on tightly. "Thank you, Uncle."

He hurried out, and Daanir took the abandoned chair. He drummed his fingers on the tabletop, then met Tarjiaan's eyes.

"Your sister is the strongest person I think I've ever met," he said softly. "I understand where her head is right now, and... well, I haven't had a chance to react yet. But... I might be there, later."

"How close are you to falling apart?"

Daanir grimaced. "Half a hair? Maybe? I'm holding on, but..." He closed his eyes. "Narrick. It was fucking *Narrick.*"

"You don't have to tell me more," Tarjiaan said. "*Wave Runner* showed us the footage from the submersible."

Daanir nodded. "I can't get my mind around it. And... remember how we didn't know what happened to the mancers?

Ilaris recalled them all, and we didn't know where they were? I know now. And... Jiaan, we're it. We're all the mancers that are left. Me, Ishantar, the children. And now Aanaji. We're the only mancers left."

Tarjiaan sat up so abruptly that Tripod had to jump onto the table to avoid falling off his shoulder. "What?"

Daanir shrugged. "I don't know if he was lying. I'm going to have to find out. But... I don't think he was. I think he knew he couldn't control the mancers, so... he got rid of them. He said he sent them to the Emperor." He rubbed his face. "Mothers below, I'm tired."

"Have you let Nika or Navi examine you?"

Daanir grinned. "Navi wouldn't let me off the submersible unless I let him make absolutely certain I was healthy. Aanaji laughed, so I'm not complaining. I'm just... tired."

"Go to bed." Tarjiaan suggested. "I'll join you when I can."

"Not alone," Daanir said. "I don't want to be alone when I break. And I know I will. I'm tired enough that I'll break." He tipped his head back. "I knew you'd find us." He took a deep breath. "Oh, before I forget. Kaapi is still on the *Chimaera*. Before we left, Marikaar asked if I'd allow her to stay. He was worried that the *Chimaera* wouldn't make it to the dockyards without a mancer on board. He wanted me to stay, but I didn't think it would be good for Aanaji to stay on the *Chimaera,* and she made it very clear that she wasn't going anywhere without me. She needed to be out of there. Wil said it was a good thing I did. She needs a fresh start."

"She'll have that," Tarjiaan said. "She'll have anything she needs. Including a place away from me, if that's what she needs."

"It isn't," Daanir said. "You cannot send her away, Jiaan. She wants to know you. She regrets everything he made her do, and she's afraid you won't want her anywhere near you. But she wants to know you. And Nika. She told me that she likes Nika. She was worried that you and me together was going to hurt Nika."

Tarjiaan smiled. "That's good." He stood up and came around to stand in front of Daanir's chair. He leaned down and rested one hand on Daanir's cheek, running his thumb over his cheekbone. Daanir closed his eyes and whimpered softly as Tarjiaan kissed his lips.

"You... you need to stop," Daanir said softly. "I... not yet."

Tarjiaan nodded, but didn't drew back. "I was so afraid I wasn't going to be able to find you," he whispered, resting his forehead against Daanir's. "I didn't know what I was doing, and Kyraath couldn't explain it in a way that worked."

"You found us," Daanir said. "And... if you stay this close, I'm going to kiss you again. And then I'm going to shatter, because it's safe, but I can't yet because you have work to do."

"I love you, mancer mine." Tarjiaan paused, then kissed the tip of Daanir's nose. He stood up, reached over and picked Tripod up off the table, and put the cat into Daanir's lap. "Pet the cat. It helps."

Daanir looked down at Tripod, who sat up and reached out with his front paw, batting at Daanir's chin. He laughed, petting the cat. "What else can I tell you, before you go out and be the king?"

"I think you need less reporting time and more time petting the cat, so I'll let you be. I'm going to go to the infirmary and see how Logiri and Rathsafa are."

"I'll come with you. I don't want to be alone right now. And just to warn you, Logiri wasn't doing well. He reacted badly to the gas that Ilaris used to take him, Rathsafa and Naajir," Daanir said. He put Tripod down and stood up. "Go play with Gossamer, Tripod. I'll pet you more later."

Tarjiaan led the way out of the day cabin, wandering over to the rail overlooking the *Chimaera*. There was a crewman on the deck, and she waved when she saw him. He waved back and kept walking, weaving around the crew moving this way and that.

"Captain!" Antivar made his way across the crowded deck.

"How are you feeling, Antivar?" Tarjiaan asked, slowing down so that Antivar could fall in next to him.

"Better," Antivar answered. "Still... not entirely recovered, but Navi won't let me push."

"Having a healer as a spouse means that they do take care of you," Tarjiaan said.

"He's not my husband yet, Captain. That's one of the things I wanted to ask you," Antivar said. "We're going to war. And I want to be married before we do. If we could have the ceremony?"

"Antivar, I promised you that months ago, and it floated clear out of my mind," Tarjiaan said. "I'm sorry. Do you want it now, or when we get back to the dockyards? Your mother is here, so we can do either."

"I'll ask Navi, and let you know. And... the other thing I wanted to ask." Antivar paused, then took a deep breath. "Marikaar asked me to stand as his First Mate on the *Chimaera*."

"He did?" Tarjiaan stopped walking. "Antivar, that's wonderful! Congratulations!"

Antivar blushed. "I... I don't know if I should take it," he admitted. "I mean... Nika said that one of the men we rescued today is her father. Navi is going to meet his father for the first time, and I don't want to separate them so soon after meeting."

Daanir coughed. "Wait, Navi hasn't met Rathsafa yet?"

"Navi was on the submersible, and Rathsafa and Logiri came back by launch," Tarjiaan answered. "And I'm not entirely certain where Navi is at the moment."

"He's in the infirmary," Antivar answered. "And the last I saw of him, he was trying to hide behind Wilaanger. He's waiting for Nika to be available to introduce him, and she has been busy."

Tarjiaan nodded. "We're going to the infirmary. Walk with us." He started walking again. "So, my advice for you? Tour the *Chimaera* before you decide, Antivar. It will be good for you to learn about the belowships before you make the decision, and if you decide to take the rank, you can rejoin us when we move on the Empire."

Antivar nodded. "That... makes sense. I don't know what to expect, so how can I make an informed decision? Should I stay there until we reach the dockyards?"

"That's not a bad idea," Daanir said. "And since we'll be escorting you back, if you have any issues with being below, you can just come back here."

"Issues?" Antivar frowned. "Oh. Because it's entirely enclosed?" He cocked his head to the side. "I'll talk to Navi. See what he thinks." He stepped forward and opened the infirmary door. It was quiet in the infirmary, and Tarjiaan paused inside to let his eyes adjust to the dim light of the outer room. The inner door opened, and Chel peered out.

"Captain," she said, smiling. "Just the man I wanted to see. Logiri is asking for you." She looked past him. "Ah, Daanir. Just the other man I wanted to see. Lady Aanaji was asking about you."

"I thought she would be with Naji," Daanir said.

"She is, and asked if you would join them." Chel gestured. "Last bunk on the left."

Daanir nodded and looked at Tarjiaan, who smiled. "Go on. I'll come find you after I look in on Logiri." Daanir walked away, and Tarjiaan turned to Chel. "Where am I going?"

Chel pointed. "Second on the right. For the record, he's not alone. Lord Rathsafa is sitting with him."

Tarjiaan paused. "I... I'm not even going to speculate."

"You're not doing it very loudly," Antivar said. "Chel, where's Navi?"

Chel grinned. "He's in the back. Officially, he's getting things ready for the *Chimaera* crew who are going to be sent over. Unofficially, he's trying not to be obvious about the fact that he's hiding."

"Chel, Marikaar says that he's seen Lysson," Tarjiaan said. "He'll be coming over with the crew."

Chel closed her eyes and covered her mouth with one hand, her calm facade cracking. "I... thank you," she murmured. "I didn't want to ask."

Tarjiaan squeezed her shoulder, then went to the door she'd indicated and knocked before opening it. Inside, Logiri was sitting up in bed. He looked older, thinner, and not well at all, but his smile was warm when he saw Tarjiaan. Rathsafa sat in a chair next to the head of the bed, and he bowed his head when Tarjiaan came in.

"Captain," Rathsafa said. "Ah... Your Majesty?"

"You don't have to call me anything but my name," Tarjiaan said. "You are, after all, my father by marriage. You're family."

"I told you," Logiri murmured. He turned and looked at Rathsafa, a fond expression on his face. "Nadar, he will never stand on formality. Not from those he considers family."

Tarjiaan studied the two of them for a moment, then asked, "So... that target you refused to take...?"

"Was Nadar," Logiri said. "We grew up together, and... I couldn't kill him." He took a deep breath and sighed. "I apologize, Tarjiaan. I tried to deal with Ilaris, but I couldn't get a clean target. And apparently, he knew where we were hiding the entire time." He snorted. "I'm getting old, Jiaan. I've lost my touch."

"Then it's a good thing we won't need you in that capacity anymore, Logiri. He's dead." Tarjiaan leaned against the wall. "We've all got some recovering to do, and not much time do it in. We'll be heading to Sualiman as soon as we rejoin the fleet."

Logiri looked startled. "Why?"

Tarjiaan smiled and gestured to Rathsafa. "Because King Rathsafa's people want him back."

Rathsafa sat up straight in his chair. "What? My people... King? What?"

Tarjiaan nodded. "Lestalt has risen in your name, and Sualiman is allied with them. There's war on land, and we're going to join the fight and end this once and for all. Right now, the dockyards are full of Lestalti refugees, fleeing the war and Imperial forces. Women, children, old men. Logiri, you remember Antivar?"

"That promising young Imperial officer?" Logiri said. "The one who wouldn't stay? Yes."

"He's one of us now, and he and his men helped save me from the Imps." Tarjiaan decided not to tell Rathsafa that they were talking about his future son by marriage. "And we found his mother among the refugees at the dockyards. As soon as he tells me he's ready, he's going to marry. Then he'll be sailing out with us to war."

"Poor girl," Rathsafa murmured. "A bridal bed and then... what?"

"Actually, he'll be marrying a healer who'll be going with us." Tarjiaan paused, then sighed. "And the rest isn't mine to tell you. But you'll meet them soon enough."

"Meet them... Tarjiaan, I'm told my son is here. That you found him, and he's a healer. That means he's here in the infirmary, doesn't it? Where is he?" Rathsafa looked at the door. "I... does he want to meet me? Does he think I abandoned him? I know Nika was... wary of me, because of the lies they told her. What does he know?"

There was a light knock on the door, and Antivar peered inside. "Captain?" he said. "We were outside and... his Majesty's voice carries. May we come in?"

"He's ready?" Tarjiaan asked. He stepped back, and the door opened fully. Antivar came inside first, with Navi behind him, clinging to his hand. At the sight of him, Rathsafa stood up.

"Ysnavin?"

Navi looked up at Antivar. "Tell," he whispered.

Antivar nodded, putting one arm around Navi's shoulders. "Sir, you should know... Navi and I have been together for almost a year now. He was a healing slave on a warship, and he protected me from discovery, and was beaten nearly to death when he refused to reveal who he'd been with. He doesn't talk very well anymore, but he understands perfectly."

"And you love him?" Rathsafa asked.

Antivar smiled. "With everything I am. We'll be married once we get back to the dockyards." He looked at Navi and smiled. "Your son is a wonderful man, and the strongest healer I think anyone has ever seen..."

"He beat Tears of the Sunset," Tarjiaan interjected.

"He did *what*?" Logiri gasped.

Navi looked up at Antivar, then stepped forward. "I... do not... know... you," he said slowly. "I... worry..." He grimaced as gestured to himself. "Not... not good."

"No," Rathsafa breathed. He stepped forward, held out his hands. Navi hesitated, then took his hands. Rathsafa pulled him closer, studied him for a moment, then smiled.

"You have so much of her in you," he said, his voice hoarse. "Masthaka. You have her eyes." He rested one hand on Navi's cheek. "And you're a healer, as she was. My son, I don't care how well you speak, or how strong a healer you are. You are my son, and I have missed you." His voice cracked on the last words. So did Navi – he burst into tears. Rathsafa gathered him close and held him tightly.

Tarjiaan left the room and closed the door behind him. He wasn't surprised to find Nika in the corridor.

"They need some privacy," he said. She nodded.

"I will see him later," she said. Then she gestured. "Aanaji wants to see you."

Chapter Thirty
Appeasement

TARJIAAN TOOK A DEEP breath, then tapped gently on the door.

"Come in."

He opened the door, expecting to see Daanir and Naji, but Aanaji was alone, sitting on the bed. The last time he'd seen his sister, she'd been impeccably dressed in mourning red, her hair coiffed perfectly, her cosmetics artfully done. Now? She was curled up on the bed, and her posture reminded him of Kaapi, not of his composed and elegant sister. Her clothes were dirty and rumpled, her hair was caught in a messy tail, and her face was bare. He could see bruises, and the still-red mark that had once been a long cut along her cheekbone.

"Oh, Aani," he murmured. She looked up, clearly startled by his use of the diminutive.

"I..." she faltered, then waved one hand. "Sit. You should sit."

Tarjiaan nodded, then looked around. Small chair. Narrow bed. Nothing that would hold his weight. He crossed to the wall at the head of the bed and sat on the floor, stretching his legs out and crossing them at the ankle.

"There's room on the bed. You can sit up here," Aanaji protested. "You don't need to sit on the floor!"

Tarjiaan grinned. "If I sit up there? We'll both sit on the floor. It won't hold my weight while I'm in armor, and I can't easily take it off here. Better to be on the floor."

"But... you're the king—"

"And it's my floor," Tarjiaan pointed out. "I can sit on it if I want to. And I don't have anything to prove. Not to you." He looked up at her. "I know that now. But then, I never knew you, did I? Not really. The last time I saw you was... Mother's funeral. Then I went to the crèche."

"That was also his doing," Aanaji said. "Ilaris, I mean. I asked Uncle to let you stay with me. I didn't want you sent away, Jiaan." She sighed. "But he wanted me alone. Because he wanted me. You were in the way, so he had Uncle send you away."

"Aani—"

She shook her head, and he fell silent, waiting for her to take the next step. "Do you hate me?" she asked, her voice barely audible.

"No, Aani," Tarjiaan said. "I was afraid of you for a long time. Afraid to be alone with you, because you knew how to hurt me in ways no one else ever could." He thought about the past, about the wasted years. "I thought you hated me," he added. "Because I survived, and Ranji didn't. That's what you said in... in the closet. But... that wasn't you, was it?"

She shook her head. "No. And... Jiaan, I can't remember everything that happened while he controlled me. But... but I remember everything he made me do to you. And... I don't understand why you don't hate me!" She turned, swinging her legs over the edge of the bed so that she could face him. "I almost killed you!"

"That wasn't you. That was Ilaris. Ilaris almost killed me," Tarjiaan corrected. "Multiple times. And when it came to the end, you killed him to save my life. To save both of our lives. All of our lives." He held his hand out to her. "Come down here. Sit with me."

She hesitated, then took his hand and slid off the bed, sitting down next to him on the floor. Tarjiaan shifted slightly and put his arm around his sister. She stiffened, then shivered.

"Too much?" Tarjiaan asked.

"No," she answered. "I just wasn't expecting it. Wasn't expecting you to... to not hate me. I thought you were going to send me away. Daanir said you wouldn't, but... I didn't believe him." She looked up and smiled slightly. "I see what you see in him."

Tarjiaan laughed. "He's mine, Aani."

She giggled. "I know! And he's too young me for me But... he's a good man. Ranji told me he was, but I never had a chance to see it until he tried to protect me from Ilaris, and started teaching me to protect myself." She shifted closer. "Consortage, he told me. That's brilliant. And Nika is fine with that?"

"Nika actually proposed something similar the morning after our wedding. She understood our past, and didn't want to stand in our way," Tarjiaan answered. "Somewhere in the twenty-three days they spent in close quarters coming after me, they fell as much in love with each other as I am with the both of them. She calls us her men. And she's our wife."

"That's good." She paused, then poked him in the ribs. "And a baby?"

"Who told you?"

"Daanir did."

"Did he tell you that there's a chance of twins?" Tarjiaan asked. She stared at him, and he smiled. "Nika is a twin. Have you met Navi?"

"I've heard his name. He's another healer. And he's Nika's brother? How did you find him?'

"Long story," Tarjiaan said. "I'll tell you once we're underway for Sualiman. If you want to come with us?" He hugged her gently. "What do you want to do?"

"I..." Aanaji paused. "Do you want me to stay? I will understand if you don't. If you want me to stay at the dockyards. Having me here... I don't want to make you uncomfortable."

"You won't. And I asked what you wanted, Aani."

She smiled. "Daanir offered to train me. He says I could be a mancer. He says that I'm quick, and that he'll enjoy training me. And... I think I want that. I want to be something more than the precious only girl of our generation, and the mother of the heir." She took a deep breath and let it out as if she were blowing out a candle. "I've never been just... me. I'm not even certain who that is."

Tarjiaan shifted so he could turn and look at her. "I never... Aani, how did I not notice that they treated you like that?"

"What, like something to put on the shelf and admire?" She shook her head. "Jiaan, you were so young when we lost Mother. And you were the youngest of all of us. I never expected you to notice! Not at that age. And when you were old enough... it was all different. Because you were the only one left. They treated you... much the same way as they treated me. You had more freedom, because you were the Sea Prince, and the people had to know you. But you were as constrained as I was. Just... differently." She folded her legs, rested her elbow on her knee, and propped her chin on her hand. "Naji told me that he wants to abdicate. And he told me that you're going to let him."

"I told him that I want him to be fully trained as heir, but that he does not need to stand as the Sea Prince once the baby comes," Tarjiaan said. "He's agreed to that. And he and Kaapi have been having lessons with... well, I suppose Istin is my first mate now, since Marikaar is now commanding the *Chimaera*. Istin was a teacher before he was arrested for speaking out against the Emperor."

"Istin... the man with the patch? The one with the cutters?" Aanaji asked. "I'll have to meet him properly at some point." She paused, then smiled. "Naji also told me that you gave him a viol. Thank you."

"Thank you for telling him that he should emulate me. I had no idea that you thought so highly of me and my music. And I really had no idea you played hammers!"

She rolled her eyes. "Not think highly of my musical genius brother? Jiaan, please! And my musical abilities aren't as impressive as yours." She shifted, rubbing her hands against her skirts. "Is there a place I can wash up? And perhaps change? I itch."

Tarjiaan slowly stood up, being careful about where he put his feet. As he held his hand out to Aanaji, he realized that she'd been watching his every movement.

"It's so fluid," she murmured, letting him help her up. "Your armor. I... can you feel anything? How do you know where you're walking?"

Tarjiaan smiled. "In reverse order, lots of practice and no. When I was first learning to walk again, I had a walking frame, and then a pair of canes. Part of what makes me stable is the size — I have a larger, heavier foundation. I do have to think about walking, about where I'm putting my feet and how I'm standing. And I might have to relearn all of that once Daan and Kaapi and Naajir finish the new armor they're making." He led her out of the tiny room and into the corridor.

"New armor?"

"Smaller," Tarjiaan added. "So I'll be able to wear it below. If I ever need to go below, that is. Wil!" He smiled as the older man walked into view. "Is Aanaji able to leave?"

"And go where?" Wilaanger asked. He reached out and grabbed a chair, sitting down heavily. "How are you feeling, Aanaji?"

"Better," Aanaji answered. "Now that we've talked. Still raw, but... better."

Wilaanger nodded. "Remember, Chel is here to talk with you whenever you need it. She has a bit more experience than Nika in this regard, so I think she'll be the better choice. Now, where are you off to?"

"The day cabin," Tarjiaan answered. "Aani wants to wash up, so I thought she could use the palace."

Wilaanger laughed. "Oh, is that what you're calling it?"

"The... palace?" Aanaji repeated. "What does that mean?"

"You'll understand when you see it," Tarjiaan replied. "Well?"

"Go on," Wilaanger answered. "Nika's already gone, by the by. She went to go and eat something. She said to tell you that she's sending for enough to share, so you should go and eat with her."

Tarjiaan nodded. "*Wave Runner*? Where is Daanir?"

[He is with Naajir, and asks that they not be disturbed,] *Wave Runner* answered. Next to him, Tarjiaan heard Aanaji gasp.

"Thank you, my dear, If you would, please tell him that there's food? Tell him once he's available. Don't interrupt him."

[I will tell him. Captain, he says that there are no more mancers. Is that true?]

Tarjiaan sighed. "I don't know, *Wave Runner*. We'll find out the truth."

[I hope the bad man was lying.]

"So do I, *Wave Runner*." Tarjiaan offered Aanaji his hand. "You've never seen the *Wave Runner*, have you?"

"She talked to me," Aanaji said. "I thought I was going insane. But she sounds the same as she did when she spoke in my mind." She took Tarjiaan's hand. "Introduce me properly to your ship."

They walked out onto the deck, and Aanaji shaded her eyes with one hand and looked up at the sails. "It's been so long since I was last on an above ship. I... Jiaan, I think it might have been before you were born!"

Tarjiaan grinned. "Was that when you were at the dockyards?"

She turned and stared at him. "How did you know about that? Yes. Mother and I came to spend time with Father and Ranji while the *Marauder* was at the dockyards. I was nine..." She frowned slightly. Then she blushed. "Oh..."

"Oh?" Tarjiaan studied her for a moment, wondered at the look on her face.

"How much younger than I am are you, Jiaan?"

"I... oh!" He started laughing. "That's an uncomfortable current to sail. So let's not. Naji told us about a picture of you wearing a green and gold dress. Same trip? It couldn't have been. You wouldn't have been wearing that dress at nine."

"I... oh! I'd forgotten about that trip! No, that was from my second time at the dockyards, and that was my first real formal gown. I hadn't been allowed to attend formal events before that dinner. Why?"

"Because Nika wore it when we had a formal dinner at the dockyards."

"Oh, that must have looked wonderful on her!" Aanaji said. "I'm surprised that it's still wearable. It's been close to thirty years."

Tarjiaan nodded, turning when he heard someone call, "Captain!" He smiled when he saw Istin coming toward them. The man stopped and bowed.

"I was coming to look in on the lady," he said as he straightened. "Captain, if you'll present me?"

Tarjiaan nodded. "Aanaji, allow me to introduce my new First Mate, Thistintal, late of the Empire. Istin, my sister, the princess Aanaji."

Istin bowed again. "It's a pleasure to meet you properly, your Highness."

She smiled. "The feeling is mutual. Thank you, Istin. You put yourself at great risk for me. And I'm told you're tutoring my son? Was it you who taught him to brawl?"

Istin smiled broadly. "I did, my lady. Where did he show that off?"

"He almost broke Ilaris' knee."

"Oh, we'll have to work on that," Istin said. "Almost isn't quite good enough. Naji is a good boy, my lady. He's a joy to teach. I could say the same of Kaapi." He paused. "Except that she's not a good boy."

Aanaji burst into giggles. "No, she is not!"

Istin laughed with her. "Those two, though. They'll make the wind blow backwards if they put their minds to it." His smile softened. "Glad I could make you laugh. If you don't mind my saying so, it seems you could do with more laughing."

Tarjiaan glanced at Aanaji, who was blushing. He turned back to Istin, and was about to say something when a shiver ran the length of his spine. Before he had a moment to try and understand the sensation, Istin's eye widened. "Captain!" he yelped, pointing. "They're back!"

He turned, and saw the ghostly ship in the distance. "Oh. Aani—"

She followed his gaze, and grabbed his arm, swaying slightly. "That... that's Father's ship! That... Daanir told me, but... I thought he was joking!"

Tarjiaan led Aanaji to the rail, then fished in his pocket for his earpiece and put it on. "*Wave Runner,* tell Daan I need him on deck now," he said. "Tell him the *Marauder* is back."

[He is on the way, Captain.]

Daanir appeared at a run, with Naajir on his heels. He stopped at the rail and stared out over the water. "I thought they said their duty was done! That we wouldn't see them again!"

"I know," Tarjiaan said, watching as the *Marauder* sailed toward them, her sails swelling with a wind blowing in the opposite direction of the one driving the *Wave Runner*.

"Are they coming for me?" Aanaji asked softly. "It's my fault."

"It isn't," Istin said firmly. "It's that mage's fault. And if their duty was to make the Empire pay for what they did? They're coming for him."

Aanaji looked over her shoulder at him. "He's dead."

Istin nodded toward the approaching ship. "Doesn't seem to have stopped them at all."

Her eyes widened, and she turned back around. The ship was close enough that they could clearly a figure in red armor waving at them. Aanaji moaned, and Tarjiaan put his arm around her shoulders.

The crowd at the rail grew as the *Marauder* got closer. Tarjiaan felt a hand on his arm, and turned to see Nika. Behind her, he could see Navi, Antivar, Logiri and Rathsafa. Further back, Tommen and Reeshi stared in wonder.

"That... that is truly the *Marauder*?" Rathsafa asked, his voice just barely audible. "I thought that was a story!"

At Rathsafa's proclamation, Aanaji snorted. "Stories have their roots in truth," she murmured. "But this... how?"

"You'll have to ask the Great Mothers, because I have no idea," Tarjiaan answered.

The *Marauder* sailed past them, cutting across their bow and circling the *Wave Runner* before drawing up alongside between the *Wave Runner* and the *Chimaera*, keeping pace with them. At the rail stood Taarik, who smiled sadly.

"My little Sea Star," he called. Aanaji burst into tears.

"I'm sorry!" she choked. "I... I couldn't stop him! I couldn't fight him and I killed you!"

"No, my Star, you didn't." Taarik sighed. "I wish I'd known. I wish I'd been paying closer attention to you. I should have defied the King and brought you above, but... there's no turning back the tides. We know that it wasn't your doing, Star. It was never your doing. And... you needed to hear that from me. From us." He glanced back as Aaranji joined him at the rail. Aaranji leaned on the rails and nodded.

"Everything he said, Aani," he said. "There's nothing for us to forgive."

"That's why you came back?" Tarjiaan asked.

Taarik nodded. "Part of it." Then he grinned. "So... threatening the children with me?"

"You heard that?" Tarjiaan gasped. Then he laughed. "It worked."

"It did, and it amuses me that I'm the scary ghost grandfather. I like it." He looked around. "We will be going on this time. But first, we have some work to do, and..." He stopped, looking past Tarjiaan, who turned to see Kyraath had come through the crowd.

"Never thought I'd see you again, Rik," Kyraath called.

"Kyr. I... how I didn't know you were there, I don't know." Taarik paused. "I should have known you'd find your way. You always did."

Kyraath huffed out a laugh. "And you always did have too much drama."

Taarik shook his head. "This one wasn't my doing. Unless you think I wanted to spend fifteen years hunting Imps and never going to my rest?"

"No... that's a bit much, even for you," Kyraath drawled. He paused, then sighed. "The old man went back to Mother Ocean missing you, Rik. He was wrong, and he knew it. And he knew what you did, and he was proud of you, in the end."

Taarik closed his eyes and nodded. "That... that's good to know." He opened his eyes and smiled. "So just how did you meet your nephew?"

"What?" Tarjiaan turned and stared at Kyraath. "You're *what*?"

"You didn't tell him?" Taarik asked.

"You said you were done with your kin, and I wasn't about to disrespect your choice. But when he came to me and asked to learn about the gifts, I couldn't say no. So I've been teaching him best I know, but I didn't tell him who I was." He looked up at Tarjiaan. "He's just like you, Rik."

"We are going to talk," Tarjiaan said. "You, me and Aanaji. You... you could have told me!"

"Same thing I said to your da. He made his choice, and I respected that choice." Kyraath smiled. "But now that he's said it, I can acknowledge it. Your da and I were twinborn."

"Oh," Aanaji murmured. "I'd always wondered... Ranji and I were the only twins ever in the royal family."

"That's why," Taarik said. "Your mother knew. I should have told you, but..." He sighed and shrugged. "It's not something I spoke of. Ryk, tell them for me, will you?"

"Father, we've a job to do," Ranji said. "And not much time left."

"True." Taarik nodded. "True." He turned and looked around. "You may want to send the children out, Tarjiaan."

"No." Naajir came forward. "I think I have the right to see what you do to him, Grandfather."

Taarik smiled. "As you wish." He turned, walking away from them, going to the bow of the *Marauder*. Aaranji followed behind him, drawing his saber, standing back as Taarik stopped at the very point of the bow, right above the carved figurehead. He rested one hand on the rail, and with the other, he pointed at the water.

"The Great Mothers and Mother Ocean reject you!" he shouted. "Come forth and face your punishment."

His voice echoed, and the water started to churn and spin, fast enough that a void formed in the center of the vortex. But instead of pulling things down, the vortex spat them out — a pair of bodies appeared.

"Two?" Aanaji murmured. "Ilaris and...?"

"Ishian," Daanir said. "That... that's Ishian."

The bodies rose on a column of water, and Taarik stepped back from the rail as they drew level with the deck. They stayed there for a moment, then a fountain threw them both over the rail and onto the *Marauder*. As they landed, both started to move, taking on the same ghostly appearance as the Demon Captain and his First Mate.

"Aaranji? He's yours."

Aaranji smiled with the cold, feral look of a hunting shark. "Thank you, Father. Daan, I'll make him pay for the pair of us." He stalked forward, reached down and grabbed Ishian by the shirt front, lifting him up. Ishian looked at him, recognized who he was, and screamed....

And they both vanished.

Taarik nodded, then looked over his shoulder. "I assume you want to take this piece of shit?"

"Thank you, Taarik." The familiar voice came out of the air, and Ikaanaji appeared between one step and the next, walking forward to stand over Ilaris' prone body. "You've made a very grave mistake, Ilaris."

Ilaris rolled onto his side, looked up, and gasped, "Father, no..."

"No," Ikaanaji interrupted him. "No, you do not get to call me that. Not after I came to you and begged for your forgiveness for how you and your mother were treated. Not after I offered you a place at my side and you refused to allow me to acknowledge you. Not after you betrayed our kingdom and murdered me. Now get on your feet and hear your punishment."

Ilaris got to his feet and stood in front of Ikaanaji. He looked sullen and defeated.

"The Mothers refuse you. They reject you completely. You will never find your rest with them," Ikaanaji said.

"Your fate shall be a warning to everyone who sails the sea." Taarik stepped forward to stand with Ikaanaji. He gestured to the *Marauder*. "The demon ship shall have a new captain... and a new mission."

Ilaris looked around. "I don't understand."

Taarik smiled. "You will." He gestured. "This way... Captain." He walked toward the quarterdeck and the helm, with Ilaris following behind him. Unwillingly, it seemed — he moved like a motorized doll, protesting the entire way, stumbling up the stairs until he stood at the wheel. Ikaanaji followed, standing at the top of the stairs.

"Put your hands on the wheel," Taarik ordered. Ilaris' hands rose, and as he took the spokes, the compulsion that drove him fell away. He started to struggle.

"I can't let go!"

"No, and you never will." Ikaanaji started to fade from view. "From now until the seas are dry and the Great Mothers have been forgotten, this ship shall sail the oceans. You will never know a moment of peace nor a moment of rest. You will never again speak to another living being, and your screams will carry the message that some ambitions are not worth the cost. That some choices come with the direst consequences. This, Ilaris, is your punishment."

Ikaanaji vanished, and only Taarik remained. He folded his arms over his chest. "Are you ready for the last part?"

Ilaris whimpered. "No! No more!"

"Yes, more." Taarik drew his saber. "You murdered me, my oldest son, and my crew. You raped and abused my daughter for years. You tortured my youngest son, and it's only by the graces of the Mothers that he survived any of your attempts. For that... this is a small price to pay...." The saber flashed, and Ilaris screamed. Taarik turned and walked away, coming back down the stairs to midships.

"It's time and past time for me to take my rest, my children," he called. "I love you all."

Then he was gone, and the *Marauder* started moving, accelerating at an impossible speed. As it passed, Tarjiaan heard Ilaris' screaming.

"No! My eyes! I can't see! No!"

Chapter Thirty-One
Promises

"THAT WAS..." AANAJI'S voice tapered off, and she looked up at Tarjiaan. He nodded.

"That certainly was," he agreed. Then he turned and raised his voice. "Back to your posts! It's over. Destirian, set course back to the dockyards. We have a fleet to meet. Istin, comm the dockyards and let Mentiras know that the problems have been dealt with and that I will fully brief him when we dock." The crowd slowly scattered, crew returning to their work. Tarjiaan offered his arm to his sister, then turned. "Logiri, come with us. There are a few updates you need to see. And news that you need to hear."

"May I join you?" Rathsafa asked. "Nika and Navi are going back to the infirmary, because the crew from the other ship are coming over. I don't know enough to help them or to not be in their way, and I have nowhere else to be."

"Of course." Tarjiaan gestured. "We can talk." He led them to the day cabin and as he walked in, Tripod came yowling out of the bedroom.

"Jiaan," Aanaji gasped. "Who is this?" She went to one knee and offered her fingers to Tripod, who sniffed them, then bumped her hand and started purring loudly.

"That's Tripod, and he decided that he was mine while we were in the dockyards. And where Tripod is..." He stopped, smiling as a clumsy ball of gray and black striped fluff appeared through the open door. "Gossamer follows."

"Oh, she's precious!" Aanaji sat on the ground, and immediately had a lap full of cats.

"You've always wanted to bring a ship cat on board," Logiri said. "Now we have two?"

"Tripod made it very clear that he's the captain's cat," Tarjiaan said as he took a seat, "and Gossamer chose Nika the moment they met."

Logiri nodded. "I assume this is part of what I needed to see?"

"Yes, and the rest is in the bedroom."

Logiri looked quizzically at him, went into the bedroom. He came out a moment later. "What did you do?"

"Daanir decided that the existing bathing room wasn't meeting my needs, so when we were in the dockyard for repairs from battle and from the storm, he added the bathing room to the list. Nika calls it the palace—"

"The palace is your bathing room?" Aanaji asked.

"And you're welcome to use it." Tarjiaan looked up. "*Wave Runner*, please ask Aranti to bring clothes for my sister?"

[Of course, Captain.]

Aanaji moved the cats off her lap and stood up. "Thank you, Jiaan." She went into the bedroom, and Tarjiaan laughed as both cats followed her.

"You said that you had news," Logiri said once the door had closed.

"Sit, Logiri." Tarjiaan waved at the chair that was usually Daanir's. "Rathsafa, please. Sit. There's... quite a lot to tell you." He paused, getting his thoughts in order. "I won't be returning to the belowships. I can't be in an enclosed space anymore. We tried desensitization, and... this time, it's not working." He took a deep breath. "When Ilaris gave me to the Imps, he told them about my trouble with enclosed spaces. And they used that against me."

"Jiaan, you've gone pale," Logiri said, just as Rathsafa caught his breath.

"Oh, no."

Logiri stared across the table. "Nadar?"

"I... there was a box. The priest brought it onboard, and didn't tell me what it was or why." He turned to Tarjiaan. "It was so small. They didn't... they *couldn't* have...."

"Twenty-three days," Tarjiaan said softly. "They held me in that box for twenty-three days. There were spells on it, they told me, to keep me from dying in there." He paused, swallowing hard. "Daanir, Wilaanger and Nika got the children away from the *Chimaera*, and they found the *Wave Runner* and the Imp ship. They saved my life. Nika..." He looked at Rathsafa. "You'd have been so proud of her. From what Daan told me, she took command. She came up with the plan to get to me. She saved Daanir, and she saved me. She... I could not have asked for a stronger queen to stand at my side."

Rathsafa smiled. "She is her mother's daughter. I can't wait to truly get to know my children." He looked down at the table, then frowned. "Tarjiaan, they brought the box onboard with them. Does that mean that they knew what I was planning?"

Tarjiaan frowned, then shook his head. "I don't know. Perhaps? Perhaps they allowed you as much freedom as they did because they knew it would open an avenue into Meradon. I can't imagine Ilaris being able to contact them under Daanir's nose."

"My nose isn't that big," Daanir said from the doorway. He smiled slightly. "He wasn't. I'd have known if he was. The only transmissions into Imperial territory were ones that Wilaanger assured me were from the King. Which doesn't mean they weren't actually Ilaris." He came to the table, leaned down and kissed Tarjiaan, then sat down next to Logiri.

"Daan, go to bed," Tarjiaan said gently.

Daanir grimaced. "No. I need..." He stopped, tipping his head back and pressing the heels of both hands into his eyes. "I don't even know what I need."

"Food," Logiri said, standing up. "Rest. Have you been seen by a physician?"

Daanir smiled slightly. "Navi wouldn't let me off the submersible unless I let him check me over. I'm healthy." He paused. "Tired. Heartsore. But healthy."

"Then we'll treat that which ails you," Logiri said. He turned to Tarjiaan. "You haven't moved the tea service since I was last here, have you?"

"Your cabinet is safe," Tarjiaan said with a grin. "And there's a new tea blend in there for you to try. Oh, Mentiras got married."

"Did he?" Logiri moved to one of cabinets along the wall, opening it to reveal a water spigot, a kettle, and a small burner plate.

"Yes, and we both know his wife. Remember Tyvvin?"

Logiri looked over his shoulder. "From the *Sea Wolf*?"

Tarjiaan nodded. "She's Tyva now, and she and Mentiras are married. She mixed that blend up."

"I thought you weren't drinking tea anymore," Daanir murmured. "That reminds me. Logiri, we owe you a wealth of thanks."

"You do?" Logiri didn't turn from his work as he filled the kettle and set it on the burner. "And why is Tarjiaan not drinking tea anymore?"

Tarjiaan sighed. "Remember how I told you that Navi beat Tears of the Sunset?" he asked.

"Tarjiaan!" Logiri gasped, turning and nearly dropping the cup in his hands. "You... you were *poisoned*? An Antar poison? In Meradon?"

"At a formal dinner," Tarjiaan said. "One of the servants, and she killed herself before we got an explanation, or found out how she got an Antar poison. You were right, by the way. It didn't set off the poison sniffer. When I woke up and found out what had happened, I made a comment that I was never going to drink tea again, and Daan keeps reminding me that I said it."

Logiri sighed. He put the cup down and came back to the table, and Tarjiaan braced himself for what he knew was coming — a resounding slap to the back of the head. Daanir was on his feet in a shot, his pistol in his hand, and Logiri took a step back, his hands held up.

"Stand down, Daan," Tarjiaan ordered. "I earned that, and I'll take it. I was careless." Daanir stared at him for a moment, clearly not understanding. "I told you, remember? That Logiri would have slapped me for taking a full cup from someone?"

"I... you were serious?" Daanir lowered his pistol. "I thought... I didn't think you meant it." He holstered his pistol and sat back down. "I apologize, Logiri."

"Apology accepted, Mancer Royal. And yes, I made certain my lessons made an impression," Logiri said. "Although, apparently, not one that was deep enough." He sniffed. "Once we're all rested, remind me to do something about your hair."

"This is better than it was," Tarjiaan said. "Tea?"

"Of course."

Aranti arrived with food and clothes for Aanaji, and Logiri served the meal as Tarjiaan recounted everything that they had learned since that last morning on the *Chimaera*. Daanir ate what was put in front of him and tried not to fall asleep. Or fall apart. They were safe now, and he was tired. He smiled slightly as Aanaji came out of the bedroom, her hair hanging in loose, damp curls around her shoulders.

"I see why Nika calls that the palace," she said. "Thank you, Jiaan. I feel better."

"Come and sit and eat," Tarjiaan replied. She came around the table, paused by Daanir's chair, then leaned down and kissed his cheek before sitting down. He jerked and stared at her.

"I... Aanaji?" he stammered.

"Was that too forward?" she asked. "Or... well, I suppose it might be inappropriate, since you're going to be teaching me. But I'm older than you, so who would be taking advantage of whom?"

"Neither of us! Nobody!" Daanir blurted. Then he grimaced. "I... I'm sorry. I wasn't expecting it." He felt his face growing warmer, and couldn't make himself looking at Tarjiaan.

Aanaji did look past him, and whatever she saw made her roll her eyes. "I'm not going to eat him, Jiaan."

"I told you. Mine."

That proclamation made Daanir turn, so he saw Tarjiaan's smile. And the worry in his eyes.

"Jiaan, I'm fine," he said, his words falling over themselves in his haste to say them aloud. "Just..."

"Stretched so thin you might as well be transparent?" Tarjiaan finished. "Once you get some more food into you, I'll get you into bed." He turned as someone knocked on the door. "Come in!"

Istin looked around the door. "Captain? We're about to dock. The *Chimaera* will make the dockyards soon, and we've heard from Kaapi. She says that everything has been just fine there. And Commander... Captain Mentiras says that he'll meet with you sometime tomorrow, once you've had a chance to rest."

Tarjiaan blinked. "I... he said that?"

Istin blushed slightly. "I might have mentioned to him that I'm not entirely certain when you slept last."

Aanaji laughed. "Tarjiaan, your crew is wonderful. Istin, have you seen Naajir?"

"Oh, Naji asked me to tell you that he's off to get some sleep," Istin said.

"Speaking of sleep," Tarjiaan said, turning to his sister, "we'll need to find you a place to sleep."

"I've got a place for her, if she likes," Istin said. Daanir coughed, staring at him.

Tarjiaan sat up straight, "Excuse me, Thistintal?"

Istin frowned slightly, then blushed sunset red. "I... no! Captain, that's not what I meant!" he gasped, and his usual, precise speech took on an accent that Daanir had never heard from him before. "Captain, I apologize! I just... there's an empty berth in the mancer quarters, and I was going to offer to escort the lady so she didn't get lost! I didn't... I would never...!" He dropped his head. "Captain, I would never dishonor the lady! If I've given offense—"

"Common isn't your first language, is it?" Aanaji asked, interrupting Istin, who fell silent and looked at her before dropping his eyes again.

"No, my lady. How did you know?"

"You have an accent, but only, I think, when you forget," she answered. "I thought I heard it before, on the *Chimaera*. Jiaan, did you hear it?"

"I did," Tarjiaan answered. "This time. But I haven't heard it before. Istin, I never asked. You're from where?"

"Tyraca. Learned Common in school, but my people spoke Tyracan at home." He sighed. "I am sorry, Captain, my lady. I meant nothing improper. I... I translated wrong, I think."

"I think you did." Tarjiaan looked at Aanaji, who smiled.

"It's fine, Jiaan," she said. "I take no offense, and Commander Istin has been most courteous ever since we met. So I suspect that you're not the only one who hasn't slept?"

"I was going to sleep once we were docked," Istin admitted. "Been running on tea and stubbornness for hours now."

"Istin, have you eaten anything?" Daanir asked. "There's plenty."

"I wouldn't presume—"

"Have a seat, Commander," Logiri said. "Do you like steamed fish?"

Istin took a seat, sitting up straight as the mainmast, his hands flat on the table. Tarjiaan smiled.

"Istin, this is something you'll get used to if you decide to stay on as my First Mate," he said. "My officers will often dine with me, and I want to hear your thoughts."

Istin smiled slightly. "It's... very different from what I'm used to, Captain. Not that I was anywhere near being an officer before." He gestured with one hand. "This is all new. All strange. I do like it, but... it takes some learning."

"You were a teacher. Learning should be second nature to you," Tarjiaan pointed out.

Istin laughed. "True, Captain. Very true. Some learning... that can be uncomfortable. But it's all worth having."

"What did you teach, Commander?" Aanaji asked. "And where?"

"At the university of Tyraca, my lady," Istin answered. "I taught history and folklore."

Aanaji looked delighted. "Folklore? You taught stories?"

Istin smiled. "Stories tell us where we came from. Who we are. Where we're going. They show us what we have in common, and where things changed along the way. Stories are what makes us people, if you look at it from the right angle."

The rest of the dinner was much more relaxed, full of lively conversation that Daanir didn't even pretend to follow. He sat and watched Aanaji as she warmed to the conversation, as she and Istin discussed and argued and bickered over things he'd never heard of before. It was like watching her come alive. Occasionally, Tarjiaan interjected a point, or asked a question. Rathsafa just sat and listened with wide-eyed wonder, until a knock on the door interrupted the flow.

"Captain?" Antivar came into the cabin, followed by Navi. "Oh, I hadn't realized you were entertaining. We can come back."

Istin laughed. "No, it's probably a good thing you came in, Ivar," he said. "I got started."

Antivar chuckled. "Lecturing again, Professor? Apologize, Istin."

"Don't you dare!" Aanaji blurted. "That was wonderful! I haven't enjoyed a conversation like that in ages!" She leaned back in her chair and yawned. "We will have to talk more. But I do love that my son has such a learned man as a teacher."

"It was truly a delightful conversation," Rathsafa agreed. "And to see two people who are so passionate about the subject, and find such pleasure in it? That's the very definition of joy."

"I agree," Tarjiaan said. "Istin, why don't you show Aanaji to the mancers quarters and help her get set up, then go get some sleep yourself?"

Istin stood up and came around the table, holding his hand out to Aanaji. "It would be my pleasure."

Aanaji blushed slightly and took his hand, standing up. She turned to face the others and bowed her head. "Good night, all."

"Good night, Aani," Tarjiaan said. Once they had left, and the door closed behind them, he leaned back in his chair, smiling.

"What are you thinking?" Logiri asked, his voice soft.

"That Istin will be very good for her," Tarjiaan answered. He straightened. "Antivar, Navi. Is this about the wedding?"

"Yes, sir," Antivar answered. "Oh, and I have a message for you. The Queen says that you're not to wait on her to go to bed, and she'll join you when she's done."

Tarjiaan nodded. "How is it in the infirmary? How is the crew?"

Antivar grimaced and looked at Navi, who sighed and said, "Not good. Nika with..." He looked at Antivar. "Girl name?"

"Oh, her name is Adalia," Antivar answered "She's... the poor girl has had a hard time of it. Nika is with her now, and I think will be for some time."

Daanir felt his stomach lurch. "Oh, no."

Antivar nodded, his face unusually serious. "I was helping where I could, and... well, I didn't hear her story, but I heard from some of the men, and... and I know what happens to girls who are young and pretty with men like that lot."

Tarjiaan paled, and he looked toward the door. "Thank you for waiting until Aanaji was gone before telling me that."

Antivar nodded. "She seemed very happy when she left. That's good."

Tarjiaan nodded. "What did you want to ask about the wedding?"

Antivar looked at Navi, and took his hand. "Now?"

Tarjiaan blinked. "Now? You want to have the ceremony now?"

"Waited long enough," Navi said, his voice firm. "All here. Why not?"

"Your sister is currently busy with a patient," Daanir pointed out. "Do you want to be the one to tell her she missed your wedding?"

Navi blinked. Then he made a face. "Forgot."

Tarjiaan laughed. "Navi, I will be happy to celebrate your marriage in the morning. When we can be assured that your married life and mine won't be shortened drastically because we didn't tell Nika."

Navi nodded. "Thank you." He looked up at Antivar. "Tell Mother?"

"We'll go tell my mother." Antivar looked back at Tarjiaan. "Just to warn you, it... might be a double ceremony. Tommen asked me if he could marry my mother, and I gave them my blessing."

"Very good! Tomorrow, we'll celebrate everyone. Now go to bed, the pair of you."

"That sounds very much like a hint," Rathsafa said. "Gir, where am I sleeping?"

"I'll show you." Logiri turned and smiled. "Captain, if I may be excused?"

"It's good to have you home, Logiri," Tarjiaan said. "Good night."

Logiri and Rathsafa left, and the silence filled the empty spaces of the room. Daanir closed his eyes and let the weight of it settle on him.

"Are you ready to go to bed?" Tarjiaan asked softly.

Daanir nodded. He got to his feet slowly and held his hand out. Tarjiaan took it and led him toward the bedroom door.

The tears started before they were halfway there.

Tarjiaan held Daanir as he cried. As he mourned the mancers — his mancers, he called them. The guards who had been kind to them. Narrick, and the person that Daanir had thought he'd been. Finally, Daanir cried himself out, and fell asleep in Tarjiaan's arms.

It wasn't the first time that Tarjiaan had fallen asleep in his armor, but he wasn't usually lying down when he did it. It wasn't entirely comfortable, but if he moved, Daanir would wake up. He could manage for one night. Or was it morning? He had no idea what bell it was, or how close to dawn. He let himself drift off, secure in the knowledge that they were safe.

When Tarjiaan woke up, Nika was curled up against his other side, her head pillowed on his shoulder. He had no idea when she'd come to bed, or how she'd gotten into bed without waking him. He shifted slightly, trying not to wake either of them, putting his arms around them both. Daanir stirred, whimpering softly in his sleep. Then he jerked, coming awake all at once.

"Easy," Tarjiaan murmured. "You're safe."

"I..." Daanir propped himself up on his elbow. "Dreams."

"I understand." Tarjiaan tugged him back down. "You know I understand."

Daanir settled with his head on Tarjiaan's shoulder, then reached across and covered Nika's hand with his. "When did she come in?"

"I have no idea. She didn't wake me. And I don't want to wake her." Tarjiaan heard the ship bell ringing twice. "Two bells. Two bells past dawn, or two bells past mid, I wonder?"

"Does it matter?" Daanir asked. "Wait... weddings."

"And Kaapi will be wanting to see you. The *Chimaera* was due in shortly after we docked. She might be onboard—"

Daanir nodded, then laughed softly. "She is. And *Wave Runner* isn't about to wake Nika up either. She whispered in my ear that Kaapi is waiting for me. So I should probably get up and wash." He shifted, then froze when Tarjiaan took a fistful of his shirt and pulled him back down. "Jiaan!"

"Two more minutes. Just be with me," Tarjiaan whispered. "I was terrified I wasn't going to be able to find you in time. That we wouldn't make it. Just stay with me a little longer."

Daanir leaned over him and kissed him. "I knew you were coming for us. I knew you would find us. I never doubted it...." He grimaced. "Not until I saw how far away the *Wave Runner* was when they brought us up to the ring. I'm sorry for that."

Tarjiaan took a deep breath and nodded. "Apology accepted. I'm sorry it took us so long." He tugged Daanir closer. "We're going to war, Mancer mine."

Daanir sniffed. "We've been at war. Our entire lives. We're not going to war, my king. We're going to peace." He smiled and rested his hand on Tarjiaan's chest. "And to a pair of weddings. You need to get up."

"I don't want to wake..." Tarjiaan turned and laughed. "And how long have you been awake?"

Nika smiled slightly. "Only a few minutes. Weddings?"

"Antivar and Navi. Then Tommen and Reeshi," Daanir answered as he got off the bed. "Navi wanted it last night, but we pointed out that you were busy."

"And I will continue to be busy, so we should all get up and get ready. I will need to go back to the infirmary after." Nika sat up, then visibly shuddered. "Biscuits?"

"I've got them." Daanir handed a ration pack to her. "I've got to wash up. Kaapi is waiting for me."

The crew assembled on the deck to witness, and Tarjiaan stood by the mast, waiting. Antivar and his mother were in the day cabin, while Navi was in the infirmary with his father and Nika. Daanir had gone with Antivar to coach him on what was expected, while Logiri was doing the same with Navi.

The day cabin door opened, and Daanir slipped out, coming to stand on Tarjiaan's left. "He's ready," he whispered. "I've told the infirmary."

Tarjiaan nodded and raised his voice. "We come together today to witness the marriage of Commander Girantivar and Prince-Healer Ysnavin. Let them come forth!"

The day cabin door opened again, and Antivar came out, with his mother on his arm. Reeshi's smile was brilliant, and Antivar looked the happiest Tarjiaan had ever seen. He turned and saw the group coming from the infirmary. Rathsafa in front, with Nika and Navi behind. Nika had her arm linked in her brother's, and she leaned in and whispered something to him that made him laugh.

They reached Tarjiaan at the same time. Antivar turned and kissed his mother's cheek, while Navi hugged both Nika and his father. Then the two stepped forward, facing Tarjiaan.

"Our ways are much simpler than the Imperial ceremony," Tarjiaan said. "This is a promise between the two of you. We're just here to watch."

Antivar smiled and turned to face Navi, taking his hands. "I, Antivar, son of Reeshi and Ivanik, ask that you accept me as your husband. I swear by Sun, Sand and the Great Mothers that I will honor you and protect you, and that I will be a good husband to you. Will you accept me, Ysnavin?"

Navi took a deep breath and nodded. "I do." He paused, then nodded again. "I... Ysnavin... son of... Masthaka... and... and Rathsafa..." He paused, scowled slightly, and continued, "Ask.. ask to be accepted... as husband. Swear... I will honor and protect, and be... good husband." He smiled. "Accept me, Antivar?"

Antivar looked as if he was about to cry. "That's the most I've heard you say in a year!"

"Yes?" Navi prompted.

"Yes!" Antivar pulled him close and kissed him, making the crew cheer. And in the lull that followed, Tommen's voice was clear: "Is it our turn now?"

Chapter Thirty-Two
Sualiman

"LAND! LAND HO!"

Tarjiaan didn't need the lookout's call — he had known when he'd woken up that morning that they'd make landfall today. He could feel the distant shore, solid and steady at the edge of his awareness. Now he could see it, and he smiled as he studied the dark smudge on the horizon. With any luck, there would be news tonight, and they'd have a better idea of what was facing them. There had been no messages since they left the dockyards almost a month ago, no communications outside of the ships of Meradon. There had been nothing but the time that he and his kingdom had both desperately needed. He was recovering. Meradon was recovering. And soon, the rest of the Four Sisters would be able to recover. Once they removed the poison that was the Emperor.

For now, though? There was the fleet and the sea, and land in the distance.

"Captain." Istin came up the stairs to the helm. "Orders, sir?"

"Send a message to the fleet and on to the Sualimani watchtowers that we'll be dropping anchor off the coast this evening. Don't expect an immediate answer from Sualiman," Tarjiaan answered. "Sualimani comm tech isn't as strong as ours, and they'll receive the message, but they won't be able to respond until we're closer. Not unless they send one of their ships out to meet us. Which they might. We might get an escort." He adjusted their course, then looked at Istin. "Now tell me what you really wanted to ask. Because you could have commed me to ask that. You wanted to talk."

Istin blushed. "I'm clear as glass, aren't I?" he asked. "I... I was wondering when the Lady Aanaji and the children would be back?"

Tarjiaan smiled. Since they'd left the dockyards, Istin's growing attraction toward Tarjiaan's sister had been obvious to everyone on board — the First Mate was clearly completely besotted with her, and the two often would be found together when they had overlapping free time. Ever since the mancers had gone to tour the belowships in search of surviving mancers, Istin's pining had been both noticeable and painful.

"They should finally be back sometime today," Tarjiaan answered. "Truthfully told, I'm missing them, too. But Daanir commed this morning. They'll be here today."

"Oh, now that's excellent news!" Istin smiled, then looked out over the rail. Without turning, he said, "I miss them. Aani and the children. I never thought I'd have a family. Never thought I'd live long enough to have the chance." He looked at Tarjiaan. "You understand?"

Tarjiaan nodded, wondering if Istin even noticed that he'd used the affectionate diminutive of Aanaji's name. When had *that* started? "I do understand. And... have you talked to Aanaji about this?"

Istin smiled shyly. "Scared to," he admitted. "I mean... I don't know the details, but I know that she's been through a time. I know she might not want a man's company ever again. And if all she wants from me is to be... a friend, and someone she can talk with about folklore? I'll be disappointed. I just... don't want to ask for the disappointment."

Tarjiaan nodded. "What about Ilenwy?"

Istin shook his head. "We were done before we ever left the dockyards." He shrugged. "She wasn't after anything long-term. She wanted new and different. I was new and different... until I wasn't. She had two more after me before we ever sailed away. That's... surprising in a woman, isn't it?"

"Maybe if you're not used to women having that sort of choice and control, but here?" Tarjiaan shrugged. "There were girls when I was young who tried to run the entire fleet of princes, starting with my oldest cousin and ending with me, hoping that they'd land one." He paused. "There were six of us, Istin."

"No!" Istin gasped. "Truly?" He paused, then grunted softly. "Huh. Makes sense, I suppose. If it's behavior that's acceptable for a man, and a woman has the same rights as the man, then... she can have the same behaviors. Even the questionable behaviors." He folded his arms over his chest. "I... I should talk to Aani. See what she wants. And... if she says yes, I'll be asking your permission to court your sister, Captain."

"You don't need my permission, Istin. I want her happy. If she says yes, then that's all you need."

Istin smiled. "Thank you, Captain. I'll go send those messages."

As the day grew older, the smudge on the horizon grew larger, more distinct. Started to gain finer details. Tarjiaan could see sails in the distance, the distinctive, triangle shaped sails of the smaller ships that the Sualimani used for fishing and trade. He couldn't see any of their deep-sea ships, and wondered why.

[Captain, the mancers are back on board.]

"Thank you, *Wave Runner*," Tarjiaan said. He'd felt a submersible coming in to dock, but there was so much traffic between ships that he hadn't been certain which submersible was which.

[First Mate says that Destirian is on her way to relieve you, Captain.]

Tarjiaan smiled. "Give him my thanks."

A few minutes later, he was on the main deck and heading for the day cabin. He heard the commotion behind him, and turned to see Naajir and Kaapi running toward him. Kaapi reached him first, throwing her arms around him.

"Papa-Captain!" she crowed. "We missed you!"

"I missed you, too." Tarjiaan hugged her tightly, then hugged Naajir. "Was your search successful?"

"Sixteen mancers in training and two instructors," Naajir answered. "And twelve more who might be mancers in a year or two."

"Naji, that's my report to give," Daanir said as he reached them. He looked tired, but satisfied. Behind him, Aanaji looked relaxed, rumpled, and completely at peace. It was a good look for her. Tarjiaan held his hand out to his sister, and she smiled as he pulled her in for a quick embrace.

"We missed all of you. Come into the day cabin," Tarjiaan said, letting Aanaji go. "Daanir, you can give your report there, and we'll get something for you all to eat."

"Logiri is going to take one look at me and fuss," Daanir grumbled. He took Tarjiaan's hand and sighed. "It's good to be back. I missed you. I'll show you how much once we're inside."

Tarjiaan turned toward the cabin, only to stop when Aanaji called his name. "Jiaan?" She waited for him to face her, then smiled. "Would you mind if I wasn't in this meeting? I don't think I'm needed. I don't have anything to report."

Tarjiaan fought the urge to laugh. He should have expected this. "You're dismissed, Mancer Aanaji. And I think you'll find Istin in comms."

Her eyes widened. Then she blushed. "Thank you," she murmured, before hurrying away. Towards comms, he noticed.

"Uncle, we're going to go see Istin, too," Naajir said. "He sent us lessons to do while we were away, and we need to report in."

Tarjiaan coughed. "Ah... why don't you and Kaapi go and wash up first? Change your clothes and get settled?"

Naajir frowned slightly, then yelped when Kaapi poked him. "I'll explain on the way," she said. "Come on." She grabbed his hand and dragged him off.

Daanir laughed. "I wonder how she noticed and he didn't?" he said as they started toward the day cabin. "Is Nika in the infirmary?"

"She's not on duty at the moment," Tarjiaan answered. "It's been quiet. She's resting."

"Resting?" Daanir repeated. "Is she sick?"

"Just tired," Tarjiaan answered. "Chel says that she's fine." He stopped at the day cabin door and knocked, then opened it, and was immediately met by Tripod, who chirped, then stood up on his hind legs and planted his front paw on Tarjiaan's left leg. Tarjiaan laughed and leaned down, picking the cat up and letting him climb up to sit on his shoulder. "Nika? You have visitors."

"Visitors?" Nika came out of the bedroom, and her smile lit up the room. "Daan!" She stopped, her eyes wide. "Who do I greet first?"

"Give me a moment," Daanir said. "I haven't kissed our husband yet, and I saw him first."

"You saw him years before I did," Nika quipped. Tarjiaan laughed and turned to Daanir, pulling him close and kissing him. It wasn't nearly enough to make up for Daanir being gone, but it was a start.

"I missed you," he murmured. Daanir nodded.

"I missed you all, too. But it had to be done." He turned and opened his arms to Nika, who came to him and held him tightly.

"You have not been eating," she said. "You need to eat."

Tarjiaan looked up. "*Wave Runner...*"

[Logiri is on his way.]

Daanir laughed. "Logiri is going to fuss at me. I'm not used to being fussed at."

The door opened and Logiri came in. "I suggest that you get used to it," he said as he looked Daanir up and down. "I also suggest a bath and a change of clothes. A meal will be ready when you are done."

Daanir took a deep breath and let it out. "A bath... sounds very good right now," he said. "Where are we, anyway? I've been on so many belowships in the past however many days that I've lost track, and I'm too tired to look."

"We'll drop anchor in the Queen's Bay tonight," Tarjiaan answered. "Do you want company in the bath, or do you want to get through it quickly?"

Daanir frowned slightly, then sighed. "I want to eat. So I probably shouldn't have company. I'll be quick." He kissed them each again and went into the bedroom.

"Where is Aanaji?" Nika asked as she went to a cabinet and opened it, taking out two bowls. As she put them down, Tripod launched himself from Tarjiaan's shoulder to the table, and from the table to the floor. "Only one of those is yours, Tripod," Nika called. She went into the bedroom, then came back out with Gossamer at her heels. "She was on the bed, and she is still too little to jump so far."

"She went to see Istin." Tarjiaan answered, sitting down. He smiled when Nika went to another cabinet and took out a familiar pouch. "Are they done?"

"I finished Daan's this morning," she answered. "I will give them to each of you when he is finished." She smiled as Logiri placed a cup of tea in front of her. "Thank you."

Daanir came out of the bedroom dressed in shabby clothes that hung loose on his frame, barefoot and with his hair wet and uncombed. He slumped in his chair and sighed.

"It's good to be back," he said, smiling as Logiri put tea in front of him, then left the cabin. "So, Naajir told you my report. Sixteen students, two teachers, and twelve little ones that we need to monitor because they might have the gift, but it's too soon to tell."

"And how did people take the news of the purge?" Tarjiaan asked. "I understand why you didn't want me to make a fleetwide broadcast, and let you bring the news to them directly, but that was a lot to ask of you."

"It was a lot." Daanir tipped his head back. "I didn't realize how many of them were married. How many parents were still out there. I didn't realize that I don't think about parents. Probably because I never had any. Not that I remember. I had to tell Westin's mother that he was gone, and... that near broke me." He smiled. "Aanaji was a rock. She truly was."

Nika took the pouch out and opened it, laying the contents on the tabletop. There were two lengths of intricately knotted bands, each one finished with a clasp. "I have something for you, Daan," she said. He opened his eyes and looked at her, then looked down at the table.

"What are... wait. Wait. Is that...?" He looked up. "Is that a collar? A Sualimani marriage collar?"

"Yes." Nika smiled. "I wanted to give these to you and to Tarjiaan before we met my grandmother. If the collar is not comfortable for you, it is long enough to wear around your wrist twice."

Daanir sat up straight. "You made me a collar, I'm going to wear it! Put it on me?"

Nika smiled and stood up, picking up the collar and coming around the table to fit it around Daanir's neck. She closed the clasp, then leaned down and kissed him.

"I love you," she murmured. Then she stood up and came back around the table to pick up the other band. "Jiaan? Your left hand."

Tarjiaan held his left hand out, watching as she put the cuff around his wrist and clasped it. "This should have been here from the start," she said. "I should have let Ishantar show me how to do this sooner."

"It's here now," Tarjiaan said. He reached out and pulled Nika into his lap, putting his arms around her. "We are yours. And you are ours."

She sighed and rested her head on his shoulder. "I am trying not to think of what will happen after we meet my grandmother. You will be going to war. And... I presume that I will not be going with you."

Tarjiaan sighed. "You presume correctly. You need to stay safe in Sualiman." He rested one hand on the slight swell of her belly. "You all need to stay safe."

"I will stay with you, my lady," Logiri said, bringing a cart back into the cabin. He set a bowl on the table. "I'm too old to go to war, and I've realized that my skills are no longer up to the challenge. I am better suited to be guard than an assassin."

Tarjiaan looked at him. "Thank you, Logiri."

Logiri smiled. "Now you should eat. Then I suggest you rest. Once we reach the bay, you'll be busy."

Tarjiaan woke first, and for a change, he was not underneath a pile of people. They had put Daanir in the middle, and Tarjiaan woke up against Daanir's back, while Daanir was curled around Nika. Neither of them stirred as Tarjiaan moved to the edge of the bed, spread his banyan over his chair, and shifted from the bed to the chair. He pulled the banyan on, arranging the too-long length of it to not snag in his wheels, then went out into the day cabin. He rolled up to the table, looked at the door, and silently started to count as Tripod jumped up to sit in his lap.

Logiri walked in before he'd hit twenty.

"You either have *Wave Runner* telling you when I'm awake," Tarjiaan said, "or you're a mage, and you just never told me."

Logiri smiled and went to the cabinet, starting to make tea. "Neither. I know you. And I need to do something about that banyan."

"I'd appreciate that." Tarjiaan closed his eyes as he stroked the cat, feeling the water around them. It was far shallower than he'd expected. "How long were we asleep? Are we at anchor?"

"It's been several hours, and yes," Logiri answered. "Your new First Mate is a very capable man."

"He is," Tarjiaan agreed. "What have I missed?"

"Not much," Logiri answered, putting a cup in front of Tarjiaan. "A submersible from the *Chimaera* arrived, and Commander Antivar and Prince Ysnavin are onboard. Apparently, life in a belowship doesn't agree with Navi. Not to the same degree as you, but while we are in the harbor, they will be above." He paused, turning toward the door as someone knocked. The door opened, and Istin came inside. He looked both excited and oddly nervous.

Tarjiaan put his tea down. "Istin? What is it?"

"Ah... Captain? You... we... we have a visitor." He glanced back, then swallowed. "A royal visitor." He came the rest of the way inside, then bowed deeply as a woman entered the day cabin.

Queen Ysnia was beautiful in much the same way as Tarjiaan saw his dress saber as beautiful — graceful and deadly all at once. She was solidly built, very nearly as tall as Tarjiaan in his armor, and she was the very last person Tarjiaan expected to see onboard the *Wave Runner*. He sat up straight, suddenly very aware of how unkempt he was, and of the fact that he was dressed solely in a knotted bracelet, a banyan and a cat.

"Your Majesty," he gasped, bowing from the waist. "You honor both me and my ship! I would have come to you!"

"Tarjiaan," she said, and her smile softened her stern expression. "I was told that you were taken by the Imperial forces. And I was told that you were dead. I am very pleased to see that both tales are false."

"Only one was false. I was taken, and I was held for twenty-three days before I was rescued." He gestured to the table. "Please, sit. Logiri, some tea for Her Majesty. And... send for him, please?" Logiri's eyes widened, and he nodded once. He poured the tea, setting the cup on the table before he bowed and hurried out, taking Istin with him.

Ysnia's eyes widened, and she came to the table and held out her hand. "You have married?" she asked as she sat down. "Let me see?" He put his left hand into hers. "You have married a woman of my people? Tarjiaan, I am surprised! Who?" She frowned slightly. "Not Ishantar?"

"No, your Majesty." Tarjiaan smiled. "Ishantar was a member of my crew. That would have... complicated things."

"Then who?"

The bedroom door opened, and Nika came out, tying the belt on her robe. "Jiaan, who are you talking to?" she asked. Then she saw the woman sitting at the table. "Oh!"

Tarjiaan smiled. "Your Majesty, if I may present my wife—"

"Tarjiaan," Ysnia breathed, standing up slowly. "Tarjiaan, what have you done?"

Tarjiaan continued as if she hadn't spoken. "Ysnika, daughter of Masthaka. Queen of Meradon. Your granddaughter."

The outer door opened, and Logiri came back in. Behind him was Rathsafa, followed by Navi and Antivar. Ysnia turned toward them, and gasped in shock, covering her mouth with her hand. Rathsafa stepped forward, bowed deeply, then met her eyes.

"Mother," he said, his voice cracking. "I tried. I tried to save her. I—" His voice cut off as Ysnia pulled him into her arms, holding him tightly as they both started crying. Tarjiaan held his hand out to Nika, and she came to his side and put her arm around his shoulders.

"Did you know she was onboard?" she whispered.

"No, or I'd have warned you," Tarjiaan replied. He looked at the bedroom door. "Where's Daan?"

"In the bath," Nika answered. "I will..."

Ysnia turned toward them. "Ysnika. And... is this Ysnavin?" She looked at Navi, who bit his lip and smiled shyly as he nodded. "And... you are?"

"Girantivar, your Majesty," Antivar answered, bowing deeply. "I am married to your grandson."

Ysnia looked puzzled. "Does my grandson not speak for himself?"

"Not... not well," Navi answered. He tapped his head. "Hurt. Now... not talk good. Ivar talk... for both."

"Has a healer seen to this injury?" Ysnia asked.

"It was a year ago, your Majesty. And... Navi was a healing slave on a warship. They thought doing anything more than keeping him alive was a waste of resources," Antivar answered. He put his arm around Navi's shoulders. "He's working with Honored Physician Wilaanger, but there is little to be done for the injury at this point."

Ysnia looked troubled as she turned back to face Tarjiaan and Nika. "I will admit that this reunion was not what I was expecting," she said, taking her seat again. "I came because I wanted to know the truth of what has happened on the sea, and if the Sea Prince yet lived. I hoped to find you alive, since at long last Meradon has returned to the land to join the battle."

"The Sea Prince is now the Sea King," Tarjiaan answered. "My uncle has gone to the Great Mothers, murdered by someone he trusted. The same someone who gave me to Imperial forces. The traitor is dead, and my uncle is at peace."

"This is good," Ysnia said. "And I assume that it was you who slew the traitor?"

"No, it was my sister who dealt the killing blow," Tarjiaan answered. Ysnia nodded.

"This is as it should be," she murmured. "Now, have you come to join the battle?"

"We have, your Majesty," Tarjiaan answered. He turned, seeing movement in the inner doorway. "Daanir, come out and meet Queen Ysnia."

Daanir opened the door and stepped out, bowing slightly. He had clearly been lurking, and wore only his trousers and the collar around his throat. Ysnia smiled when she saw him, and her smile broadened when she noticed the collar.

"A pair?" she said, turning to Nika. "Granddaughter, well done!"

"They are my favored males," Nika answered. She smiled at Tarjiaan, then held her hand out to Daanir. He blushed as he joined them, color spreading down his chest. "This is Lord Daanir Meranas, the Mancer Royal, our Royal Consort, and Tarjiaan's battle companion."

"And I should... put some clothes on," Daanir murmured. "I..."

"Stay, Mancer," Ysnia said, her tone brooking no argument. "I have seen the male form before, and we have much to discuss. Sit, all of you."

Daanir and Nika both moved to sit across the table from Ysnia, while Rathsafa, Navi and Antivar joined her on that side of the table. As they took their places, Tarjiaan said, "Your Majesty, I attend," as he rested his hands on the table. In his lap, Tripod reached up and hooked his claw into one sleeve, pulling Tarjiaan's hand back down. Ysnia chuckled.

"Your pet has opinions." She smiled. "What do you know of the battle on land?"

"We know that it's happening. There are refugees who have made it to Meradon who have told us as much. But we do not know more than that, and any information that we have is a month old. How fare your forces? Does the Empire still stand?"

Ysnia paused and picked up her tea, taking a sip. Logiri moved behind them, setting out more cups, pouring more tea, clearly listening intently.

"Lestalt is free," Ysnia said after a moment. "And Tyraca is free. It was... almost appallingly easy to defeat the Imperial forces. They are impoverished, malnourished, and some of them surrendered the moment our forces were within striking distance. Yet the Emperor still lives, and he has retreated to the only stronghold that remains to him." She looked at Tarjiaan and continued. "The Palace of Meradon. Apparently, he anticipated an attack, and planned for it. The landward walls have been rebuilt and reinforced, and our forces have not been able to breech them. But we do not think that he did the same to the seaward approaches, and there has been no signs of the Imperial navy. He is trapped, and the time to strike is now, before they arrive."

Chapter Thirty-Three
Palace

TARJIAAN PICKED UP his own cup and drained it. "The Imperial Navy rests on the floor of Mother Ocean," he said. "There will be no forces from the sea save for my own."

Ysnia smiled. "Oh, that is a wonderful thing to hear. And this is your palace. Do you know the way?"

Tarjiaan shook his head. "I don't," he answered. "I've never even looked on it with my own eyes. But...." He looked up. "*Wave Runner*, please tell Wilaanger I need him immediately." He paused, then looked at Daanir. "*Wave Runner* can access the archives, can't she?"

"Of course she can," Daanir answered. "Why... oh! *Wave Runner*, we'll need any blueprints or floorplans of the Palace of Meradon."

[It may take me a long time to locate those,] *Wave Runner* replied. [The archival records are expansive.]

"How long is a long time?" Tarjiaan asked.

[Five minutes,] *Wave Runner* answered. [Perhaps as much as ten.]

Tarjiaan bit back a laugh. "Do your best, my dear."

[Of course, Captain.]

Ysnia arched a brow. "That is a long time?"

"To a machine? Yes." Daanir smiled. "That was the voice of our ship. She's advanced enough to have woken up."

"Intriguing," Ysnia murmured. "And she is female. Appropriate."

"All of our ships are female," Tarjiaan said. "Even the ones that aren't awake yet." He leaned back in his chair, one hand resting on the purring cat in his lap. "I've heard stories about the Palace, and about the Water Gate. The royal belowship and the flagship were supposed to be able to sail right into the Palace and dock. So we should be able to sail straight in. But if we do, he'll know we're coming. It's not like he can miss a ship of this size entering the Water Gate."

"If a belowship can sail in, would a submersible be able to do the same?" Antivar asked. "The way we took over the *Chimaera*?"

"I don't know enough to answer that," Tarjiaan answered. He paused, then nodded. "I'd like to adjourn this discussion for long enough to assemble all of the officers. Marikaar too, if he can leave the *Chimaera*. If we're going to plan an assault, I want to do this properly." He looked down at himself and laughed. "And I'd like to put on some clothes."

When they reconvened at the table in the day cabin, Tarjiaan was dressed in a formal uniform and his armor. In addition to Daanir, Nika, Rathsafa, and Ysnia, seated around the table were Marikaar, Wilaanger, Antivar, Istin, Theonus and Nyssa. Logiri moved around the room, filling cups with tea and water, making certain that there were writing implements and paper.

As he took his seat, Theonus looked up. "Mancer Ishantar sends her love, *Wave Runner*."

[Thank you for carrying the message. Please tell her that I miss her, and that I hope she is doing well.]

"I will do that," Theonus said. He grinned. "I'm enjoying having a ship that can tell me what she's thinking."

Tarjiaan nodded. "I agree. Now, if everyone is here, we'll begin. For the benefit of everyone who was not here earlier, I would like to present Queen Ysnia of Sualiman, who honors us with her presence."

"A great honor, indeed," Wilaanger murmured.

"May I report on what you told us, Your Majesty?" Tarjiaan asked. She nodded, and he turned to face the others. "The fighting we were told of has driven the Emperor to ground. Tyraca and Lestalt have both thrown off the rule of the Empire, and the Emperor has retreated to the only stronghold he has left — Meradon. He has locked himself away in the Palace, and the forces on land cannot reach him. But we can."

Wilaanger coughed. "You're thinking of the Water Gate?"

"Yes," Tarjiaan agreed with a nod. "Now, this is not going to be an easy endeavor. We cannot just sail the *Wave Runner* up to the gate. Not without alerting all of his forces. There was a suggestion of bringing in an assault team using submersibles—"

"There's only one docking port in the Water Gate," Wilaanger interjected. "Because the only belowship that was ever supposed to use it was the *Chimaera*."

"Which means we need to plan for how we're going to get in. And once we do get into the Palace, we have the issue that all of my men were born to the waves. They have never fought on land. None of us know the Palace, and we don't have the time for them to acclimate to land the way I did when I lived in Sualiman. So... recommendations?"

"Captain," Antivar said. "You're only half right about your men. The forces that you command who were born to the sea have never fought on land. But your adopted forces are all land born, and trained on land before we ever went to sea. If your strike teams are mostly refugees, that should counter the Meradonese native... lack of experience at land-based warfare."

"And if we lead the assault on the Palace the same way we led the assault on the *Chimaera*," Istin added, "we should be able to get in under cover of darkness, and have no one be the wiser."

"You mean using launches?" Marikaar said. "How many can we assemble? How many would we need to take the Palace?"

"How many men does he have inside?" Wilaanger asked. "That's going to inform our numbers." He frowned. "And... there's another problem. Tarjiaan, do you know how the Water Gate works? How you open it?"

"I just barely know that it's there," Tarjiaan admitted. "That was on my list of questions to ask. How does it work? Is there a transmission code, and do we have it? Or is there something on the *Chimaera*?"

Wilaanger folded his hands on the tabletop. "There is no code. No signal device. The only way to open the Water Gate is for the Mancer Royal to do it."

"Oh." Daanir looked thoughtful, then nodded. "I see how that lends a level of security. I don't see this as a problem. I can open the gate, and I can hold it open as long as it needs to be held." He frowned. "I've never asked. What sort of tech does the Palace have? I assume it's all fifty years out of date, but is there a central core, like on the ships? If we can tap into the core, we can find out how many people are in the Palace, and better plan an attack."

"That's not something I can answer," Wilaanger said. "I never paid much attention to the mancer's arts. Not until we were out at sea."

Tarjiaan frowned. "*Wave Runner,* see if you can find mancer records on the Palace while you're looking for the floorplans. If there's a central core we'll need... what, Daan?"

"Schematics," Daanir answered. "I'll need to see if we can interface our tech with what's on land. Which might mean using wire, spit, and a crowbar, but I won't know until we see what's there."

[I have the floorplans,] *Wave Runner* announced. [I am still looking for schematics and records.]

"We need a monitor." Daanir got up and went to the cabinet, coming back with the monitor. He set it up at the foot of the table. "Show us what you found, *Wave Runner.*"

The screen lit up, showing meticulous plans of rooms and corridors. Tarjiaan studied them, then frowned. "Wil, I'm still not certain of what I'm looking at. You're going to have to guide us."

Wilaanger looked closer, then nodded. "These are the plans for the main floor, which has access to the courtyard and the land side entry gates. *Wave Runner,* I need the plans for two levels below this. If it's labeled, it'll say that it's the water level."

The image changed, and Wilaanger stood up and moved down the table to better reach the monitor. "This is the entry from the Water Gate," he said, pointing. "There are guard positions here and here, and a watertight door that can seal this area from the rest of the Palace. Once we're past that, the water stairs are here. Those are the first of the grand staircases." He paused, then slowly said, "We'll need to do something about all the stairs once we're actually in control of the Palace."

"Not something we need to worry about at this moment, Wil," Tarjiaan said. "I'm not leading this assault from my chair."

"You could," Daanir murmured.

"Of course I could," Tarjiaan replied. "But I anticipated stairs." He turned back to Wilaanger. "Go on."

Wilaanger nodded. "*Wave Runner*, I'll need the main level again." Once the image had changed, he pointed once more. "The water stairs come out here, in the courtyard. This part is open to the sky, but it's inside the inner curtain wall. Guard stations at the top of the stairs, here at the curtain gate, and here at the inner doors. This, I think, is where we'll start to see resistance." He traced his finger over the floorplans. "I've skipped the service level, but that's between the water level and the main level. That's where we find the servant quarters, the guard barracks, the kitchens and the armory. Kitchens have access to the dining rooms and the great hall, back here. On the main level, we have the great hall, the council chamber, and the throne room." He paused, frowning. "The throne room is the most secure room in the Palace. If he's anywhere, he's there."

"What's above that?" Theonus asked. "There's more than just the three floors. I know that. I've seen drawings, and it's taller than that."

Wilaanger smiled. "The next level was the Queen's solar, the King's study, the library, and the Mancery."

Daanir made a soft sound that Tarjiaan heard as a whimper. "I've read about the Mancery," he said. "I never thought I'd get to see it."

"You're not only going to get to see it, that will be your domain," Tarjiaan said. Daanir grinned. Tarjiaan rested his hand on Daanir's and turned back to Wilaanger. "Take us through the rest, Wil. Let us get an idea of what we're facing."

Wilaanger nodded, leading them through a short tour of the Palace, having *Wave Runner* change the floorplans as he talked. Finally, he had the ship put the main level back on the monitor. "I don't think the upper levels will be of concern to us," he said. "Your Majesty, when Gondarishan fled Tyraca, do you know what sort of forces he had with him? Or attendants?"

Ysnia frowned slightly. "I did not lead the final assault on the Imperial Palace, and the reports that reached me were not as detailed as I could have wished. It appears that when he left, it was with his personal guard and his body servants."

"Captain, if I may?" Logiri said. "Rathsafa might be able to speak to how many that would be."

Tarjiaan nodded. "*Wave Runner,* would you ask Rathsafa to join us?"

Soon, there was a soft knock on the door, and Rathsafa stepped inside. "Captain?"

"Father, we were hoping you might be able to provide some information," Tarjiaan said. Rathsafa smiled broadly.

"I am at your service, my son."

"Rathsafa, what do you know of Gondarishan's entourage?" Ysnia asked. "His guards and his attendants?"

Rathsafa frowned slightly, folding his arms over his chest. Then he blinked. "Oh, when he ran, did he take his bully forces and personal slaves with him?"

"It appears so." Ysnia looked amused at the description. "How many of each were there?"

Rathsafa nodded. "His personal guard... there were usually between ten and fifteen. Never more than that. And he always had two slave girls and a body servant. Usually a boy for that. I doubt he took his secretary with him, but that's possible. And his secretary was Antar." He glanced at Logiri. "It was Antarlogirat."

"Irat?" Logiri sniffed. "I'd wondered where he'd ended up. It was either going to be in a position of power, or strangled by some jealous husband."

"You know him?" Tarjiaan asked.

"My youngest brother," Logiri answered. "Have you ever heard the saying that the oldest is the father's pride, and the youngest is the mother's pet? That was Irat. Mother's pet, and spoiled beyond all belief. He is sloppy in his work, careless in his manner, and should never have been granted the rank he holds."

Tarjiaan nodded slowly. "And... what threat will he be when we hit the Palace?"

Logiri frowned, cocking his head to the side. He slowly shook his head from side to side. "I will not say he will not be a threat. To discount any of my kin is to court the kiss of the Sand Queen. But I do not think he will be an effective threat. I believe that he had... overinflated opinions of his own prowess, but I also cannot say that I ever saw him actually face a challenge. And remember, I last saw him nearly twelve years ago."

"Which means we have to treat him as a larger threat. He might have changed. He might have gotten better." Nyssa nodded. "He'll need to be put down quickly and completely." She grimaced and turned to Logiri. "Sorry."

"You need not apologize," Logiri replied. "I agree with you. My father and my uncles would tell you that the Antar hold themselves to the highest of standards. Irat... does not, and when last I saw my family, my father was gravely disappointed in his youngest son."

Tarjiaan nodded. "So, it's Gondarishan and at the most nineteen others. Fifteen guards. One assassin secretary, and three servants who may or may not be threats." He looked around the table. "Is there anything we're missing?"

"Rumors," Ysnia said. "The rebellion has taken a toll on the Emperor. I have heard that his health is failing, and that he has been executing any healer who fails to reverse his deterioration. I have heard that he has been consorting with mages and medical pretenders, trying to extend his life. And, most disturbing, we have confirmed that all of his mages were put to the sword before he fled Tyraca."

"Did you hear anything about mancers?" Daanir asked. "Ilaris said that he handed all of Meradon's mancers over to the Emperor. Are they imprisoned somewhere?"

Ysnia looked thoughtful, then shook her head. "I have heard nothing. We have heard only about the deaths of the mages."

"If that's true, it doesn't make sense. He knows we can't fight mages. Why take away that advantage?" Tarjiaan shook his head. "Antivar? You had an idea about what men to send?"

Antivar licked his lips, then reached out and picked up a piece of paper and a pen. Istin slid an inkwell closer, and Antivar started scribbling, making lists, crossing things out. Making new lists. He frowned, nodded, then took a fresh piece of paper and rewrote his list before passing the page up the table.

Tarjiaan took the page and looked down at the list. Eight launches. Eight men per launch. The majority were men who had been under Antivar's command, and who'd come to the *Wave Runner* during the last battle against the Imperial Navy, but leading each launch was someone from Meradon. "Antivar, this is very complete. An attack force of 64 should be enough to secure the service levels, and to deal with the number of guards. The rest of the fleet will secure Half Moon Harbor and the Meradonese coast, in case he gets past us and tries to escape by sea." He passed the pages to Daanir, who read through them, then passed them on.

"What about the land approach?" Rathsafa asked.

"The people of Lestalt and the people of Tyraca have been laying siege to the gates of the Palace since shortly after Gondarishan took shelter there," Ysnia answered. "My people will join them in time for your assault from the Water Gate, and if the land gates can be raised, we can join in the fight."

"Tarjiaan, there's one change I want to make to this list," Wilaanger said, looking down at the page. "I'm coming with you."

"You are not!" Tarjiaan gasped. "Wil, you were going to stay in the dockyards! You said you were getting too old for this! You need to go with the healers, not into battle!"

"I do have to go with you. I'm the only one you have who has ever set foot in the Palace. I can show you all the floorplans, but in the heat of battle, you're not going to have time to look at a map. You need someone who knows the way." Wilaanger set the page down and looked at Tarjiaan. "Jiaan, I need to do this. I wasn't there for Ika. I failed him. I refuse to fail again."

Tarjiaan started to protest, only to stop when Daanir rested his hand on his arm. "Jiaan." Tarjiaan turned, and was surprised by the intensity in Daanir's eyes. "It's his last chance to serve Ikaanaji. Don't take this from him."

"Agreed," Nyssa said. "Captain, this... you aren't the battle companion. This isn't something you'd understand. We do." She smiled. "I'll stick with him."

"You need to stay with your companion," Wilaanger said. "I don't need minding."

Tarjiaan took a deep breath, then nodded. "So be it. Ysnia, how soon can we move?"

[Captain, Mancer Aanaji is looking for you.]

Despite *Wave Runner*'s message, it took far longer than Tarjiaan expected to find Aanaji. He was about to ask *Wave Runner* to locate her when he saw her standing at the prow. He walked forward to join her.

"For someone who was looking for me, you certainly made it hard for me to find you," he said as he reached the rail. She smiled and looked up at him.

"Your ship is beautiful," she said. "But it's hard to find a place to be alone with your thoughts. And... I've had a lot to think about." She took a deep breath. "This is goodbye, isn't it? I heard the report from land that Queen Ysnia's forces are in place and ready to move. That means we need to move, too, and you and Daanir and... and you're going to attack the Palace."

"And we'll be back, Aani," Tarjiaan said. "This won't be goodbye forever. But we will be sailing north to Meradon tomorrow midday, so that we can be in the right position to have the launches in the water at sunset."

She nodded. "And where do you want me to be? I can't stay here. I'll be in the way. Naji and Kaapi have already gone to the *Chimaera*, and I thought about going with them, but...." She blushed. "I understand you a little better now, I think. I thought about going back to the *Chimaera*, and... I can't do it. I can't go back there. But that leaves me wondering where I can go?"

"I was actually going to ask if you would go with Nika." He leaned on the rail and turned his head to look at Aanaji. "She and Navi and Rathsafa are going with Queen Ysnia. They'll be leaving in an hour. They'll be with the healers. Close to the Palace, but far enough away to be safe."

Aanaji turned her back to the rail, leaning against it. "Does she want me to go with her?"

"She hasn't said it explicitly, but I think she'd appreciate having you with her. And I'd appreciate having you with her. Having someone there to take care of her, and to make certain that she doesn't push herself too hard. Logiri is going with her, too. But... I think you'll be more of a help."

"Especially with the cats?" Aanaji added.

Tarjiaan smiled. "She'll probably appreciate help there, too." He paused. "Has Istin talked to you?"

Aanaji blushed. "I... he told me. And... Jiaan, I don't know what I want. I told him that. And he said he'll wait for me to know." She hugged herself. "He's a good man. A wonderful teacher. Naji adores him. And..."

"And what do you think of him?" Tarjiaan asked. "How do you feel about him?"

She looked down, swaying slightly from foot to foot. "I think I could be happy. No, I know I could be happy. He makes me happy. I could talk to him for hours about anything and nothing. Just being in the same room with him is... is wonderful. But... Jiaan, it's terrifying!"

He nodded. "It is. But I learned that it's incredible, too." He smiled and stood up. "I've learned that it's truly amazing to have someone who sees you, who sees your truth and accepts it, and who loves you even when you're broken. Loves you enough to help you pick up the pieces of yourself and find how they fit."

"Daanir?" Aanaji said.

"And Nika. Daan knew me before. With Nika, I was terrified of what she would say when she saw me without my armor, and without the shell of my chair to hide behind. And... she just accepted me. Completely and without reservations." He looked out at the small, Sualimani ships anchored nearby, bobbing slightly with the waves. "It still surprises me. Still scares me, a little. There's still some small part of me that wonders when she'll tell me she doesn't want me anymore. But that voice is getting quieter." He rested his hands on the rail. "Istin is like that, I think. And he'll wait for you to be ready. And if you decide you're not ready? He'll still be there. Because you make him happy, too." He sighed and looked up. "I need to go say goodbye to my wife. Will you go with her?"

Aanaji nodded. "I'll go with her. But first... I need to go and put together things to take with me. Then... I need to talk to Istin before I leave."

Tarjiaan walked with her across the deck, back toward the day cabin. He could see bundles and baskets waiting there. One of the baskets was loudly protesting.

"Gossamer doesn't like the travel basket?" he asked as he reached them. "Or is that Tripod?"

"That is Fancy," Nika answered. "Gossamer and Tripod both curled up and went to sleep." She looked up and tried to smile, but he could tell it was forced.

"Aanaji is going to come with you," he said. "And I will come to you as soon as I can."

She nodded. "I know you will. Be careful, Jiaan." He went to one knee in front of her and opened his arms, and she threw her arms around his neck, holding on tightly.

He wrapped his arms around her, breathing her in. This was his reason to fight. His wife, and their child. This was his future, and he wasn't going to give that up so easily. "I promise, I will be careful."

She nodded, her hair brushing against his cheek. Then she took his face in her hands and kissed him, her lips lingering against his long enough that he could taste her when she moved away. He let her go and stood up, seeing that Daanir had joined them. Nika went to him, and Tarjiaan took a look around, seeing a similar goodbye happening between Antivar and Navi. He saw Aanaji reappear on deck, carrying a bundle that she brought over to add to the pile. She turned around, saw Istin standing among a group of other former Imperial sailors, and set out for him like a compass needle toward true north. He looked startled, standing up straight as she approached. Tarjiaan couldn't hear what she said, but Istin's face lit up like a lamp. He bowed deeply, took her hand, and kissed her palm. Which, apparently, wasn't good enough for Aanaji, who reached out with that same hand, grabbed Istin by the front of his shirt, and pulled him in for a kiss. Istin's gasp of surprise could be heard clear across the deck before it was drowned out by the cheers of the men around them, which doubled when Istin put his arms around Aanaji and kissed her back.

"I was wondering when he was going to do something more than yearn after her," Wilaanger said as he came up behind Tarjiaan. He'd put aside his healer robes in favor of the royal uniform, and for the first time in his memory, Tarjiaan saw Wilaanger as a battle companion.

"Apparently, it's been mutual yearning," Tarjiaan replied. "I wish we had time for them to have more than this now that she's accepted him. But it's time to move."

Chapter Thirty-Four
Into the Palace

THE VIEW OF THE PALACE over Half Moon Harbor as they approached from the sea should have been impressive, if only they could see it. The night was as dark as the bottom of a barrel, and Tarjiaan was navigating by instinct and reckoning alone.

"Launch six, you're drifting to port," he murmured into the comms. Everyone in each launch had been issued an earpiece, and they were all in constant communication.

"*Correcting now, Captain,*" Istin replied. "*How much farther?*"

"We're about to open the gate," Tarjiaan answered. "Everyone, be ready to move." He nudged Daanir. "Ready?"

Daanir snorted. Then he went silent, and Tarjiaan heard a distant, tortured screech of metal on metal.

"Oh, no," Wilaanger murmured from behind him. "That's something we never thought of. There's been no one to keep the gates in good condition."

"Daan—"

"Working!" Daanir snapped. "The mechanism is frozen." More screeching, and a distant crash. Then... silence. "Gates are open!" Daanir wheezed. "Move!"

"All launches, full speed ahead!" Tarjiaan called, and accelerated toward the open gates. He could see lights ahead now, illuminating the way. "Daan, did you do that?"

"They're tied in to the gate mechanism," Daanir answered. "They go on when the gate opens, to better guide in an above ship. With the noise sounding the alert, I didn't think the lights were going to make things any worse. They already know we're coming."

"But now they can see us." Tarjiaan increased their speed, ordering the others to do the same. The gates were wide open, and as they drew closer, he anticipated an attack at any moment...

But nothing happened. They sailed through the gates and up to the dock without being challenged. They assembled there, watching for defenders that never appeared.

"Where are the guards?" Antivar murmured.

"Would there be any?" Istin asked in response. "There's maybe twenty people here, we think. There can't be enough guards to spare. We'll face them further in."

"Agreed," Tarjiaan said. "Right. Teams, proceed as planned." He drew his force pistol and started forward.

"The portcullis is down. That's where we're going," Wilaanger said from behind him. Tarjiaan nodded, gesturing for his forces to split, sheltering on either side of the passage while Daanir forced the heavy gate to rise, the mechanism screaming in protest at being forced to move after so long.

"That's another reason there's no one on guard down here," Antivar said. "They couldn't get out this way."

Tarjiaan nodded. "Daan, once we're through, seal the gate again. Don't leave an escape avenue."

Daanir looked at him. "What if we need an escape avenue?"

"If we need one? We're well and truly fucked," Istin muttered.

"Istin," Wilaanger chided. "Language."

"Least of my worries, Wil," Tarjiaan said. "Let's move."

Despite all the noise, they met no one as they moved through the corridors to the water stairs. Istin and his half of the attack force went first in order to secure the service level, while Tarjiaan and his men waited in the shadows of the silent stairs. It wasn't long before Istin's voice came through the comms.

"Captain, there isn't anyone here, and I don't think there has been for years," he said. *"Most of these rooms have dust deep enough to lose your ankles. The kitchen shows some use, but there's no one here now. All we've seen are mice. Stairs are secure at the front and the back of the level."*

Tarjiaan glanced back at Wilaanger, who shrugged and shook his head. "I don't know," he said. "But we can't take chances."

Tarjiaan nodded. "If it stays this quiet when we get to the main level, I want to send a group to get the front gates open and let Ysnia's forces in," he said. "Theonus?" He looked around, saw the other man was looking slightly green.

"I thought you were joking about being land sick," Theonus muttered. "I'm fine. Am I taking the front gates?"

"Yes, and be careful," Tarjiaan answered. "Your balance is off, and you're not going to be able to shoot straight."

"All the more reason for us to get out of the way," Nyssa said. "I'll keep him safe, Jiaan. I'm fine."

"Wilaanger, tell them where to go once we're on the main level." Tarjiaan listened with half an ear as Wilaanger described the route that they'd need to take to get to the gatehouse. Where were the guards?

"Daan, have you gotten into the palace central core?" he asked.

"I've been looking, and I don't think there is one," Daanir answered. "At least, not the way we have them now. I can feel something, but it's barely there."

"Is it there enough to tell us where everyone is?"

Daanir frowned, closing his eyes slightly. "There... no. I'm not getting anything that makes sense. I'm getting power readings, but no sense of people. Power reading is highest one level up, and toward the rear of the palace. Ah... the throne room, I think."

"Jiaan, we're ready to move," Theonus said. "I know the way."

"Take what men you think you need, and get those gates open. Once they're in, your orders are to secure the upper levels and the water gate." Tarjiaan looked around. "The rest of us will head for the throne room. That's where we'll find him."

They ascended the stairs to the main level, and Theonus led his team toward the walls, while Tarjiaan and his men went further into the Palace. Footsteps echoed in the high-ceilinged hall, where not a single guard waited to challenge them. Tarjiaan started to wonder if Ysnia had been wrong. Was the Emperor here at all?

Was this a trap?

"Hold," he murmured, stepping back into an alcove. Daanir fell in next to him, and Wilaanger and Antivar joined them, while his other men moved into similar hiding places around the room. "Istin, we're going dark for a moment."

"*Understood, Captain.*"

Tarjiaan turned off his comms and waited until the others had followed suit.

"What is it?" Daanir asked.

"Are we absolutely certain that he's here?" Tarjiaan asked. "I trust Queen Ysnia, but we've had no resistance at all."

"There's something here," Daanir insisted. "There's a power signature unlike anything I've ever seen up ahead of us. The closer we get, the more certain I am that it's not Meradonese tech. I just can't tell what it is."

"The Queen said that her people put the Palace under siege when the Emperor took shelter here. He cannot have gotten out by land, and we just saw that he cannot have gotten out by water. He must be here." Antivar looked over his shoulder. "But... there's a chance that he's alone now. After all this time, I wonder how many of his guards are still alive?"

"Why do you say that?" Wilaanger asked.

Antivar grimaced. "In the Emperor's court, killing is a form of sport, and gladiatorial battles are common entertainment. The Emperor... enjoys hurting people."

"Gilded skulls," Tarjiaan murmured. Antivar nodded.

"Exactly." He frowned. "That might explain why there was no challenge. There's no one left to challenge us."

"Then let's keep moving." Tarjiaan turned on his comms. "We're moving. Be ready for anything."

They started out again, heading toward the rear of the Palace and the throne room.

"*Captain,*" Istin's voice came through the comms. He sounded... off. "*We just found... bodies.*"

"How many?" Wilaanger asked.

"*I... I don't know!*" Istin's voice took on a heavy tinge of panic, and his accent was very strong. "*They... they're in the larder. We hadn't looked there before. But... they've been butchered and hung like meat!*"

"Easy, Istin," Antivar crooned. "Easy. Close the door. Leave them be. We'll deal with them later." He looked at Tarjiaan, clearly alarmed.

"Close the door, Istin," Tarjiaan repeated. "That's an order."

"*I... yes, Captain.*" The comms went quiet, and Tarjiaan took a deep breath.

"This needs to end," he said softly.

"Then let's end it.' Daanir rested his hand on Tarjiaan's shoulder. "For them. For us. For everyone we love."

Tarjiaan nodded. He looked down at his pistol, checked the charge, then drew his saber. "Mancer, open that door."

Daanir grinned. "With pleasure." He gestured to several of the men, and they formed up around him as they walked toward the door. Just outside, they stopped. Daanir shook his head. "It's not locked."

"Not locked?" Tarjiaan started forward.

He never reached Daanir's side. The doors exploded outwards in a rain of metal and wood, and Daanir and the men with him vanished in the smoke and debris. Tarjiaan would have screamed, but the silhouette visible in the smoke froze his voice in his throat.

Twice as tall as a man.

Heavy armor.

Rounded helmet.

An *Executioner.* It marched out of Tarjiaan's nightmares, coming toward him with its weapon raised. He could see the growing glow as the weapon readied to fire, but he couldn't move....

Everything happened at once. The weapon fired. Something hit Tarjiaan from the side, hard enough to knock him off balance. He felt heat, all along his right side. Then he landed hard with a body on top of him, and time started moving again.

Unfortunately, his armor refused to do the same. He was trapped on his back, pinned under...

"Mothers below... Wil?" Tarjiaan pushed as hard as he could, and Wilaanger's body shifted off of him, letting him reach the emergency release on the armor. He pulled the release, but nothing happened. He tried to sit up, and got far enough to see that most of the right leg of his armor was gone, sliced away just below the point where his leg was seated. The Executioner moved closer, standing over him, and Tarjiaan's world narrowed to a single point of focus, and the awareness that he was going to die. Tarjiaan raised his own pistol, knowing it wouldn't do anything, but refusing to die helpless.

"Captain!"

He could hear Antivar, but couldn't see him. All he could see was the Executioner. It raised its weapon once more...

And laughed.

"Well, well. If it isn't the pretender king of Meradon. You are exceptionally hard to kill." Tarjiaan stared. The thing was *aware*? But... how? It was powered by magic. It didn't have a central core to awaken. "Tell me," it continued. "How is my worthless son?"

The shock of recognition almost drowned out the fear. "Gondarishan?" he gasped. "You... you're *in* there?"

"Surprised?" The nightmare machine laughed again. "You inspired this, you know. The man in the machine. I've known about your armor for years now. It took some doing for my mages to replicate it, and I have your mancers to thank for the final touches. Now I'll live forever. I am finally the immortal Emperor. And once I'm done with you and that bitch Ysnia, there will be no one left to challenge me."

It was futile. He knew it was futile. But Tarjiaan fired anyway, watching the shots flare and fade against the metal shell. Gondarishan laughed again.

"You amuse me," he said. "You're trying so very hard not to die. Not like the others. They were boring. Even the Antar was boring in the end. They all just laid down and gave up. You... you won't stop until I squeeze the life out of you." He laughed again, slowly leaning forward, one metal hand outstretched. "Let's see how long that takes."

Tarjiaan started firing again, aiming for the face, the seams at the neck, anything that might slow the metal monster down. He saw movement, saw Antivar running toward them, firing at the Executioner's back. Gondarishan straightened and swung, backhanding Antivar across the room. Tarjiaan pulled the release on his armor again, but it refused to open.

"Do you think I'd have left that flaw in place?" he demanded, turning back to Tarjiaan. "This machine is unstoppable! I am unstoppable!"

Tarjiaan felt the sound before he heard it, felt it in his teeth and his ears, a high-pitched metallic whine that grew in intensity until it was audible. The floor under his back was vibrating... no. No, it was his armor vibrating! The release hissed, and the armor opened enough for Tarjiaan to shift, to pull himself out and away from the Executioner. Gondarishan straightened again, looking around, ignoring Tarjiaan.

"What is that?" he demanded. "Where is that coming from?" He shook all over, like a mechanical dog. "That... that *hurts*! That's impossible! You cannot hurt me!"

"You're not unstoppable."

Chapter Thirty-Five
Executioner

DAANIR SHOOK HIS HEAD and winced, feeling warmth running down his face. He pushed himself up on his hands and knees, debris sliding off his back. He'd felt the power surge a heartbeat before the door exploded, had no time to shout a warning or get out of the way. Someone had known they were coming. Something—

"Captain!"

Daanir's head shot up. Antivar's shout was nearly drowned out by a mechanical laugh.

"Well, well. If it isn't the pretender king of Meradon. You are exceptionally hard to kill. Tell me. How is my worthless son?"

Who... what was talking? Daanir frowned, reaching out. Machine. Distantly familiar, but he was distracted by Tarjiaan's voice. "Gondarishan? You... you're *in* there?"

"Surprised?" That mechanical laugh again.

Daanir lurched to his feet and saw the shadow through the haze of dust. For a moment, he couldn't move, seeing back through fifteen years to the last time he'd seen that shape. An Executioner? And... and it was the Emperor? How?

"You inspired this, you know," the Executioner said, clearly talking to Tarjiaan. "The man in the machine. I've known about your armor for years now. It took some doing for my mages to replicate it, and I have your mancers to thank for the final touches.

419

Now I'll live forever. I am finally the immortal Emperor. And once I'm done with you and that bitch Ysnia, there will be no one to challenge me."

Daanir went cold. *This* was what Ilaris had done to his mancers? Ilaris had given the mancers to the Emperor to create this... monster? This was why his people had died? Gunshots flashed in the haze. The angle was wrong. They were coming from the ground. Tarjiaan was on the ground? Why wasn't he getting up? He felt for Tarjiaan's armor, and couldn't find it, then realized that the reason Tarjiaan was on the ground was that he was trapped. Trapped in his ruined armor, the same way he'd been trapped before.

It was happening again.

No.

Not again. Never again.

The last time Daanir had faced an Executioner, he'd been nobody, a half-trained soldier dizzy in love and desperate to prove himself. He'd seen the flaw, but destroying the machine had nearly cost him everything. This time? This time he wasn't just a Mancer, he was *the* Mancer. He could stop it. He could change it.

More mechanical laughter. "You amuse me," he said. "You're trying so very hard not to die. Not like the others. They were boring. Even the Antar was boring in the end. They all just laid down and gave up. You... you won't stop until I squeeze the life out of you." The Executioner stepped forward, one hand extended. "Let's see how long that takes."

More shots from the ground. Shots from behind, and the Executioner turned and lashed out, knocking whoever had been trying to stop it away.

"Do you think I'd have left that flaw in place?" The Executioner turned back and lurched toward Tarjiaan. "This machine is unstoppable! I am unstoppable!"

"No," Daanir murmured. He let his power flow, splitting his focus. Part of him studied the Executioner as the rest reached for the remains of Tarjiaan's armor, forcing the release to open. He saw Tarjiaan pull himself out, dragging himself away. Good. Daanir turned his full attention and the full force of the power of the Mancer Royal on the metal monster. He could feel the machine now, feel how it was assembled. How the wires flowed through the conduits with the coolant tubes. How the joints fitted together. It would have been a masterwork if it hadn't been horrific.

"What is that?" the Executioner demanded, turning awkwardly, flailing like a loose sail in a high wind. "Where is that coming from? That... that *hurts*! That's impossible! You cannot hurt me!"

"You're not unstoppable."

"Daan?" He heard Tarjiaan's voice, but ignored it for the moment.

"You are not unstoppable," he repeated, walking forward. "And I can hurt you." He stopped as he gathered all his power, then smiled and reached out with both hands. "This is over. You will not take him from me again." He closed both hands into fists.

The monster screamed as it crumpled, as bare metal responded to Daanir's will. Or maybe it was the consciousness inside the metal screaming. For a single, sickening moment, Daanir *reveled* in that scream. It was, he imagined, the same sound his heart had made when he'd been ripped from his Prince's side. And it would never happen again. He studied the twisted mass of metal, then opened his hands.

The Executioner exploded.

Tarjiaan pushed himself up on his hands, trying to see where the voice was coming from. "Daan?"

"You are not unstoppable," Daanir repeated. He limped out of the smoke, his face covered in blood. "And I can hurt you." He stopped. Smiled; if you could call that a smile. It was an expression Tarjiaan had never seen on Daanir's face before, and he prayed to the Mothers that he never saw it again.

His wife wasn't the only one who was terrifying.

Daanir stretched out both hands, his fingers splayed as if he was reaching for something. "This is over. You will not take him from me again," he snarled and closed his hands into fists.

The Executioner crumpled, reminding Tarjiaan of the paper balls he made for Tripod to play with. Gondarishan shrieked, a sound that might have been pain, rage, fear, or a combination of all three. The sound made Tarjiaan flinch, but Daanir showed no reaction. He studied the twisted mass of metal, then flicked his fingers open.

Metal shards flew everywhere, and Tarjiaan ducked, hearing whistling missiles flying overhead, hearing them clatter like rain onto the broken tiles. Then... silence, broken only by soft wheezing.

Not wheezing. *Breathing!*

"Wil?" Tarjiaan dragged himself to Wilaanger's body. The older man was struggling to breathe, his face a mass of blood and burns. He turned toward Tarjiaan's voice.

"Jiaan?" he croaked. "Jiaan? I... I can't see."

"I'm here, Wil." Tarjiaan rested his hand on Wilaanger's chest. "I'm here. I... comms. My earpiece is gone. We'll get you to the healers. You'll be fine." He swallowed, knowing he was lying. "It's over, Wil. He's dead."

Wilaanger coughed out a painful sounding laugh. "I know," he wheezed. "Heard it. My King. I... so proud of you." He coughed again, blood staining his lips. "My son."

Tarjiaan blinked, feeling the tears. "Stay with me, Wil. I... we need comms. Daan? Antivar?"

"I'm here." Daanir dropped to his knees on Wilaanger's other side. "Help is coming. Antivar needs a healer, too."

"We'll get you to the healers," Tarjiaan repeated. "Both of you. You need to be there to meet the baby, Wil. You need to be there to be a grandfather."

Wilaanger smiled. "Sorry. Time... Ika... I see you. You promised... Ika...." He shuddered. Then he fell still, and the wheezing stopped.

Tarjiaan blinked back tears and reached out to close Wilaanger's eyes. He coughed, then softly began to sing the *Farewell*. Daanir sang with him, softly, his voice cracking, the harmonies broken. By the time the song was finished, they were both crying, and they were no longer alone. Tarjiaan looked up to see Istin was standing behind him, tears streaming down his face.

"Captain," he said, his voice thick with grief. "The Sualimani forces are inside. We've taken Antivar out and sent him off to the healers, and they're working with other injured. What... what do we do with Honored Wilaanger? I don't know what's proper."

Nyssa came running toward them. "Captain!" She skidded to a stop, her eyes wide. "Mothers below. Oh... oh, no."

Istin turned toward her. "You know what to do?"

Nyssa looked at him, touched his arm and nodded softly. "I'll help. You've done a fine job, Istin. You can stand down."

"Where's Theonus?" Daanir asked. He wiped his face and grimaced at the blood on his sleeve. "I'll need the healers, too. I think. I'm pretty certain that this is all mine. All of my team were injured. We'll need litters to take them," Daanir answered. He looked at Tarjiaan. "You're not hurt?"

"I'm sore, but I think that's from how I landed when Wil knocked me out of the line of fire." He looked down at Wilaanger, then leaned down to kiss his forehead. "I don't know how I'm going to tell Nika."

"We'll tell her together," Daanir said. He stood up, swaying slightly as he got to his feet.

"Sit down, Mancer," Nyssa said. "I'll get the litters. And Theo's trying to convince himself that the bench he's sitting on isn't caught in the worst storm of his life. I've never seen him be this sick, the poor man." She turned to Tarjiaan. "Captain, what do you need?"

Tarjiaan considered the question, then shook his head. "My armor is destroyed. I'll need my chair. Eventually. For now... another litter. And... and I want that armor given to Mother Ocean. It can't be repaired, I don't think." He glanced at Daanir, who shook his head. "Then it needs to be retired." He sighed. "And I need someone to give me a report. How many dead? How many injured?"

"Outside this room? Everyone else is fine," Nyssa answered. "Other than being completely horrified by the servants quarters. We all heard Istin. That... we'll need someone with a strong stomach to go in and deal with that." She shook her head. "Later. For now, I'll get the litters."

"I'm fine." Tarjiaan lost count of how many times he'd repeated those words once they reached the healers camp. He was brought to a tent, settled onto a bed, and someone brought him a jug of water and a bowl of something to eat that he wasn't certain what it was and didn't touch. Then they left him, with someone occasionally stepping in to see if he'd spontaneously injured himself and needed treating. He sighed and shifted around until he was lying down. His shoulder and back were sore, but that was minor.

It was over. The Emperor was dead. The Four Sisters were free. Now what?

Gondarishan had left behind broken kingdoms torn by war and famine. How could Meradon help? What could they offer that no one else had? Could their hydroponics support the people until the land was healed enough to start producing crops again? He'd have to talk to Daan, talk to the caretakers of the farm ships. They could set the systems up on land, teach the people to use them.

It would be a start.

Someone scratched the side of the tent to let him know that they were there. The sound was accompanied by a yowl; Tarjiaan smiled as Tripod came through the tent flap, bounding over to the bed and jumping up, purring fiercely as he headbutted Tarjiaan. The tent flap opened again, and Nika came into the tent.

"They told me you were here," she said softly. "I am sorry I couldn't come sooner."

"I understand why," Tarjiaan assured her. "Come and sit." He shifted over on the bed and let her sit down facing him. She rested one hand on his chest, and he covered her hand with his own. "I'm fine, Nika."

She nodded. "Daanir will be released soon," she said. "And Antivar will live."

"He was that badly hurt?" Tarjiaan gasped. "I didn't realize!"

She nodded. "Several broken ribs, and internal injuries," she said. "But he will be fine. Navi is making certain of that." She swallowed. "I am sorry, Jiaan. About Wilaanger."

Tarjiaan nodded. "He saved me. He put himself between me and Gondarishan."

"I thought that the Emperor was ill?" Nika said. "How could he cause so much damage?"

Tarjiaan took a deep breath. "By having his mages and the captive mancers make him into an Executioner."

"What?" Nika gasped.

"He was in there, Nika. And... that's probably why he killed all the mages and the mancers. So they could never duplicate what they'd done, or remove him from the machine. He was in there, and... and Daan tore him apart."

"I wasn't going to let one of those things take you from me again," Daanir said as he came into the tent. His skin was clear and whole, but his uniform was still torn and bloodstained. He smiled slightly. "Is there room for me?"

"Always."

Daanir sat down on Tarjiaan's other side. He took deep breath. "So... now what do we do?" he asked. "We've been at war our entire lives. What do we do now?"

"I was thinking about just that," Tarjiaan answered. "The people in Tyraca are starving. How soon to you think we can get hydroponics set up and producing?"

Daanir's eyes widened. "Oh! I... oh, I'm not certain. I... oh, that's a good idea. And there are ways to grow that aren't as water intensive. It's dry in Tyraca, isn't it?" He frowned. "I'm sorry about the armor, Jiaan. I agree with retiring the old set, but the new one isn't anywhere near ready."

"I don't want you making it priority, Daan," Tarjiaan said. "The people have to come first. My chair is fine. And I'm fine with just my chair."

"What about the stairs in the Palace?" Nika asked.

Daanir smiled. "I have some ideas about those...."

Epilogue

THE ROYAL COURT OF Sualiman never stayed in one place for very long, so there wasn't really a palace. There were gathering houses, though, and it was in one of those that Tarjiaan met with Queen Ysnia and various nobles from Tyraca and Lestalt. On Tarjiaan's side of the table were Nika, Daanir, Rathsafa, Navi and Antivar. The only person he recognized on the other side of the table was Ysnia, who had apparently warned the others – none of them even batted an eye when Tarjiaan entered in his chair.

"Tarjiaan," Ysnia said. "Thank you for joining us. I would like to introduce you to what remains of the Tyracan Royal Council, and the Lestalti Privy Chamber."

"A pleasure," Tarjiaan said, inclining his head in their direction. "I had hoped to meet with you all."

"I..." One of the older men frowned slightly. "First things first. Do you intend to take the Imperial throne?"

"Great Mothers, no!" Tarjiaan gasped. Then he laughed. "I apologize. I'm a soldier and a sea captain, gentlemen. And lately, a king, although it's not a role I was born to take. I have no desire to be Emperor. The Four Sisters are free, and will remain so. All I intend to rule is Meradon."

"But, we have no one," another man said. "The entire royal house..."

"Of Tyraca?" Tarjiaan asked. When the man nodded, Tarjiaan gestured to Nika. "May I present my wife? Queen Ysnika, daughter of Masthaka and Rathsafa. You may be more familiar with Rathsafa by the name he bore before his marriage — Gondanadarish."

Nika smiled. "Gentlemen. It is my pleasure to meet you."

"Excuse me?" A third man spoke, one that seemed somehow familiar. "Your wife is... *his* granddaughter?"

"My wife is the last living daughter of the Tyracan royal house," Tarjiaan said. "And the union of her parents was, I believe, sworn to by Queen Ysnia herself."

"It is so," Ysnia said. "My granddaughter and namesake is the rightfully born queen of Tyraca."

"And I am happy to be nothing more than her first favored male," Tarjiaan added. "And we will travel between Meradon and Tyraca as the seasons change, so that neither is neglected."

"You've given this some thought," the third man said.

"We've been discussing little else," Nika answered. "How to best support my people, and provide them with food. How best to transition the Meradonese people from their undersea kingdom back to land. How to rebuild homes and alliances that were torn to shreds. There is so much healing to be done."

"We have rather a lot of notes," Daanir added. "And, for the record, I am Daanir Meranas, Mancer Royal and Consort of Meradon, and favored male number two."

The third man chuckled. "Well, you certainly know that tradition," he said.

"Have we met?" Nika asked. "You seem very familiar."

He bowed. "We have not, my lady. I am Antarthirakin, head of the house of Antar."

"That's it!" Daanir blurted. "He looks like Logiri."

Antarthirakin's jaw dropped. "You know my son?"

Tarjiaan nodded. "Logiri has been my closest friend and greatest ally for almost eleven years now. He has saved my life more than once."

Antarthirakin shook his head. "I thought he was dead. Tell him... tell him that his father wishes to see him, if you would?"

"I will pass on the message," Tarjiaan replied. "Now, Tyraca has a queen. Meradon has a king. The people of Lestalt have claimed their king in Rathsafa."

"And I will take my mother's throne," Rathsafa added. He glanced to the side. "And I have asked my son Ysnavin to stand as my heir. He is a talented healer. However, he is married to a man, and as such..." His voice tapered off.

"Navi and I have discussed this," Nika interjected. "My first son shall follow his father to the throne of Meradon. My first daughter shall take Tyraca when it is her time to rule. And my third child shall follow my brother, should he have no heir of his own."

"Although my mother is hoping," Antivar added, and a wave of laughter rippled through the room.

"You have been thinking about this," Antarthirakin said. "I'm interested in hearing more of your plans, and how we can assist."

"And just how you intend to have three coronations in three separate countries," someone else asked.

"It will be mine to arrange," Ysnia said. "And it will not stress any of you."

"And none of them are going to happen until the people are taken care of," Tarjiaan added. "We have work to do."

Tarjiaan worked alongside Nika and Rathsafa, planning what was best for their people. It took months. Months of travel. Months of work. Months of meetings and arguments and petulant nobles from all Four Sisters, each of whom was firmly put in their place. Meradon was deliberately left for last — the Meradonese people were safe and comfortable in their undersea homes, and could wait until the people who needed more were treated first. When a

Meradonese noble arrived on the *Wave Runner* with a complaint about what he called preferential treatment of outsiders, Nika patiently explained to him that, as a healer, it was her duty to treat the most gravely injured first.

Throughout it all, Ysnia provided raw materials. More food. Support and guidance. Homes were rebuilt, the work shared between Lestalti carpenters, Tyracan stone masons, Sualimani craftspeople, and Meradon's mancers in training. Food distributed from the Meradonese farm ships, and hydroponics systems were imported into Tyraca and Lestalt. Experts from the farm ships patiently trained anyone interested in learning the new farm systems how to start the matrix, how to maintain the systems and provide for the people while they also worked to restore the land. When the time finally came to start rebuilding Meradon, Daanir focused his attentions on the Palace of Meradon, working to make it habitable and accessible, allowing the King and Queen to leave the flagship and formally take residence, an act that signaled the last stages of rebuilding. That same night, in an intimate ceremony attended only by family and friends, Crown Princess-Mancer Aanaji married the newly-ennobled Lord-Commander Thistintal.

When the winter rains settled over Lestalt, they celebrated the first of the coronations as King Rathsafa claimed his mother's crown, taking the throne, then surprising them all by naming Antarlogirish his consort. The second coronation came with the spring, when Nika, now very pregnant, made her slow and stately procession into the Queen's Palace, followed by her favored males, and accompanied by cheering and thrown flowers.

The morning of the third coronation dawned bright and clear, with a crisp summer breeze off the sea. Tarjiaan sat in his powered chair on the balcony of his study, letting the breeze muss his hair. His new valet would fuss, and make noises about being presentable, but just being alone with the sea was worth the fuss, and Oona didn't fuss nearly as much as Logiri had.

[Captain?]

The familiar mechanical voice made Tarjiaan smile. The *Wave Runner* was moored inside the Water Gate, but Daanir had given her control of the Palace's new central core. Tarjiaan wasn't entirely certain what happened when they left — was there part of *Wave Runner* still in the Palace? Was she aware of being two places at once? He didn't know how to ask, and wasn't entirely certain he wanted the answer.

"I hear you, *Wave Runner.*"

[Healer Cheladra says that it is time, and that you need to come to the Queen's chambers right now.]

Tarjiaan sat up straighter. "Now? Right now?" He turned his chair and went back into his study, stopping only long enough to pet Tripod, who was asleep on the couch. "Tell her I'm on the way. Have you told Daanir?"

[He has just left the Mancery.]

Tarjiaan headed for the door, which swung open as he approached. Outside, waiting for him, was Daanir, who grinned.

"Looks like the coronation is going to be a little late?"

Tarjiaan nodded. "*Wave Runner*, comm Mentiras and let him know we're delayed. Let him know why, and tell him to apologize to the nobles on my behalf. I'll be there as soon as I can."

[The Steward says congratulations, and he will explain to the attendees.]

"He's settled in very well," Daanir said as they hurried to the stairs. Tarjiaan nodded, rolling onto the platform that was one of the first things that Daanir had installed. Clamps closed on the wheels of his chair, and the platform started moving, gently gliding up the stairs to the next level.

"He ran the dockyards for however many years. There are far fewer moving parts to a Palace." Tarjiaan looked up the stairs. "It's just that I want to get there. I know it. But I swear this is slower today."

"The new armor is almost ready for testing," Daanir said as they reached the top. He waited as the platform released Tarjiaan's chair, and they started down the corridor. "Another few days, I think. Sorry it wasn't ready for today. You're sure you don't want a ramp on the dais?"

"No ramp on the dais. There's no point – I can't transfer to the throne, Tarjiaan said. "And the throne will still be there once I can climb the dais stairs." He stopped outside the door to Nika's suite of rooms. "Ready?"

"Are you?" Daanir asked with a grin. Tarjiaan smiled back and rolled forward, and the doors opened to let him in to the large sitting room. As the doors closed, an inner door opened, and Aanaji came out.

"Aani? How did you get here before us?" Tarjiaan asked.

Aanaji looked puzzled. "I've been here for most of the morning," she answered. "Nika asked me to come have breakfast with her, and I was here when her waters broke."

Tarjiaan looked at Daanir, then back at his sister. "How long has she been in labor? And why were we only just called?"

"Because it's not Tyracan tradition to have the men in when there's a birth," Chel said from the doorway. "However, I managed to convince her that you'd want to be here. Come inside." Tarjiaan followed Chel into the bedroom, where he could see the wide windows out onto the balcony were open. The curtains were blowing in the breeze, and he could see Nika outside, sitting on a bench. Chel rested her hand on his shoulder. "Go on. She's waiting for you."

"Daan?" Tarjiaan looked up at him. "Are you coming with me?"

"Not for this." Daanir leaned down and kissed him. "This is for you to do. I'll be out here."

Tarjiaan nodded and rolled out onto the balcony, stopping next to the bench. Nika had her head tipped back, her eyes closed. She smiled as his chair stopped.

"I can hear you," she said. "When you are on the balcony. It is right below us."

"Then you could have shouted and told me to come up sooner," he replied.

She giggled. "That is undignified. You should not stay. You will be late for your own coronation."

"So? You're more important."

She opened her eyes and turned to him. "I love you, Jiaan."

He reached for her hand and kissed her palm. "I love you, too. Are you ready?"

She ran her nails through his beard, scratching his cheek. "I think I have little choice in the matter."

The coronation finally started three hours past when it had originally been scheduled to begin, but the guests had been plied with food and drink, and everyone was eager to hear the news. Mentiras refused to say anything about the baby, and a betting pool had started among several of the younger nobles. Daanir slipped into the room, and was immediately joined by Naajir and Kaapi.

"Papa?" Kaapi whispered. "And?"

"And... I'm not spoiling it for Tarjiaan. He'll tell you all when he comes in" He smiled and hugged his daughter to his side. "What have you heard?"

"Four to one odds that it's a girl," Naajir answered. "Papa Istin is trying to place a bet, but no one will take his money. They think he knows."

Daanir snorted. "That's ridiculous. I didn't even know, and I was there for almost the entire pregnancy."

A bell chimed, and a rush of chatter passed through the crowd as everyone hurried to find their places. Daanir led Naajir and Kaapi toward the front, escorting them to the edge of the dais. Then he took his own place, standing to the left of the Coral Throne.

Another bell chimed, and the double doors at the rear of the throne room swung open, framing Tarjiaan in the opening. He sat tall and proud as the chair rolled forward toward the throne, and a hush fell over the room as people noticed his precious cargo — there was a blanket wrapped infant in the crook of each arm. As he reached the dais, he turned his chair, and Daanir came down to meet him. Tarjiaan looked up at him, smiled, then turned back to the assembled nobles.

"My lords, my ladies," he said. "Thank you for your patience." He smiled down at the bundles in his arms, then looked up. "In preparing for my wife's coronation, I learned that there is very little ceremony to a Meradonese coronation. There is no grand procession. No blessings. No ritual or bells or special words. There is only the declaration." He paused, then smiled. "I, Tarjiaan, son of Taarik and Aajinisa, do claim the throne of Meradon, as is my right as my uncle's acknowledged heir and as the last son of the royal line. I swear before you that I shall serve Meradon to the best of my abilities until the Mothers claim me as their own. How say you all?" The cheers of assent were perhaps a bit more subdued than Daanir expected, but it appeared no one wanted to wake the sleeping babies. Tarjiaan bowed his head in assent, then smiled. "Thank you. I wish that my uncle had lived to see this day. Lived to see the Palace once more. It was his greatest wish, and I hope that he is smiling on us today." He paused and looked down again, his smile softening. "It gives me more joy than I could ever express to introduce you to the reasons we're running late." His smile broadened. "I claim these children as my own, born of my wife, Queen Ysnika. Firstborn, a daughter for Tyraca. Thaanika, daughter of Ysnika. Secondborn, a son for Meradon. Jiaadan, son of Tarjiaan."

"What?" Daanir whispered. "What?"

"I didn't know either," Tarjiaan admitted. He turned back to the assembled nobles. "Now, before all of you, I do honor the request of my nephew Naajir, and name my son as heir to the throne of Meradon. Let him be known as the Sea Prince from this day forward. And now, my lords and ladies, I invite you to celebrate with us. I will join you presently." Tarjiaan smiled. "First, I need to put my children to bed."

Safe Harbor

(TTTO: *My Fate,* as performed by Owain Phyfe)

Go bid the compass true north to neglect
That with assured reliance it did embrace
Go bid the still water cease to reflect,
Go bid the stars their paths no more to trace.
And when these all shall be convinced to do
Then shall I cease, cease to love you.
Seek not my course in wind and wave
To navigate my way, seek not the sea
But mark your place, and find there all I crave
For only there is my truth and destiny
Seek not the stars that race throughout the skies;
But guide me through the stars, the stars of your eyes.
Should charts all go blank and all anchorage fail
Should storms and winds do threaten, I've no fear,
Whate'er force or squall shall me assail,
I know in truth that my, my heart is here.
Though may our voyage be rough or calm
Trust that I'll return,
To the harbor of your arms.

Pronunciation Guide

IMPERIAL NAMES ARE Family name Given name. So in our world, Girantivar would be Antivar Gir.

Meranas (Mer-ah-nas) is the surname used by the Meradonese royal family and their fosterlings.

Nessunre (Ness-oon-ray) is the surname used for an unclaimed orphan.

Characters, in order of appearance/mention

Tarjiaan: Tar-zhahn (pronounced like the French name Jean. Think Jean-Luc Picard. Tar-Jean)

    Ishantar: Ih-shan-tar

    Meradon: Mer-ah-don

    Girantivar/Antivar: Gear-ant-e-var/Ant-e-var

    Marikaar: Marry-car

    Logiri/Antarlogirish: Low-gear-e/Ant-ar-low-gear-ish

    Ikaanaji: Ick-ah-na-zhee

    Ilaris: Ill-ar-es

    Daanir: Dah-near

    Kaapi: Cap-ee

    Riguaarin: Rig-guar-in

Quentas: Quen- tas (Quen as in quench)
Aaranji/Ranji: Ah-rhan-zhee/Rhan-zhee
Aanaji: Ah-na-zhee
Naajir/Naji: Nah-jeer/Nah-gee
Taarik: Ta-rick
Sualimani/Sualiman: Sway-lee-mon-e/Sway-lee-mon
Wilaanger: Will-anger
Rathsafa: Wrath-sa-fa
Gondarishan: Gone-dah-ri-shon
Gondanikaranthia/Nikaranthia/Nika:Gone-da-knee-kah-ran-thee-ah/Knee-kah-ran-thee-ah/Knee-kah
Lastalti/Lastalt: La-stall-tee/La-stalt
Masthaka: Mass-thack-ah
Adalia: Ah-dahlia
Falian: Fah-lee-ann
Aajinisa: Ah-jin-ee-sah
Cheladra/Chel: Chell-ad-rah/Chell
Lysson: Lyss-on
Gondanadarish/Nadarish:Gone-dah-nah-dar-ish/Nah-dar-ish
Tishaya: Ti-shy-ah
Ysnavin: Es-na-vin
Ysnika: Es-knee-kah
Ysnia: Es-knee-ah
Ilijiaan: Ill-e-zhahn
Alyaan: Ally-ann
Larina: Lar-eena
Thistintal/Istin: This-tin-tal/Is-tin
Ishian: Ish-ee-an
Destirian: Des-tea-rhi-an
Mentiras: Men-tir-as
Theonus: Thee-own-us

Nyssa: Knee-sah
Gellan: Gell (rhymes with yell)-ann
Narrick: Nah-rick
Rothga: Wroth-gah
Kyraath: Keer-wrath
Tommen: Tome-men
Reeshi: Ree-she
Tyva/Tyvvin: Tee-vah/Tih-vin
Ilenwy: Ill-in-wee
Oona: Un-ah
Owain: Owen
Antarlogirat: Ant-ar- low-gear-rat
Antarthirakin: Ant-ar-theer-ah-kin

The Coral Throne Soundtrack

IF YOU WANT TO LISTEN to all the music I listened to while writing this book, check out my Spotify playlist: https://open.spotify.com/playlist/7IpAkfv1UCtBu23PW7dDo7?si=aeef999a07284b1d

Also by Elizabeth Schechter

Heir to the Firstborn
Worlds Begin
Written in Water
Forged in Fire
Bones of Earth
Wings of Air
Visions in Smoke
Children of Dreams
Valley of Shadows

The Coral Throne
The Sea Prince
The Coral Throne

Standalone
The Rape of Persephone
Fools Rush In
Her Captive
To Market
Infernal Machine

Chains of Light
The Chronicles of John Zebedee
Snowbound

Watch for more at elizabethschechterwrites.com.

About the Author

Elizabeth Schechter has been writing award-winning Romantasy since before the word was coined. Her writing credits include the award-winning steampunk romance *House of Sable Locks*, the Celtic fantasy *Princes of Air*, and 2021 VIVIAN finalist *Written in Water*.

She was born in New York at some point in the past. She is officially old enough to know better, but refuses to grow up. She lives in Central Florida with her husband and son.

Elizabeth can be found online at http://elizabethschechterwrites.com, or on Facebook at https://www.facebook.com/Elizabeth.A.Schechter.

Subscribe to Elizabeth's newsletter at https://www.subscribepage.com/k4u7k2

Read more at elizabethschechterwrites.com.

www.ingramcontent.com/pod-product-compliance
Lightning Source LLC
Chambersburg PA
CBHW031027030726
47497CB00004B/1039